THE FALL

TRACY TOWNSEND

THE FALL

an imprint of
Start Science Fiction

Published 2019 by Pyr®

Cover illustration © Adam S. Doyle
Cover design by Jacqueline Nasso Cooke
Cover Design © Start Science Fiction

Inquiries should be addressed to

Start Science Fiction
101 Hudson Street, 37th Floor, Suite 3705
Jersey City, New Jersey 07302
PHONE: 212-431-5455
WWW.PYSF.COM

Paperback ISBN: 978-1-63388-498-4
Ebook ISBN: 978-1-63388-499-1

10 9 8 7 6 5 4 3 2 1

Printed in the United States of America

For Joe Maynen, my found family.
You wanted what happened before and got the middle, instead.
Now you have to stay for the end.

BEFORE

Our better part remains
To work in close design, by fraud or guile
What force effected not: that he no less
At length from us may find, who overcomes
By force, hath overcome but half his foe.

—John Milton, *Paradise Lost*, Book 1

4TH ELEVENMONTH, 276 A.U.
THE CATHEDRAL COMMONS, CORMA

It was a wonder the aigamuxa was still alive. A wonder, but Haadiyaa Gammon did not go so far as to think it a miracle. Miracles ought to have more pieces turned the right way round.

It *was* a miracle that so many of the Reverend Doctor Phillip Chalmers's notes had made it to the ground below the Old Cathedral of Corma intact, fetching up in threes and fours against the feet of trees and under the seats of park benches. Gammon had sent a constabulary page running up and down the Commons for the better part of an hour, gathering them up in a canvas evidence envelope.

She crouched beside the broken creature half-buried in a mangled hedge, staring at its juddering chest, the rickety bellows motion every moment on the verge of ceasing, then reached for the signal balloon in her jacket pocket. So many stories circulated of the aigamuxa being all but indestructible. Perhaps they were true. Perhaps you couldn't hope for gravity alone to end a creature born to climb and stare down on the world from the soles of its feet.

Behind her, a gendarme whistled—the awed, two-note falling sound of a man who wasn't sure if he wanted to step in closer or clear off altogether.

"Reason bless me, Inspector," he muttered.

"Best hope it blesses him, instead." The signal balloon lay across her hand, a foot of sturdy twine connected to a tiny, rubberized chute, an alchemist's globe, and a cylinder of gas.

Gammon rose, backed away from the boxwoods, then checked around for tree limbs hanging in the flight path. She shook the globe hard for ten seconds—long enough to ensure the chemicals within would have agitated to a proper, sun-yellow glow—and pulled the cylinder's sealing pin. The device sputtered, a tiny, blue-white tongue of heat licking her palm before she could cast the whole contraption into the air.

She shook out her singed hand and watched the bright bubble rise over their location and into the sight lines of their scouts posted all around the Commons.

The gendarme stared at her in naked confusion.

"You're calling a new medevac, Inspector? Why?" He patted his sidearm. "I've got what we need to sort him out."

Gammon fixed the man with her iciest stare. He looked away and let his hand fall from his belt. "He's wanted for questioning," she said.

A new light hovered into the far edge of her vision. A red-gleaming globe, two hundred yards off and around the corner of the Cathedral's porch. Gammon tracked the signal chute, reading the response in its color. *No medical services available.* Of course not. They'd had their hands full scraping the Alchemist up from the clerestory roof.

"Inspector," the gendarme began.

Gammon looked back to the aigamuxa's twisted body, curled up on itself like a dead spider. Was it only her imagination that the breathing had slowed? She spat a curse in one of the Indine dialects she knew only well enough to keep up with her chacheras' running mouths when she visited her mother's family. She finished in Amidonian, more for the gendarme's benefit.

"The Constabulary crankcarts have stretchers on them. Get me three more men and a driver to take us north of the Commons. There's someone I know who lives nearby."

Jane Ardai sat on the edge of an examination table beside the trestle Gammon and her gendarmes had made for the broken aigamuxa, her head cocked like a puzzled bird. She studied the creature, now fastened to a steam-driven bellows that pumped its lungs. It lay surrounded by hanging pouches of fluids pushing substances Gammon had little hope of pronouncing into its compromised system.

Jane's insolent mouth turned into a crooked smile. She patted the space beside her hip and crooked a finger.

"Haaaaaaaaadi," she crooned. "What have I told you about bringing in strays?"

"That I shouldn't."

"And yet you do always bring me the nicest things."

Gammon looked at the space on the table beside Jane and slid herself into the space between her knees, instead, pressing close to the physick's apron.

One eyebrow above Jane's perfect, coal-black eyes twitched. Her plump cheeks dimpled. "You were to join me for luncheon on Sabberday," she murmured.

Gammon leaned closer.

"I'm so sorry. You wouldn't believe—"

"I'll give you hell for it later. Shhhh."

Jane's hush died away as her lips met Gammon's. For a long moment, there was only the hungry press of their mouths and the breath that passed between them.

Finally, Jane pulled away. The physick's hair had fallen from its disorderly bun in locks that smelled of iodine and lister soap.

"Tell me all about this one," Jane murmured.

"Nasrahiel, chieftain of one of the aiga tribes squatting in the Aerie.

He tried to kill me. Tried to kill most every human he came in contact with tonight."

Jane jerked back, the ironic serifs written across her face blotted away. "He tried to kill you and you brought him to me to *fix?*"

"I'm going to need him."

"To make a second go of his plans?"

Gammon considered the creature on the table, tethered at death's door. "I need him because of what his plan *was*. There's more I need to know about it, and if I'm lucky—" she nodded toward the ragged bag of notepaper slouched beside the door, "—I'll find something to convince him he needs to know more than he thought he did."

Jane's nose wrinkled in distaste. "So I'm only keeping him alive, bringing him back to consciousness?"

"I need him working—completely. Just as he did before, or near to it."

Jane's sour expression deepened, as if something more foul than usual wafted up from her lurid work.

"His legs—where his eyes are." She stopped, sighing. "Haadi, this won't be fast, or easy, or cheap."

"I've always kept a little put away with you, just in case."

"This is much more than *a little*."

It was Gammon's turn to look affronted. "I can find a way to pay—"

"And you will, love. But first, explain to me why I should want to take a monster that wants to twist your head from your shoulders and turn him from 'off' to 'on'."

Gammon frowned. "Is Julian here?"

"Out with a friend at the public down on Bleeker. Why?"

"This is the sort of story that goes better over a drink. You might not have enough to make it go down well if we split the bottle three ways."

Resurrection Jane Ardai slid from the table and glared up at Haadi-yaa Gammon, all five feet three of her radiating disapproval. "The next time you want to compensate for missing a luncheon, you needn't go so far to get my attention."

"If only you knew."

"Jules has barely been gone an hour. There's time enough for you to spin quite a yarn, and I want to see every stitch."

Jane, Gammon reflected, had a very particular relationship to stitches. She might have sewn more things closed in her career than a whole garment district of tailors. After this job, that might rise to two garment districts. And like any good tradeswoman, she knew her price.

Gammon was sure down to her marrow she'd be a long time paying it.

9TH ELEVENMONTH, 276 A.U.
OFF THE SHORES OF MISERY BAY, CORMA

The turnkey who dismissed Beatrice Earnshaw from her cell hadn't been a real turnkey. Bess had only done the first three days of her sentence in the rusted hold of the prison hulk *Accursius*, but she'd seen enough to know real turnkeys in the employ of the Court and Bar never had such tidy uniforms. Every crease was pressed and every button stitched tight on this young man. Three days had been enough to teach Bess that even the newest, greenest guards and screws were outfitted in hand-me-downs. The dark-eyed young man who passed her a bundle of things as she stood shivering on the boarding plank to the skiff bound for the shore looked too unworn by that shabby place, full of screams and stinks. She'd stood holding the bundle, which contained something odd and jabby—something other than the rumpled ball gown in which she'd been arrested, interrogated, and perfunctorily tried—and watched, wordless, as the boy pivoted back toward his station on *Accursius*'s main deck.

He had, Bess realized, an odd hitch in his gait. His left side. Lamed, somehow. *Surely not a real turnkey.*

But hells. Bess wasn't about to complain. "Beatrice Earnshaw" wasn't even her proper name. Who was she to whinge about cutting the corners off the truth so it could wedge into tight spaces?

She sat as far from the other just-released prisoners as the rails framing the skiff allowed, and tried not to stare at the pair of aigamuxa chained to the ship's oars, their eyeless brows furrowed against the push and pull. What might they have done? It wouldn't have taken much more than just being aigamuxa to land them on that bench, she supposed.

Bess's prison jumper was an itchy, baggy mess stitched of old sailcloth, repurposed from some air galleon whose sprits and mains were too shabby to hold wind any longer. They were full of enough holes, it was a wonder they could even hold in people. Every prisoner—no, ex-prisoner—had an Engine punch card pinned to their jumper's front, giving their name, their release date, and where the Court and Bar had determined them bound to go now. Workhouses, for a sentence reduction. Temporary tenements, for the employable in need of a start back in everyday life. Names of family who had sworn to take them in and see to their good conduct in the future, for really lucky ones.

Bess had no idea what was on her card.

The skiff lurched on through the choppy Elevenmonth waters, cutting a furrow in the gray foam. The prison hulks *Accursius, Proculus*, and *Salvius* shrank in the wake until they seemed no larger than Bess's hand, all hunched together on the high waves. Each ship was large enough for two thousand prisoners apiece. *Accursius* had held two thousand eight hundred and nine. Bess had taken turns using the bed with her two cellmates. All of them had been sentenced to the rope, though the Trimeeni girl who had been there long before Bess arrived had just been taken off the swinging list, since physick had done an examination and found her pregnant. The second girl, a bucktoothed blonde from the south quays, murmured that the Trimeeni had been making eyes at every male turnkey on shift for a month trying to get a tumble out of them. Finally, it had paid off.

Bess had already been on her blood. No hope of Smallduke Regenzi having done her some unintended favor. And then, the boy with the bundle and the punch card for her jumper came, and everything changed, all at once.

Bess jerked free of her reverie as the skiff butted against the quay. The aigamuxa's chains were slackened enough for them to clamber out and tie off the boat. Four guards split the task of disembarking, two watching the aiga, two marching the nearly released prisoners toward the security office at the dock head down a path shoveled through the building snow.

The security office was about the size of a cobbler's tent in a bazaar, though it had walls and a proper roof holding up a shelf of city-gray snow. There was room enough inside for a tall, teetering table, the clerk sitting at it, and the mass of levers and switches and dials and pumps and brass and ivory that was the Algebraic Engine behind her. The guards plucked the ex-prisoners' cards off their jumpers and passed them to the clerk through a narrow window. She fed them one by one to the Engine, which punched out a duplicate card with additional nodes and holes adding date and time of processing, the names of the guards—all manner of things, Bess supposed. The Engine would rattletrap out a set of orders from a printing reel whose pages bore a surreal resemblance to actual handwritten script, a font all in curlicues and serifs, linked awkwardly by a machine. Then the prisoner would be sent off with a shove on the back and instructions in hand.

The lucky ones could even read them.

Bess breathed in relief. That, at least, she could do.

One of the officers from the skiff jabbed Bess's hip with his truncheon, nodding toward the security office's window. She edged forward and tried not to flinch as the other officer snapped her card off its pin, tearing at her jumper's seam.

The clerk inside the tiny, Engine-crowded hut looked older than the hulks themselves, a tiny, wizened lady whose puckered eyes and mustard-brown skin made it hard to tell where she'd come from, eons ago. No one, as Bess had learned in her years running for Ivor, actually *came* from Corma. It was a destination, or an intermediate stop—*a fly trap*, she thought bitterly—but not really a point of origin. Just a muddle of folk from all ends of the Unity, toeing or stepping over the line as survival demanded.

The Engine's input slot snapped up Bess's card. She heard the *rattle-whirr-buzz* of it being read, duplicated, modified.

And, she hoped, approved.

The boy with the limp had been so young, so tidy. Something was wrong, wrong, wrong—

"Here," the clerk said. Bess looked down at the folded paper pressed into her hands.

If there had been anything unusual in the release orders, the old woman didn't seem to notice, or care. She stared at Bess with a patience polished by Reason-only-knew how many years sitting on this stool, processing other people's futures.

"Thank you," Bess murmured.

She tucked the order sheet against her bosom and scurried a few paces off to try to do something with herself and her bundle of discharged things. The urge to tear open the folded paper and read her fate was almost unbearable, but Bess knew if she didn't attend to her welfare in the moment, she might not live long enough to make good on the orders, whatever they were. Flakes of snow had begun to wander down from the iron-gray clouds again, half storm and half smoke, gathering over the city's spires. The Elevenmonth wind cut straight through her jumper. She turned the drape-skirt of her useless ball gown into a sloppy sort of shawl, then tugged on her embroidered gloves, hoping they'd provide at least a little protection against the cold. Everything else in her balled-up kit was worse than useless, barring a lucky pawn at a second-hand clothier's shop.

And then, her hands found the jabby thing she'd been too afraid to search the bundle for earlier.

The pistol's pearly, ladylike handle didn't quite offset its ugly, snub nose. An alley piece, with just one shot and a hammer-trigger and *oh, Reason, she needed to hide it straight away.*

Bess still shivered as she put her back to a stack of barrels, cutting herself off from the wind whipping in from the sea. She wanted to jam the alley piece back into her bundle of cast-offs, but if she pulled the trigger by mistake, God only knew what trouble that would bring, even if no one caught a bullet. Looking all around, she wrapped it carefully and tucked the bundle the boy had given her under an arm.

Definitely not a turnkey. Had the gun been meant to help her, or get her into worse trouble? Bess had almost dropped the release paper as she swaddled the pistol. She knelt down, unfolded the note. Only the fear of losing it on the breeze kept her fingers clamped tight.

> Gooddame Audrea Carringer, 108th on Lower Hillside, Street 19.

The boy had been too young, too fresh and decent. That strange limp and the release order coming of nowhere—

Hanged.

She was meant to have been hanged as a poisoner that very spring, as soon as the queue before her was cleared.

Hanged.

And now, somehow, someone had seen fit to set her free, and give her a gun, and send her to the exact address she'd been given the last time she'd been trapped. She hadn't been wise enough to walk through the door the Alchemist had left open for her.

It could not possibly be a coincidence.

Bess scrambled to her feet and stuffed the order under her jumper's belt. They were in the northernmost curve of Misery Bay, fully a mile north of Rotten Row and the sewer-mouth that was Blackbottom End. If she legged it hard, she might make Lower Hillside before the snow came down thick and after she'd unsnarled the questions tangled in her brain . . .

Bess ran.

The neighborhoods surrounding Oldtemple had had other names, four or five generations back, or so Bess had heard, when she ran packages for Ivor Ruenichnov of New Vraska Imports. The region itself had been not one place, but a fusion of many. Boroughs made up of Hasids and Tzadikim and Mohammedeans living at odd, jutting angles to one another, with a Jennite or Hindoo enclave slipped between, had been compressed together like so much silt turned into coal. The neighborhood name Bess had heard most often was Bet Navah, which must have meant something among those people. Now, folk just called it Lower Hillside.

It wasn't nearly so pretty a name as Bet Navah, but the crowded streets paved with mossy cobbles had their own charm. And it was still far better kept up than the rest of Oldtemple Down.

Street 19 snuggled in a little valley of cross-paths and avenues that formed the borders of Oldtemple proper and the rest of middle Corma. It wasn't properly a street, being too narrow to admit more than a single crank-rick or hansom carriage, and so it fared no better than the rest of the lattice of pathways around it, where earning a name was concerned.

Number 108 was a tiny, tidy ladies' necessary shop, with demure, curtained windows taunting with vague suggestions of what fabric fancies awaited within. Audrea Carringer's name glinted from a well-polished brass plaque beside the building number. The pasteboard sign propped against the glass showed the store was open another quarter-hour.

Bess entered, panting, and ran her fingers through her hair to pull out the sodden tangles left by melting snow.

She felt only the rough burr of the haircut she'd been given after her delousing three days prior, and winced. *Accursius* had taken so many other things, she kept forgetting about her hair.

"Holy Reason, get back on the mat, girl!"

Bess shrank backward. A broad-hipped woman with a pert nose and olive skin bustled around a corner where a kind of chifforobe had concealed her presence. Bess was only a little better than sixteen, but she was already a hand taller than the woman she presumed to be Audrea Carringer.

"*Tsk.* Here," the lady said, snapping a dainty vanity towel from a rack of embroidered necessaries.

Bess opened her mouth to thank her, only to find herself being scrubbed as heartily as a terrier caught leaping in mud puddles. The woman sniffed and cursed in a thoroughly unladylike fashion as she roughed the girl up and down.

Dazed, Bess stared at herself, chafed dry and pulled in front of a tall mirror set in an elaborate brass frame. She hadn't seen herself in a proper glass since her arrest.

It was so much worse than she'd imagined.

Before *Accursius*, Bess had boasted a tumble of russet curls and waves down her back. Now, her coiffeur was reduced to a ragged shave and some odd, long-hanging pieces of leftover hair. The tooth she'd chipped after bucktoothed Sadie thrust her face-first into the washing bowl on her first night shipboard snaggled, fang-like. She gaped at the spectacle she made, pale-browed, red-cheeked, her nails blackened by oakum and thumbs pricked by sail-stitching needles.

"You look a proper damned mess," the woman-who-might-be-Carringer sighed, not ungently. "Keep the towel. It'll do for a handkerchief if you need a cry. I put the kettle on an hour ago, after Jules let me know you had your walking card, so I hope you don't mind taking your cup on the strong side. Ah, yes. There it is."

The woman plucked Bess's card from where it peeked out of her bundle and wagged it at her. "They pin these to released cons so no matter how stupid or mad the hulks have made them, they can't lose their pass. But that doesn't make it wise to carry it out in the open. *Honestly*. One would have thought Ivor'd teach you better."

The name roused Bess from the shock of her own appearance.

"You—you know Ivor, Madame Carringer?"

"Knew. He's dead now, and you'll pardon me if I'm not sorry for it. There isn't a bolt or hinge I put into his arm I wouldn't gladly have taken back, but his money was good, and I needed it, at the time. Now whoever told you I'm Madame Carringer?"

Perhaps, Bess considered, she had run mad after all. Ivor's arm? Bolts and hinges? She looked around, as if expecting the walls of the necessary shop to fall away like some prop-board set in a kinotrope play.

"There must be some mistake. I thought I had come to Madame Audrea Carringer, 108th Lower Hillside? Street 19?"

"You would have, if there were such a person. But it's Seventh-day, and so it's my shift, and so you have me."

It was an answer, though it didn't seem to fit the question Bess had asked.

The woman put her fists to her hips and shook her head. Then, for the first time, Bess noticed her glossy black hair was done up not with hairdressing pins, but with tiny, glinting clockmaker's tools.

"You look about to fall over, Beatrice Earnshaw. How about you do it in an armchair while I turn the sign and teach you a little something about the Dolly Molls of Corma?"

"Is that . . . some kind of union?" Bess found her way to an armchair set near a little curtained stall.

The woman was at the door, drawing the curtains fully and turning off the gas tap to the lamp on the shop's stoop.

"There comes a time in a young woman's life," she explained, "when she realizes the only people who will help her out of a tight spot are ladies who have been cinched up just as tight themselves before."

And she smiled. "We're a union of very particular skills and particular renown. Anyone looking for Audrea Carringer has been sent looking for us, even if she doesn't know it."

"And you're . . . what? The president?"

"It's Seventh-day, as I said, if you'd been listening. I handle Fifth-through Eighth-days, every month. It's how I pay my dues back. How we all do. Any girls who are called in or sent to us on Fifth- through Eighth-day are mine to see to."

Bess blinked. "Yours to see to?"

"Haadi told me you'd be in need of a position, once she pushed your papers through, and she knew I needed an extra pair of hands for a very, very big job."

A very, very big job. They were just the sort of words Bess had learned to yearn for, and to dread, in her years running for Ivor Ruenichnov. Everything good or bad that had ever happened to her had started with some *big job* or other.

As casually as she could, hoping it passed for a nervous tic, Bess twisted the little vanity towel her hostess had left with her into a kind of short rope. She'd seen other girls do that in the community washroom, if someone showed signs of giving them trouble. If she was fast, she could simply run, and if not, she could loop the towel around the woman's neck and pull tight.

"What kind of *big jobs* do you do?" Bess asked warily.

The smile reached the woman's eyes at last. "Only the very biggest. My name is Jane Ardai. You've probably heard people call me Resurrection Jane."

Bess's fingers slackened. The towel fell back in her lap.

"The sawbones?"

Resurrection Jane's lips pursed tartly. "Better than that, I hope. Haadi has quite a job for us, and I'll need someone with your experience to help me gather up all the right parts from all the wrong sorts of places." She crouched before Bess and rested a hand on her knee, precisely like a doting aunt, if the aunt were a mad-eyed physick known for replacing a pound of flesh with a stone's worth of steel.

"We're going to rebuild an aigamuxa."

There were a great many things involved in rebuilding anyone, Bess was to learn, and Reason only knew how much more complicated the patient being an aigamuxa made the job. Jane Ardai—not, she was quick to correct, Doctor Ardai, and certainly not Reverend Doctor Ardai—seemed somewhere between perturbed and elated at the prospect. Bess Earnshaw had no opinion at all about her new situation, save that a very strong cup of tea had been sorely overdue. She followed her first with three more, and if Resurrection Jane minded refreshing the leaves and warming the pot over the pilot burner again, she gave no sign.

Bess held her teacup with two hands, as if it were an anchor. Jane Ardai's explanation for herself and the not-quite-existence of Gooddame Audrea Carringer rolled in like high tide, wasing over the table between them.

"You've heard of the Savoyard's Social Brotherhood?"

Bess nodded. Sweeps with any sense put in for a membership with the SSB as soon as they'd worked the chimney pots long enough to be eligible. "They take complaints about customers who won't pay their bills and such to the Court and Bar on behalf of sweeps."

"Among other things, yes. And there are the Mainspring Men for clockworking, the Dockworkers' Union for longshoremen. That lot even takes aigamuxa, in some cases, I've heard. Have you heard of the union for—" Jane paused, considering "—ladies who are self-employed?"

Bess shook her head. "No, I don't think I—" And then she came up short, realizing what being *self-employed* likely meant. "Oh. No, well. I mean, my mother was a mistress in a gentlemen's salon. That's where Ivor found me, all those years ago."

"Girls in salons and clubs aren't usually part of our merry number. Their line of work being in a proper shop-space affords some protections the independent contractors among us lack."

"I don't understand," Bess interrupted. "I thought you were a sawbones, not a bawd."

Jane laughed hard enough, she had to set down her own teacup for fear of spilling on the lacey tablecloth. She'd put a meal together with almost frightening efficiency, whipping tea, kettle, cakes, and napkins from various cubbies beside the till as if she were rushing to collect the instruments needed to prevent someone bleeding out on the operating table. Then she had set into the meal, like a lioness gutting a kill— unselfconsciously thorough and mercilessly swift. That laugh was the first time Bess had seen her attitude of utter command broken. A smile, she realized, fit very well on Jane Ardai, sitting in the brackets of a round-cheeked, rather wicked face well accustomed to them.

"My sexual recreations have never given me much experience learning to please men. Well, apart from Jules's father, I suppose, but that was a long time ago, and I should have known better. No, Bess. I'm no bawd, and despite what you were run down to the hulks for, I don't think you are, either. Then again, most of the Dolly Molls aren't, once you take a full and proper census."

"And the Dolly Molls are—?"

"Us." Jane gestured between them. "Lady misfits. Independents.

Oddballs in our trades. A few of us are bawds and escorts and such, yes. Registered courtesans or companions. But there are plenty of others, too. Midwives, alchemists, tinkers, peddlers, antiquarians, even Kneeler academics. All sorts of people who don't fit, all of them ladies. We had to have some kind of an organizing principle, you understand. We're utterly competent and damned important and still the world of the EC and the governors and their peerage can't be bothered to give us the time of day. They'll use our services, of course. But given even a quarter-chance, well . . ." She shrugged, sighed. "You've learned for yourself what they'll do to us, if we become more trouble than they think we're worth."

"And Inspector Gammon arranged to send me to you?" *And the Alchemist before her, too*, Bess thought.

"She knew I'd be here this time of the month. There are no dues you pay, in the usual sense, for the help of your fellow Dolly Molls. It's not about money. We staff this place round the clock, and a few others—satellites, of a sort—so there's always a place to send for help. There isn't any 'Audrea Carringer' now, though there was about sixty or seventy years ago. She was the first of us. Now, for a few days every month, we take our turns being her at one of the safehouses, and keep ready to be of use to whosoever comes."

"The Constabulary knows about the Dolly Molls?"

"Once Haadi came along, yes. There was never the right sort of person at the helm before. But we took a bit of a gamble on her. It's paid off very well—or did, until she tendered her resignation. Now we're back to keeping our heads lower."

"This isn't the first time someone gave me your—this, I mean—address," Bess admitted. "I used to deliver packages in Westgate Bridge, out to the Stone Scales."

Jane Ardai's brow lifted. "The Alchemist. Well. There's someone I haven't heard from in a long, long time. Not since Rare."

Bess frowned. "Since what?"

"He adopted a girl who'd had a very bad go of it, years ago. Her mother had been one of ours, and we couldn't leave her without a family after what had happened. What kind of sisterhood would we have been? It almost worked out." She sighed. "Almost."

"So he really was trying to send me to help," Bess murmured.

"Oh, yes."

"I thought . . . I don't know what I thought."

"I think," Jane announced, "you need one last cup of tea, and to learn a little something about the work I need done. But the second part can wait until after you've had a hot bath."

Bess made her way to the apartments tucked up above the garment shop. (There were crates and shelves of garments in a little room off the kitchen stair—though it stood to reason the clothes and goods within were meant for outfitting wayward Dolly Molls rather than selling for a tidy profit. She wondered where the money to keep the place going came from. A question for another time.) She cranked the hot-box, setting the alchemical material within aflame and stoking the tanked water up to temperature. A few minutes later, she was sliding into a hot bath, pointedly ignoring the bruises and scratches tattooing her body. The bath was heaven. Her body barely felt like her own. Her mind most certainly wasn't, colonized by questions that refused to keep silent.

Why did Gammon throw me in the hulks if she meant to set me free? Then again, had she? Bess didn't think so. Not from the start, anyway. She'd spent enough time in the interrogation rooms of the Constabulary's central office, the City Inspector could easily have dropped a hint that Bess wouldn't have long to worry over her situation.

No, Gammon hadn't planned to spring Bess. So why do it at all? So she could play errand-runner for her Dolly Moll friend? There had to be more to it. The question jabbed at her, like the alley pistol she'd left on the vanity's edge.

Gammon must have assumed Bess would be safer traveling to Old-temple Down with a gun in easy reach—and had also gambled that Bess's anger at the conviction and prison time wouldn't move her to use the alley piece on Resurrection Jane.

Down the winding stair to the shop below, the sawbones's voice joined in conversation. Two other voices. A man's, or perhaps an older boy's. And—

Bess's hands closed on the lip of the tub.

Gammon.

She had little enough hair that a rough pass of a sudsy soap cake over her scalp was enough to finish her toilet. Bess climbed from the bath, still steaming, jerked the chain to drain it, and dressed in the frock and shawl she'd taken from the storage room.

She scarcely bothered to towel down. The edges of her vision had gone hot and blurry. Tears, but furious and full of acid. If they were going to burn her, she'd make sure their flames touched at least one other person.

The voices took on clarity as Bess descended the stairs.

First, the boy, tenor and relaxed. ". . . afternoon, give or take a few hours. It might be better to leave them waiting a bit than turn up early and seem overeager."

And Gammon. Bess pictured her in her Constabulary blues, straight as a mast, her voice prickly with splinters of caution. "Don't be too sure of how far you can push them, Jules."

Jane cut in tartly. "Yes, it's bad form to rely on someone for help and then stand them up without the least explanation."

"Jane, I meant to answer your invitation—"

Bess rounded the foot of the stairs into the shop's fitting salon, finding the sawbones with her hand raised, cutting off Gammon's response. She wasn't wearing her Constabulary blues after all. Indeed, she looked more like a groom or valet than a copper, knee boots and trousers capped off with a fitted jacket whose pin-tucks were better suited to a man's chest than a woman's. No epaulets. No hat. No gun straps and no jacket heavy with braids.

Gammon turned her hooked nose Bess's way. The pained look Gammon had been wrestling with settled in properly.

"Well," Jane said, seeing Bess's arrival. "I'm not the one in need of your apologies, in any case. You'd be better off saving them for my new apprentice."

"Miss Earnshaw," Gammon began.

Bess lifted her chin. "Inspector."

"Just Haadiyaa now. I've resigned my post."

"I can't imagine why."

"You've every right to be furious with me."

Bess puzzled over the word. A tear was already running down her cheek. "*Furious?*"

"Angry," Gammon explained, "didn't seem sufficient to the task." A long silence. Bess held Gammon under her gaze, like a creature pithed in an EC lab. It said something that she didn't try to slip away from Bess's stare. "Clearing the charges against you was the last official act I took."

"I suppose you had very good reasons for letting me dwell for days in a lightless hole, fending off turnkeys' paws and bunkmates' fists. I suppose you were *busy*."

Gammon shook her head. "I can't claim I did the right thing in the first place, but I did what I might to make good on it later. I'm sorry." She turned plaintively to Resurrection Jane. The other woman dusted her hands and sniffed.

"Oh, I'm not saving you from this. You know my feelings about that Regenzi nonsense."

"We need your help," Gammon said instead, turning back to Bess.

Bess frowned. "For something to do with an aigamuxa. Rebuilding it?"

"Properly speaking, I'm the one who needs your help."

Bess followed the voice to the boy leaning by one of the gas lamps ensconced on the wall. Tall and whipcord-thin—eye to eye with Gammon, and she was no trifle—his hair kept slipping into his eyes, more in a moppish manner than a fetching one. The eyes had the same shape as Jane Ardai's, suggesting one of the Asian provinces bordering Old and New Vraska across the Western Sea. Bess squinted, then recognized him as the too-young, too-tidy turnkey, the pomade washed from his hair.

"I'm Julian. Jules, to most people," he explained. "I run Mother's shop."

Bess tried to visualize him settling ledgers for the ladies' necessary shop.

"I keep my proper business on East End, near Deacon's Lane north of the Commons," Jane explained. "Jules is my machinist." The next came out not with a mother's pride, but cool, professional haughtiness—the sort of tone Bess had heard over and over again at Regenzi's ball. "He's the finest prosthetics engineer in all of Amidon."

Jules rolled his eyes and unseated his hip from the wall. Bess noticed a hitch as he resettled his weight. His left trouser leg seemed slightly less occupied, less filled-out, than the right, though he stood without a prop and crossed the distance to take Bess's hand without a pause in his gait.

Bess was in no mood to play at niceties. She invited herself to a good look at Jules's leg, ignoring his proffered hand.

He let the hand drop, lifting his trouser leg a few inches, instead. A bundle of pistons and cables passed down into his boot and stretched up toward the knee.

"The whole leg, clear down from my hip," Jules said. "There was an accident during my delivery, and nothing for it but to amputate."

Bess stared. She knew she shouldn't, but—

"He's your son and. . . your patient?"

Jane raised an eyebrow. "Lucky to be one, too. Though after he outgrew my second design, he wouldn't let me draw up his new legs anymore. Jules has a much finer sense of craft than I do. He does all his own work, and most of my clients', too. I only perform the installations. And now I need him designing some very unusual things."

"For the aiga."

"Not just any aiga," Gammon said. "The one we'll need to keep a war from breaking out."

"I don't understand."

"You will," Jane said. "Julian can't waste time finding and negotiating part costs when he'll need to be working on prototypes for hours every day."

"You've worked with fences before, Bess?" asked Jules. "Ever come across one called Sticks?"

She almost laughed. "That old lanyani fraud? Every bird knows him, around Blackbottom End. He up-charges by at least fifty percent and tries to make you feel grateful when you get him down to forty."

Gammon raised an eyebrow. "And what have you gotten him down to?"

"Fifteen."

Julian grinned at Inspector Gammon and Resurrection Jane. "She's perfect. When can she start?"

1.

The bell over the Stone Scales's door jingled, waking Rowena from where she dozed, propped on a stool behind the till. Shouldered close to its neighbor buildings, the Scales never had a cross-breeze to speak of. Sevenmonth's steamy air had sunk deep into its plastered walls, sweating up from its floorboards.

The man at the door wore a dusty pair of gabardine trousers and a linen shirt whose rolled sleeves and damp collar clearly displayed his own reaction to the heat. Rabbit startled up from his tight curl under the counter and zuffed, all tail and earnest charm.

The man reached for his straw gambler's hat. Its shadow came away from his sunburned face and Rowena darted from her post.

"Master Meteron! Where've you *been?*"

Anselm Meteron offered his one-shouldered shrug, crouching to ruffle the snuffling dog's ears. "Traveling," he said. "Some acquisitions overseas."

Rowena wrinkled her nose. "What kind of . . . acquisitions?"

"An island."

She gaped.

"It's between the latitudinal parallels where Amidonian and Lemarckian taxation policies are in play. It'll be a few years before the political balance is sorted out, so in the meantime . . ." Meteron smiled. "He who owns the land makes the rules. The details make for dastardly boring conversation, cricket. All that matters is it's the perfect place to build a resort."

"What's a 'resort'?"

"A little something I dreamt up recently. It'll be news to others, as well, I think." Something in Rowena's expression must have looked particularly odd, for he raised an eyebrow. "Problem, cricket?"

"You're just, um . . . different. When you en't gussied up."

Meteron thumped Rabbit's exposed chest one last time and rose, looking about. "Hardly any call to overdress on the most miserably under-conditioned steam liner in the whole western fleet. I slept above decks to keep from stifling in the cabins." He glanced at her. "You're rather different when you *are* gussied up."

Rowena looked down at herself. The fact that she put very little thought to how a pea-green seersucker dress compared to her britches and blouses of a few months before was a measure of how she'd grown into them, she supposed. They felt ordinary now—though she still kept her little knife tucked into a strap of her ankle boots. Meteron studied her with his measuring gaze, moving the balances about as he so often did. His sunburn and a faint patina of coal dust deepened the lines by his eyes. Slowly, his face tilted into a knowing smile.

"Um." Rowena gripped her skirt and swished it experimentally, as if she'd only just put the garment on. "I actually, um . . . with my own money. Bear keeps telling me I can have my pick of what's here, Leyah's and Rare's old things, but I just don't have the figure, and—"

"You look lovely," he said.

The word froze Rowena, though if it had any weight in Anselm Meteron's vocabulary, it was unremarkable. He dusted at his trousers with the brim of his hat, as if he'd already forgotten what he'd said. "The Old Bear about?"

"In the yard. He's started this project, y'see, and it's a bit physical . . ."

Meteron started for the back of the shop. Rowena followed, ducking after him through the curtain separating the public from the private face of the Scales. She could hear the scowl in his tone.

"The old fool has project enough with you about. He's hardly in condition to take on anything more."

Rowena smiled to herself. It had been eight months since she first met Anselm Meteron and the Alchemist. In that time—much of it spent caring for the Alchemist as he mended from the dramas that brought her into his company—she'd learned the surest sign of their bond was how badly they dogged one another. Her life as a courier bird hadn't afforded much experience with friendship. But if it was typical of old companions to become overfamiliar in their scoldings and possessive in their stubbornness, the Old Bear and Ann made a model couple.

"*A project,*" Meteron snarled. "What exactly are you here for, cricket? You should know better."

Rowena spread her hands. "If you just have a look—"

He opened the yard door, raising a hand to shade his eyes against the sun.

And then he stopped, staring. Just as Rowena knew he would.

After the late-fall snows had been cleared from the streets and the Alchemist had weathered two weeks of bed rest, Rowena came back with him to the Stone Scales. Its little cobbled yard, a roughly hexagonal piece of land with two alleys shunting into it and a shuttered old machine shed hulking in one of its corners, had boasted little more than a pile of cordwood and a bin for Rabbit's bones and rags. When the frost melted and the Alchemist was on his feet again, the old man took to the yard's maintenance as if it required a reprimand and he had its switch picked and trimmed for the job. By the second week of Fourmonth, he'd turned up a quarter of its cobbles and built the planters—and set Rowena to work with him.

Rowena grinned behind her hand as Meteron scanned the yard, the summer heat having turned it into a veritable urban jungle. There were ever-blooming lilacs framing the door, still short and stubby since their arrival off a barge from the Midlands, but bursting royal purple and lily-white all the same. There was a sunny spot beside the machine shed, certain hours of the day. That was where the Alchemist had constructed tiers of shelving for an array of herbs, raised up on planks built of old shipping crates and housed in containers that ranged from cracked crockery and patinaed kettles to beakers of tempered glass that gave a twisting view of the roots within. Along the Scales's walls, trailing vines and dwarf hedges and creeping lattice-flowers and peas and snap-beans mingled, thriving as if they'd been planted there many seasons.

The Alchemist worked beside a hole trenched in the ground, the clay soil once hidden beneath the cobblestones and gravel half-buried again under the heap of amendment piled in its place. Rowena's smile broke into a scowl at the sight of him down on a knee beside the hole, flanked by a barrow holding a stubbornly flowering bush.

He glanced at them and passed a hand over his damp, dark brow. "Nearly done. Any customers lingering?"

"Just this one," said Rowena.

"Hmph." The Alchemist eyed Meteron with mock suspicion. "Seems a rough character."

"*You* shouldn't be down—"

"Go turn the shingle, girl," he instructed. "You can sharpen your tongue on anyone who tries to slip in for late purchases. Ann, pass me this rose-of-Sharon. I'll be done in five minutes with another pair of hands."

Rowena looked at Meteron. "Sorry. Didn't think you'd get roped into some dirty chore."

He shrugged, checking his rolled sleeves as he crossed the yard. "It won't have been the first time I've had a little dirt under my nails. The *second*, perhaps."

Rowena lingered, watching Meteron standing by the barrow, taking instruction from the Old Bear as he gestured to the underside of the hemp-bound root ball, the garden shears lying in the barrow beside it. There was a certain solemn efficiency between them when there was a job to be done.

Well.

Better the job be in a garden yard than a perilous old basement or a reeking tunnel. She turned back to the Scales to start closing up shop and spied the Alchemist's cane left leaning in the doorframe.

Or the roof of some damned cathedral, a voice not quite Rowena's own murmured in the back of her mind.

"Come on. Let's see about the shop," she whispered back.

To her relief, neither Meteron nor the Old Bear heard her, or had to wonder to whom she was speaking. *Better to keep my own counsel.*

And to keep back from whom it came, as well.

"When the girl said you had a project, I assumed I'd find you busy killing yourself with something or other."

The Old Bear grunted a general assent and took the unbound shrub from Anselm, who heaved it up for an awkward hand-off. Anselm watched him settle the root ball in place, angling the plant this way and that.

"Disappointed?" the Alchemist asked.

Anselm crouched beside him. "Only surprised. I hadn't expected to arrive so late. You've already moved on to your resurrection." He smiled. "You look very well."

The grunt again. It was the closest thing to agreement the Old Bear would willingly part with, facing down a compliment.

But it was true. When Anselm departed Corma three months prior, his old partner was still a paled version of himself, whittled down by a conspiracy of injuries that allowed little good rest and scarcely any means of speedy recovery. Anselm had quietly despaired of his friend regaining much more than a badly hampered mobility. That was more than a little of what had set him on his journey, researching ways to keep the dangers he was sure his friend could no longer weather at bay.

Those worries might as well have applied to some other man entirely, given what Anselm presently saw. The Old Bear put a hand on Anselm's shoulder without preamble and leaned into him, rising gingerly off the knee he'd cushioned with a folded blanket. But once he had his feet, he was very much himself. He'd quite sweated through his linen shirt. Through it, Anselm saw the return of muscle, the planed edges of hard work and stubborn restlessness. Erasmus unrolled a sleeve to mop his brow and shrugged. "I am better than I was." He offered Anselm a hand, hauling him up, then nodded toward a pump attached to a pipe by the machine shed. "Bring the hose over. We'll give her a good soaking before the backfill."

They worked in silence, passing items between them, Anselm taking little direction. He was no gardener—there had been staff for such business in the house where he'd grown up—but he'd worked with Erasmus Pardon too long not to know how he liked a job to proceed, and thus, as soon as a task was done, he tidied after it, gathering tools and sweeping away debris. There was a comfortable quality to the silence he could keep with his old partner, an assurance in his constancy and concentration that said much more than words ever would.

Before long, they sat side by side on the shale stoop, a cask of ale from the cellar cracked and poured. Anselm stripped off his sodden shirt, hanging it from the bracket of a downspout.

He'd watched Erasmus's movements carefully as they finished the day's work. A discernible limp, yes. A tendency to favor the right leg. Still, the transformation of the yard and the industry of keeping it up boded well for his recovery.

Behind them, beyond the shop's kitchen and its curtains, came the clatter of Rowena locking up and ringing out the till.

"She's come along nicely since last I visited. Cooks for you, I hope?"

Erasmus snorted into his ale. "The dog is as fat as he is and I'm as lean principally because of it. Practically poisonous in the kitchen. I took it back from her a month ago. It was that or be starved by her kindness." He glanced over a shoulder, back toward the shop. "And yes. She's come along."

Anselm gestured with his mug to the alley yard bursting with greenery. "This is all very nice, Bear, but I can't say I see the point in it. You'll be fighting against the coal dust and the seep from the tide every day just to keep it all from dying, and for what?"

"For her."

"You've put a roof over her head. That's what she was wanting."

"She's *had* roofs before. She's never had a home."

Anselm smirked. "The Bear is nesting. How quaint."

"Go to hell, Ann."

"This *isn't* what we discussed."

Erasmus's eyes met his, sharp and raptor-clawed.

"When we talked back in Fourmonth—" Anselm pressed.

"I've had a change of heart."

"I can bloody well see that, thank you."

"I cannot just take her away."

"And, pray tell, *why not?*"

Erasmus studied the depths of his drink, as if it were empowered to offer up a reply. "What would I tell her? I've no sensible cover for a move. The business is profitable. She's more than enough help to keep it running."

"Old memories. You want to leave this place, forget the past."

"I've made my peace with it. No one knows that better than her."

For a moment, anger flared in Anselm's chest. The suggestion that anyone apart from the two of them, husband and brother, might understand what losing Leyah had meant—what losing *Rare* had meant—

But he recalled the roof of the Old Cathedral, and the strange trance Rowena had fallen into over Erasmus's fallen form. The days of deepest sleep that followed, and the oddly knowing girl who had emerged from them. He swallowed his words and their heat. Whatever had happened, happened. And he had not been a part of it.

"This city's no place for a child," Anselm suggested instead. "You've said that half a hundred times."

"It's *her* place. It's all she knows."

"Say you want to broaden her bloody horizons!"

 "And what of her mother?"

Anselm closed his teeth on a curse. Clara Downshire was settled in the Mercy Commission Home for Convalescent Gentrywomen in Southeby, a morning's ride on the iron rail to the southwest. In his letters, Erasmus had indicated through various codes and signals that the girl visited once a fortnight and that things seemed very well between them. Anselm had paid a few visits, himself—many more than he had owned up to. He felt a pang at how long away from Clara he'd been, and quickly stifled it.

"The Downshire woman's proximity will hardly matter if her daughter's a corpse," Anselm snapped. "They *know* she's staying with you, Bear, and they damned well know they can find you here. My father's people. The aigamuxa. You can plant Rowena all the forests of Leonis. Much good they'll do when she's dragged off running some gouty customer his medicine."

"I know."

"Then for God's sake, man, take my advice! I've found a place hardly anyone knows about, and I've paid the bribes to keep it off the maps. It's yours. A whole island, with good land and a favorable climate. You couldn't ask for a safer refuge."

"What cause," Erasmus said, with a patience Anselm found instantly galling, "am I to tell her we have for seeking refuge in some remote place, away from the family you've already taken pains to dispose of within her reach? What perfectly ordinary, *unsuspicious* reason should I give?"

Their gazes locked a long, silent moment. Anselm snatched up his ale in his four-and-a-half-fingered hand, sloshing over the rim. "I've no idea," he admitted.

"To keep the secret safe, she needs to *believe* that she's safe, Ann. Not that she's a target. Targets wonder why anybody would bother to aim at them. They ask questions."

"Let her believe whatever you can make her believe. *You*," Anselm said, shooting a scolding glare at his friend, "need to think more like campaigner."

"And less like a father."

"I didn't say that."

The Alchemist sniffed and finished his drink in a long draw. Anselm set his aside. *Damned mind-reading bastard.*

Anselm surveyed the yard, painted in amber by streaks of sunset. The Old Bear had a point, much as he hated to admit it. The girl had had her life of running from trouble already. And so had they. What she needed was something quieter. More ordinary. More complete.

Ordinary, he thought, *is not likely to be forthcoming.*

"We've had post," Anselm announced. He reached into his trouser pocket and drew out a thrice-folded letter penned on heavy stationery. It had survived the sweat of his journey remarkably well.

Erasmus looked at it, clasped between the stump of Anselm's index finger and his curled middle, and took it slowly, as if it were an adder fanged.

He'd unfolded it and read enough to curse over its contents when Rowena's shadow appeared behind them.

"That looks fancy. What's it about?"

Erasmus crushed the letter in his fist and returned it, thumped in a wad against Anselm's chest. "Lord Roland can go to hell." He levered himself to his feet and grabbed his cane, as if it had done something particular to offend him.

The girl's eyes shifted between the Old Bear and Anselm, lingering for a moment, after which Anselm recalled his missing shirt. He shrugged an apology and plucked it off the drainpipe. The letter fell between his feet.

He waited, knowing it wouldn't take long.

And it didn't.

Rowena trotted down the steps and plucked the crumpled mess up.

"That," Erasmus snapped, "is no concern of yours, girl."

Rowena blinked at the formal script for a moment, then read, with surprising clarity and speed: "The Greatduke Jonathan Roland and his lady Greatduchess Simone request your presence at their summer ball, twenty-fifth of Sevenmonth. They would be most gratified to attain personal audience with—"

Rowena looked up, grinning. "*Bear!* There's a pair of peerage asking you and Master Meteron to a *ball?* You'll go, won't you?"

Anselm shrugged. "Well, there is the matter of his acquiring an escort. Part of the etiquette." He smiled at the glower Erasmus flung his way. The morning glories fairly wilted under it.

"You planned this, you conniving bastard."

"An escort," Rowena broke in. "What's that mean?"

"Unwed gentlemen who do not intend to open themselves to . . . overtures, let's call them . . . from interested, eligible ladies are understood to bring a female escort," Anselm explained. He smirked at Erasmus. "Unless I've made the wrong assumption of you? It *has* been a long time."

"I could be your escort, Bear!" Rowena cried.

Erasmus's jaw clenched. "*Rowena*—"

"I had hoped, actually, that you would be mine," Anselm said.

If he had a daguerreo-box ready to take the girl's portrait, Anselm Meteron would have picked the look on her face at that moment to preserve. She turned, her lips parted, and blinked at him, eyes wide as blue moons. Her hands tightened on the invitation, the little lock-picker's scars on her knuckles whitening.

"I . . . me? You want me to escort you?"

"You do not have my permission," Erasmus said flatly.

Anselm spread his hands. "Technically, we don't need it. You're not her father, and you haven't apprenticed her. The decision is entirely Miss Downshire's."

Rowena looked down at the paper in her hands, then up at Erasmus, who loomed nearby with a face like a storm cloud. "Well, why shouldn't I go?"

Anselm crossed his arms victoriously. "That's an excellent question, cricket. Why not?"

Some part of Anselm knew that if anyone else had visited this consternation on the Old Bear, they'd have been turned inside out by now—but it was too good a sport to see the man chewing at the problem to deny himself the pleasure.

"Rowena." Erasmus lingered over the girl's name, clearly stalling. He seemed to marshal himself, wringing the neck of his cane. "The greatdukes and greatduchesses do not invite just anyone to their balls. The guest lists are very exclusive—bishop professors and landed gentry and others of the peerage. Foreign dignitaries . . ."

Rowena tossed her curls and glared. "Better folk than me, you mean. More important."

"That is *not* what I said. Not better people—"

He looked at Anselm. His expression was almost enough to break his friend's resolve. There was a furious, silent pain in it—and, written clearly enough for him to read, the answer the Old Bear would not give aloud:

Not better people. More dangerous *people.*

He was right. If there was any place they could expect to find a link in the chain of power stretching back to Bishop Meteron's conspiracy, it would be with the Rolands and their peers. If there was any place *more* dangerous to take Rowena, Anselm was hard-pressed to imagine it, short of the aigamuxa Aeries themselves. And yet, to refuse the invitation would be worse—a declaration of secrets withheld. Of ulterior motives.

"They are people one does not refuse lightly," Anselm noted.

Rowena gave Erasmus a look prickling with daggers. "And you say I can't go."

"I say you shouldn't."

The girl threw her hands up, the invitation almost flying from her fingers. "But *why?* D'you think I'll embarrass you? Or . . . or not talk proper? I'll clean up my mouth then. No more cusses and en'ts. I can do it, I know I can!"

"It's dangerous company, girl."

"Dangerous? Little fancy drinks and string quartets and . . . and . . . those little food-things people pass 'round?"

"Canapes," Anselm offered helpfully.

"*That's* dangerous?" Rowena cried.

Erasmus reached for her, consoling. "Rowena, if you went, you'd only find your way into trouble."

The girl slapped his hand away. "If I'm such a disaster, you can keep clear and pretend we've never met." She turned to Anselm with a stiff back and jutting chin. "I'll go with Master Meteron and keep my mouth sewn tight as a deaconess's drawers." She slackened, then, uncertain. "Unless you've changed your mind?"

Anselm sketched a little bow. "Never, cricket. There's a week to gather the proper effects. May I take you tomorrow to fetch a dress?"

"I've even saved a little money up lately, so—"

Anselm waved the suggestion away and retrieved his hat from the stoop. "My invitation, my expense. And no arguments." He winked at

Erasmus. "We've had enough of those. Do put a little thought into what you might wear, old boy? Lady Simone's waited ages to see you again. Best not to disappoint."

2.

Anselm Meteron's list of errands to attend upon his return to Corma involved a certain amount of delegation (Miss Ennis was surely due a raise, especially given the snags she'd been forced to navigate as he negotiated for a substantial island that now seemed unlikely to serve its intended purpose). Certain tasks, however, required the personal touch.

He stood before a vast, curious desk, considering its many dials and levers—the focal point of the Reverend Doctor Charles Wyndham's office in the Mercy Home at Southeby. The Doctor reminded Anselm very little of Phillip Chalmers, lacking in the younger man's fragile dignity and ready fluster. Wyndham was a professional—a stern-faced man, Leonine dark, with even less humor than the Old Bear, God help him. Anselm considered the field of thin, gray pins massing at the desk's framed center, their dull, slightly rounded ends forming an undulating surface, the shape reminiscent of a cloud or a plate of haggis—

Or a brain.

"All right, Doctor. Enlighten me. At what, exactly, am I looking?"

Wyndham loomed over an array of controls off to Anselm's right, dialing this and nudging that. The field rippled like wheat in the wind, the pins riffling low, disappearing into a plane of tiny holes from which the dull gray pins obediently rose. The entire prickling field seemed to sigh, collecting itself. Resetting.

"Look here," Wyndham said, more to his switchboard than Anselm. "It's simplest to begin with the beginning."

The pins shot upward, creating a single, level expanse under a sheet of tempered glass. And then they disappeared.

"This, Master Meteron, is an ordinary, healthy human brain."

A cluster of pins, very much like the ones that provoked Anselm's initial question, rose from center stage. They assumed a topographical pose, their baited ends forming a rolling surface of bunches and coils, the unmistakable landscape of humanity's chief organ.

"This is an image of Clara Downshire's brain."

With a hushed *ssnnnnkkkkkk*, pins lowered, raised, shuffled into place. The brain's rough outline remained the same, but part of its surface near what might have corresponded to the woman's left temple region appeared mashed and flattened. The pinheads glowed softly, a current of electricity turning the field orange and pink and even shining white in places, clusters of tissue highlighting obediently to underscore Reverend Doctor Wyndham's narrative.

"This is the region of the brain responsible for processing information about time. Or, more properly, it's *one* of the regions of the brain responsible for processing information about time. Time is not an abstraction, Master Meteron—it's very real, and we have objective means of measuring its passage. Planetary positions. Tides. The sun cycle. So on. Still, how we have chosen to *divide* time into pieces, and how we relate these pieces to each other, are both concrete *and* abstract things. What is a day but a collection of hours? What's an hour but a collection of minutes? What is a minute but—?"

"Understood. Units of time are agreed-upon falsehoods we use to subdivide a real phenomenon into comprehensible, but fundamentally arbitrary, parts."

Doctor Wyndham stared at Anselm Meteron as if he had just squatted and shat out a live bird. Anselm sighed.

"I may be a vaguely legitimized criminal, Doctor, but I'm a damned well-educated one. Smoke?"

Wyndham blinked, stone-faced. "No. Thank you."

Anselm retrieved a packaged cigarillo, thin and black and banded in gold, from a case on his hip. His recent travels had furnished a few novelties he'd yet to have exhausted entirely.

"Carry on, Doctor."

"This is one of the many areas of the brain that process the convenient fictive reality of time, Master Meteron. You can see that here." Wyndham gestured to a pink-glowing area. "And here." An orange one. "And here." The white-hot ones. "There is a physical pattern of damage that suggests just how profoundly impaired Mrs. Downshire's cognitive processes in this realm actually are. Now, watch the shifting landscape of colors here." The doctor returned to toggling oddments on his switchboard. "This is a playback of data gathered during a conversation one of our nurses engaged Mrs. Downshire in."

Anselm frowned. "You've been experimenting on her?"

Wyndham glanced up from the controls, entirely unabashed. "Ordinarily, we don't investigate our patients' organic situations so closely, unless we feel doing so would result in a viable treatment plan. But you made quite clear that you wanted to know more about Mrs. Downshire's state of mind, and—"

"You went poking about because I'm paying you," Anselm finished.

"It's quite harmless. A few electrical leads attached at the scalp. It looks rather like a shower bonnet. She wore it during a chat over tea."

Anselm watched the field of pins, waiting for the promised changes.

The pins kept their physical positions, but a wave of shifting, mottling colors played across their heads, like a jellyfish undulating in some deep, unseen current. Pinks, oranges, whites blurred over the featureless gray surface. A passing haze of red, then a fade to orange—

Wyndham did something with the switches and dials and the colors froze, keeping the highlighted portions bright, suspended in some critical moment. Anselm's nose prickled with the acrid tang of hot metal.

"Look!" the doctor cried. "There. Do you see?"

Anselm squinted. He drew on his cigarillo. It was an evil, tarry thing, and he held onto its smoke a long time, thinking.

"I see," he said at last, "a lot of shiny pins."

Wyndham grimaced. "What you're seeing," he explained with a condescension Anselm found much harder to dismiss than his rueful expression, "is Mrs. Downshire's cerebral response to a conversation that focuses on the events of her afternoon tea."

Anselm had a difficult time imagining that afternoon tea at a convalescent home for ailing gentlewomen would feature much of anything that passed for "an event." "And?" he pressed.

"The pattern of neural activation suggests that Mrs. Downshire's brain was accessing the areas of the mind associated with past, present, *and* future events. Recall and prediction."

"That seems reasonable. When one is in a conversation, one frames one's statements based on some basic prediction of possible futures. If I decide I want your esteem, I'll ignore the stain on your cravat and flatter your ego in some way. If I decide I'd like to dress you down for being a pompous ass, I'll point it out rather loudly when your assistant comes in the door."

Wyndham studied Anselm for a long moment, as if attempting to ascertain how hypothetical his example really was. He'd gone a bit stiff in the effort to avoid examining the state of his cravat.

"My point, Master Meteron, is that the degree of activation across the areas of Mrs. Downshire's brain that process distinct time-states is far too extreme. The kind of social maneuvering you are suggesting, however probable in another patient's case, seems quite outside Mrs. Downshire's present faculties. Moreover, the activity is deeper and more sustained than such fleeting associative decisions could account for. Interpreting this image requires another hypothesis altogether."

"And that is?"

"I believe," Wyndham said, shutting down some circuits and winding a clattering reel down, the modeling pins dimming slowly and the glass panel above them cooling in response, "that Mrs. Downshire is actually experiencing data drawn from past, present, and future simultaneously."

"I'm talking to you now, with knowledge of our past relationship and our present circumstances. I am considering how the information you are attempting to provide to me, however dubious, will dictate my decisions in the future. Such as, for instance, maintaining Mrs. Downshire's residency here and, thus, my funding of your institution." Anselm fixed Wyndham with a calculating stare, his eyes boring through a faint blue haze of cigar smoke. "Come to a point I can't explain away with layman's logic, Doctor. I bore so easily."

Wyndham cleared his throat.

"Master Meteron, I'm afraid Mrs. Downshire can see the future."

Anselm turned the cigarillo in his hand, then looked back toward the field of pins. "All right, Doctor. You have my attention."

Clara Downshire stood at the edge of a pond overlooking the Mercy Home grounds, her back to the path Anselm walked. It was, he was certain, a pose—a choice she'd made to position herself just so. Not long before, he wouldn't have believed the woman capable of such minute social manipulations. He had seen too much evidence to the contrary.

"Good afternoon, Mrs. Downshire," he said as he neared. She tilted her head toward him, smiling the warm, seemingly guileless grin that never failed to prickle the hairs down his neck.

"Master Meteron." Clara gathered her skirts up for a curtsy, then froze before she could complete the gesture. "You don't like it when I do that," she murmured. The smile went brittle.

Anselm put a hand on the lacy sleeve of Clara's dress. He'd meant to stay her, soothe her. She stiffened like a cornered doe, instead.

"Clara, it's all right."

"But you hate it when I do that," she insisted. She shrugged his arm away, chin lifted in an approximation of dignity.

God, she was beautiful. A few months before, if the thought had come upon Anselm unbidden, he would have squelched it, but that seemed such a long time ago. He had watched the curve of her neck in the afternoon sun too many times since then, seen the perfect little brackets hugging her lips when she smiled, and the slender, sloping shoulders under the shadow of a parasol.

Anselm reached for her again. This time, he took her by both shoulders, turning her by gentle degrees to face him completely. Slowly, very slowly, Clara yielded. The wild, darting thing that came into her eyes fled as she looked at Anselm steadily, as if it hadn't really been him she'd been talking to before. Perhaps it hadn't been. There were a great many men living under the jagged staircases of her mind, it seemed. After talking to Dr. Wyndham, he had a growing sense of why.

Clara blinked. She smiled shyly and slipped her arms over his neck. She had to reach down a little to do it. Barefoot, she would have stood an inch or better over Anselm. In her wedge-heeled walking shoes, her chin brushed his forehead as she drew him close.

"Oh, Master Meteron," she laughed, as if only just recognizing him. "Bless, it's *you*. Of course."

"Of course."

They kissed. It was a fleeting thing, a brush of lips and a flicker of tongue. He could taste the talc of tooth powder and feel the smooth balm of her lip stain. And then it was gone. Anything longer, more fervent, and they could well be seen. The staff likely had their own theories as to why Anselm Meteron had taken such an acute interest in the widow Downshire's personal affairs. That didn't oblige Anselm to confirm them.

Clara stroked Anselm's cheek. Then she stepped back to the length of her arm to study him with wide, blue eyes. "You've been gone so long, I worried over you. Pined, really. Truly. It's too early for that. Not time for that again."

Anselm guided Clara toward a bench some yards off. They sat, her fingers twined through his like a lovestruck schoolgirl. She lingered over the stump of his right forefinger, fascinated by its rough, scarred tip.

"You've said things like that before, Clara. What do you mean?"

Anselm's obsession with Clara had begun with just such cryptic statements—things being on time, or too soon, or coming, or past due. When she smiled at him, a clean, well-fed woman, scrubbed and plaited and corseted with the finest clothes his money and the Mercy Home's modesty codes would permit, she sometimes faded into the scrawny, mat-haired specter he'd met in the bowels of Oldtemple. "*She needs you here awhile, before she needs you there,*" she'd told him, peering through the bars of her cell. *She needs you here.* Rowena, she'd meant.

In the eight months since the Cathedral, Anselm had traveled four times, twice at length. Every visit after, he would pry for some comment about his comings and goings from Clara. And yet her responses were so damnably ordinary, it was plain his promised journey was yet to come.

Clara blinked at him, smiling innocently. "What d'you mean? What things have I said before?"

Anselm pinched the bridge of his nose, thinking. Clara stroked his other hand, waiting patiently.

"Something wrong?"

"Clara, when you look at me, what exactly do you see?"

"Ice," she answered. The immediacy of the response was jarring. As if she'd been dying for him to ask, all this time. "And air and shadows. I smell things, too," she added helpfully.

The woman sat alert as a greyhound spoiling for the chase. Anselm frowned. "Go on."

Clara leaned close. Her lips hovered by Anselm's ear, breath warm and teasing.

"Brimstone," she whispered. Clara sat back, her gaze shyly fixed on her tangle-fingered lap. "But there's a great many things around you with that smell and not all *really* you, I'm sure of it. Smells are hard because they're all from us and not all from us, too. It's just the way of them."

"Did Doctor Wyndham tell you what he meant to discuss with me today?"

"No. I leave the collars to their own business. It's always seemed best."

"He thinks," Anselm said, measuring his words, "that you have something wrong in your brain. He thinks it changes how you see time, and what you see in it."

Clara went unnervingly still.

"I think he suspects you know things other people can't, Clara."

"There's always at least one," she murmured.

Anselm arched an eyebrow. "One what?"

"One person who is . . . and who en't." She licked her lips and squirmed on the bench, as if she wanted to slip her skin and walk free of it. She let go of his hands. Something in that haunted fidgeting and the lost, wandering beam of her eye made Anselm's missing finger ache.

"It's not like I get *to choose*," Clara insisted. She rounded on Anselm. "S'not like I have *a say* in what happened already and nobody's seen but me."

Anselm covered Clara's hands with his. He squeezed. The pressure jolted her free of the petulance that had so suddenly seized her. She gaped at her lap, puzzled to find Anselm's hands there—as if they had fallen onto her skirts from the sky above.

"So Wyndham is right? You see things differently?"

"You already knew that. S'not what you mean to ask. So ask."

"I don't know what you—"

"*Ask.*"

Anselm studied Clara's face a long, silent time. "Can you see the future?"

"It en't the future." She shook her head. "The future is things that haven't happened."

Anselm sat back, letting his fingers slip free of hers. Relief seeped into him slowly, and he savored it.

Until Clara sighed and turned toward the pond.

"It en't the future," she repeated, "when it's already done and nobody's told you yet."

Anselm froze. "I'm sorry?"

"S'a pity the Creator keeps giving me men who don't know already they're dead," Clara continued, more to the pond than to Anselm. "Maybe He wants me to let them down easy for Him. But I don't see why it ought to be my job."

"You think I'm going to die."

Clara laughed once, a high, tinkling sound like a champagne flute dropped from a height. "*Everybody's* dead, Master Meteron. Didn't anybody ever tell you that's how all the stories end?"

Anselm stood abruptly. He felt sure that if he could only move around a little, he would evade Clara Downshire's pronouncements, step away from them as he might a cloud of dust thrown up by a passing carriage.

Incidental litter. Crumbs. That was all. She didn't know a thing. She was mad, and lost, and terrifying, and he'd tried to inoculate himself against her by breathing in the perfume of her hair and unlacing her bodice, lying with her under the trees by the Mercy Home's pond. She'd reached for him, and taken him, and yet it hadn't helped. It had only ground her deeper into his skin.

It's nonsense. Nonsense.

"I really am sorry," Clara murmured. She rose, closing the distance between them. She held Anselm with her gaze, bolting him to the earth with an electric charge so real, he could smell its ozone tang.

Clara lifted his chin with one slender finger and kissed him, her body easing into the curve of his. Just as Anselm finally willed himself to respond, her mouth drifted up over the plane of his cheek, lips brushing hot and sweet.

"I'm sorry," she repeated. "But you make such a lovely corpse, even now. It's not so long. You'll keep very well. The season's good for it."

Anselm jerked away. He tried to say something—to curse her, or shout her down, or beg for something—mercy or answers or silence or her body to rinse his mind clean. But his breath had left him, and all he had were ragged, panting gasps.

They were enough to remind him he was alive now, though.

"Madame," Anselm said, voice shaking, "it's a long ride back into town. I must take my leave for the day."

Clara nodded solemnly. "Of course."

He stepped backward, hunting about the ground under the bench for his hat, only to realize he was still wearing it. Anselm adjusted his grandee, trying to shade his eyes.

"I'll see you next Sabberday," he murmured.

"No." Clara shook her head. "I'm afraid you won't."

Anselm Meteron could count on one hand the number of times he'd fled from a woman. Now he would need to keep that count on his uninjured hand, if he meant it to be true.

3.

Two seasons past, the lanyani of Corma had called the great edifice of glass and iron towering over the northernmost reaches of the city "Crystal Hill." But much could change in two seasons. It could bring about an ordinary wilting—or an uprooting. It was a matter of perspective.

Dor knew a great deal about perspective. More than she had known two seasons ago, for certain.

The copse clans had gathered, filling the place lanyani now called "the Gathering Grove" to its limit. Even the volunteer tribes had made the trek in from the foggy, wooded mountains north and east of Corma. With no loam left in the hothouse for their roots, they vined up the glass ceiling's skeleton beams, their bodies drawn into fibrous lengths like wool on a skein, dangling beards of moss, their eyes distributed across buds that winked down into the shaded grove, fringed by petals half-wilted in the summer heat.

"The count?" Dor asked Lir.

Her lieutenant reviewed the space with his eyes, but it was his feet, rooted deep in the hothouse soil, which did the real census-taking.

"Three hundred nine . . . ten . . . eleven. We had expected two hundred."

"News travels," Dor mused. "If I had sent the call earlier, we would have twice as many. We would have had to gather in the Commons."

"The Men and their Constabulary—"

"They no longer matter." She reached to the twiggy bundle growing from her right hip. A latticework of slender branches held close the book that had begun her quest to muster the lanyani of western Amidon.

Dor looked back into herself, feeling in her body's new layer of rings and sap the time that had passed. Winter had been an utter loss. She had gathered her people by the dozens and preached to them, not as the Men did, from lecterns and laboratories and street corners, but through the air and the soil. So much had been planned, but the branch-snapping cold of a bitter season kept her intentions as dormant as her rallied troops.

But as soon as the frost melted, they were ready. As the summer swelter intensified, they turned the earth of the Pits, added new bodies, fed them to worms and fungi. In another month, their numbers would be doubled. The cuttings her people had made in the fall were nearly ready to uproot, and then—

"Let us begin," she said.

Lir raised his spindling arms high above his head. A haze of pale, golden pollen sighed from his fingertips. The digits, imitations of human anatomy adopted for convenience's sake, wore away like so much dust in a wind. The bark of his arms rippled, grew dense, and crawled forth to replace the fast-disappearing matter of his fingers.

Through their connection in the grove's deep, black earth, Dor felt the furious hunger of Lir's body sucking at the soil. She had to fight to keep the area around her own roots warded from his ever-reaching twiggings, lest his powerful need to build and disperse and rebuild endanger her own strength.

Thus, the colloquy began—not with words, but with air and essence. The pollen settled on the plants of the grove, settled in the cracks and fissures of the lanyani ringing all around. There, it quickly infused the tree-people, making them ready for the message that was to come—a message more complex and nuanced than their shimmering language of leaves and boughs could easily muster, and one more vast than a single speaker could transmit through the earth to a crowd such as this.

Conversations of this size demanded a hive.

Dor lifted her hand from the bundle at her hip that held the book and let it rest instead on the slatted ceiling of the wood-framed beehive. She had been rooting beside it for hours, meditating on the book, turning its pages, letting her body flourish with blossoms and be touched by countless, tiny insect feet come to her on paper-fine wings. Now, the hive knew her plot as well as she knew herself. Lured by the bounty of Lir's pollen cloud, the bees surged forth from the hive, spiraling out to every plane and angle of the hothouse. They landed on lanyani, danced along their keeper's fibrous skin, skirled and turned in the air, kissed wooden flesh and brushed themselves deep into crevices, humming and pirouetting Dor's message to every tree-person they touched or passed. And so the message ran:

"My friends, you are welcome here, in the home of my roots, at the core of my being. The seasons have been bitter and we have suffered for it, thinking the land had forsaken us.

"It has not. But it has forsaken Men and their houses of stone and metal, their cities built not by the strength of their matter, but by tools and forges. They have mistaken knowledge of natural law for permission to break it. They have mistaken the practice of science for the worship of a God.

"But we know the truth. We knew it ten thousand seasons before Man rose up from his jungles and valleys. We serve no God but the skies above and the earth below."

The grove itself seemed to rally, stirring as if a gale tore through it. The earth thrummed with her people's approval.

Dor's bees spoke for her again, spinning and alighting, spreading her words by the brush of their delicate feet.

"You have come here because I promised to share something that would give us all new power. Something that shows our place in this Man-ravaged world. This."

The branches lacing her thigh opened, became like the arms of a spider, passing the book upward until it settled in her outstretched hand. She held it aloft. Low-hanging volunteer tribesmen vined downward, drawing as near as they could without tearing their far-reaching forms to splinters. The grove became a coiling mass of twigging eye-stalks, broad-lensed parasites, leaves the size of palms that flashed open and shut, surrounded by fringes of moss, gathering pollen hungrily and drawing Dor's bees to them for a share of that second sight.

Nearby, a Pit Master of the old Crystal Hill rumbled darkly.

Dor tilted her face toward her elder and nodded. "You speak true. It's a blasphemy to bring this pulp of our people's flesh before you, and yet—look."

She fanned the pages, paused at the proper place, then reached higher and higher, her arm twining upward.

A shudder of leaves. A gasp. Or the nearest thing to one a people without lungs might muster.

A line of serif-heavy script marched like ants across the page. As little as the lanyani used the written word—scrawled on hides and scraped, gently, into fallen wood—they had their own language. The words on this page came from that language.

Something that almost passed for a smile tugged at Dor's face.

"For years, reverend doctors of the humans' so-called Ecclesiastical Commission struggled to translate this text. I have read its pages many times over in the months since the book . . ." She paused. The bees hovered uncertainly for a moment. Dor focused herself. *A little omission. A small lie.* "Since it was given to us. Who can guess if the Men who held this book for so long know half of what I saw in a single afternoon? Each day, the book grows, and I learn more."

A shimmer and rustle of birch. Dor glanced at the cousin looming there. "More of what, indeed?" she echoed, hearing its question. "More of the people the Creator has made us to find. The Vautneks. The Nine."

One of the vining volunteers hanging above wound itself into something like a pair of pseudopods with a taut cord of tuberous flesh between. The pseudopods inflated, then deflated, pushing air through a crude bellows.

"The Nine are an invention of Mankind," the pseudopods moaned. "They are an excuse to hold our world in fief."

"You are right in your second claim, if not the first, brother. They are a legend used to prove how precious human lives are—how any one of them might be the cornerstone of the world. But we are lanyani! We have no need for cornerstones or buttresses or columns or walls. We have roots. And this book calls on us to make them grow."

The brother lanyani's pods deflated in answer. "You have not looked around this place, if you believe we have no use for walls. What do you mean?"

"What I say." Dor's swarm of bees clustered over the book now, as if to emphasize the tie between her message and her matter. "It's time we left the hothouses and seedling groves. They are crutches we lean upon so we can dwell among Men and feed ourselves through their appetites. But this book proves the Creator means to speak to us directly—to show us the places we must go to grow." The bees' buzz transformed from a sonorous drone to a jagged roar. "And to show us the lives we must prune to find our place."

Dor nodded to Lir. He had spent himself sending out all that pollen, and so he pushed air through the crevices of his craggy face, his words piping out in piercing, dagger tones.

"We send emissaries of our people tonight to the quayside below Old-temple Down. We start there. Our partners will be waiting for us."

And with that, the colloquy ended, lanyani vining and twining back into themselves in their dozens and scores.

You are sure this is wise? Lir asked Dor through the soil. *Remember what became of the last messenger we sent to these . . . partners.*

Of course I am sure.

In truth, Dor could only hope her claim that the aigamuxa would be waiting was true. Rahielma's response to her last communique had been . . . not entirely what she had hoped. But if what she understood of the chaos that marked the Old Cathedral months ago was even half-true, it could still be more than enough to have thrust the hot coal of vengeance down the aigamuxa chieftess's throat.

Rahielma was a widow now, and she knew very well whom she had to blame for it.

4.

From the vast network of the Aerie, linked across rooftops and fire escapes and balconies, knitted up with old fishing nets and even older sails, Rahielma peered down into the quayside alley, waiting. She had always been a superlatively patient hunter. Indeed, half the retinue of guards she had begun the night with had since left, scuttling themselves back to their families with various excuses.

It mattered not to her. She was chieftain, absent her mate, and chieftains carried the weight of the tribe alone, even when a hundred strong-backed aigamuxa gathered around them. In the end, it always came down to the chieftain.

From her place deeper in the lattice of nets and ladders, Sunbelma thrummed for attention.

Like sparks in the night, a half dozen pairs of pink eyes flickered open and turned, feet angled to the street below.

Rahielma answered Sunbelma's rumble with a curt whoop and worked her way lower, arms picking through the maze suspended above the shabby neighborhood as her eye-heels probed this way and that, the right scouting out a safe path to traverse and the left scanning for the intruders Sunbelma warned of.

There.

The quayside was only a half-block away, perpendicular to this wing of the aigamuxa's Aerie. Dark as the night was, it could not hide the ripple on the water from the aiga's keen gazes. They were hunters by nature, though fishing had never been well suited to their bodies or methods.

The ripple turned into a tumult of parting water. What rose from it was not prey. It was lanyani. One, two, three members of a copse clan, then more. They walked out of the River Corma with slow, sucking steps, their long-spun limbs reaching down like stilts to the river's muddy bottom. As they drew nearer to the shore, the limbs shortened and thickened, the matter of them pulling inward and coiling back up, like the rope wound round the pilings of the pier.

Rahielma barely suppressed a shiver at the sight of them. No lungs. No muscles to starve of air, to burn and shut down. They had walked under cover of the water, their root-feet digging like claws into the muck and murk. Fully two miles traveled, and not a soul above the water's surface aware of their passage.

Sunbelma turned her eyeless face toward Rahielma, her brow puckered. "Monsters," she hissed. "You trust them, my chief?"

"No," Rahielma murmured. "But they have their needs as we have ours. Men stand in the way of both."

Sunbelma sighed. "May the enemies we share make us friends."

An old saying. Time had proven it true more than once, Rahielma recalled.

Still . . .

The lanyani, now six strong and dripping river water that reeked of all the dead dogs and charcoal leavings the city had to spare, formed up to tread down the alleyway, pausing at a distance suited to parley. Some of the same old chiefs who had spoken of friends and enemies taught that the tree-people had no souls of their own. They were born when the unquiet dead, dishonored by their families, rose up and joined with a tree to walk the earth in search of recompense. It was but one of a half-dozen stories told to explain the lanyani, but it suited the creatures altogether too well. How many humans had died in their composting pits, become slaves to their black market goods, been robbed of all they possessed by these slow, cunning, all-absorbing creatures?

"I will meet them," Rahielma announced, with a boldness she did not feel.

She had crossed her legs before her, ankles turned out, eyes to the quayside where the lanyani gathered, shushing and rattling at one another, the pollens they would use to transact their conversations too sodden to cloud the air around them. Out of the corner of one eye-heel, she spied Sunbelma's incredulous look and bared teeth.

"I will be careful," Rahielma added hastily and—afraid of what her second-in-command would do to stop her if given a chance—dropped down from the Aerie netting to the street below.

She landed hands first, her legs already curling up along her spines, and a moment after impact was waiting in the pedestal position. High above, Sunbelma and three others worked lower in the Aerie's riggings, though none came to rest at Rahielma's side. It was not the aigamuxa's way to stand beside the chieftain without express leave.

The lanyani people were so like the weeds they resembled. They might spring up singly between the cracks of forgotten places and thrive in gravel and clay, or they might be spread all across the land around them, as far as the eye could see. Rahielma had never been to the old lands of Leonis, but her grandsire told her stories of the lanyani clans in the forests her people once called home. Thick under the canopy. Over the canopy. They had *been* the canopy. Now, the lanyani messengers crowded shoulder-to-shoulder, moving as if they were one rhizomatic being. They finally stopped one long leap away from Rahielma's claws.

It wasn't fear that stalled them there, she knew. The lanyani feared very little from the aigamuxa. No axes, fires, or chemicals to ruin them. What did they care about teeth and claws? Perhaps, if Rahielma could only close her hands on their willowy limbs, she could split them like wishbones, sunder them with the lightning of a sudden rage.

The tallest of the group sidled forward, only a foot or so from the rest of the copse.

It—no, she; this one had fashioned herself with the plane of breasts and curve of unneeded hips, almost luridly detailed—she expanded her chest, the hair-fine fissures of her bark opening for an instant as something like a bellows expanded inside her. With rustles and undulations of a twiggy hand, the lanyani sang its words, mezzo soprano.

"We sent a messenger with a request and did not receive a response."

Rahielma blinked her eye-heels. She shifted her hands, raising and curling fingers until each of the thirty-eight knuckles cracked in turn. "You did not receive your *messenger* back, either, if the story my tribesman told was true."

The lanyani tilted her head. "We received the messenger. Though it was in several more pieces than it had been before."

"I apologize for that," Rahielma answered. She ducked her head once, and the lanyani copse echoed the movement as if they had been bent in a sudden wind. "None of my tribe has my permission to bring violence down on others without my leave. Certainly not upon a messenger."

The lanyani leader nodded, inhaled, and sang out again. "It would be easier if we had the methods Men use." Her tapered, many-fingered hand fluttered by her shoulder, indicating the sky above, crackling in the summer heat with galvano-graph lines sparking words across miles, and air galleons carrying post, and the magnetic hum of vox boxes.

Rahielma spat.

The gobbet landed in the space between herself and the lanyani leader. The tree-woman's expression bent like a bow toward a smile that did not reach the white, irisless eyes above it.

"I am called Dor. I come from the Gathering Grove, once called Crystal Hill. I speak for the lanyani."

"For which lanyani?"

"All of them," sang another tree-person, though which in the tangle behind Dor was hard to say.

"It is true, friend chieftess," Dor agreed.

"I am not *chieftess*." This, Rahielma nearly spat, as well. "I am a chieftain like my mate before me."

The sound that answered from Dor's acoustic body might have come from some strange musical drone. "You will forgive us, I hope. Perhaps our messenger angered your tribesman in its asking, for that was the word I gave it to use. It is most difficult to understand your ways and Man's both, where these genders are concerned."

Spoken like a proper Tree, Rahielma thought. Men added their foolish "-ess" and "dame" qualifiers to draw lines between men and women playing the same roles. The aigamuxa did not. Either way amounted to little more than curiosities of language to the lanyani. What use were such things to a people whose bodies were complete unto themselves, genderless, self-sustaining, perfect engines of identical reproduction?

They used pronouns with a kind of lazy interest and abandoned them freely, like curiosities from a cheap market stall.

"You are Rahielma," Dor continued, "and the lanyani wish your alliance against Man."

The chieftain snorted. "Against? We dwell in their cities. We may hate them, but you cannot be fool enough to believe we can undo them."

Dor's head tilted, strangely like an aigamuxa in its thoughtfulness. "Your mate, who was chieftain before you, believed we could."

"He believed in fairy stories and magic," Rahielma answered bitterly.

Dor reached a hand out on a level with her shoulder, spindly digits held flat as a serving platter. One of the lanyani copse behind her stepped forward, placing on her hand something wrapped in a piece of leather that might have been a scrap of some lost soul's coat. With a street conjuror's attention to style, she unwrapped the bundle to reveal—

Rahielma's breath caught in her throat only long enough to become a roar. She catapulted herself toward the lanyani. They crashed together, a bull charging through a shanty made of sticks, and under the red of her fury, the flailing, disoriented non-sight of her eyes pressed close to the cobbles, Rahielma could see *the book* in Dor's hands.

"Give it to me! My husband died for that useless heap of papers! You carry his corpse, you kindling, you driftwood—"

Her words were barely words anymore. Hands with claws and hands with thorns joined in hauling Rahielma back. As her upper body was torn away from Dor, who was still rooted to the filthy cobbles, Rahielma's legs swung forward, and her eye-heels spied a wave of action—one of Dor's clan-kin crowding close to Sunbelma, the other aiga tribesfolk split between protecting Dor from her and protecting her from Dor's people as they rattled and hissed, their leaves spitting curses.

"Enough!" Dor cried.

Her voice was lightning striking heartwood. The book lay in a puddle beside her, surely soaked by the rainwater. And yet, her twiggy hand closed over it, and it seemed dry as she turned it over. The lanyani woman stayed in a crouch at a gutter-head, her irisless eyes boring into Rahielma's furious face as the chieftain struggled to her pedestal pose.

"If you feel such rage at your mate's destruction," Dor hummed, "why suffer the one who killed him to live? All these months, and yet the human who fell with him remains."

Rahielma locked her jaws, her saw-teeth clamping down on the first words that sprang to mind. But her tribe was there—Sunbelma and Nassunbel and all the rest. Their eyes pressed into her, their expectation needle-sharp, all but drawing blood.

"We have our laws," the chieftain answered. "Nasrahiel died in open combat, a conflict he began. If we did not let his death stand as his due, our battles could continue forever, every death demanding vengeance. We cannot protect our people if we live in endless bloodshed."

And yet, how many nights had Rahielma slipped away from the nest where her children slept and prowled across dark rooftops toward the narrow alleys of Westgate Bridge? How many hours had she spent peering at the Alchemist's shop from across the quay, watching shadows move in its lamplit windows? One lame old man and a feckless girl. Nasrahiel had deserved a better death—a stronger final foe than his own arrogance. Only the stain of dishonor at felling such weak, helpless prey had stayed Rahielma's claws this long. Her sons had already lost so much. She could not cast away their family's good name, too.

"And so your chieftain died for fairy stories and magic," Dor concluded.

"So it seems."

"Tell me," Dor said, very quietly, "about the stories your husband believed."

"He believed that we could prove to God that mankind is unworthy by destroying their nine representatives. Proving they were unfit for His Experiment. That once we did, God might leave the world to us."

Rahielma did not specify that Nasrahiel had been thinking most particularly of the aigamuxa. He would not have begrudged the lanyani a place in the world he wished to build for their children. He was a good chieftain, and wise enough in that respect. The aigamuxa needed the trees. What were the nets and ladders above them now but a poor reminder of that?

Dor nodded. "That is an outcome much to be desired." She lifted the book before her—but not too far. Not as an offering. Out, and then back to her chest, and then she stood, with a queer angular movement no Man or aiga could have managed. "I am the prophet of my people. I found this book. It is marked for me."

"It is marked with Nasrahiel's blood," Rahielma snapped.

"And for that, I grieve with you."

Rahielma could not imagine a creature more incapable of tears, more alien to grief. She rose, putting feet to the cobbled street, relieved to take her gaze away from the lanyani prophet. Rahielma smelled something of the tension among her own people, their pheromones passing quick messages. She heard the rustle and snap of tree-people making conversation, too. Suspicion. Anger. Need.

A great deal of need.

Rahielma closed her eyes and pressed her heels into the stones. It hurt. Her vision flared with bursts of light and swimming colors, but it grounded her, blacked out any thought of seeing beyond the right course of action.

The lanyani leader was not content to leave Rahielma to her thoughts. "Your Nasrahiel's life brought my people this book, and for it, we are grateful. It will show us the path to the ones the Men call the Nine. If your wise husband was right, their undoing will be the undoing of all their kind. We, the lanyani, have been called to do this thing. But we will need your help."

"My help," Rahielma echoed. She sniffed. Her flat, flaring nostrils pulled in . . . something. A smell muddling the pheromones of her people and the chatter laced inside them—*leave, don't trust, join, no, yes, revenge, safety, revenge, revenge.* The smell, she realized slowly, came from the lanyani. Their pollen. A secret idea circulating among them, not as secret as they imagined.

She was not chieftain for nothing.

"You said you speak for the lanyani," Rahielma said, having found the conversation beneath the one already spoken. "I speak only for my own tribe, and perhaps for the ones who followed my husband.

There are many others of my kind in the city. How great an aid do you seek?"

"As great as you can give."

"And what task would you ask of us?"

The smile had entered Dor's voice. It was every bit as awful to hear as it was to see, sitting lifeless on her face. "The task of your heart's deepest desire. To dismantle the power of this city. To make it free for our peoples. To make the world as dangerous a place for Men as it has been for us."

Rahielma tilted her head. She let the thought sift deeper into her mind, trailing skepticism and concern behind. "What good does this do you?"

"A Corma trying to save itself from destruction," the lanyani answered, "will have no attention to spare for the members of our people who go forth to sow destruction for these Nine. When all the gendarmes and all the constables and even all the Ecclesiastical Commission's advisors to the Governor are wound up in keeping the city intact, what time will there be to save nine unfortunate souls, or even to remember what might make them significant?"

"It will not bring my husband back," Rahielma murmured, after a time. "But it will bring his vision to life."

"It will."

"Then tell me how we must begin."

5.

Pain was not the first thing to return to Nasrahiel. The light came before it.

It poured in through his head somehow, seeping into his mind. He remembered it as he remembered the lash wielded by men who made a servant of him long before Regenzi. The light scored a path through his vision. That was when the pain took hold in earnest.

It began with knowing that the light in his head had something to do with seeing.

He struggled to sit up, to pull his legs toward him and cover his eye-heels with his hands, but something bound him in place. A long, heavy strap. A voice bound him, too—soft, strong, and low. A woman's voice. Human.

"Lie back."

The chieftain might have laughed at the futility of the order, but pain rang through his body like a bell. If the voice spoke again, he did not hear it. The darkness came and took the place of the light filling his skull.

Pain—pain that flooded his joints and ran in his blood like fire— came the next time he woke, and the time after that. The voice came, too, every time.

"Rest."

Or "Sleep."

Nasrahiel knew little of what had happened to him since the Alchemist wrapped him in a desperate embrace at the top of the Old Cathedral. There was the roof, then the sky, then open air, and then . . .

Ground. There had been the ground.

Later, on some other night or morning, Nasrahiel awoke. There were no straps to hold him, no voice resting on his chest like a purring thing, heavy as lead. He placed his hands right and left, flanking his sides, and pushed slowly up to a seated position.

He noticed, before anything else, that he saw the room *wrongly*. He should have awoken looking at the dim outline of the door on the opposite wall, for that was the direction he felt his body stretched out beneath the linen sheet. It was where his feet pointed. *Sitting up* should have changed nothing.

Sitting up, he realized, should not even have been his first instinct. But he had done it, and it had changed everything.

The room was now upright, and so was he, and yet he could detect its dimensions as he might in the pedestal position. He had not curled in upon himself. Why? What did his body know that he himself had yet to learn?

The door opposite his makeshift bed—a high trestle of some kind, improvised, as the beds of Men were far too small to accommodate even an aigamuxa stripling's form—the door he had seen first not at all, and then head-on—opened.

The woman who entered was short and well-curved, her broad-waisted dress dotted with pockets and sleeves for various implements. Her hair coiled about the crown of her head, held in place with innumerable tiny clasps. Her dark eyes watched him carefully. Dispassionately. She set a metal tray down beside his bed and reached, wordless, for Nasrahiel's arm. He stared at her.

As the woman's fingers covered his wrist and her eyes studied her chronometer, counting out the beats, Nasrahiel realized something on his face—no, something *in* his face—had been moving.

He fumbled back, tearing his arm from the woman's grip. Though his body felt out of use (how long had he lain there, insensible? how wasted and weak had he become?), he was strong enough to break her meager hold.

His hands covered his face. All at once, he understood why his skull had ached, why the light had poured into it.

Above the flat, flaring span of his nose, something cold and hard pressed against his long, reticulating fingers. He heard a tap-tap-tapping, as if he probed some instrument from the Reverend Doctor's lab. The sound made him flinch, and with the flinch came another reflex.

A blink.

Something metallic snapped at his fingertips. It sounded like a kinotrope lens snapping shut.

Nasrahiel screamed.

The woman looked upon him with absolute exhaustion. The door behind her opened again, and two humans—a male and female, juveniles—gaped inside. The boy said something and lurched forward, but some little glass vial had already appeared in the adult woman's hands. There was a sharp pinch at Nasrahiel's throat.

The darkness came again, blotting out the light.

Eventually—an hour, a day, a year, a century later—gray fog crawled away from the his vision, and he woke, blinking only to wince at the sharp, snapping sound his monstrous eye made.

The woman was there, seated at a writing desk beside the trestle bed, scanning papers. Records. Something. The alchemical lamps ringing the room had been dialed higher. Night, then—almost certainly night. Nasrahiel's head roared, though the pain was gone. Its absence made his stomach clench. He longed for the pain, for its reassurance that his body had been wronged—that it knew things were not as they should be.

"Why did you do it?" he croaked.

The woman did not look up, now jotting with a tiny, surgical steel ink pen.

"If you uncover yourself, you'll see why straight away," she replied, sounding flat and bored. Human voices were expressive, though they lacked all other virtues. Nasrahiel closed his eye. He did not uncover himself, but he did move.

When they were still, his legs felt like his own, but under the sheet and moving, he heard their steel on whetstone ring and knew what the woman meant. He opened his eye and stared at the foreign shapes jutting, still hidden, beneath the cloth.

"After the fall," the woman began, squaring her papers and setting them aside, "you were scarcely alive. Both legs were broken, though they might have survived purely locomotive repair. The trouble was the particular nature of your fractures damaged the optical nerves running from your brain stem along your spine and into the ocular organs situated in your feet. The left eye-heel was pulped in the fall. Even if the vision in that leg could have been restored by closing the nerve gap, there was no eye left to do the work. Your left spinal array was badly twisted and the pelvis broken, though that in three rather convenient parts not too difficult to reassemble. But your legs themselves were, for all practical purposes, beyond hope, and given your species' peculiar anatomy, that meant quite a lot of . . ." She paused, searching for a word, as if she had suddenly decided to bother with something like a bedside manner. "It meant a lot of auxiliary augmentation to restore your sight."

Nasrahiel shifted himself into a seated position and pulled the linens away.

The sheet slithered to the floor, revealing two spindly structures of polished brass and steel—pistons and gears, hinges and springs—attached to his body, grafted into two scarred stumps that terminated just below his pelvis, flanking his sex.

Perhaps the scream he had given before was the only one he had. He stared at the mechanical legs with mute hatred, studying their every detail so he might commit them to memory and damn every Man-forged part.

With a flinch, he realized he was able to count the minute coils making up his ersatz toes. A faint whirring in his head and a buzz like pins and needles told him his eye's lens had focused and extended, magnifying the image of his monstrous legs.

"You might have left me as I was," Nasrahiel murmured. "Let me die. What was it to you if another ape died in your city?"

The woman shrugged. "Nothing to me personally, except a challenge. You'd be better served to ask what it was to *her*."

The woman nodded toward his left, across the room. Nasrahiel saw they were not alone.

City Inspector Haadiyaa Gammon sat, her long legs crossed and hands folded on her lap. She was not, for once, in the uniform of the office Nasrahiel never believed she'd earned. She wore ordinary clothes tailored for a human male—trousers and jacket and waistcoat.

"You weren't in a position to give your consent," Gammon said.

"You might have left me still one of my people," Nasrahiel continued, rounding on the first woman—a doctor of some kind, no doubt. She smelled of disinfectants and looked as if she knew better how to address her papers than another of her kind. "You took my legs. Why not build them back as they were meant to be? What am I without my eyes turned toward the earth my people were given?"

The doctor sighed. "Your *brain*, which is *here*," she jabbed a finger toward Nasrahiel's violated skull, "is still where visual information is processed. It's not as if approximating nerve tissue with bioelectrical conduit is easy, or cheap. The filaments are desperately tiny and tear with the least misuse until they're properly installed. The farther I had to string the stuff to reach from optic nerve point to occipital lobe, the more likely I would do it badly and leave you blind in any case. It was much simpler to drill you a proper occipital cavity and build up an ersatz with just a few inches of conduit." She crossed her arms, tossing her head. A bit of her hair fell free from its arrangement. "It's very likely the finest visual organ I've ever made. The telescoping feature is both powerful and only mildly intrusive, and the multistage lens approximates appropriate depth perception to a very tolerable margin of error."

As if she expected him to ask how she might know this, the doctor added crisply, "I tested it on a cat gone blind with glaucoma. It was quite a mouser again for a while."

Nasrahiel looked to Gammon, his teeth bared in a snarl. "What is this ghoul you've brought me to?"

"Nasrahiel." Gammon rose, squaring her shoulders. "This is Jane Ardai, Lieutenant Colonel, Amidonian Army Medical Corps, honorably discharged and now serving in private practice."

Nasrahiel wrinkled his nose. "Resurrection Jane."

Jane Ardai crossed to a long wall full of cabinets and countertops. She filed her papers in a drawer and reached up, unpinning her hair. Nasra-hiel's eye focused in close without his choosing and saw her drop surgical sutures from her hair, one by one, into a shallow dish of lister.

"It's a crass nickname." Ardai sighed wearily. "But it's good for busi-ness. Suggests a certain reputation." She cast a narrow-eyed glance back at her sulking patient. "It's earned, you know. You're living proof."

"How long since I fell?"

"Eight months."

Nasrahiel stared.

"You're easily the most involved reconstruction I've ever attempted, in no small part due to your ocular dilemma. It took almost three months to redesign my standard bio-conduit so your immune system wouldn't reject it, a month waiting for my machine apprentice to finish the design for the legs and another two weeks getting him to hammer out his errors after some basic tests. That's completely ignoring the time my courier spent fetching supplies from local dealers and standing her ground in negotiations for the really tricky parts. You owe that young lady rather a lot, I should think. After the surgery and installation, you needed weeks for all the grafts to take hold and mend you up again. All the while I had you feasting on my best intravenous and subcutaneous feeding solutions and kept your natural musculature from going flaccid through regular electrical stimulation." Ardai crossed her arms under her heavy breasts and tossed her head again, as if she'd won some victory and the right to gloat over it. "You've been almost the entirety of my professional practice for months now. And I don't come cheap."

That last, Nasrahiel saw, was directed past him and toward Gam-mon.

"We had an agreement," the other woman answered. Her tone was soothing, almost apologetic. Gammon's eyes lingered lovingly on Resur-rection Jane. Something in them answered a suspicion Nasrahiel had nursed about the officer when they first met.

"Yes, well. If only I knew then what I know now," Ardai scoffed, though she seemed more playful than put out, "I'd have held out for more." She dusted her hands off, lifted high in the air, as if to make the point that she was well and thoroughly done. "The sooner Nasrahiel makes his merry way out of my care and into yours, the better. My electrical stimulus regime is quite effective, but those legs will take getting used to and that can't happen lying flat in my infirmary."

Ardai marched toward the door, snapped its handle open, and paused on the threshold. Her smile showed teeth, and a little claw, too. "Out by week's end, Haadi, my love. If I come back from Sabberday lectures and find six hundred pounds of aigamuxa still here, you'll find out just how much a resurrection can *really* cost."

And with that, the woman left.

In the silence that followed, Nasrahiel stared at Inspector Gammon with his alien eye, wondering if he had strength enough to fling himself from his bed and break her neck.

It was a struggle to form the words—a struggle against rage and nature and the horrifying realization that there would be no narrowing tunnel of red in his vision. No rush of blood to color his sight. Never again. He was a creature of passions and they felt more distant than ever, just as he needed them most. He reached for the fury, and it was a cold thing, limp and unfamiliar. He held it, oozing, between his fingers.

Cold as the clipping iris of his mechanical eye, Nasrahiel found his words at last.

"Tell me why you had her save me."

Jane Ardai's work had made a freak of Nasrahiel, but he could not deny that reading with an eye placed like a human's was easier than reading in the pedestal position. His hands were free to lift and turn pages, to leaf and shift. His long, many-knuckled fingers moved shakily, fumbling the ragged pages' edges. Confidence using his body had yet to return. And so much of his body had been changed. Ardai had been all too pleased to share the notes describing his case. There was a lacing of surgical steel netting over the bones of his spines, mending their breaks and protecting them against further injury. His arms felt changed, too, and he could see the faint tattoos of suture scars near elbow and wrist—some amendment to his musculature.

Focus. The pages. He directed his attention back to the ragged sheaf Gammon had given him as explanation: the reason he'd been saved, lying there before him.

The pages kept slipping between his fingers, but his eye took in the figures and facts quickly. He was no scholar, but among his people, Nasrahiel was known to be wise.

"Does the Reverend Doctor know you have these notes?" he asked the woman standing warily by his trestle bed.

Gammon shook her head, gathering some of the ragged sheets Nasrahiel had set aside. "I left the Constabulary . . . unexpectedly. I haven't seen Chalmers since the night at the Cathedral—or, rather, he never saw me, up until he left Corma altogether. The Decadal Conference ended in a scandal—his kidnapping uncovered, a mass exodus of much of the EC's leadership in the dead of night, the final day of programming entirely scuttled. Chalmers refused any interviews, spent a few weeks convalescing at Regency Square, and emerged back on the public scene with a joke of a paper adapted from the talk he was meant to have given for the keynote. He didn't stay in the city long after that, and no one in the EC is very interested in looking for him. He'd probably have trouble getting work tutoring at a finishing school now, let alone qualifying for grants. There's been talk of scheduling a new 'Decadal Conference' next spring to make up for the loss of this most recent event."

"None of that matters to me," Nasrahiel growled.

"I imagine it wouldn't. As for the notes, I've pieced the pages together as best as I can. We seem to have portions of Chalmers's records related to Subject One, Two, Four, and Seven."

"*We.*" Nasrahiel ground the word against the rasp of his voice.

"We," Gammon echoed. She pulled a sheet out, seemingly at random, and thrust it into Nasrahiel's clawed grasp. "Focus on the coordinates for this one. What do they tell you?"

"Nothing," the aigamuxa snapped. "I have no atlas, no map of this

. . . Man's world. You could as well bid me to read tea leaves or find water with a rod."

"Look again. You should be able to tell something easily, if you try."

Nasrahiel's eye clicked and whirred. He bristled at the numbness it rattled into his flesh, but the feeling passed, and he found himself looking at the coordinates on the page, a splash of ink the size of a thumbprint.

"It is far from here," he announced petulantly.

"*Very* far," Gammon agreed. She pulled out another page and compared it against the first, laying it on the trestle beside him. "These coordinates are much closer, still in the western hemisphere and still in the north. Those others are in the east, south of the equator. If you compare them against a proper atlas . . ."

"Leonis," Nasrahiel murmured. "Deep in the jungles. There are no Men left there. My people saw to that long ago."

The former City Inspector leaned over the papers now, her hands braced to either side of them. She looked up, her dark Indine eyes locking on his mechanical gaze. She deserved some credit, this frail, human thing. *She sees horrors and does not flinch from them.*

"Exactly my point," Gammon said. "Pierce and Chalmers were so busy gathering data and deciphering it, they scarcely bothered examining what it actually showed. They assumed all nine subjects would be human. But here—" she tapped the coordinates that pointed to a faraway home Nasrahiel had never known—the place from whence his father's father had been dragged in chains. "And here—" she tapped the set on the other page, "It's clear that can't be. This region of northern Amidon is still unsettled. The lanyani tribes hold sway there. There are raiding parties to drive off settlers. No human habitation has been founded there and lasted more than two seasons since John Amidon came to the continent with the first Unitarians. It's all wild game and rivers and mountains."

"And trees," Nasrahiel added. "And tree-men."

Their faces were very close—close enough that Nasrahiel could clutch the woman's neck, the pulse-point pounding, inviting the pressure he *should* use to end her.

His fingers ached, not for the first time since his waking.

"When last I saw you," he growled, "you were shooting down my kinsmen. How much smaller is my tribe now, turncoat? How many body weights shall I tie to your feet, before I throw you to the river?"

"Eleven aigamuxa died at the Cathedral. Three were my doing. I maimed more than I killed, by the time the night was done."

The woman's perfectly uninflected ownership of her crime brought Nasrahiel up short. He tilted his head, an old habit of his thinking, and puzzled over the change it wrought. Strangely, his gaze turned, too, unbalancing the woman in his field of vision, shifting her right, then left.

He bared his teeth.

"You," he said, at last, "are a bold creature, woman. I thought you Regenzi's puppet."

"And I thought you were just a pet waiting to bite his hand," she parried. "But you're more than that, Nasrahiel. You're a prophet to your people. Their hope."

Nasrahiel looked away. He closed his eye. "I have failed at that."

"How many tribes followed your mission—believed in the theory of destroying mankind by destroying the subjects in the Grand Experiment?"

He turned back, glaring. "You have been gone since the Cathedral. None who were there know where you are, you claim. How do you know of my aims when you were not there to hear my claims?"

"I can make sense of the evidence before me. And I've been keeping watch over Chalmers. That's shown me enough to fill in the gaps."

"Four other tribes."

"All in Corma?"

"Two in Corma. Two beyond."

Gammon nodded grimly. "They'll carry out your mission, with or without you?"

"They saw me fall," Nasrahiel observed with a savage snort. "We have laws against retribution after the end of a war, but these are already . . . flexible, in a sense. One could say my quest against the Nine is itself a retribution for the harm done to my people. It might itself violate our

law. Whether my fall will be read as proof that I was judged for my retribution, or as a martyr's death that demands a response, I cannot say."

"That's why I needed Resurrection Jane. You set this in motion
among your people. You're the only one who can stop it."

"Why would I want that?"

"Two of the four subjects in these notes are almost certainly nonhu-
man. One is clearly an aigamuxa. If there are nine subjects, and three
races, it stands to reason all three are being watched, and each race has
three representatives. The sample size is smaller than Chalmers ever
imagined, but its scope is much bigger. If you tamper with the Experiment by slaying the humans, you tamper with an experiment in which
you are actively a part. It's a risk you can't afford."

Nasrahiel sneered. "You saved me so I could save *you*."

"There are many things you could save. Who do you think has taken
leadership of the tribe in your absence?"

A knot pulled closed in Nasrahiel's heart. He pried it open with brutal will.

"Rahielma."

"Among others."

Nasrahiel studied the woman through a steadily narrowing gaze, like
the spyglasses and microscopes he had seen cluttering up the scientist's
cell at the Old Cathedral. He looked for tension in her jaw, or the line of
sweat at her brow that could prove this all to be lies.

He breathed deep and smelled the tang of resolve, not fear, surrounding Haadiyaa Gammon.

"You have a plan," he said. It was not a question.

"The beginnings of one. I'll need your help. I can't carry it through
without you."

He nodded slowly. "Be it as you say, then. First, I must know what
has become of the girl."

Gammon frowned. "Girl?"

"The maps Chalmers drew. His notes. What of the girl?"

Gammon pursed her lips. "The one from the Cathedral? Rowena
Downshire?"

"Her."

The woman drew near, leaning over the papers again. Nasrahiel knew he had spoken too soon.

Fool. Idiot.

Gammon appraised him cautiously.

"Does she matter," she murmured, "for the reason I'd expect?"

"That and more. You'll need to find her before your Bishop does. The old Meteron."

"And if I don't?"

"Then none of this—" Nasrahiel gestured—taking in the room, his metal legs, the bedraggled leaves of notes. The world itself "—will matter, after all."

6.

Erasmus Pardon was standing in front of the small shaving mirror propped on his chest of drawers when he heard a small, insistent cough.

Rowena hovered in the doorway, a hand clamped at the small of her back. The two long ribbons of her corset's stays waved disobediently behind her. "I, um." She smiled ruefully. "I need help? And there's nobody else here, so. . ."

He had been finishing his cravat, but as Rowena's need seemed to have left her poised at the edge of indecency, Erasmus abandoned it over one shoulder. "Turn about."

She obeyed. He frowned down at the line of hook-and-eye clasps that formed the corset running over her underslip, working them closed from bottom to top before cinching the runaway ribbons. It was scarcely the first time he'd been asked to wrestle such a device into service. There had been Leyah, and even Rare, on a few occasions. Neither had trembled with such fretful energy, though.

"Nervous?"

"S'pose. Excited, too." Rowena put a hand to the doorframe, rocking a bit in the heeled dress boots Anselm had purchased. "Is that, um . . ." She glanced over her shoulder. "Is that all, then?"

"As long as there isn't an over-corset, yes."

"Master Meteron said I'd disappear turning sideways if I had any more cinching-up."

"He's not wrong."

The girl turned, smoothing down her slip's cream-colored silk. Though it wasn't meant to be seen, it boasted near as much lace and ribbon as the gown itself. Erasmus had long been absent from any social event's invitation roll, but he remembered enough of their details to be certain of that much.

Rowena had already pinned up her hair with clasps limned in mother-of-pearl and gold. They gleamed against her mass of dark hair, less unruly than Erasmus was accustomed to. She wore a little powder but seemed otherwise unpainted, which met with his grudging approval. He would have words enough for Anselm once they had a moment out of Rowena's earshot. Cluttering up the argument with sartorial complaints was beside any practical point. And yet—

It had not yet been a year since Erasmus first laid eyes on the scrawny, bruised guttersnipe girl, boldly silencing a pub full of Westgate Bridge's most unflappable regulars by interrupting the Alchemist's supper. He marveled at how much only a few months had done.

Some things had *not* changed, of course. Her rough beginnings would always be written on her hands, crossed with pale scars, and the break in her left eyebrow where a little pink line showed how a guard had opened her face up against the grating of Reverend Chalmers's cell. She could hide the first with her gloves and the second with a bit of painting, but the street would always linger on her tongue. It was coated with the rushed slang of Oldtemple and Blackbottom End, weighted with vowels dropped like puddled iron. But Rowena held herself with a certain stubborn pride, too—something an order of magnitude greater than the audacity he'd seen in her that first night at the Abbey. Something earned. It fitted her better than any gown.

"You look lovely," he said, his voice catching. He turned back to the shaving glass and his neglected cravat.

Rowena looked down at herself, twisting and swishing the underskirt with evident pleasure. "S'nice, en't it? Just the first bit, though. The rest of the dress is—"

"Anselm's coach will arrive soon. Best finish up, girl."

Erasmus felt Rowena's gaze strafing his back—and something else pressing at him, too. A peeking-in she must have imagined was coy, but was really more akin to throwing the shutters open on a bedroom at noon. "If there's something you want to know," he murmured over the knot in his hands, "you'd be better served to ask *aloud*."

He saw her studying him in the mirror. Sometimes, the temptation to . . . visit . . . was too much for her. The connection they'd forged in a desperate moment after his fall from the Cathedral had somehow never broken. Having pushed her way through his barred doors once, she assumed they'd never be properly shut again. Curiosity awakened by some oddment, Rowena would reach for his mind, try to touch it—try to ask without words things she couldn't quite say.

You were the same way, once, he reminded himself.

Erasmus Pardon had been nearly eight years old when he finally determined why his head was always filled with the clamor of other people's thoughts and fears, a discovery that transformed a terrifying childhood spent as far from other people as could be managed into an entirely different kind of isolation. What had been his curse became his crutch. Never a talkative child—indeed, so silent and distant most of the people in his boyhood home of Long Meadow had assumed him dull-witted—he became all but mute, giving up the inefficiencies of speech. If it was hard to find the right words to say, he needn't bother searching them out. He would reach, and the shorthand of mind-to-mind would translate for him.

Small wonder that Rowena, who had discovered that cold night atop the Old Cathedral that she could do in his mind what he had done for decades in the minds of others, found it hard to resist the same temptation.

"I didn't have a question," she answered hastily. "I wanted you to know that you look . . . Well. *Saying* it seemed so odd, so—"

His cravat finally tamed, Erasmus swept his dress coat up from the rack. "Rude?" he suggested.

Rowena pulled a face. "*No.* For being a mindreader, you're a lousy judge of intentions."

He grunted, shrugging into the coat. Rowena's hand touched his sleeve.

"I *was going* to say you actually look quite handsome."

Erasmus arched an eyebrow. "Well."

"*Well?*"

"You've terrible taste in men."

"*Be-arrr . . .*"

"There *are* worse problems, I suppose."

Rowena gave his shoulder a clout that stung more for the boniness of her knuckles than the strength of the blow.

"Arse."

A knock echoed up the stairway from the Stone Scales's front door.

"Oh, pissbuckets," Rowena gasped.

Erasmus hooked his cane off the coat rack, scowling. "Put on the last of your dress and see if you can scrub clean your tongue. We won't be at this party long if you can't dress up what comes out of your mouth." Then he assayed the stairs to the back room, teeth gritted, telling his screaming right knee it would have to register its complaints another time.

"Dog-wanker! Fuckwit! Turd blossom!" Rowena taunted, laughing, from the room above.

Anselm stood just inside the shop door, tucking the key back into his wallet. He nodded toward the stairs.

"Having a row already?"

"Just clearing the verbal mechanism."

They assessed each other in a quick sweep—tailed coats and brocade vests and pocket chains. Anselm Meteron had been born to such style. Erasmus felt more like an actual bear kitted out for a circus.

He consulted his inner pockets, taking a superfluous inventory for pipe and reading spectacles and a cache of chemical conveniences his hosts might be less than pleased to have on their premises. "Tuck the alley piece strapped to your arm closer to the wrist," he told Anselm. "It's bunching the sleeve near the elbow."

Anselm unbuttoned his coat sleeve and made the adjustment. "God's balls, you'd think I'd just signed my first campaigning license."

"No one without our experience would have noticed."

"And the Rolands might have finally hired better security. They've learned a lot since '63."

Haven't we all? Erasmus thought. He didn't share the thought aloud, or even reach out with it. With Anselm, he rarely needed to. They shared a look, and it was a whole conversation, Anselm's pat on his arm its punctuation.

"All right," Rowena's voice called from the stairs. "I'm coming down, but someone ought to stand at the bottom to catch me when I trip and break my face."

Anselm smirked at Erasmus, who rolled his eyes in response, waving him on. "Go rescue the girl."

From his vantage point, all Erasmus could see was Anselm waiting at the end of the stair rail, his face—always ten years too young, a lie taken for granted in a life of deceptions—turned upward. His expression shifted, the whetted edge of his knife-smile turning. It was a look that would have earned another man the drubbing of his life, had Erasmus caught him using it on Rowena.

"God's balls, cricket. There was a girl under that grime after all!"

She stepped to the landing, dressed in cartridge pleats of emerald green and a bustled hem that showed a provocative helping of calf. She put out her elbow, though at too steep an angle, as if she might jab it up into Anselm's throat any moment. *Not an altogether bad plan*, Erasmus supposed.

Anselm took the proffered arm and levered it down through his own. "Ready, Bear?"

"God help us all," Erasmus muttered.

He opened the door and let his companions usher themselves out and down the street to where the carriage had been forced to park, lacking proper clearance so deep in the highstreets of Westgate Bridge. He closed the shop door, turned the key, and set, at the top and bottom of its frame, resting just inside the jamb, two alchemical spheres. He'd come up with them some months before, and only used them when he knew the shop would be empty a long while. They'd never been tried in a moment of need, but his laboratory tests had never yet lied to him. They had proven the little devices quite the match for even the most unlikely intruder.

⋈

Anselm Meteron's carriage driver and footman snapped to attention as soon as Master Meteron emerged round the bend with Rowena on his arm and the Old Bear coming up behind. After handing Rowena up to the carriage box like the proper lady she hoped very much to be taken for, they were off, filling the street with the clamor of chimes and clattering gear-works.

Inside the carriage, Meteron flicked a look at his old friend and smirked. "Didn't you wear that suit at a ball fifteen years ago?"

"More than likely. I don't own another."

"Huh."

"What?" the Old Bear growled, wringing the head of his cane rather like a neck.

"Surprised it still fits."

"I am just full of surprises," the old man muttered.

As they rode to the Greatduke's villa at the far east of Corma proper, Anselm chattering amiably at his friend, poking and winking at the Old Bear's expense, Rowena enjoyed not being noticed by her companions. She was afraid of what they might see, if they really looked. *My gloves are too long and they're sliding down my arms, but I can't take them off or everyone'll see my hands. I should have chosen the ones that stop at the wrist. Why did I have to get all fancy? Stupid, stupid . . .*

After a half-hour's journey, the city parted like an opening zipper, the jagged teeth of towering buildings falling away to either side. Rowena caught sight of the Rolands' mansion, and in the same moment lost her breath.

Rowena had been alive long enough to know folk seemed in the habit of debating how to measure what a man was made of—what made him important or grand or what-have-you. It wasn't money; it was esteem. It wasn't esteem; it was grace. It wasn't grace; it was propriety. It wasn't propriety; it was connections. Sometimes, when folk in the Abbey really got down into their cups, they'd decide it wasn't any of these things because it all came down to clockworks and carriages and caskets full of clink.

Rowena might have chosen any of a dozen different measures. In each of them, Greatduke Jonathan Roland would have fared a damn sight better than anyone had a right to.

Staring past the carriage's drawn sash, Rowena took the measure of Greatduke Roland in units of courtly guests, and glimmering decorations, and rows of courtesy carriages fetching the most honored guests from their homes at his expense.

Seeing this villa broke the spell Master Meteron's carriage had cast. It was not that his carriage—appointed all in brass and mirrors and gilt details—was anything shabby. But it was a singular thing, and the Greatduke's estate was ringed with that carriage's perfect mates, drawn by stolid, steaming fore-engines or stamping clockwork beasts, built not just into the shapes of horses, but all kinds of fanciful designs. Ostriches and rhinoceroses, unicorns and griffons, tigers and wolves, and, yes, even one with a brace of bears done all in shining silver. They looked like polar bears, lumbering along with unhurried dignity.

The greatness of the Greatduke surged like the tide. When the footman opened the carriage door and ushered Rowena gently down, it closed upon her, swallowing her whole.

She didn't even realize until the Alchemist's hand rested on her shoulder, a handkerchief secreted in his palm, that she had begun to cry.

Wordless, Rowena stole her fingers through his, drawing the handkerchief from his weathered hand. She touched it to her eyes, hoping she hadn't made a ruin of her powder or the little tracing of kohl she'd dared to try out. She knew so little about how to wear it in the first place, she stood next to no chance of repairing it.

Rowena felt the Old Bear's voice in her mind.

Are you well?

I'm fine. I think. It's just . . . It's so pretty and I'm just . . .

He squeezed her shoulder. Master Meteron took her arm again.

"Are you ready for this, cricket?" he whispered.

Rowena blinked. There was a line drawn between his eyebrows. It took a moment for her to realize that he wasn't upset at her dithering. He was worried.

She sniffed and stowed the Old Bear's handkerchief in the bosom of her dress.

"Lead the way, Master Meteron."

He did, the Alchemist following a few paces after. Rowena struggled to keep her eyes from darting around and snapping up the thousand reminders great and small that this was *not* where she belonged.

"Tonight," Anselm said, looking forward and nodding at a tall, wasp-waisted woman with a pale, powdered face, the veritable twin of the many strangers milling all around, "you'd best not call me that."

"If I can't call you Master Meteron, what should I call you?"

He shrugged in his one-shouldered way. "Uncle Anselm. Most people know I had a sister, and a niece. They don't know that was Rare."

Rowena detected a hitch in his tone that she might have missed if a certain, shadowy voice inside her had not known what to listen for. It was a presence that knew Meteron far better than she did, and it was at least as uncomfortable as she was in the swirls and eddies of the Roland mansion.

"All right," Rowena said. She smiled. So what if that smile was her own affectation? She'd need it here. All the polished, pretty faces, all the gilded grins, and she hadn't yet seen the first button on the Great-duke's jacket. She'd need a great deal more theater to make it through the night.

And so it began. Anselm Meteron introduced her to the curious, the kind, and the clearly dissembling. In less than a quarter-hour, his confidence made the words "This is my niece, Rowena" seem nearly true. Even Rowena could have believed it.

Meteron was a guest at the ball, but he was more its master than anyone else gracing its halls. If the Greatduke and his Greatduchess had descended from their rooms above the spacious gathering halls and parlors and wine rooms, they hadn't made themselves known. The ball abhorred that social vacuum, snatching Meteron up eagerly as its replacement host. Notoriety and grace and the devil's own wit made it easy for him to hold court. Standing so close to his ambient social heat, Rowena caught herself wishing she really was his niece.

Before long, he turned her out onto one of the several dance floors, teaching her the paces of the minuet. More than a few very eligible-looking young women lingered at the periphery, feigning disinterest badly. They kept well supplied with iced cordials and glared at Rowena over the lace of their fans. In only a fraction of the night, Rowena had gone from terror at being noticed to reveling in the power Master Meteron had granted her. It teased out her wickedest smile, which he must have noticed. He leaned close, murmuring in her ear during her next close and turn.

"Tell me which of these vultures watching you with such envy is wealthiest. I'll give you a clue: you can't tell by the dress."

Rowena flicked her gaze over to them, scanning up and down. "'Course you can't," she sniffed. "You can get really nice dresses on credit, if you're keen to. Jewelry, too."

"And therefore?"

"Gloves and hairpins prove it best," she whispered. "Nobody lends gloves because they get all soiled holding hands in dances or picking up refreshments. And nobody just drops their fancy borrowed choker and doesn't notice. But hairpins fall out all the time." She pointed her chin toward a curvaceous woman in an ecru gown chased with rose and ivy patterns. Her ginger hair was a confection of jewel-studded clips and curl-pins. "She's probably got a couple thousand sovereigns poking out of her head, and they drop out all the time. You have to be a special kind of rich not to care about shedding sovereigns like hairs in a brush."

"Very good. That's the Greatduchess Avergnon—the new Lady Avergnon, I should say. Her great-aunt did her the favor of dying in her sleep back in Threemonth and leaving a surprisingly vague will behind. She's very eager to consolidate her position with a suitable match."

"You?" Rowena suggested impishly.

He snorted. "She might like my money but not its rate of exchange with her reputation." Another step, turn, pass. "Try the same game again, cricket, but with the gentlemen. Tell me what to look for."

"Pocket chronometers—ones without yellowed faceplates. And what the buttons on their waistcoats are made of."

Meteron's laugh showed his teeth for one, unguarded moment. "If I didn't know better, I'd think you had spent your life casting for wealth at the gentry's balls."

"More like on the streets."

"Well. Over there are two ministers from the Governor's cabinet and a visiting dignitary from Iberon. Shall we introduce you?"

Rowena blinked. "Um . . ."

He took her arm and winked. "Be as confident talking to them as you are talking about their clothes and you'll do better than most, cricket."

Somewhere in that blur of niceties, Rowena lost track of the Old Bear. It was two hours after their arrival when it dawned on her she hadn't spotted him in a long while. Master Meteron was engaged in prolonged repartee with a socialite lady—some cousin or in-law or something of the Governor, Rowena remembered overhearing—and though she'd been afraid to move beyond his orbit, a different gravitation pulled at her. It started with simple curiosity, but soon it grew into guilt, and something a little like fear.

Rowena peeled away from Meteron, hugging the edges of conversations and scanning the room for her Old Bear with an eye for crowds she'd honed years before. Her knack for sorting out the bustle of a space served her well, and after only ten minutes of what must have looked like wandering to anyone else, her careful system led her to a terrace with an open set of glass and iron doors. She knew the shape of him, silhouetted against the moon. It was past Reason how often she'd slipped from her bedroom above the Stone Scales to look for him in the dark of night. She would always find him, if not in his bed, then stretched out in the driftwood chair by the kitchen stove, reading by the light of a clockwork lamp.

She knew the cast of his shoulders turned against the wheel of hard thinking. One hand cradled his pipe, gesturing, leaning into the balcony railing. He looked over the crowds and the lights of the distant city, a curl of smoke rising around him.

Still a dozen paces off, Rowena smelled the sweetness of marjoram and fennel, the damp earth of burning tobacco. She smiled. And then, she frowned, considering his hand in motion once more.

Gesturing?

Yes. There was no hope of hearing him from where Rowena stood, but the Alchemist gave every appearance of carrying on a conversation with someone who wasn't there. Her desire to creep up behind him and surprise him with a pinch faded, replaced with a memory of the collapsing library of his mind when they were atop the Old Cathedral months before, the destruction everywhere—what was left behind.

And who she had found in it.

Rowena, the voice in her own mind chided gently. *Don't.*

Rowena ignored it. She'd become good at that, especially in the Old Bear's presence. She'd had to. She'd seen the look in his eyes as he'd tried to keep Leyah with him even a moment longer. To know that they had lost each other again, finally and for their own good, only to find a piece of her so close . . .

Rowena moved toward the Old Bear on the terrace, ransacking her brain for the right words to ask impossible questions—or she would have, if things hadn't gone very wrong. The terrace lay off the top of a staircase, frequented by scurrying serving staff and footmen. Rowena might have heard the butler coming if the roar of repartee from a hundred voices and the chamber orchestras woven in among them had not chewed up sounds more than an arm's reach away. As it was, just as she'd crossed the tiles that linked that narrowing piece of the hall to the uppermost landing, a portly server bearing two trays of *vinas* barreled around from Rowena's left. They collided, and he slammed the wind out of her without spilling a single glass.

She staggered, hunting for her balance. Her heels found the edge of a slick marble stair, instead. Rowena's yelp disappeared in the buzz of the partygoers. She tumbled down four stairs, a tangle of skirt hems and petticoats and scrabbling feet—

An unfamiliar pair of arms snapped her up from the edge of the fifth stair.

Rowena's hair had fallen half out of the combs previously pinning it back. Through a tumble-down skein of waves and curls, she stared at a boy of about her age.

"Are you all right?" he asked.

"Ehm," Rowena answered. Her flush could've set the lace collar of her gown afire.

She'd meant to say, "I'm fine," but hadn't quite gotten her breath or her bearings. The boy had been climbing up the stairs just as she'd made her unexpected trip down them. He'd staggered back against the sculpted rail, stopping her from carrying them both down to the bottom.

"Here." He levered Rowena onto her feet and stepped back.

"Thanks," she said. Rowena looked back to the top of the stairs, but the serving man had gone, probably scurried off to act as if someone else had knocked a guest down the stairs and killed her. "Stupid butler clobbered me good there."

The boy's head tilted curiously. Rowena cringed. *Eejit.*

"I mean, rather, thank you," she corrected, sanding down the sharper street corners of her accent. "I'm afraid I'm a little . . . um . . . out of sorts." She pawed at her hair, trying to sort it into something proper and purposeful. That only made her feel stupider, so she dropped a tidy curtsy, hoping that was the gesture being saved from a broken neck called for.

A bite of pain in her left ankle sent her teetering back to the rail.

The boy reached out to steady her. Rowena waved him off.

"S'nothing. I think I might've just cranked up—turned, I mean, my ankle. Bugger . . ."

She winced again, this time from the pain as much as her tongue.

"Here," the boy said, slipping round to take her left arm. "Going down will be easier than coming back up. There's a garden below. Not many people are there."

For a moment, Rowena considered refusing the boy's arm. She remembered Master Meteron somewhere above, holding court with a press of hangers-on. He would notice she'd gone, eventually. And then there was the Old Bear, alone on the terrace, far enough off not to have witnessed her tumble, and—perhaps—less alone than he seemed.

She met the boy's eyes, meaning to give him her apologies. He smiled again.

"All right," Rowena answered.

All the way down, she leaned into him, wondering who he was, and if there was a proper way to ask without sounding like an idiot, given she was already hanging on his arm. Something in his gait seemed off. A limp, maybe? She glanced back up the staircase. As they rounded a bend in the stair to the courtyard below, the angle afforded her another view of the terrace. She saw the Old Bear's backside, holding up the weight of some unseen world, and something else, too. Another figure moving onto the terrace.

The moon was high and full, painting the scene silver.

Somehow, the cut and gather of the woman's gown around her pregnant belly were lovelier than the svelte, swaying ladies in the hall beyond, cinched up tight in corsets or puffed out with crinoline cages. As she came into view, the Old Bear straightened, leaving his pipe on the railing. Then he did something Rowena had never seen him do before.

He bowed, and when the stranger lifted her ungloved hand, he kissed it with perfect solemnity.

Rowena had to turn her head back toward her feet to keep from missing a step and tumbling all over again.

It seemed the Alchemist was having a meeting of his own.

The courtyard was a precise square built into the center of the manor house. It lay at the bottom of a shaft cut straight through the building, four stories tall, with the balconies and terraces above spiraling toward its greenhouse roof, crowned by a mighty cut-glass skylight. The doors to the outside had been propped open, letting warm Sevenmonth air plume in on a cross-breeze.

The garden itself was geometric, a tribute to mathematical ingenuity and horticultural patience, with statues arranged under trailing ivies like points on a graph. There were well-trimmed hedges and tiers of tall, fronded plants Rowena suspected came from the tropics, someplace far from Corma and its salt winds and coal-black dusk. Purple lilies with white throats and pale yellow something-or-others grew on lovely, twining trellises until they reached the stone pillars of the spiraling floors above, joining with moss and ivy, the last evidence of wilderness in their well-trained forms.

The boy conducted Rowena to a stone bench and knelt down before her. She stared at him in the moonlight. His sandy brown hair looked rough and tousled, as if whatever he'd done to slick it back hours before had come as undone as Rowena's combs. It drifted down into eyes of an oddly familiar shape, like the Nipponese traders Rowena had seen around the docks and quays of Oceanside. He tossed his head to cast the hair out of the way.

It fell impudently back.

"Could you move your skirts just a little, so I could have a look?"

Rowena straightened, glaring. "*Hells not*, you arse."

He blinked, then blanched, putting his hands up to fend her off. "Oh, no. I meant—I meant have a look at your *ankle*. My mother's a doctor. I know a little about caring for injuries."

"Oh. Oh, in that case, yeah. I mean, yes. Here."

Rowena gingerly adjusted her skirts. She hadn't worn a very high heel, partly because she hadn't the least notion if she could keep her feet in them, and partly because Master Meteron might be forced to look her directly in the eye if she had tried.

The boy's hands paused over the buckle of her ankle boot. He offered a hand to her instead, smiling.

"I should have introduced myself. I'm terribly sorry," he said. "Julian Ardai, if it please you."

Rowena smiled. It was unkind, perhaps, but she couldn't resist.

"I can't imagine what your name has to do with my pleasure," she answered, with an air of mystery she hoped did justice to the Old Bear's first private words to her. A little thrill followed at the boy's uneasy expression.

She took his hand, feeling a little guilty. But only a little.

"I'm joking. Rowena Downshire. It's a pleasure to meet you, Master Ardai. Or . . . is it Doctor Ardai?"

"No." He laughed, shaking his head. "Or not yet, in any case."

Julian Ardai removed Rowena's foot from her shoe as carefully as if he were setting a bone. He turned her foot this way and that, watching her face and the joint at intervals, stopping whenever Rowena twitched in pain.

"It's only a sprain, though a right nasty one," he concluded. He was about to put the shoe back on when Rowena spoke again.

"Wait. Since you're down there already—could you just, um . . . ? Could you do the other?"

"You turned that one, too?"

"No, it's just I en't ever—" She bit down on her words and tried again, a little more slowly. "I *haven't ever* worn shoes like these before, and I swear my feet want to fall clean off."

Julian freed her foot from her other boot and set it beside its mate under the bench. He turned that ankle, too, rubbing his thumbs into the soles of her feet. Rowena stared at his hands, puzzled.

"You really don't have to—"

Julian froze. "I'm sorry. I thought if they were hurting you, I might—"

"Oh, they are. They're murder." Rowena shrugged. "I just didn't want to bother you . . . You're not bothered?"

"Not particularly."

"So you're in the habit of giving strange ladies foot-rubs at fancy dress parties?"

Julian shrugged one shoulder and dug deep into her arches. "Every habit starts somewhere. You're not part of the usual crowd."

"That obvious?"

"It's not a bad thing."

Rowena sniffed. "So you say. This place seems all about the usual crowd."

"It is. Places like this *always* are." Julian finished his work on her feet and rose, gesturing to the space beside her on the bench. "May I?"

Rowena shuffled left, making room. She tried threading her hair back into her pearled combs, hoping she could piece her coiffeur together without a mirror. Julian sat beside her, watching the operation with unconcealed interest.

"Is staring usual for the usual crowd?" she asked tartly.

Julian looked away. "I'm sorry. I'm making you uncomfortable. I just could swear I've met someone like you before."

Peddling lucifers out behind a public house maybe, yeah, Rowena thought bitterly. She gave up on her hair and hoped Julian wasn't mistaking the heat on her cheeks for her turning all swoony.

"So what brings you here, Rowena?"

There was a speech she'd been drilled on, and Rowena launched into it, folding her gloved hands primly on her lap. "My uncle. My mother's been pestering him for months to take me out for my debut—he goes to a lot of these functions, you see—and he finally decided now was as good a time as any." Julian studied her. Flustered, she wheeled off something spontaneous, spinning the thread to stitch up loose ends. "He was nattering away with some heiress or other—he's a bachelor, my uncle, and tends to gather up some notice. I decided I would rather look for something more interesting for a while."

Rowena smiled, as if it were a form of punctuation. *There.* It was even more than halfway true. She wondered, remembering Anselm's caution in the past, if she'd blinked twice or not.

"Your uncle," repeated Julian.

"My uncle. That's right."

"I should probably take you back to him. He'll be wondering where you've gone."

"No. I mean—he won't be."

Without quite knowing why, Rowena felt absolutely certain the last thing she wanted at that moment was to be returned to her wondering not-uncle.

"I don't get out much," she explained, too hastily. But it was honest, at least. Was it possible she could carry on the whole conversation without telling a pack of lies? If she rationed herself a steady stream of half-truths, would that leave her only half as much a fraud? The idea blossomed in her, warm and thrilling. "I live with my . . . my parents. My father tends to keep a close watch of me. He's a good man, and he means well by me, but it can get a little . . ."

"Stifling," Julian completed. He spoke the word with conviction, as if he knew it well—carried it and pulled it out for regular consideration, like a well-wound chronometer.

"A bit."

"I know exactly what you mean. My mother's work puts her much in demand. She's training me in it. Mostly the mechanical side of things."

"I work in my father's business, too," Rowena said. "An alchemist's shop."

As soon as the words came out, the bloom of truth withered and went cold.

Rowena's mouth snapped shut. However credible her story was, if she was the niece of a man whose sister had married down to be an alchemist's wife—worse, a *shopkeeping* alchemist's wife—then she wasn't much of anything to be on debut. A quarter-hour earlier, that wouldn't've bothered Rowena Downshire one spit. But a quarter-hour earlier, she hadn't yet tumbled into the arms of some doctor's son and settled into a lovely little garden to have him rub her feet. She wasn't fool enough to draw up designs beyond that. She just didn't want him to look on her the way she knew she deserved to be.

"Bugger." Rowena knotted her hands into fists.

Julian put a hand over hers. Rowena glanced at him warily.

"It's all right." His voice was low and earnest. "Everyone knows my mother's not *really* a doctor. Not the sort with a title from the EC."

Rowena blinked. "What sort, then?"

He shrugged—one shoulder, only half a dismissal. "A special sort. Complicated jobs. Reconstructions. Greatduke Armando Elanti had three serious bouts of dropsy in less than two years. Mother gave him a replacement heart last spring. He's at the party tonight—his first gala since the operation—but you wouldn't know he'd been so far gone just a year ago."

"She *made him* a heart?"

"Well, she ordered the design and installed the pump when it was done. I did the building. That's my job—biomechanicals. The EC haven't a formal program of study for it, so it's all retired army surgeons and lay-physicks and engineers driving the field. That's where Mother got her start, back in the Coal Wars over in Vraska. We're tradesfolk, too."

Now, Rowena knew she was staring again.

"Holy Proof. You're *that* Ardai? Your mum's *Jane Ardai*. Resurrection Jane."

"Is . . . that a problem?"

"No! I mean, it's grand," Rowena insisted. "I should have recognized the name straight away. I've heard stories about Resurrection Jane for ages. They say she can do anything." She straightened, tilting her head as a thought ran like a marble down from one side of her mind to the other. "Actually, a lot of that is you, isn't it?"

"Mother can build the replacements herself, but the work goes faster if she can focus more on the medical part. I started learning how to read her schematics and use the materials when I was ten or eleven. That was forever ago."

Rowena wrinkled her nose. "'Forever' nothing. How old are you, fifteen?"

Julian bristled. Something about the twist to his lip made Rowena laugh. That only made his scowl deepen.

"*Sixteen*," he answered.

"Oh, well, that's *completely* different!"

"It is to me!"

Rowena smiled apologetically. "I'm fourteen." The news seemed to surprise him. "And a half," she added. "My birthday was back in Twomonth. I'm very mature."

Julian studied her for a long moment. Rowena looked back, doing her best to screw her own face down into a mask of absolute conviction.

They both cracked together, laughing until they were out of breath.

"And a half?" Julian gasped. "That's a sure sign of maturity. *Counting halves.*"

Rowena nodded, sputtering between giggles. "That's right. And I'll bet you don't even shave."

"I do! Here, see?"

He grabbed Rowena's hand and pulled it to his cheek, pressing her fingers close.

They both froze. Silence closed around them like a curtain.

Rowena stared into Julian's face, blinking back the tears laughter left in her eyes. His hand went slack and was about to fall away from hers, his eyes wide with shock at what he'd done.

Suddenly, without knowing why, losing hold of Julian's hand seemed like the worst possible ending for Rowena's evening. Her fingers tightened around his. They sat, staring at one another. She wondered if she had ever breathed so loudly before.

You should go find Anselm. Or the Old Bear.

As soon as the thought came to Rowena, she knew she wouldn't follow through on it. She wanted to sit here all night—to be near Julian and his youth and his earnest, lovely face. She'd had enough of old wounds and gray hairs and scolding father-fondness. They could wait their turn. They would keep.

She wanted something else entirely.

Somewhere in the garden, a bullfrog burbled. The fireflies had come out—or they had flown in from the great glass doors cast open on all sides of the courtyard.

"I'm sorry," Julian murmured. His fingers moved under Rowena's, as if they might slip free. "I shouldn't have just grabbed—"

"I can't really feel it," she blurted.

He blinked. "I'm sorry?"

She pulled his hand down, still twined in hers, and unlaced their fingers. "My glove. You wanted to prove it, but I can't . . . my glove."

Julian pulled at the glove's lace, teasing it off, one finger at a time. The right glove came off, slithering down Rowena's skirts and pooling on the ground between her cast-off shoes.

Rowena put her bare hand to Julian's face. She traced his cheekbone with a thumb, trailing her fingers along the line of his jaw. A soft rasping answered her touch. The pale, fine stubble whispered against her skin.

"Your razor en't very sharp," Rowena murmured. She pulled her hand back.

Julian's face followed it, drawing nearer. She watched his warm honey eyes close, the lashes so fine and clear she might have counted them.

Julian had teased off her other glove, leaving her hands bare. Rowena closed her eyes and felt his presence, the warmth of his approach, one hand drifting to pull her to him, and then—

For a long moment, nothing happened. Rowena opened her eyes and found Julian at a more proper distance, his hands back in his own lap, cheeks flushed.

"I'm sorry," he said again. "That was—I'm sorry, I shouldn't have presumed."

Rowena smiled, hoping to conceal her disappointment. "It's all right. Honest."

Julian looked round with his whole head and shoulders, sweeping the courtyard for any sign of the kiss-that-wasn't having been noticed. Only the bullfrog and the drifting fireflies attended them, a thin rattle of crickets chirruping from the long fronds of palms and tiers of begonias.

"We should find your uncle," he said, sounding sullen. "He'll be looking for you soon."

"But what about you?"

Julian blinked. "What about me?"

"It's just," Rowena continued, "I don't know . . . Will I see you again?"

He smiled.

"Tell me where you live, Rowena Downshire," he vowed. "And I promise you'll see me again."

"By the Highstreet quay in Westgate Bridge. The Stone Scales."

Julian gaped. Rowena went cold, frozen by her foolishness.

"The Alchemist is your father?" he asked. There was none of the usual provincial wariness in his voice—none of the tremble she'd come to expect after any mention of her position. Julian Ardai had most definitely reacted to that address, but reacted how, Rowena couldn't say.

A familiar voice cut the air. "The Alchemist isn't her kin, boy. I am."

Anselm Meteron stood at the foot of the stairs they'd descended earlier, his expression flat and inscrutable.

To Rowena's great surprise, Julian rose and walked in his oddly hitched way toward Master Meteron, laughing, his right hand outstretched.

"Uncle Anselm!" he cried. "Blessed Reason, you scared me near to death!"

Rowena watched, dumbfounded, as Master Meteron shook the boy's hand. It had been some kind of a put-on, the cold look and hard voice. He slapped Julian on the shoulder with the rough familiarity of an old friend.

"How are you, Julian? Been taking care of your mother?"

The boy smiled. "As much as she lets me, sir. She said to expect you'd be here, but I thought you must have turned the invitation down."

Master Meteron quirked an eyebrow. "Oh?"

"There was still wine enough to go around."

"Arse." Meteron gave Julian another slap on the back and strolled down the path toward Rowena, his smile so sharp it could've skinned a cat.

"I see you've already met Rowena."

Julian blushed. Rowena hoped the heat rising on her cheeks didn't show half as clearly. She tugged her gloves on, fumbling for dignity, but her trembling hands had other ideas.

She wasn't afraid of Master Meteron judging her. He could take his sneering suspicions straight to the devil for all she cared. She was trembling from something else—something hot and yearning still tumbling around inside her.

"Yes, sir," Julian said. "I hadn't realized she was your relation."

"And my escort," Meteron added. "You've left me defenseless against the most shameless widows and ambitious spinsters, cricket. I'd have escaped their clutches ages ago if I'd had your comfort to beg off on."

Rowena righted herself with a few unceremonious tugs at her bodice and skirts. "You wouldn't have so many hangers-on if you just let someone make an honest man of you."

"That's entirely impossible, I assure you. Character *is* a mitigating factor." He winked. "I'm sure any one of those ladies would be very happy to apply for the position of Anselm Meteron's deeply bereaved, unspeakably wealthy widow."

"You don't really think they'd marry you just to murder you, Uncle," Julian scoffed.

"By degrees, as quickly as they could manage," Meteron said. "They'd make sure the help kept my cups and my plates full, and once I grew old and fat enough, my wicked heart would cave under the weight of its many sins. An eligible bachelorhood may be the only thing keeping me alive."

Master Meteron took her hand, and Rowena rose, only to wish she hadn't. Her ankle lit up in a flare of pain. She buckled against his chest.

Meteron's brow creased. "I'll have a devil of a time explaining to your *mother* if you've gotten stumbling drunk on the night of your debut." He leaned into the word, making clear that he meant the sort of mother who was two hands taller and four stone heavier than himself.

"It's my ankle. I tripped on the stairs and Master Ardai kept me from going down the whole way."

"Hmm. Well done, boy."

"Thank you, sir."

"Well. As it happens, we've our audience with the Greatduke and his wife to enjoin, and we're already late, given the time I spent looking for you. Best be along, cricket."

"I know where the receiving room is," Julian volunteered. "Mother was there earlier this evening. Here—it's faster if you go up the east corridor."

They started that way, Rowena using Master Meteron as a prop as unobtrusively as she could manage. Putting her shoes back on seemed like more trouble than it could be worth—at least until they were about to enter into the peerage's audience directly—and so she carried them in her left hand, swinging them a little, as she might a market basket. As they went, Rowena looked between the Masters Meteron and Ardai, trying to parse the relationship. Julian wasn't any more Anselm Meteron's nephew than she was his niece. Of that, she was sure. She wondered what unspoken understanding had earned him that particular identity. Surely the missing finger of his right hand was proof he hadn't called on Resurrection Jane's personal services. She wasn't the type to leave a job half-done, if the stories about her bore any truth. As they walked, Julian nattered away, trying to impress Master Meteron with his recent work, talking about something called a polymer and how he'd figured out how to use it to substitute for cartilage. Rowena felt the familiar weight of facts sifting through her brain, working into the crevices like a bit of sand nagging an oyster, forming the pearl of an idea.

It might be . . .

She frowned, thinking, and pursed her lips. Julian was taller than Master Meteron, with a face made more for unguarded truths than the high gloss of social theater, but his jaw tapered much the same way. If only he could summon an ironic moment, Julian's smile could well be the sharpened edge of a dagger, too.

The boy conducted them to a pair of gilt mahogany doors. There he shook Meteron's hand again, then turned to Rowena, smiling warmly.

"It was a great pleasure meeting you." Julian took her hand and bowed, kissing the tips of her gloved fingers.

He looked up at her through the untidy fringe of his hair, the shadows from the gas chandeliers above falling just so. A fist clenched in Rowena's heart.

"Thank you," she replied.

They watched Julian disappear down the wide, shining corridor, weaving back toward the murmur of the party and the tinkling of glasses lifted in toasts.

"*Uncle* Anselm," Rowena said.

She stared a challenge at Meteron. His cold gaze pinned back her ears.

"His mother and I were friends once." His voice was too level to be anything but a threat.

"Nice of you to keep in touch."

"If I were you, I'd hold my tongue when it comes to matters I know nothing about." He examined her minutely, and most unkindly. "Unless I arrived later than I believed, and you've already learned a few things for yourself?"

Rowena coiled to snap back, but Master Meteron opened the parlor door. Her curse at him changed into one for herself. He hadn't given her a moment to put on her shoes again. Too late now. The people within the chamber turned at once to look their way.

Ears burning, Rowena took Anselm's arm, trying to hide her dangling footwear behind their backs. Her clenched teeth made for a very toothy smile.

8.

Greatduke Jonathan Roland stood nearly as tall as the Old Bear, despite his rounded shoulders and stooped posture. He was young—or youngish, anyway. Rowena supposed nearly everyone she met seemed younger than her Bear, who wasn't so much old but somehow outside of time, weathered and inscrutable. Roland, she guessed as she tried to hide a thoughtful squint behind a yawn, was probably less than forty.

Lord Roland stood to greet Rowena, muttering some pleasantry over her hand as he bowed her into the room, trailing her past the Old Bear seated in a chair beside the unlit fireplace. How many hands had he been forced to kiss and how many to shake that night, Rowena wondered. There were no fewer than three hundred guests or she was the Governor's wet-nurse. Hardly sanitary. And to think the quality called folk from her side of the street dirty.

Still, Rowena said, "It's an honor, milord," though perhaps a moment later than she ought to have. The Greatduke eyed her curiously. She wondered how long she'd left him waiting as her mind wandered.

"Rowena Downshire," she blurted, managing a wobbly curtsy on her aching ankle. Master Meteron cleared his throat. She blinked at him, then realized he'd almost certainly *already* given her name.

"I'm sorry," she added stupidly.

The Greatduke had grace enough to pretend he didn't hear her second—third?—gaffe of their brief acquaintance.

"This is my lady wife, Greatduchess Simone Roland," he said, gesturing to a woman.

The woman, Rowena realized. Pregnant, and very far along, too. She had the wide, round face and opalescent eyes of someone born far from Amidon, her near-black hair arranged in a topknot, studded with dangling copper bells that tinkled softly as she nodded her greetings.

Afraid of another misstep, Rowena kept her response to a curtsy and a held tongue.

Roland turned to the bar where a statue-still lanyani draped in a robe of cascading moss awaited his orders. It looked very much like one of the statues arranged in the grottos of the Rolands' indoor gardens. Slowly, it dawned on Rowena those "statues" might very well *be* lanyani instructed to stand sentinel and spy on the guests' comings and goings—especially in a place where they might assume themselves to be alone. *You should have been more careful*, she scolded herself.

With a gesture, Roland directed the lanyani's attention to the assemblage. The creature set about pouring five flutes of *vinas* from a tall silver ice bucket into even taller crystal cups. It made a circuit of the room, setting glasses on tall, inlaid tables set between the guest chairs near the empty fireplace.

Rowena took a smaller wing chair between Master Meteron and the Old Bear.

"We're very grateful you could accept our invitation, Master Pardon," Lady Roland began.

"The pleasure is all mine," the Old Bear answered. There could not have been less pleasure in his voice if Lady Roland had just dropped a set of balances on his foot.

"My husband and I will always be grateful for your service to our house," the lady went on, unperturbed. Rowena noticed that she had an accent—very light, carefully schooled. She wondered where it came from. She imagined more lovely women like her, wherever that place was, their eyes wide and cheeks smooth as velvet. "Without you and Master Meteron, I would never have arrived safely in Amidon." She touched her belly. "My lord and I are expecting our fifth child. I'm hoping to Reason it's a daughter. This house could hardly stand another son, though I'm sure my husband is happy to know his line rests so secure."

"Indeed," the Old Bear said flatly.

An awkward silence followed. Rowena bit her lip.

"You understand, my lady," Meteron said, his voice pouring honey over the sour moment, "that our experience on the *Aeropagi* was a less happy one than yours. But we're glad of the happiness it's bought you since."

Roland bristled at those last words. *Bought.* He leaned in, scowling. "You were paid for your pains." His gaunt hands curled into the arms of his chair. "And you knew the risks."

"We did," the Old Bear agreed. Rowena saw the tightness in his jaw, grinding his anger. "My wife paid them for all of us."

Something stirred inside Rowena, pressing her to soothe him, or silence him, and she knew at once that it wasn't herself.

Not now, she begged. *Please, I can't right now. I'm sorry.*

"It was business," Roland was saying. The glass of *vinas* the lanyani had set beside him sweated in the summer air. "I can appreciate the depth of your loss. That's why I was disinclined to heed my wife's request that we hire you again."

That, at least, is probably true, the voice in Rowena's mind murmured.

Meteron regarded Greatduchess Roland. "As to that point, I'm afraid there's been a misunderstanding, Milady. We're retired."

The lady smiled. "I've heard that. I also heard of something happening at the Old Cathedral last fall. Something involving two unusually well-prepared campaigners. And a girl." Her gaze met Rowena's before settling on the Alchemist. Her expression twisted with sympathy. "I can imagine how seeing me brings you pain, truly. But we've come into a situation that requires specific help—yours."

The Alchemist fingered his *vinas*. Rowena had never seen him drink the stuff. He studied the glass turning in his hand. Lady Roland wasn't wrong. Something in him ached so bitterly, Rowena could feel it rising from him like heat. The voice that had lived in her for months began to quietly weep.

But the Alchemist said nothing.

Master Meteron leaned forward. "Who has asked after us? Why?"

"In recent years, Lady Roland and I have been in the business of funding experimental research," Lord Roland replied. "Most of it has been more based in practice than theory, but after the Decadal

Conference, we decided to focus more pointedly on . . . investigative branches of Holy Reason."

Rowena joined her companions in an exchange of glances. She read in them the whole play of possibilities: suspicion, interest, worry, hostility, hope. She wasn't entirely sure what look she contributed, but it wouldn't be anything simple. Of that, she was sure.

"Investigative," the Alchemist echoed. He had lost his feigned interest in the *vinas*. His hand twisted around the neck of his cane. "Any specific cause of that new interest?"

"Things are afoot," Lady Roland replied. "We intend not to be left behind."

"The Decadal Conference, for all its scandal, represented an opportunity," Lord Roland continued. "A sea-change in the relationship between the peerage and the Ecclesiastical Commission. Some efforts have been made to suppress the details of what happened the night the keynote was to have occurred, but conjecture offers its own explanations." He sat back, studying his guests intently. "And we have good reason to believe this conjecture nearly as useful as fact."

"What manner of investigative research?" the Alchemist pressed. Rowena realized he had moved almost imperceptibly closer to her, shifting in his seat as if his shadow cast across her were some kind of ward.

"We have a certain sympathy for displaced scholars," Lady Simone said quickly. More uneasily than before, she smiled. "I was one, back in Khmer, before . . . Well, before."

"I remember."

Rowena glanced at Master Meteron. The conversation seemed to be flowing between the Rolands and the Alchemist in a straight line, as if neither she nor Meteron were there to hear. Was this what it had been like, back when they had campaigned? The Old Bear—the Younger Bear, she supposed—brokering the deals, and Meteron playing the silent partner? It was utterly the reverse of what she expected. At any moment, the Anselm Meteron she knew was due to break into the conversation, piqued at being disregarded, and disarm the lot of them with some deadly verbal riposte.

But he didn't. He watched, instead, and Rowena caught only the barest glance from him, a flicker of his steely gray eyes.

Just listen, they said.

And so she did.

"I had to approach him, you see," Lady Simone was saying. "After I read that paper, I knew something had gone very wrong. It was a lie. It takes an excellent scholar to lie so very poorly in print, you know. It's a sign of how much dissembling in his research is against his nature."

"Bloody Proof," Meteron groaned. "You mean Chalmers."

"He had a project to carry out, and it required travel," Roland said, nodding. "To Lemarcke."

"We sent him and heard nothing more, for a time. Then, four weeks ago, he sparked us," Lady Roland explained. "He had found materials quite important to his continuing studies but needed to make a rather . . . challenging journey to make use of them. He felt he needed protection."

"We would never have suggested you," Roland interrupted. The words could've come off as a slap, but he seemed the sort of comfortable, scientific bloke who spoke facts without much regard for feelings. Blunt. Direct.

"He *demanded* you," Lady Roland explained. "Insisted. Given the nature of the work, he said it had to be the two of you, or he would abandon the project entirely."

Meteron sat back in his chair, his thumb running circles over the stump of his missing finger. "What project?"

Roland snorted. "You can dispense with pretense, Meteron. We know. And so do you."

The Alchemist and Meteron exchanged a guarded look. It grazed over Rowena strangely, lingering for an uncomfortable moment. She tried to place what was wrong about it.

"I think," Meteron said at last, "we need a moment to confer. Alone."

The Rolands rose, the lady still smiling with unnerving calm. *She's sure they'll take the job*, Rowena realized. *She doesn't care a whit about flouncing off to humor them. She knows she's got them already.*

"There is some urgency to the decision, you understand," Lord Roland said.

Given the grit of the Old Bear's jaw, Rowena was shocked he hadn't cracked a tooth. "Ten minutes."

And thus, the Rolands turned to depart.

"My lady," the Old Bear called.

They turned. Lady Roland's head tilted, curious as a spaniel.

"Might I trouble you to take Miss Downshire with you, for the time being?"

Rowena started, staring. "Bear, I—"

"Of course," Lady Roland answered. "My dear?"

She extended a hand toward Rowena, waiting. It was too far away for Rowena to simply take it. She considered pretending the gesture hadn't been clear—that she hadn't noticed it.

"I was there with you," Rowena hissed at her companions. "I know *all about it*, remember?"

"He's right," Meteron cut in. "Go on, cricket."

Rowena stood as if propelled from her chair, wobbled on her bad ankle, and swore. Over her shoulder, she heard Lady Roland hiss at her effrontery. Rowena glared down at the Old Bear. The gas lamps flickered, catching the stone in his gaze and the horizon line of some inscrutable emotion, just out of reach.

Rowena turned, ignoring Lady Roland's hand, and cut ahead of her hosts, sharp as a knife. She'd seen the door already and didn't much care if it was indecorous or uncouth to pass through it first. She only cared about getting away from those two old bastards and their secrets and stares before something welled up in her eyes—something knotted up and complicated.

Rowena did have the presence of mind, at least, to pause on the threshold and hold the door to the anteparlor for her host and hostess. When she let it fall closed, she saw the Old Bear levering himself from his chair and Anselm Meteron eyeing the waning space between the door and the jamb, his face troubled.

"So," Rowena said, leaning as close to the Old Bear as the carriage's jostling gait allowed. "*Are* we taking the job?"

"You have this fascination with the word 'we,'" Master Meteron drawled. He stared out the window at the shadow of Corma proper passing by. The city grew as the carriage rolled along, the spires and colonnades of the manor houses dotting its outer limits blurry in the pale hues of dawn.

Rowena crossed her arms and flounced back. *Fine.* If Master Meteron wanted to take up the Old Bear's part of the conversation, he was welcome to it. The Alchemist had been all but mum after the ten terrible minutes she'd spent alone with the Rolands. They had stretched into twelve, actually, but Rowena had done her best not to crane her neck toward the anteparlor's mantel clock more than once or twice.

Or three times.

The Rolands, as it happened, weren't really so awful. Lady Roland had asked questions, trying to be civil and curious about Rowena, but the more she probed for the sake of hospitality, the more Rowena's stomach seized with worry. Some of her questions and statements made no sense: whether she remembered much about her mother, and how the lady was sure she'd have been proud to see her grown into such a fine young woman. And then it dawned on Rowena that Lady Roland had mistaken her for Erasmus and Leyah Pardon's adopted daughter. She must have known they had a child. Apparently she hadn't any idea that Rare was already Rowena's age when Leyah and the rest of the Corma company went off on whatever job it was that spelled the end of their campaigning days. Rowena only knew it had ended badly, in blood and searing light and terrible pain. Some kind of an explosion on an airship. It had killed Leyah and concussed an emotional hole in the Old Bear and her brother, Anselm—one that had never properly healed. Even seeing the Rolands again battered at nerves they'd probably thought dead for years.

Rowena did her best to play along with the lady's assumptions. She'd never been more grateful to see Master Meteron's face when the door finally opened. He'd stood on the threshold, offering the little bow that was really a nod, and said only, "Send the papers in the morning. Use the old address."

After that, everyone murmured goodbyes, and Rowena found herself swept along to the carriage house, where the footman and driver were busy smoking themselves to cinders. She wondered how long they'd been told to keep the clockworks wound and the wheels unbraced.

Now she was spoiling for a fight. She'd come to the ball entranced, only to grow bored, then find herself knocked down the stairs and then . . . Well, she didn't even *know* what had happened with Julian. And now this.

"Is there a *problem* with my thinking of us as a 'we'?" Rowena demanded.

Master Meteron shook his head. "Nothing beyond it being impractical, naïve, dangerous, foolhardy, and ridiculous." He yawned, lolling his head toward his partner as if a proper turn were too much exertion. "Am I missing any appropriate adjectives?"

"We're taking the job," the Old Bear said.

Rowena blinked. "We *three*, or we *you*?" She braced to be told she'd have to stay behind. She wondered what they'd do with her. Find some finishing school? Set her up in the Mercy Home down the hall from Mama? Had—oh, *Proof* forbid—had the Rolands offered to take her in as a cut-rate governess to their brood of snot-nosed lordlings?

"We three." The Old Bear looked up from his pipe, which he'd been handling with obsessive attention the whole ride. It was close quarters for smoking. He was trying to be conscientious. He also had a look on his face that said he'd throw a man under the carriage wheels for a slow pipe and a deep drink.

Rowena looked back and forth between them. She'd been ready to fight. During her exile with the Rolands, better than half her brain had been assigned to assembling case points and rebuttals. The carriage ride was to have been her battleground. She was almost disappointed.

"But why?"

"For God's sake, cricket," Meteron cried, "isn't this what you *want?* The sort of thing you've griped for in the past?"

"Well, yes."

He threw up his maimed hand in disgust. "You're bloody welcome, then. You're in. Once we reach Lemarcke, you'll be a licensed, bonded, and insured campaigner. It's your rutting mercenary bat mitzvah."

Rowena looked back at the Old Bear. "I don't understand."

"The standard contract names all the parties involved," he explained. "There are always spaces to allow the core contracted group to write in additional parties—subcontractors, if you like. Not every core group covers every needed skill set, and so it's wise to give your campaigners latitude to hire additional muscle at their discretion. We'll be writing you in when the papers arrive."

Rowena smiled. "I'm the 'additional muscle'?"

"It's fucking *hilarious*," Meteron complained. "The Rolands will think you're mad, Bear, and I'm inclined to agree."

"This was *your* idea?"

The Old Bear arched an eyebrow. "Is that so surprising?"

"En't you usually the one trying to keep me from losing my head or getting into scrapes?"

"I am," he allowed. He wrenched the window open a few inches, at last, stuffing his pipe and lighting it. The smell of marjoram and fennel filled the carriage box. "But . . ." He sighed. "I can hardly do that if I'm on the other side of the Western Sea and you're back here."

Meteron smiled wanly. "I was going to pass you off to Mrs. Gilleyen, down at Coventry Passage rectory. I understand she has some horrid, horse-faced granddaughter who runs a girl's school outside Southeby."

"Another niece of yours?" Rowena quipped.

He snorted.

Intermezzo

I had never imagined there would be so much space in here. I find another hallway—cluttered with debris, of course; everything here is such a fantastic wreck now—and I walk it, expecting that its next curve leads to an end. But there never is one. If I turn back, the path I walked before has changed. There is a staircase I never crossed, or even a lift. There are windows where once stretched long corridors of chipped plaster. It's always night outside those windows. The landscape changes, even in the space between one casement and the next. A broad meadow under moonlight, then a creaking old port city, then a military encampment, until I reach a place that can't possibly be of this world, with trees growing down from drifting islands in the sky or platforms of waterfalls climbing up against gravity.

There's more than enough space here, Father, but you might at least have tidied up after the mess you made, all those months ago.

You needn't worry. I'm doing it for you. I remember how Mother keeping her things all helter-skelter around the shop made you grind your teeth. When I was little, I tried to put things in order for her, just to keep you from having your little spats. You told her she was losing track of her tools for want of a proper system, and she resented that. She had good reason. She was losing her things because I kept putting them away, but never told her I was doing it, or where I had thought they best belonged. It was supposed to be a surprise, like when the little elves in the fairy stories you used to read me set the poor cobbler's shop aright and he thinks it's all some miracle and is grateful and everything turns out perfectly without his ever knowing why.

Things didn't turn out so perfectly for us. I'd put things away and hope she'd notice how nice it was, but I might as well have thrown all her hones and lathes and hobs into the river, for all the good it did. Mother would storm about, muttering over you moving her things, and

I'd never fess it was me, because the only thing worse than trying to end a fight only to stir it up again would be *admitting* how thoroughly I'd ballocksed the job.

Well.

There's no one left here now but me. If you won't—if you can't—put things back the way they were, maybe I can. I have nothing but time, and nothing standing in my way. Nothing to hide from you. You already know I'm here. I think you appreciate our time together, though you'd never say it. You're not really one for sentiment, are you?

At least, I never thought you were before. Then I started stripping these rooms down to their wallpaper.

God, why didn't you tell me? If you had only told me what it's like, I'd have understood why you opened that door and waited for me to walk through it. I think I'd have wanted me gone, too, after all the raging and crying and cursing I'd done. I thought I was behaving better then—had put the grief over Mother deep inside where it wouldn't bother anyone anymore. Why couldn't you just say how much worse that would be—how you could feel it all boiling in me, scalding your own raw wounds? Why did I have to learn it in this place?

It gets lonely here, sometimes, especially with Mother gone. You're wondering where she is, I suppose. I haven't had the heart to tell you. Maybe the part of you that's still a hayseed Kneeler boy wants to believe she's gone to a better place. That she's been set free.

That's not really how this works.

I am pleased to say she's had a change of scenery, at least. It's a little smaller in there, but that's only because the space is so young and new.

Ah. I see now you understand. Did you think Leyah was only giving you the silent treatment? Did you think your little Rowena couldn't keep such a secret from you, all this time? Don't be surprised. Big as this place is, there's barely room in it for the both of us now. Three would have been a terrible crowd. You should thank the girl for giving Mother her new home. I doubt she had any idea what she carried with her when she fell into this place, or who had burred into her mind when she finally found her way out again.

You *could* tell her. Teach her. Try to spare her feeling the power the way you do. But you won't, will you? You secretive old bastard. *Caving.* Mother called it "caving," and called you "Bear," and we were all meant to think it was sweet. But did she know before she was trapped here, too, how dangerous a place a cave can be? I remember Ann telling me once: *Life doesn't afford many second chances.* He's right, of course. He's usually right.

Well. There comes a time when every daughter has to take certain decisions away from her father for his own good. I'm putting a lot of goddamned effort into fixing you up properly, Father. You might show a little fucking gratitude.

I don't *have* to put things back the way they were.

9.

Bess held the printed spark, checking the message again, as if there was some chance it had magically transformed. She felt surreally certain the letters could have rearranged into anything. It wouldn't have surprised her. Nothing surprised her, anymore.

"*Don't be so stupid,*" she hissed, shaking herself. She stuffed the spark into her reticule and strode up the winding lanes of Westgate Bridge's highstreets toward the Stone Scales.

"Every Dolly Moll pays her way as she can," Resurrection Jane had said. She'd meant it, and seen to it that Bess paid her share to the rest of the girls in the eight months since her release from *Accursius*. She minded "Audrea Carringer's" shop on the ninth and tenth of every month, sometimes turning its shingle so she could gather girls up from the back stoops of gentlemen's clubs, armed with a parcel of sovereigns as powerful as a pair of chain-cutters. Clothing the opium-eaters, feeding their nearly orphaned brats, cleaning up the sick of both, and looking the other way when the best of intentions couldn't put an end to the worst of habits. She had known all her life Corma was full of desperate, damned souls no amount of Reason could save. Hells, half the folk she knew lacked schooling enough to even read the knowledge the EC peddled as paving on the road to understanding Creation. Small wonder they kept finding ways of killing themselves by degrees. And then there was negotiating with Sticks, and Stones, and a half-dozen other slats in the city's fencing network. For that task, Jane wanted more than results. She wanted miracles, and believed all in her employ should serve them up to her as readily as she scattered them over broken bodies.

When Jane told Bess that morning that she'd had a call for a Dolly Moll suited to a long-term job, Bess had just been grateful to leave behind scrapping with fences over this mechanical or that. Nasrahiel was built. It—*he*—seemed likely to hold together. Nothing Jane could ask of Bess now could be harder than finding all his bits had been.

She'd been wrong.

Now Bess stood before the grated window of the Stone Scales again, for the first time in nearly a year. It looked . . . very much the same. Bess herself didn't. Though her hair had finally grown out evenly, it was only long enough to take a few pin curls in a tight coif that left her feeling practically naked.

"Walk in, or don't," she said, loudly enough that a man passing down the lane glanced up from his chronometer.

"Not you," she muttered, glaring at his retreating backside. He hustled past the Scales in a way that suggested he was a newcomer to Westgate Bridge—full of rumors about the Alchemist and very few proper facts.

Bess knew at least one thing about the old man now. He needed something from her.

The bell over the door tinkled as she entered. Bess ducked into a room of shelves as tall as a man, spaced just wide enough for two to walk abreast. The shop walls were checkered with framed maps and shadow boxes of insects, or displays of bones, brass, and glass. It was a cacophony of oddments and formulae as sorcerous as scientific.

This time, the Alchemist wasn't calling from the back room or the top of a ladder. He was there, just on the other side of the door, a ring of keys in his hand, not two feet from Bess's nose.

Bess squared her shoulders and managed a curtsy.

"Master Alchemist. Sir."

The old man's stolid face shifted. It took Bess a moment to realize that flicker of expression, quickly smothered, might have been confusion.

"Beatrice," he said.

And all at once, she was crying. The part of her that had snatched up his hand months before forced her to keep her chin up and her voice strong. But the kohl around her eyes was already stinging.

"I'm sorry to bother you so late in the day," she said, her voice wobbling. "I meant to come before you closed up shop, but Jane said—"

"Jane. Of course. Come in."

And this time, it was the Alchemist who took her hand, guiding her back toward the same damned stool at the same damned counter. Bess's tears hiccuped into a sob. Once again, the old man crouched before her, but this time, he took the position more gingerly. Bess saw there was a cane tucked in the crook of his arm and wondered how he had come to need it.

He scowled over her again, pressing the pad of her thumb, watching the nail color take its color again (was she dreaming? was that why this was all so familiar?). This time, though, the scowl seemed . . . kindly? Was that even possible? Or had it been the same before, and she'd been too terrified to notice?

"I went to jail," Bess said.

The Alchemist placed two fingers just below her earlobe, pressing for the pulse.

Bess closed her eyes and sucked in a slow, sobering breath. One look at him, and Blackbottom End came rushing toward her, the past surging uphill. Memories of Ivor's hawthorn, and the prison hulk's jailors, and the Trimeeni girl fucking the guards sideways, hoping a baby in her belly would keep her from the gallows pole. All of that because she'd set foot in this shop and taken a tonic and note that could have given her a whole different future. And she'd poured all three down the drain.

"I never meant you to come to harm," said the Alchemist.

"I believe you." She did. That was what made the crying so hard to stop.

The Alchemist levered himself up, leaning into the counter, and disappeared beyond its drop-leaf. Crockery and a hissing noise suggested he was putting the kettle on. He came back a moment after, holding a jam jar with a measure of something brown and fierce-looking at its bottom.

Bess took it, her fingers touching his. Neither said a word.

Bess sniffed. Brandy. She threw it back all in one go and winced. A blooming warmth followed a moment later.

"Shouldn't you . . . ?" she gasped, "Shouldn't you wait for the harder stuff until after lockup?"

"I've turned the shingle already."

He settled beside Bess on a stool like her own. "So you found your way, after all."

"To Gooddame Audrea Carringer."

The Alchemist nodded. "I am glad you are well, though I wish it had come about differently."

Their eyes locked for a long, uncomfortable time.

"I'm well enough," Bess agreed, at last.

The old man frowned, more custom than ferocity in the look. "Resurrection Jane sent you here."

"You called on her. Asked if there was anyone she could spare from the Dolly Molls. The job she gave me's been done for some time, and I'm no use in her lab." Bess folded her hands, trying to arrange herself properly. She nearly fumbled the jam jar, then set it on the counter. "She said you needed a girl for the shop for a while. Is it because of your, um?" She gestured vaguely to his leg and the cane resting against his thigh.

"I'm leaving Corma and will need someone to take over the Scales while I'm gone."

Bess felt her jaw go slack and cinched it back up with a snap. "You mean run the whole shop?"

"I've contacted my current suppliers and arranged for the stock to be replenished once a week, based on the usual consumption. There are customers who take deliveries and their schedules to mind. I've prepared their prescriptions in large supply and set them aside for regular distribution."

"How long do you mean to be gone?"

The old man's hand tapped the head of his cane. "What I mean and what may come to pass are different things. Two months, most likely. This should be only a little more complicated than running a market stall."

Bess couldn't help it. A bark of laughter, sharp and incredulous, escaped. "I doubt that. May I . . . ask why you're leaving?"

"A client."

"I wasn't aware you made house calls?"

The Alchemist's face curdled. "I might live the rest of my days without hearing that quip again and die a happy man."

Bess was about to apologize, but the rattle of a key meeting the Scales's lock closed the door on her words.

The lop-gaited old hound Bess remembered from her previous visits trotted through, with someone else—a girl, or a small woman, or—

"Rowie?" she gasped.

The door framed Rowena Downshire for only a moment before she bolted forward and threw her arms around Bess's neck, toppling her stool back against the hinged counter. Bottles rattled off their racks to roll along its scarred surface.

For a time, they were a knot of limbs and yelps and faces pressed to noses and utter confusion. At some point, a scratching sound took Bess's attention, and she looked up from staring at Rowena's face—where had she gotten that scar across her eyebrow?—to find it had been a simultaneous clearing of throats, baritone and tenor. The first belonged to the Alchemist.

The second man was a stranger, except . . . Bess straightened up, untangling herself from Rowena. She'd lived above New Vraska Imports and ducked behind the curtains of gentlemen's club suites too often not to know him.

"Master Meteron," she said, dropping a curtsy as well ordered as a bundle of sticks. Bess cast a reproving glare at Rowie, hissing for her to do the same.

Rowie wasn't giving the quality his due, and Meteron didn't seem to care that Bess had tried. Instead, he took Bess by the arm and pulled her up, not as gently as he might have done.

"Ann—" the Alchemist said, his voice full of caution.

"If you're not in the hulks, it's her doing," Meteron said.

Bess stared, confused. "You mean Resurrection Jane?"

His brow furrowed. "I mean Gammon. I have some unfinished business with her. Where is she?"

Bess looked between the three almost-strangers. Rowie, looking clean and fed and utterly perplexed; the blade-eyed Master Meteron, with his hand closed too tightly around her arm; and the Alchemist, whose dark hand closed on Meteron's shoulder, pulling him away. Meteron glanced back at the Alchemist and, reluctantly, released Bess, still waiting for her response. She wasn't sure what she'd done to make him angry—or if Gammon had angered him, why she ought to answer for it.

"I think, perhaps," she said slowly, "things are a bit more complicated than I realized here?"

Rowie's darting eyes caught Bess's. *You have no idea*, they said. "I'll put out supper, and maybe we'll let her explain?" she said to Meteron and the Alchemist. "Okay?"

Silence.

Bess felt her hackles rise. The dog, forgotten, whined at her feet.

Suddenly, arguing over clink with Sticks and Stones seemed an acceptable pastime. So did minding the opium-eaters and hustlers done wrong by their pimps. Nearly any job Jane Ardai might have given her seemed preferable to the hornet's nest she'd unknowingly bestirred.

"You do that, girl," the Alchemist told Rowie. "I expect this is going to take some time."

10.

It was dusk and still murderously hot when Anselm Meteron pulled on the last of the black, tarry cigarillos he'd purchased abroad, hoping something evil in his lungs would steady the blood in his veins. Thus far, it seemed determined not to.

Perhaps, he considered, planting his arse on a tomb slab for the last quarter-hour had been none too good a plan, either, where tending a black mood was concerned.

"Fucking woman," he sighed through a cloud of smoke, grinding the cigarillo butt into Briar Hill Cemetery's gravelly earth. Its monuments were only a few decades in service, with barely any moss or rust stains to give them the character he'd come to expect of cemeteries during his childhood in Rimmerston. But Rimmerston was an older town than Corma, part of the first, abortive wave of Amidonian settlement that stalled for two generations when pre-Unity medicine struggled to treat the maladies of the southeast's swampy climate. The EC had eventually returned to Rimmerston, dignifying it as they'd done the west once they'd conquered the continent's western shores. Still, that plantation town had its roots sunk past the foundations of the Unity. Some of its monuments still boasted angels, though properly contrite families had slipped sets of balances or calipers or astrolabes into the figures' delicate hands, hoping to discourage public murmurs of a Kneeler past. Anselm found most cemeteries rather scenic, even the ones with doctored histories. But Corma's Briar Hill was little more than a seismic upheaval of granite and iron.

More than cemeteries, Anselm loved theatrics—provided, of course,

they were his own. A meeting at sundown in Corma's oldest bone-
yard appealed to a certain morbid, dramatic instinct lodged between
the thorns of his innermost self, but waiting there because it had been
Haadiyaa Gammon's plan was an offense to his considerable dignity.
Impractical, foolish, and clichéd. Even as he critiqued her idea, he stifled a
jealous pang that, really, he should have thought of it first.

"You were hoping to outdo me," the former City Inspector's voice
called out, as if privy to his thoughts.

Anselm turned a razored look over his shoulder, watching Gammon's approach. The almost-evaporated spice of the Indines rested on
her polyglot tongue, some residue of whichever parent had come to Amidon and mingled with the Unity. She stood on a rise a few yards off, a
bundle tucked against her hip, summer storm clouds gathering over the
iron arch marking the cemetery grounds behind her.

Anselm snorted. "Since when did you develop a penchant for melodrama?"

"Conspiracy, perjury, betrayal, disappearance." Gammon closed the
distance down the hill in a few long strides. "They occasion some aes-
thetic adjustments. I've been studying up."

Anselm considered Gammon's bundle. Something bulky in a canvas
shoulder bag. It looked about the right size. The lingering heat in his
blood iced over. He stared at his feet, wishing he hadn't run through his
cigarillos.

"I meant to bring her to you sooner. Things have gotten out of hand."

Gammon placed the bag on the insteps of his shoes. *God's balls.* It
weighed far, far too little.

"I used a private facility instead of the Constabulary's crematory. It
seemed more appropriate."

The sack's drawstring opening had fallen slack, revealing a wooden
box corner. Knotty pine. A dovetail joint. *She always fancied quality
goods,* Anselm thought bitterly.

"How much do I owe you?"

"Pity's sake, Anselm—"

"I pay my debts, Haadi," he snapped.

The look Gammon wore under her tricorn's brim was as well sanded as Rare's urn. "This time, she paid for you."

She didn't mean the crematory fees, of course. Naming everything Rare had paid for—Anselm's arrogance, his presumption, his expectation of control—would take all night, and most of the day after. It was a red ledger stretching back thirteen years, settled with claws and fists.

Gammon sat beside him, slumping on the tomb lid as if she'd dropped a heavy load. Anselm slid left, giving her space enough to put her elbows on her knees and rub at her temples.

"You're not dealing with the pain in your usual way," she announced. "Which means you aren't dealing at all. Which means Bess's message about your wanting a meeting is actually you wanting closure. You think I can give it. So." She looked at him, her mouth a hard line. "What do you want to know?"

Anselm frowned.

"How do you know I'm not *dealing* in the usual way?"

"Surely you know I had a tail on you between our meetings, as often as I could spare a man."

Anselm ticked them off on his right hand, skipping the stump of his index finger. "The Indine boy, probably a mail page in the Constabulary offices. You'd usually set him out bussing tables in restaurants and cafes. The fat secretary, who you liked to use in market spaces. Some indifferent-looking, brick-faced lout on the street, selling smokes or posing drunk."

"And Giezelle."

Anselm arched an eyebrow.

Gammon shook her head. "If you didn't notice her, I won't ruin her cover. She's still with the Constabulary and will take a sideline from me, if the money's right."

"I'll be damned. She's good."

"The very best."

"And, to return to the subject, how do you know I'm not dealing with my pain?"

Gammon searched the slow-gathering clouds. "I always knew when you and Rare were in a row because you'd go on a spree with some other girls, trying them on for size. Taller than you, usually blonde. Younger, by varying degrees."

Shame had burned out of Anselm Meteron long ago. It lingered in him more as a memory, an essentially theoretical conceit. If Gammon meant to color his cheeks like some silly schoolgirl, she'd chosen the wrong tack.

"You haven't been doing that lately," Gammon finished.

There was no buxom almost-Rare taunting him now, true. *But still.* He pictured long, black hair, haunted eyes, a body hardened by hunger. *I'll see you next Sabberday,* he'd said. But he hadn't. And she'd known it would be that way.

"Not really," Anselm sniffed. "Haven't had the time."

"You're the one who wanted to meet. If this isn't about closure, then what?"

"I can get *closure* in my own way," he said, the word itself suddenly grating. *Fucking women.* He had taken Gammon for something less predictable, but there she was, talking like some half-clink romance reader. "I want to know what you know about His Grace's involvement in the events of last fall."

Gammon took her time composing what next to say. Then she shook her head.

"Almost nothing. Bishop Meteron was Regenzi's spur and financier. I'm aware of his research denouncing the Vautnek theory back in the '30s and '40s, and read some of it, though I'll confess most of the mathematics he uses to substantiate his arguments are over my head."

"Topological reasoning applied to socioeconomic and organizational theory," Anselm murmured. His mind drifted back to uncountable boyhood hours in his father's study. The tutoring, recitations, examinations. *God's balls,* he wanted a smoke. Gammon eyed him with the scrutiny of a copper sizing up a lead.

"I don't follow much of it, either," he lied.

She let that go.

"The book is still lost," Gammon continued, fanning herself with her hat. "Though I'm working on some leads salvaged out of Chalmers's notes. You're about to travel abroad, so I'm assuming you have something brewing, too."

"Unless whatever tail you've put on me doubles as a precognitive, I don't see how you think you could know that. Call up Miss Ennis. All my appointments in Corma are intact through the end of the year."

Gammon shook her head. "First, you and I both know I'm not calling anyone on the voxes or sending a spark under my own name. As far as the Constabulary, the Court and Bar, the Governor's offices, and the Ecclesiastical Commission know, I've disappeared off the face of Amidon. Second, if you think I could deal with you all these years and not figure out that you keep four separate calendars, only two of which contain anything remotely like your actual schedule of activities, you haven't thought enough about how I earned my job."

Anselm raised an eyebrow. "*Haadi.* You're positively galvanizing when you've spent the final shit you had to give. If you keep this up, you'll inspire me to soothe my grief with you."

"You'd lose another finger trying."

"I've risked far more for much less. The grass is dry and we're both passably young."

"Not on your life."

"Pity." He sighed. "But your insistence on being provocative dodges the question of why you're so sure I'm about to leave the city."

"Because the Alchemist called on the Dolly Molls for a shop-sitter ready for a rough neighborhood, and he'd only do that if he were leaving. Putting aside your message coming back to me through Bess Earnshaw herself, I saw the look on your face when the Alchemist was dying on the Cathedral roof. You'll never let him go anywhere without you now."

Anselm studied her face—sharp-nosed, thin-lipped, her hair too blunt to soften her features the way they deserved. He'd put too much stock in such details, once. He should have noticed how clever the woman was—should have seen her as more than a means to his ends.

"You were magnificent at your job, Haadiyaa."

"It was a magnificent deal for you," she answered, in clipped, bitter tones. "I should have—" For a moment, the hammered-copper steadiness of her features bent. She wrung the rim of her hat, scowling. "I would do things differently, if I could go back."

And that opened the door. He saw Nasrahiel, and Rare's ravaged body, the wind whipping across the Cathedral's clerestory roof. The tide of anger rose inside Anselm again, slow enough he could build up a levee against it, try to force it below a glacial calm.

"What do Chalmers's notes have to do with rebuilding an aigamuxa?"

"*Bloody Proof.* Bess talks too much."

"I ask," Anselm continued, his words blurring hot around their edges, "because there's a certain aigamuxa I can think of in particular *need* of rebuilding. He owes me a chance to take him apart, hinge by hinge."

"I think you'd better take your little trip and let me see to Nasrahiel."

"I was promised a chance to make him pay."

Gammon waved her hat at the bag lying at Anselm's feet. "And I can promise where you'll end up, if you try."

"If you think I don't know my way around a fight well enough to put a dent in him—"

"You'll end up dead because I'll put a bullet in you now."

Anselm glared at her.

"If I have to," Gammon added, her voice quiet and fierce. "I need him. He wasn't the only aigamuxa willing to hurt a lot of people for his cause. He can find out what they'll do next, and if they'll listen to him, we can stop the avalanche before it starts."

"And if it's already started?"

Gammon smiled, the expression utterly without humor. "Be happy you'll be out of town awhile."

Anselm's hands ached. He looked down and found them clenched into fists. One by one, he worked at the joints, pausing to gentle the stump of his missing finger, feeling for the root of its phantom pain. "What makes you so sure he won't twist your head off the first chance he gets?"

"Nothing. But I have to try. I helped make this problem. Maybe I deserve to lose my head fixing it."

"You're a damned fine lawman but an apocalyptically stupid campaigner, Haadi. No job is ever worth your life."

"I stopped getting paid for this a long time ago."

"That's not what makes it a job."

Gammon made a small, knowing sound and looked at Anselm sidelong. "I suppose you'd understand something about that, wouldn't you? You and the Alchemist are taking the girl?"

Anselm recalled his argument with Erasmus in the Rolands' parlor, not even a week past.

She's safer with us than anywhere else, the Old Bear had insisted.

He wasn't wrong. But Anselm remembered the same argument coming from Leyah when Rare joined the family. The road that followed inevitably after stretched out so clearly before them, he couldn't fathom Erasmus's willful blindness.

"You'll excuse me if I decline to specify where," he replied, at last.

"I have a few educated guesses. Do me a favor, while you're turning over rocks the other side of the Western Sea. See if you can find a scholar with a background in lanyani culture."

Anselm Meteron didn't flummox easily, and he would have resented the label for this reaction, though he knew it to be accurate. He stared at Gammon, making no effort to hide his confusion. "The EC doesn't endorse any program of study for xenoculture. There's a small subset of anatomists who use the other sentients to inform human biological studies, but no one who expects to earn their collar and signet would try to connect sociology to xenospecies. The very idea is incoherent."

"It's *not* incoherent. It's perfectly reasonable, but EC doctrine assumes the other sentients are servitor species without the native resources to organize structures analogous to ours. But perhaps they're meant for something completely different than humanity—not just ecologically, but more than that. They might see the book as a means of reaching that destiny."

"They. Both the Trees and the apes."

"I'm following some leads connecting the two, and they're troubling."

Anselm pinched the bridge of his nose. "If I find such a scholar, they're almost certainly going to be a Kneeler."

"That makes no difference to me."

"I can send a name and credentials on through the Dolly Molls' usual channels, if anything turns up. There's a set of codes we've used in the past. If the message comes through while someone other than Jane's on duty, it'll be recorded without raising suspicion."

"Perfect." Gammon rose, dusting at her trousers with her hat and donning it just as the sky began to rumble in earnest. Tombstone shadows pooled on the gravelly paths, purple in the coal dust twilight. "If things go poorly here, you may have your shot at Nasrahiel after all."

Anselm's smile turned vulpine. "I feel a little torn about what to hope for."

"Don't be," Gammon answered. "Keep the girl close, and keep an eye out for the Trees. We don't know half as much as we should about how they communicate. But they already know too much, and it's spreading."

Anselm stood, too, putting the sack with the wooden urn on the tomb lid that had been his bench. His hand ached worse than before. He caught himself running his stump finger raw under his thumb. The scales of his mind shifted, trying to level the weight of mistrust and urgency, taring and clearing and tilting, the seesaw action stubbornly out of kilter. He wanted to put a finger around a trigger. Put a knife in his hand, and then through a mouth of saw-bladed shark-teeth. Take hold of the urn and its chalky ashes and bury himself with it. Find his father, and finally say what he'd meant to, twenty-five years before.

He wanted to take Rowena and the Old Bear and run.

"If you need to reach me while I'm abroad, there's a public house in Lemarcke called the Maiden's Honor," Anselm said. "We made it a business office, of a sort, back when we were for hire. They'll take my messages and pass them along, wherever we end up."

"You pay them well enough to keep quiet?"

"I own a controlling interest in the property. A nostalgia purchase on my last business trip. What can I say?" He shrugged, but it wasn't enough to slough the bitterness out of his voice, or take his eyes from Rare's urn. "I'm a sentimental old fool."

The promised rain finally started. *Melodrama*, Anselm thought, and almost laughed. Gammon was already making her way back up the hillside, her shoulders curved in against the storm.

II.

Rowena Downshire couldn't remember a time when trusting anyone to hold her things worked out well. And so, when the ship's porter waiting at the gangplank to the *Lady Lucinda* offered to take her trunk, she flatly refused, sitting on its lid with a "you'll have to shove me clean off" look to warn him away. It didn't help that the porter was an aigamuxa. The last time she'd been this close to one, she'd been dangling over the skyline of Corma from a buttress of the Old Cathedral.

She kept her stubborn seat until the Alchemist and Anselm Meteron appeared beside her, having paid the clockwork carriage driver to carry their bags to the porter.

The burly creature's face turned smug as the cat that had the cream as he tied their baggage on a barrow, his long, clawed hands moving deftly at latches and straps despite his eyes being turned to the ground. "You are certain you do not wish for help?" he rumbled.

Master Meteron raised an eyebrow at her. Rowena felt her face go hot.

"Guess I could use a hand after all," she muttered, sliding off the trunk lid.

They walked up the plank before the aiga, just in case he proved less adept at strapping up the luggage securely than he had seemed.

"Feeling all right, girl?" the Alchemist asked, limping with an emphasis she didn't like. It had been a bad morning for his knee—early, and busy, with the air humid and the gangplank steep.

Rowena shrugged. If she was honest with herself, it hadn't really been her things she'd worried over.

Going overseas seemed at first an adventure, but in the six days since the midsummer ball, it had turned first into a chore and then into an iron lump of anxiety lodged deep in her stomach. Rowena had carried it with her as she made rush deliveries to customers all up and down the lanes of Westgate Bridge, preparing for a month or more of the shop changing hands. She had carried the lump to the Mercy Commission Home to visit her mother with a kiss and to ask for her help by way of taking in Rabbit (the old dog would be a danger to himself and others on the airship, assuming he could endure the rigors of the journey in the first place, and Bess would have her hands full with running the Scales). She rolled in bed with that anxious lump, ate meals around it, woke up too early dogged by the pain of it and stayed up too late turning it over in her hands, studying it past the point of Reason. Rowena's Sabberday jaunts on the iron rail to visit her mother were all the travel outside Corma proper she'd ever done. Her world of alleys, bridges, bazaars, quays, and warehouses had seemed so vast just a week before. It had shrunk as the map of the world displayed on the Stone Scales's main floor loomed larger in her mind, the peninsula and archipelago that were their destination suddenly, overwhelmingly real.

She wasn't worried about her trunk, exactly. She was worried that her trunk would soon be the only thing left to her whose dimensions she understood.

"Didn't want 'im grabbing at my things," she answered, at last.

The Alchemist made one of his peculiar baritone notes of acknowledgement. But it was enough. Rowena smiled at him and, for the briefest of moments, saw his rare smile in return. By the time Master Meteron reached back to hand her up over the ship's rail, she felt enough like herself to be more confused than alarmed by the *Lady Lucinda*'s crew.

Perhaps a dozen lanyani moved up and down the decks, their lanky forms distending into graceful networks of branches and twigs, reaching up into the mastwork and rigging, disappearing into the ship's deck as if plunging into a puddle, or rising up from the hold with armloads of oakum rope and ballast sacks. Two of the creatures twined through the highest reaches of the rigging, where the giant gas envelope swelled like some monstrous sea creature. They looked to be adjusting some kind of firebox near the gas envelope's base, though Rowena couldn't be entirely sure, with the sun behind them, blurring her vision into a ruddy smear.

"I didn't think . . ." She looked around, blinking as much at the sight of the tree-people silently carrying out their work as the sting of the sunlight. "What are lanyani doing crewing a ship? Don't they need, like, soil and whatnot to get by?"

"They do," the Old Bear allowed. He grimaced as he turned his right hip over the side rail and, safely over, leaned against it. Meteron strode off into the thick of some of the tree-people, very much as if he knew what he was about. "The lanyani are poorly suited to longer journeys, which is why humans and aigamuxa crew travel along sea lanes. But the lanyani are better suited than men to air galleons. Less troubled by a thinner atmosphere, or the gases used to maintain buoyancy. A few crates of earth can suit the crew's needs for short-term travel, cost far less than actual food provisions, and don't suffer from spoilage. Many of the worst injuries a mammal could suffer working in the riggings—falls, lesions or amputations from unsecured lines, strangulation—are no concern to them. No need for medical supplies, no sleeping in shifts. If you need less than a tenday to get where you're bound, lanyani make better and cheaper crews."

The Old Bear delivered that speech with the almost-charming pedantry that had flavored all his tutoring since Rowena first came to the Scales. Still, at the end of it, he passed a look to Meteron that suggested there was something else about so many lanyani on the ship he wasn't prepared to say. Or at least, not say to her.

"And the Rolands know they ask fewer questions," Meteron added. He'd returned from speaking with a lanyani shaped like a yew forked by lightning. It stood further down the deck and gestured orders to its peers. One of them must have been to give the mooring line slack, for as Rowena put her head over the rail, she watched the anchor yard's ramp drift farther off, the gas envelope lifting them lazily upward.

Rowena frowned. "But the other passengers will ask questions of us, won't they?"

"They might," a voice like a massive woodwind replied. "If there were any."

The yew-like lanyani had stepped into conversational distance with their group. Its chest, knotted and creased with unshaved bark, expanded like a bellows. Another long phrase of musical language followed.

"I am Captain Qaar of the *Lady Lucinda*. Greatduke Roland owns our custom this season. We are most glad to welcome you aboard."

The Old Bear nodded. "Can you give us our itinerary?"

Rowena noticed him looking back over the railing to the anchor yard, too, his brow knitted.

The bellows-voice sighed through the air once more. "Three days to Sakhida Island in Lemarcke, with a day's leave to muster papers, then on to Nippon proper, where the Grand Library's agents will see you to your lodgings. We return to Corma by way of Vladivostoy after taking on our next travelers, guests of Lady Roland." Captain Qaar fluted out the last words. "The dock aiga have seen to your luggage in the berths below. We will drop our mooring line and ballast in thirty minutes, once the envelope is properly filled."

Rowena nodded, only half-listening as Meteron and the Old Bear saw the captain off with appropriate handshakes. She shaded her eyes against the sun, peering into the rigging, and felt as if she were a book falling open on a table, thrown all at once from darkness and privacy into glaring sunlight. *Islands and oceans and mustering papers.* Reason's rule, what did that even *mean?*

"Four days total in the air, then," Meteron said behind her. "You can manage, Bear?"

The answer was a dyspeptic sound of more than a few indelicate syllables.

Rowena glanced at the Old Bear. He did indeed look a bit bleached.

"You all right?" she asked.

"Not much of a flier."

Rowena pulled back her hair with a finger-rake and twist. "Seems stupid we can't just head to Nippon straight away."

They joined up in a line at the rail. Meteron passed a look clear across her to the Alchemist. The old man looked up from his pipe, tamping it with a thumb, and nodded approval of whatever idea his partner's look suggested.

"What? What'd I get wrong *now?*" Rowena protested.

"History lesson," Meteron said. "You're going to *love it.*"

That last came in a tone which indicated Rowena might like having her toenails drawn out better. She turned to complain that she wasn't *that* stupid and unschooled, thanks much, but the Old Bear was already making for the companionway stairs into the cabin hold, a trail of sweet smoke clouding the deck behind him.

"The maps are in my trunks," he called.

Rowena had never gotten over how quickly the Old Bear and Master Meteron could set a space into functional disarray. In five minutes, they turned their shared cabin into a riot of equipment and papers—most of that untidiness Meteron's doing as he tossed through the Old Bear's bags with the rude familiarity of a man who knew where his mates kept their knickers and what they kept in them, too. The Old Bear sat on the starboard bunk, his bad leg raised on a stool before him, cane propped in a corner like some child sent off for a punishment. Rowena could tell from the lines in his face that he was the one feeling punished, at the moment.

A map stretched over the bunk mattress like a cartographical quilt. Rowena sat at its opposite horizon, east to the Old Bear's west. Meteron flopped on the bunk across the small room, arms folded behind his head, and closed his eyes, listening to the lanyani's perfect silence amid the whistle and crack of the ship's lines.

The Old Bear tapped the map with the stem of his pipe. It left a dent on the page, an island suddenly sprung up from its waters.

"This—" he began.

"Is the Western Sea," Rowena answered smartly. "It's about three thousand-odd miles across from Corma to the nearest other land mass, and it tends calmer than the Atlantean Ocean to the east." She peeked at Meteron. "Which is where Rimmerston is, on the east coast of Amidon."

Meteron sniffed. "So you know your right from your left on a map. That's a start, cricket."

Rowena's face turned hot as a skillet. "I know a lot more than—"

"And this is Nippon," the Old Bear continued.

His pipe stem touched an archipelago: four big islands and a scattershot of small ones, all curving like a waxing crescent moon, their backs to the broader sea, bellies facing the vast body of land the Vraskans called "lower Vraska" and the Mongolian people simply called their own.

"What do you notice about Nippon?" he quizzed.

His voice had settled into the gentle baritone hum he used when the Stone Scales's shingle was turned and the shop theirs for the night. Books and maps and grammars and formulae. It had been a busy winter. A busier spring. Rowena meant to prove she'd learned her lessons well.

"It's . . . pretty isolated? I mean, there are some places kind of close by, like this land thingy."

"Peninsula."

"Yeah, this peninsula here, Koryu. And the rest of lower Vraska, too, is *kind of* close, but not really. There's still a lot of water to cross to get from its islands to the Vraskan mainland."

The old man's raptor eyes smiled, even as his mouth stayed flat around his pipe. "That kept Nippon out of the Unification Wars. History might have told a different story, if not for geography intervening."

Rowena considered the map. "But they're part of the Lemarckian Protectorate, right? Logician territory?"

"They are now," Meteron answered through a yawn. "'Unification' is a funny name for what happened after the declaration of the Ecclesiastical Commission was pinned to the high kirk in Saint Mungo, cricket."

That much, Rowena knew. It had started small, like so many things. A group of clergy. A public posting of a theory, long debated in their order's colloquia. Street preaching turning to cults recruiting atheists and academics with the promise of a way to unite the power of religion and science. Cults that turned into secret churches, which, in time, had the right kind of members in the right kinds of places—nobles and merchants and higher clergy with flexible, progressive views. And before long, the outsiders were the insiders, and the only way to insure their power was to draw a very clear, bold line between themselves and everyone else.

You could believe in the Grand Experiment, the rational nature of God's creation and His ongoing effort to teach humankind to emulate Him through the act of dispassionate experiment and rational understanding. You could believe that one's distance from the divine could be measured in precise units, recorded in significant figures, turned into data tables, framed as a hypothesis. Or, you could believe anything else and be a Kneeler: primitive, superstitious, ritualistic.

You could believe that God called upon humans to be more like Him, and gave them the tools to achieve that purpose through science. Or you could believe that God was something humans could never fully understand, and be powerless and small.

As it turned out, there were millions of people the world over who didn't see the choice quite so clearly as that.

"Unification took almost a hundred years," Rowena murmured. Collectively, folk in the many countries under EC influence called the period "the Unification Wars," but you might as well have called them purges, or pogroms, or conversion efforts. Communities reorganized under carefully designed educational programs. Families broken up, with children redistributed to households loyal to the EC—homes that could help them understand how they needed to change, and put their mothers' or fathers' ways behind them.

There were still places where the EC's hold was tenuous, at best, and some where it didn't exist at all. Meteron and the Old Bear seemed peculiarly knowledgeable about the dissidents of the world, Kneelers of every color and creed and origin. Even Anselm's family was converted—Hasids or Tzadikim. Rowena wasn't sure which, and the difference was mostly lost on her. She knew only that some of his ancestors' people still lived around Oldtemple Down, and none of them looked as if they knew half the wealth and privilege that Master Meteron's father had made shrugging a prayer shawl off his shoulders.

The Old Bear, though . . . He never talked about his people, though of course they must have come from Leonis, once. Nearly everyone in Amidon with his coal-dark skin came from somewhere on the continent Friar Leon claimed to be the "first man" to have found (never mind the hundreds of thousands of people already walking its savannahs and forests). And nearly all of those had fled Leonis when the aigamuxa rose up against the EC missionaries who had demanded their devotion, killing the Leonine natives in reprisal.

But before the EC missionaries came to Leonis, there had been all manner of others. Atavists. Mohammedans. Ecumenes, even, with their queer bloody wine and fleshy bread, or whatever that ritual was supposed to have been. It gave Rowena the creeps.

She'd never asked the Old Bear about where he stood with the EC, but he owned a great many books no proper Deacon at a free school would have countenanced her seeing. Rowena had been taught to read out of them. She had her suspicions. But she kept them to herself.

"A hundred years," the Old Bear affirmed, "and still, there were places on the globe the EC couldn't touch."

"Like Nippon?"

He nodded.

Rowena circled the sickle-shaped archipelago with her fingertip. "Lots of water. No neighbors."

"Unless you count Vraska," Meteron said. He'd opened his eyes and looked at Rowena with a knowing, crooked smile.

"Well, yeah, but Nippon's under the Logicians in Lemarcke, innit? They've got Koryu and some of the Mongolian coast—lower Vraska, I mean," Rowena corrected herself hastily. "But what's that got to do with Vraska proper?"

The Old Bear lit his cold pipe again, tamping its bowl. Soon, the room grew hazy with smoke redolent of marjoram and fennel. "When the EC itself began to fissure into subgroups—radicals within its own ranks agitating for more power, less leniency toward those who had not agreed to sacrifice their heritage for scientific progress—those radicals had to find places to rally themselves. Vraska is the second largest landmass in the world."

"The first is Leonis," Rowena blurted.

"The first is Leonis," he echoed. "But it was already well in hand after the aigamuxa were turned into a diaspora."

"Diaspo-what?"

"Scattered community," Meteron murmured. "A fractured people." There was an edge to his voice. She remembered odds and ends of things folk said back in Oldtemple when she was just old enough to pay attention to the grown people around her and some of what they said. Nobody had used the word "diaspora" for the Hasids and Tzadikim, but that sounded more or less like what they had meant.

"Oh. Right."

The Old Bear continued. "Several extremist factions headed for Vraska, looking for a place to regroup. Eventually, they found one another and put aside their differences to agree on the one thing they each cared about: the rest of the EC wasn't seeking truth through Reason seriously enough. So they called themselves the Logicians, and Bishop Professor Amabella Lemarcke made herself their leader. Before long, any territory the Logicians controlled became 'Lemarcke' by common usage, until finally the various small countries and principalities they'd gathered together formed the Protectorate."

Now Meteron was sitting up, his focus sharp as an arrow. They were talking about his expertise now: politics.

"The Logicians are the only EC faction that actually combines secular and clerical authority. The rest of the world, from Amidon to the Zairr, recognize the EC as a powerful influence on governance, but they aren't the *actual* government. The Logicians turned Lemarcke into a proper theocracy. A lot fewer roadblocks to transforming the world through the grace of Reason that way."

Rowena nodded. "So that's why everybody says Lemarcke puts Corma to shame for all its shiny doohickeys and doctorish stuff."

"I don't recall referring to the Logicians' work as 'shiny doohickeys,' nor being *everybody*," the Old Bear murmured around his pipe stem, "but yes. That's said because it is true."

"We still haven't gotten to the story behind Nippon, though."

"If you're of a mind to push science and engineering to their outer limits," Meteron said, "you're good for that only until you reach the outer limits of your own resources. Amidon had been mining for coal and drilling for oil in the high north of Vraska for a generation before the Logicians crept north from Mongolia and Koryu. When the EC and its sovereign counterparts divided up the globe, everyone imagined there would be fuel enough in Vraska to last the world a millennia. It seemed too big to be stripped bare. And, in the end, that wasn't actually the problem.

"The problem was the Lemarckian Protectorate's lands weren't resource-rich, and their technological progress depended on a greater share of what northern Vraska had to offer. But since they were in conflict with the rest of the EC, they eschewed . . . diplomatic means of obtaining their needs."

"Another war," Rowena finished. "The Coal Wars. Amidon against Lemarcke, with Vraska in between."

"With Vraska pulled both ways," the Old Bear corrected, his face darkening over the map. "Pockets of territories were claimed and conscripted by either side. Vraskan troops mustered to whatever cause rolled into town first. That was how I met Ivor."

It had been some time since Rowena last heard that name. It left a sour taste at the back of her mouth, a bile risen and never properly expelled. There was a whole story, a whole context, lurking behind the old man's statement, but she left it there. Maybe she would ask him to explain more someday.

Maybe.

"The Logicians had made some terrible weapons," the Old Bear continued. "Science was good for that. But they had no practical experience in warfare, and even less ability to organize their scattered Protectorates into a coordinated army. They needed the help of seasoned warriors, so they turned to Nippon."

He settled his back against the cabin wall, grimacing as he shifted his weight to keep his knee comfortable on the stool before him. "Geography did much to protect Nippon from the Unification Wars, but so had its reputation. Its people were accomplished, highly coordinated warriors, all the members of their noble caste trained in strategy and most in actual combat, as well. It wasn't a big nation or an especially scientifically advanced one, at the time, but it had companies of soldiers from its own internal civil wars already trained and prepared. The Logicians negotiated Nippon's entry into the Protectorate most favorably. In exchange for several thousand soldiers in smaller units that could be distributed into the Protectorate army and used as a model for training and discipline, Nippon would receive preferential employment of its researchers, schooling for its upper castes to make deacons and reverends of them, access to Lemarcke's best technologies. And, most importantly, the right to absorb the Logicians' special library collections into its Grand Library. In one political agreement, Nippon became both a Logician territory and the jewel in the Proctectorate's crown."

Rowena frowned. "And after that?"

"After that . . ." The Old Bear sighed. "Lemarcke won the Coal Wars. Amidon was pushed out of Vraska. Vraska proper became a Logician power center. Nippon became the seat of Logician information, if not of its politics."

"But what I don't *get*," Rowena pressed, searching between the two men, "is where the book that started all this fuss even came from. I mean, the Grand Library, okay, but where did it come from in the first place? Did the Logicians have it and move it there? Had the Nipponese had it all along, somehow?"

Master Meteron offered his familiar, one-shouldered shrug. "Perhaps Chalmers will know. I'm not sure that it matters. When last we saw him, he was trying to learn where the book might be now, and what else it might have revealed, and to whom. Where it used to be matters only so far."

"Only so far as it might give a clue where it's going now," Rowena challenged.

"Possibly. But I doubt the book has fallen into organized use yet," said the Old Bear. "If it had, we surely would have seen signs of it already."

Maybe, Rowena thought.

There wasn't time to think anything else, though, before the whole cabin lurched. Rowena's stomach tilted in response.

Her eyes met Master Meteron's. He smiled.

"Care to see what the view looks like, sailing from Corma in a private air galleon, cricket?"

She bounded to her feet, then paused, looking at the Old Bear.

He waved, grunting something that wasn't a word. *Go ahead.* And he put a hand under his wounded knee, gentling it into a slight bend with a wince.

"We'll be back soon," Rowena promised.

As it turned out, they spent an hour watching the ground grow smaller and the clouds grow larger, tracing the distant shoreline of Amidon with their fingers. Rowena raised a hand before her eyes, blotting the world she knew away. It had never looked so small before.

12.

Erasmus Pardon watched Rowena as she sat on her narrow bunk, oblivious to all but the book that lay before her. She stared down at her lap, a familiar line of concentration drawn between her eyes, a hand moving at intervals precise as clockwork, tucking a lock of hair behind her ear. Her lips worked the words on the page silently. The Alchemist had never acquired the skill of lipreading; a cautious graze over a speaker's distracted mind offered far better insight.

But he knew what he'd assigned the girl to read—had turned those same pages so often, they had a rhythm not unlike the beat of his heart.

The Lord is my Shepherd. I shall not want. He maketh me to lie down in green pastures . . .

Erasmus felt a twist of guilt in his stomach, as if he were being lewd standing in Rowena's half-open door. And yet the thought of breaking the spell by announcing himself was somehow worse. He admired Rowena. It was an authentic, unguarded admiration, nothing self-aggrandizing in it. He did not look upon her as his handiwork, or lay claim to her success. She had wanted everything he had offered and clutched with such a fierce intensity, it drove a pin into his heart.

Rowena was not an apt reader. She could labor over pages another child her age, educated from early years, could consume in two minutes and only grasp them fully after a quarter-hour's study. But she was determined.

Rowena's hand drifted up to her insolent lock again, tucking it away. This time, her head turned, and she spied the doorframe and Pardon lingering in it. The spell was broken.

The Alchemist stifled his regret.

Foolish, fond old man.

"I should have knocked," he said, by way of apology.

The girl shrugged. The lock rebelled and shaded her eyes again. "S'okay. I like . . . sometimes, I like just finding you there."

"May I come in?"

Rowena dog-eared a page in the book. Erasmus did his best to conceal a wince. Vigorous use could be its own form of flattery, he supposed.

Rowena shuffled over on the mattress and patted the spot beside her, inviting. He took it, as he had so many times before in her room above the Scales.

"This book is damned weird," she said, turning it over in her hands. The gold leaf on the embossed cover had long since worn away, but the curve of the B, the loops of O and E, and the angles of Y and L still remained. "It can't decide if it's poetry or stories or just really boring lists of rules. It's like Sabberday lectures, but without any posits or any of the maths and proofs, like they came from some crazy street-preacher."

"That seems to be the prevailing opinion of the text now."

"So, what's doing, Bear?"

The bank of the air galleon changed. Erasmus battled the lurch in his stomach. Why did he have to be such a miserable flier? He'd endured much worse in his life than a well-appointed airship.

If the subtle shift had disturbed Rowena, she didn't show it.

"You asked me about what we would do to pass the flight yesterday," he began.

"More books?" she suggested. She didn't sound exactly eager. *Resigned*, maybe. Probably she was worried what other doorstoppers he had packed.

"I thought you might like to stretch your legs. Come with me topside, girl."

Rowena's face lit like a flare, burning with interest. "I thought you hate being up there."

"More than I can say. But there's no room below for what we're going to do."

Rowena bounded to her feet and offered him her hand, smiling broadly. Erasmus took it. He allowed her to step back, levering him up a little. It was a small concession to his lameness, enough to keep the girl's barking at bay.

He untucked his cane from the crook of his arm and followed her through the gangway, up the companionway stairs, and into the bright, cool morning. There was no point pretending to lead the way. On the day they'd cast off, Rowena took to the riggings with Anselm, learning how to move among the beams and lines on sure, strong arms. It was not an exercise of which Erasmus entirely approved. Then again, he was not in a position to disapprove, either. Ann kept Rowena's climbs close to the deck—or, at least, had done so thus far—and focused them amidships, far from stern and prow and safely out of the worst wind shears. Pardon had planned to make a campaigner of her in name only, just for the sake of legalizing their contract with the Rolands. But Ann had returned from his meeting with the former Inspector Gammon with more than Rare's ashes. Her warnings about the Trees were never far from Erasmus's or Anselm's minds, with an entire crew of lanyani ferrying them to Lemarcke.

"We can't be her only protection," Ann had insisted.

The climbing lessons were a start on the skill sets she'd need to elude and evade, something Ann had wanted to begin Rowena on even back in Corma. Her sprained ankle now mended, he'd attacked the matter with gusto. But there were other things she needed to know, well beyond a second-story man's experience. Erasmus consoled himself that even if he did not wish Rowena a life that required such knowledge, she was fortunate to have good teachers.

Rowena stood by the main mast, hugging herself against a wind that still carried the bracing chill of dawn.

"Another climbing lesson, then?"

Erasmus propped his cane beside her and shrugged free of his frock coat. Rowena watched him closely, her eyes falling on the weaponette holstered on his left thigh. He drew it, still in its shortened position. Gingerly, he considered his footing. The flight course was steady, and the day was still young. There was strength enough in his bad leg to hold him, at least for a while.

"Here," he said. Pardon spun the weaponette in his hand with practiced ease, turning the blade toward himself, the wrapped hilt toward the girl. Its edge glinted, rippling patterns of daylight.

Rowena's hand closed on the hilt. Her fingers lingered over his.

"We started this a month ago. You want to give me more lessons?"

"I want to give you *this*."

The girl's hand jerked away, as if the blade had suddenly reared up against her. "No. I couldn't."

"Why?"

"Footwork, positions, and parries!" Rowena protested. "That's all I really know. With a stick and . . . and . . . just between the roses in the shop yard. It's not the same."

"That's why you need a proper blade."

"It's yours. I couldn't."

"Rowena." Erasmus offered her the hilt again. "You should learn properly," he insisted. "I won't be able to teach you much longer."

"You're not sixty yet," Rowena muttered sulkily. "S'not *so* old."

"Old enough. More than, for a lamed man."

Rowena shot him a stern look, the sort marms at the free schools gave their most unruly charges. "You've mended *fine*. Half the time you don't even need your cane."

"I've mended, after a fashion."

Rowena all but swatted the blade away. "Then you're fine," she spat.

"Rowena. Doctor Chalmers did his best, but even if you set a bone well, if you don't clear out the flesh around the break—if you lack the skill, as he did, and if it's catastrophic enough to be all but impossible to clear, as this was—then the wound can never truly heal. In another two years, three at the most, the bone fragments left behind will have settled into the muscle and cartilage and bored them out. A year after that and the joint will be altogether useless."

Rowena hugged herself again, though it seemed to have little to do with the morning chill. The *Lady Lucinda* had dropped a few thousand feet. The sun had burned away the clouds. The deck was shining, bright and fresh-scrubbed, the lanyani sailors rising up through it to attend their duties. The air fairly hummed with warmth.

Rowena examined the laces of her boots with an interest they hardly merited.

"Then what happens?" she demanded.

Erasmus Pardon glanced at the cane resting behind the rail of the main mast. He had made his peace with growing old years before meeting Rowena Downshire. He'd felt fortunate to do it at all, given the life he had led. Age would have its particular prices, and like all else in life, it had a prescribed, inevitable destination at its farthest shore. He had assumed time would whittle him down, layer by layer, until one day it reached his core and took a final cut. Some customer would realize the shop shingle had not been turned in a day or three, curiosity would overmaster superstition, and he would be found, wherever he had fallen—or perhaps, if he were lucky, where he'd laid down to rest and simply never woken. And that would be all. It was not something he had feared. It was not even a prospect he had mustered the will to resent. Life had been an undifferentiated string of days for so long, what was the point of counting them and feeling shortchanged?

But so much had changed for him, and so fast. He felt the pressure to take action, to make something of his time. After the Cathedral, old wounds reported their complaints with a more galling regularity. He kept busy with the project of the girl, giving himself as little time to worry over them as he might. Infirmity would still sharpen its knife in dark corners, waiting, but for the first time in longer than he cared to recall, he had mustered the will to beat it back.

"When that happens," Erasmus answered, "I'll have a choice to make. I will feel better about making it knowing I did my best by you, girl."

Rowena's jaw had set. He had not lowered the hand holding out the blade.

Her fingers closed over his, trailing between his weathered black knuckles, tracing a path as she drew it from him and into her grasp.

He smiled. "Ready?"

Rowena examined the tip of the blade in its retracted form. "You en't shown me how the zapping bit works."

"One thing at a time." He walked to the mast rail and hoisted his cane in a dueler's grip. "En garde."

Rowena snorted. "You don't mean to fend me off with *that* thing, d'you? That's just a stick."

"It's more than enough for me to make short work of you."

"Oh *really?*" She turned the weaponette in her hand, brow furrowed, and finally realized the trick. She flicked her wrist once, hard—harder than was really needed, Erasmus noted. The blade sprang forth, singing a sharp, clear note.

Rowena crossed tips with him, looking a little ruefully at the rubber-baited cane resting against her saber-end. "I thought the point was you can't do this anymore."

A flash of movement. Rowena's blade nearly rattled from her hand as Pardon's cane struck it, fast but gently to keep from damaging the sword. His cane returned to the crossed position an instant later, long before the girl reacted.

Rowena yelped. She shook out her fingers, wide-eyed. "Bloody Reason, Bear!"

"The point," he said, "is that I *can* still do this for a while longer. And that was hardly any contact at all. Back in position. I'm not getting any younger."

Smiling again, she touched blade to cane, and there was a pause.

She plunged forward.

The lesson began.

The airship sang through the sky, two figures darting forth and back on its decks like hawks clipping wings.

13.

Tucker Pettigrew was busy sweeping a pile of chadras chits into his sorting tray when the woman slid into the seat across from him. He didn't pay her much mind. The chits were all kinds of odd shapes—octagons and triangles and half-moons and such—and he knew from experience that if he didn't keep an eye on their clattersome trip from his winnings pile to his sorting tray, they'd go caroming off into every dark corner of the crowded card house.

Stupid foreign game, chadras. He could play it well enough, sure. Well enough he'd emptied three other men's trays and sent them packing after just two hours of play. The automatic trays, which could count up a body's winnings with all manner of clever clockwork tricks, were interesting little gadgets, no doubt, but Tucker made his living keeping ledgers and locks sealed tight. The thought of a simple tray replacing any part of his job seemed patently ridiculous. But it was what all the best card houses were changing out to, and so he'd been stuck with it, and damned if his fingers seemed a mite too drunk to funnel all the chits in without a spill.

Tucker blinked, staring at the strange woman in the chair opposite. His stare turned into a squint. She smiled.

A wine stem neck and a close-clipped burr of hair. Chestnut eyes and dark, lacquer-smooth skin. The smile was a spare, slight thing, as carefully policed as a street corner in Coventry Passage. She wore a tab-collared jacket of an almost military cut, a pin bearing globe, book, and scales dotting the space just below the thumbprint of her throat.

Ecclesiastical Commission, Tucker thought, first. And, *Huh*, next.

"Hello," she said.

Tucker sniffed. "H'lo. You'll need at least one more to start the table again. Prob'ly want to check the rules if you mean to—"

"I'm Reverend Doctor Deliverance Tegura."

Tucker fumbled his tray on the felt-topped table. His winnings hopped and clattered inside their maze of pins, but they stayed put. The tray's clockwork counter spun up a figure he could just blearily make out. Fascinating device, that tray. He wondered how it measured its contents. By weight? Contact points on the tray? He shook his head, remembering the woman belatedly.

"Didn't ask your name," he muttered.

"That's true," Deliverance Tegura agreed. "But the social graces require both a greeting and an introduction, and I thought at least one of us ought to observe them."

Tucker pushed back from the table, wobbled, and stood straight. He was in uniform, too, though an accountant-turnkey's Oldtemple uniform was nothing much compared to a proper EC getup. He was government. The EC wasn't law and order—it was something more than that, something outside of it, or above it. Adjacent to it. He didn't rightly know. Most folks seemed to think his uniform called for him answering to the likes of this woman. Tonight, he wasn't in the mood. He'd won, and gloated, and now he wanted to take his chits off to the exchequer and see them turned into proper clink.

"Well, hello an' goodbye, and I'm Tucker Pettigrew, by the bye. 'Night, your Reverendfulness."

"I was hoping to buy you a drink."

Her expression hadn't changed. This wasn't an advance. Tucker wouldn't have believed himself so lucky. He'd spent the last twenty years keeping books and locks in Oldtemple prison. It was an ugly place. He knew very well the ugliness it had imprinted on him in return. Pinch-faced, pale, and prone to snappish smallness. It had been years since he'd had a woman for anything other than coin.

Tucker snorted. "Bit late for that. Might be topped off for the night."

"Dinner, then? I need a little of your time, Master Pettigrew, and I would like to make it worth your while."

Tucker considered the contents of his tray. He shrugged.

"They do meals on the floor below."

They went downstairs, slipping past smoky tables crowded round with other patrons looking to fill their trays. It didn't much matter to Tucker what the woman wanted. He had a few guesses what she'd come to him for. Bribery was likeliest. There was probably someone on his level of Oldtemple she wanted sprung fast and cheap, or maybe buried deeper in the red ledger. Names and records confused, or lost. He'd done it all. Not often enough that he made a show of it, not like those other crank-headed twats working the debtors' prison. One, a turnkey named Wallace—or had it been Willis?—came up with a fee structure, and had been dim enough to have it printed on little paste cards for the convenience of his would-be clientele. He was in a cell of his own, now, but on one of the prison hulks rusting out in Misery Bay.

Tucker ordered a mince pie, an ale, and a plate of curried potato crisps. Deliverance Tegura ordered bitter chocolate over ice and milk, though she spent more time stirring than drinking it.

She let him plow through half the potatoes and three bites of pie before she bothered with questions beyond the how-do-you-dos of his job. The food was sponging up his sour mood and the stale drink clouding his thoughts. The questions, he realized, were not about confirming he was an Oldtemple turnkey, but that he was a *specific* turnkey.

"Do you remember a debtor named Clara Downshire, Master Pettigrew?"

"I do, yeah. Paid out around the end of last year. Hard to forget her."

More stirring. The woman tapped her spoon against the rim of her glass. "Can you elaborate?"

"She was daft."

"Many of your residents become at least a little neurotically agitated during their stay, if I understand correctly."

There hadn't been any particular judgment in the woman's tone, but Tucker didn't sit easy with the suggestion, however vague, that he was responsible for that fact.

"Mine no more than anybody else's," he answered sharply.

"My apologies. Could you explain a little about Mrs. Downshire's peculiarities?"

"Could. What're they to you?"

"I work for the Commission, tracking data on mental health concerns and recovery patterns in subjects of judicial discipline," she explained. "From time to time, I'm called upon to investigate specific cases in closer detail. Case studies, as it were. Mrs. Downshire's case was randomly selected."

Tucker snorted. "Begging your pardon, Reverend, but if you believe that, somebody's fed you a bloody line."

Tegura raised an eyebrow. "Explain, please."

"Clara Downshire made her share of fuss. Every turnkey in the house knew her. It's too rich a coincidence your bosses would pull a case at *random* and have it be the most notorious crackpot in the whole brick-house."

"Really." The word was as cold and flat as an iced-over pond.

"Lemme tell you a story about Clara *fucking* Downshire, your worship. You can even quote me in your records."

Tegura didn't produce a notebook. Tucker didn't care. The thought of the madwoman always heated him up. He didn't hate her—that would have been like hating an ugly wall fixture, futile and foolish. He was, in a way, almost proud of having been her turnkey. She made a hell of a story over ales on a tenday leave, always good for humor and shock and even a little twinge of horror. Clara Downshire was an interesting piece of work, and Tucker—who understood himself too well to imagine he was in the least way personally interesting—had become secondarily famous by virtue of her proximity. Life had been oddly emptier without her addled stories to pass along, amusing (or distracting) his chadras opponents.

"So, this Downshire woman," Tucker began, "she landed in Old-temple ages ago after a horse kicked her in the head and rattled her up something awful. Don't get me wrong; it weren't as bad as some I've seen. She could eat and dress and toilet herself and all. But she was daft as a goose and nearly as ornery. Had three brats all doing time with her, until they finally went their ways, off to get jobs or get dead. The littlest one, Rebecca or Regina or something like that, she was in and out every tenday at least, leaving money in her mum's coffer and checking the ledger. Made it damned hard to do anything but keep the columns honest, you know?"

The Reverend Doctor Tegura nodded solemnly. "Go on."

"So I had to deal with the little bitch whinging at me about every last quarter-clink, and her mother muttering all her usual nonsense."

"Usual in what way?"

"She'd say hello to you, and call you by the wrong name—but not altogether wrong. She damned well knew my name, I can tell you, but she always called me by my father's. Said we looked alike."

Tegura shrugged. "I'm not sure why that's a significant detail."

"My father was a sailor on a Trimeeni sky freighter. He buggered off the month I was born and I never knew aught of him, at least not until last summer. Then he showed up with his hat out hoping to play me for some sentimental arse. He'd hobbled himself with the rope off the mizzenmast, see, and hadn't money for a clockwork prosthetic. Had it in his head I'd help him foot the bill. I didn't, but I saw him long enough to see what Downshire meant. I'm his very image."

"Don't most men resemble their fathers?"

"But how would she know the blighter's *name?* How would she know to ask me about my leg all the time, whenever it rained, whenever the floor was slick from a frost? She knew things about him I'd never told her, and knew 'em before I'd ever met him. Before it even happened that he'd been crippled. And she thought that was me."

"That would be most disconcerting."

"Damned right it was. She had a bad spell of sickness—*lady concerns,* you understand—a ways back, and so we sent one of the laundresses to tend her through it. The woman flat refused to come back after the second day. Called Mrs. Downshire a witch. This laundress, she was an irrational savage, one of the last Leonine refugees off the boat from one of the Ecumenical missions—" Tucker paused, considering for the first time that Tegura might also be such a savage. "Sorry. I mean, in any case, the laundress was scared stiff as a sheet. Said Downshire told her the whole story of her childhood."

Tegura raised an eyebrow. "Not Mrs. Downshire's childhood, I take it."

"No, ma'am. The laundress's, and her whole family, too. And she knew stories about someone the laundress had never heard of, some little boy named Darby. Well, wouldn't you know, the woman turns up fat as a hen with a baby on the way a few months later, and now her Darby's living a life all but scripted from Downshire's fancies."

"Interesting you call them that. Scripted. Fancies. You believe they're hoaxes of some kind?"

Tucker scowled into his ale. "That'd be a comfort. But no. There's something to 'em, and I was happy to see the woman gone when her debt was paid."

"Do you know where she is now?"

"I concern myself with the debtors while they owe the courts and their creditors. Past that, it's no lookout of mine."

"She's living in the Mercy Commission Home out in Southeby."

"Never heard of it."

"It's very expensive. Did she have a benefactor you're aware of?"

"Her? Nah. The wee girl of hers, though," Tucker mused. "She came in around the start of Elevenmonth last year with some fancy toff. Sharp as a knife and colder than snow, that cove. I figured she must have played bed-warmer for him. A few days after, Mrs. Downshire was paid out and gone. I don't believe in coincidences."

"Neither do I."

Tucker studied the woman's smooth, studious face with a growing sense of unease. "Clara Downshire wasn't any random file your people picked."

"No, she wasn't."

"You're not looking to give me trouble?"

"Trouble? Oh, no, Master Pettigrew. You've been most helpful." She set a stack of coin between them and rose, dusting at her skirts. "I only required you for a little confirmation."

Tucker's keen eye for coin counted the stack before it even struck the table. "Confirmation of what?" he asked, shoveling up the sovereigns.

"That Mrs. Downshire has a certain insight worthy of careful research. Thank you, Master Pettigrew. And one more thing?"

"Hm?"

"We have never met, you and I."

"Don't know who you are, lady, but I'll thank you to back off my chadras tray," he replied gamely.

"I beg your pardon," she purred and slipped from the table with a tiny touch of her fingers to her forehead—a salute. A farewell.

The money lasted Tucker the rest of the night. He put it to good use, and a few hours on, had drunk enough to ensure he would forget the statuesque woman and her steady, measuring stare, after all.

14.

In her dream, Leyah walked with Rowena as she paced the deck of the *Lady Lucinda*, her body just a shadow pacing at her side. It was like this in more than just her dreams. As often as not, Rowena would wake in her room above the Stone Scales to find Leyah sitting in the chair at her bedside, tinkering with something in her lap that wasn't really there, acting out the memory of living.

And they would talk. They talked a lot. Rowena longed to speak with the Old Bear in the quiet confines of their shared mind-space, but she kept their conferences brief, afraid of what he'd see if she let the connection linger. She never told him what had happened to Leyah, after the Old Cathedral. He thought he'd let his wife go, at last.

He had. But that wasn't the same as her suddenly being able to leave this world.

Neither Rowena nor Leyah knew what the Old Bear would think about her being so near, still restless. Trapped because he'd failed to let her go for so long, she'd taken on a piece of substance beyond mere memory. Leyah had no desire to complicate Rowena's life. She rarely spoke in a way that demanded a response. Meeting the Rolands again had been a sharp, silent agony, calling up memories as jagged as the metal that had torn Leyah's life from her body. But the rest of the time, she was simply there inside Rowena, a warmth smelling of jasmine and machine oil. That suited Rowena fine. She knew all too well a woman only needed to be caught talking to herself once for folk to decide she'd lost her wits. *Half-gone*, the other prisoners of Oldtemple had called Clara Downshire.

But Leyah Pardon was supposed to be *whole-gone*.

In the dream, she paced with Rowena up and down the deck of the ship, trying to follow all the lines and cracks in its boards. Between the wind pushing against them and the ship keeling, it was no easy task. They debated without words if they should follow the seams of the boards or the knots between them, connecting them like dots on a map. The difference seemed to matter, as foolish differences always did in Rowena's dreams, as essential as choosing a fork in a road.

They traveled the deck in a circuit until they reached the edge of the companionway headed below. Someone was coming up.

A lot of someones.

There were aigamuxa, swinging forward on their knuckles, their eyeless faces smeared with blood. Their mouths bristled with jagged teeth—too many, even for a proper aiga. Even for a dream. Their lips and tongues bled from the saw-teeth bursting in all directions. Leyah took Rowena's hand, suddenly becoming more than a shadow, and pulled her away from the stairs.

Run, she shouted.

Rowena turned to flee. Out of the grain of wood and the cracks of planking, lanyani rose up, paper-thin, and turned to face her. They rippled like the sails overhead, took on dimension, unfolded into their whole and terrible selves, bristling thorns and briars. Leyah opened her mouth, but the hiss and crackle of branches was like a forest in a gale, consuming her words, and loud enough for Rowena to notice how absolutely silent the aigamuxa had become.

And then she understood. The lanyani were talking to the aigamuxa—and the aiga were *listening*.

Rowena awoke, curled in a ball so tight her back ached. She slipped a jacket over her nightshirt and padded barefoot from her cabin into the gangway beyond, then up the companionway stairs. The air above the Western Sea struck her, heavy with damp and cold, but she didn't care about that any more than she cared to go back to her bunk. The chill swept the cobwebs of sleep away. She hugged herself, squinted against the huge, pockmarked moon's glare, and saw a figure slouched against the portside rail.

Master Meteron had played cards with the ship's crew the last two nights, which might not have seemed too odd to Rowena, if they weren't a bunch of blank-eyed Trees that never spoke to anyone. They played with cards of hammered tin, with the proper figures scratched on. Meteron claimed he was making a point to lose most of the time at first, so the lanyani would invite him back—so they'd make big bets to fill up the pot, thinking they were bound to win the lot. And they had. He'd taken two big pots just before she turned in for the night, though Rowena knew he didn't need the money or enjoy the Trees' company. He was keeping them busy. Keeping an eye on them, while she and the Old Bear slept. She remembered the dream and shivered, wondering if Leyah would agree with her line of reasoning. She hadn't been at Rowena's bunkside when she jolted awake.

Anselm Meteron leaned into the rails, looking down at the sea. The curve of his shoulders spoke more of exhaustion than his usual, feral ease. Rowena wondered if he was out of his ether—if, maybe, he'd forgotten to pack it.

"You're awake?" she asked. Then she cringed. It was so obvious, she wanted to slink back down the stairs before he could turn his measuring gaze on her.

"I had better be, cricket. It would be a very bad idea to sleepwalk out here," he said.

Rowena took a piece of the rail beside him. Meteron smiled in that way that made her feel like a bug on a dissecting tray, staring at the scalpel as it descended.

"You're awake, too," he added, with a needling indulgence.

"I had a . . . I just had to get up."

"Pity. Bad dream?"

"I'm not a baby," Rowena snapped.

"You've a penchant for stating the obvious."

She pulled a face. "What's a 'penchant'?"

"Expanding your impoverished vocabulary?"

"You don't have to be like that about it."

He sighed. "*Penchant.* A habit. A strong preference or inclination."

"How d'you spell it?"

"God's balls, cricket, am I your Free School tutor?"

"I write stuff in a diary now! Sometimes, anyway. I'm learning how. Bear's teaching me."

"It's a bad idea to keep too close a record of what you do, in our line of work."

Rowena considered the chop of waves far below. "Don't know what else I'm supposed to do when you en't drilling me up in the riggings, or Bear needs to rest his leg from dueling."

Meteron studied her a good, long while, then gave his nod that was almost a bow. He spelled the word, very slowly. Rowena took it down in her mind, repeating it over and again, until Leyah murmured that she'd remember it for her.

Pay attention now, Rowena, she said.

"You never said why you're up, though."

He shrugged. "You didn't ask."

"Bloody Reason," she groaned. "You're like what Mick said talking to *girls* is like."

"Mick?"

"Big ox who worked for Ivor. He was older'n me, thank the Proof. Kept his hands and eyes from getting too interested."

"And what *did* Mick say about talking to girls?"

"'Girls,'" she recited, "'is lackwits and fuckteases, and they never just give simple answers, because if they did, you could tell they've nothing to say.'"

Meteron had been taking a pull off his cigarette, but his laugh sent the butt flying away on an air current. Rowena jerked back as its bright tip spun past, almost clipping her nose.

"That," he said, "is so perfectly pubescent, it's *almost* brilliant. Not entirely wrong, either. Not a feminist, your Mick."

"Guess not. Feminist is . . . ?"

"Women are as good as men, treat them well, all that stuff." He rolled a hand in the air, as if he were bored already of defining words—or perhaps just bored by that word in particular.

"Doesn't sound like anything you buy into."

"Not especially. But I can count on one hand the people I've been legitimately afraid of in my life, and two of them were women. It seems just to call them my equals, with equal numbers as evidence."

Rowena blinked. "But you can't have an equal count with five—"

He lifted his right hand and waggled its four fingers. She looked away from the stubby leftover of his pointer.

"You never did tell me what happened to your hand."

"Slammed it in a door."

"I en't stupid."

"Never said you were."

"Fine," Rowena countered, "I don't have to know. S'not like I care. But why are you up here in the middle of the night, anyways?"

He looked away, the silence between them taut as the jib sail's line.

Keep talking to him, Rowena, Leyah urged. *There's something he isn't telling you.*

Rowena could never sort out how she felt about Master Meteron. He was a puzzle box, full of confounding levers and catches, as likely to nip a fingertip as offer a prize. But she did care enough to push.

"Look, we're supposed to be a team. How can I do anything right if I don't know what's going on in your head? Or what you've got planned?"

He arched an eyebrow at her. "You'd make a very fine face-woman, with a bit of practice." He must have seen the question in her frown. "The business-dealer. The reasonable one."

Rowena blinked as the slides of her memory sorted into order, taking images from the Rolands' parlor and riffling them into a proper narrative. "Was Bear the face-man for your old group?"

"Well," Meteron chuckled, "it certainly wasn't Ivor, I can tell you that. And it was very useful to leave the talking to the man who had a certain insight into what people were really thinking."

"See, that's what I mean!" she cried. "I need . . . what do you call it? *Context.*"

Meteron pinched the bridge of his nose between thumb and the stump of his forefinger. "Context is exactly the problem. I was trying to make up my mind how much to tell you about what's likely to happen next." He carried on grudgingly. "This is a dangerous job. That's why there has to be a contract."

"Because of Doc Chalmers's research. People want it, and you want to know more about it, because—" Rowena stopped. "Because why? Why's it matter to you, anyway?"

Meteron fussed a thumb over his missing finger, distant and abstracted. The expression looked familiar. It took Rowena a minute to work out where she'd seen it before.

Years earlier, she'd snuck off from a delivery route to watch a trade company send a "flying freighter" ship off from the docks at Misery Bay. She was so small then, she couldn't see past the crowd's belt buckles, and had to clamber up on the coiled chains of the quay itself to snatch a view. A man stood behind her with his son sitting on his shoulders. The launch was a big to-do. Some EC squints had come up with a design that would let the gas-bubble freighter rise up from the water and fly over the sea, doing what sea ships and air galleons each could only do separately, flying or sailing back and forth in the same trip, whichever best suited the cargo or the clime. The ship bristled with rotors and gears, a beautiful riot of brass and wood. They got it out on the water, and once it had put a half-mile between itself and the quay, they started the rotors, and raised the gas bags, and then—

She'd been too young to understand what she was seeing. Something went wrong, and Rowena never knew what to look for or how to explain it. Something caught fire—the gas in the hold, or a spark from the machinery, or Reason only knew what. In an instant, the ship was a bloom of flame on the water.

The first thing Rowena saw after flinching back from the explosion was the boy and his father.

Meteron's face looked like that father's, all his knowledge and sureness seared clean away. It lasted just a moment, but she saw it just the same. He might as well have been naked. Rowena had to look away, though she wasn't sure why.

"I care about the book and Chalmers's work because it matters," he said, handling the words carefully, as if they were old, fragile things, better than half-forgotten. "Because it matters, we have to do everything possible to learn what we can, and keep what shouldn't be learned by others away from them. That means dealing with bad people. And being bad people."

It was all Rowena could do to keep from barking laughter. "*You* really believe there's such a thing as bad people?"

"I had damned well better. I'm one of them."

"But, no. That's . . . that's too simple. You know yourself. *I* know you. You're . . . you're . . ." She stopped there. *Good?* Was that really what she meant to say? Rowena couldn't seem to find the right word, and Leyah had gone conspicuously quiet, as if she, too, would hesitate to use that label for her brother.

But Meteron had the words. "I'm the sort of monster who can admit what he is. I've never kept that from you."

Rowena thought back. The rich meals, the warm bed, the charming words. The elegance of the ball, and the silk of his praise—and his sudden, needling cruelties. He had his fangs and claws, and still grazed her with them, to prove his point. To make sure she wouldn't forget.

"No," she said. "You haven't."

"I came up here because I had too much to think about. How to tell you about all the bad things we might have to do, for one, and all the bad people we might have to do them with."

"I thought we're the ones doing the right thing—protecting important stuff from the bad guys so they can't do worse things with it."

Meteron sighed. "Cricket, the worst kind of bad person is the one who is convinced they are a *good* person. The right person with the wrong convictions is a terrible creature, indeed."

Rowena tried to smile. "So are you a wrong person with the right convictions?"

"Maybe for the first time in my life."

That was when she felt it—the tug in the back of her mind that was Leyah, telling her something too urgent for words.

Rowena looked over her shoulder, toward the tug, and saw the sweeping arm coming down before she understood it was *more* than an arm.

It was a club, and it was attached to one of the lanyani crew.

"Down!" she yelped, snatching Meteron's bracers and hauling him to the deck.

The lanyani's arm crashed through the galleon's rail, showering them in splinters. Meteron and Rowena scrambled apart, him reaching for his trouser leg, her crabbing back until she thumped against something hard that lashed around her, pinning her arms against her body.

Another lanyani. One arm had transformed into something like vines, knotting around Rowena, hauling her close.

Don't fight it, Leyah urged. *Go slack.*

But Rowena's heart pounded in her throat, pushing fear up through her in a high, brittle scream. She could already imagine her bones crunching under the noose as the lanyani drew her ever nearer. Its other arm was a single giant thorn, and hooked, too, and *oh God oh God oh Holy fucking Reason*—

Rowena, go slack, now! Leyah cried.

The vines wound toward her face. Rowena thrashed her head, trying to find Meteron, shouting for him.

She only saw more lanyani snaking down the riggings, tumbling toward the deck.

Now now now!

Rowena's breath was gone, wasted in a scream nobody seemed to have heard. She slouched, sucking air, and felt herself sink lower, slipping a little from the creature's grasp.

And then she understood.

The lanyani had tried to bind Rowena up as she pushed out and thrashed, struggling to encompass the wild, flailing bulk of a human being. But it was made of wood, not rope, its green fibers too dense and stiff to wrap as tightly as a proper length of cord. Rowena played dead and slid to the deck before it could close its grip completely. She staggered away, looking for something she could use to defend herself.

"Cricket!"

She spun toward Meteron's voice. He had some kind of knife up in a guard and was weaving his way between three lanyani swinging at him with limbs turned into thorny bludgeons and whittled blades. But he didn't stab or slash. In a cold wave of horror, Rowena remembered why. Everything the Old Bear said about the lanyani being better suited to the galleons than humans. No blood, no organs, no flesh or bone. Meteron might use the knife to deflect a lanyani limb, but there was no hope of it actually injuring them.

Rowena used to think the aigamuxa were the scariest things she would ever have to fight. But at least their bodies broke the same as those of humans. At least they *made sense.*

"Belaying pin!" Meteron snapped, nearly losing his head to a swipe from a third arm turned into an ugly wooden broadsword.

She dashed to the rail surrounding the base of the main mast and snatched a pin up from its bulwark. Or tried to. It was solid iron, and she had to heave until spots exploded behind her eyes before pulling it free.

"Here!" Rowena shoved it with her bare heel, rolling it down the planks.

It raced toward Meteron, picking up speed, and would have taken him out at the ankles if he hadn't spied it coming and swept a hand down to catch it. With a grunt, he swung it round and the thorny club arcing toward his head exploded into kindling.

Rowena didn't know if lanyani felt pain, but the creature's reaction proved it knew rage. Fury roared like a flame behind the Tree's white eyes. The wounded lanyani staggered back, letting another of its kind step forward, bristling murder.

Rowena had just turned for the companionway stairs when another form cut off her path, lunging up the steps from below decks.

The Old Bear pushed the weaponette into her hands. "It's charged." He pointed toward the lanyani who'd wound her up a minute before. "Take that one. I'll get Ann."

And then he was moving past her, limping fiercely toward the fight with something that looked like a garden stake in his fist.

"What the hell good is this thing now?" Rowena shouted.

The wind took her words. She was lucky it shook a cloud of piney needles off the roper lanyani, too, or she might not have seen it coming up on her flank.

A limb flashed toward Rowena. She swatted it back with the weaponette, still in its short and stubby form, cussing herself blue.

"He's crazy," she panted, ducking, scrambling, dancing back. "You can't *stab a tree* to death!"

Smell the air, Rowena, Leyah's voice coached inside her. *It's some kind of juniper. That's why it bends so well.*

"So what?" Rowena yelped back, not caring if anyone heard her speaking to no one. Somewhere farther off came the sound of a crack like an axe splitting cord wood and a basso roar from an inhuman throat. The Old Bear had joined the fray, at last.

Junipers are conifers. *They're full of resin!*

Rowena grinned at the weaponette's leather-wrapped handle. "Oh, you brilliant Old Bear—how do I work it?"

She winced as a jagged whip-limb lashed her bare arm.

Put your index finger over the crosspiece and pull the trigger there.

The lanyani raised its arm to strike her again. This time, Rowena stepped in closer—inside its guard, just as the Alchemist had shown her in their practice duels—and jabbed the weapon's tip into its craggy chest, as deep as the fissures of its bark allowed.

She pulled the trigger.

The shock-stick hidden inside the blade flared hot in the lanyani's heartwood. Then it sparked. Rowena leaped away from the plume of flame, almost losing her grip of the weapon. She staggered against the galleon rail, but there wasn't enough of it. She'd found the broken section, the one where she'd ducked and narrowly missed being turned to pulp. Her bare foot kicked out for the deck and found nothing there. The sky and ship traded places. Rowena watched her feet flail up before her, saw the hull of the ship from the outside, and the glaring moon—

Everything jerked around, including her head on her shoulders. But the falling had stopped. Slowly, Rowena opened her eyes and saw a length of mooring rope tangled about her ankles, the bulk of the *Lady*

Lucinda swaying back and forth twenty feet above, and Meteron and the Old Bear hauling at the rope's other end.

Somewhere in all of that, she passed out, wondering if she'd ever woken up from her nightmare in the first place.

15.

Deliverance Tegura stepped down from the clockwork carriage, tipped her driver with a slip of paper he frowned at—then goggled at, once he read it—and met Doctor Montgomery, assistant to Doctor Wyndham, on the walk up the pebbled drive of the Mercy Commission Home.

He prattled. Men like Montgomery always prattled. It was such an odd consistency of character, bundled into every gentleman reverend doctor she'd met, as if packets of self-defeating agitation were the seminary's parting gifts after the final examinations. Montgomery was an indifferent, weak-chinned man with a ramrod posture and a concerningly hemispherical belly. Gaseous bloat. A slight yellow tinge to his skin. He was, Deliverance surmised, within four or five months of serious medical collapse owing to a failing liver. He lacked the saggy, muddled look of a man caught between draughts at the bottle. Medicines, then. Creator only knew how many tinctures and cordials he prepared for his lady charges daily—or how often he would tip a portion of them back for his own enjoyment.

When they reached Montgomery's office in the vault-ceilinged study just off the tea room, the doctor's gabbling finally turned in a direction worthy of Deliverance's attention.

"—unconscious for three days, after a screaming fit about killer trees," he said. "When she woke up just yesternight, it was as if she'd missed no time at all. Wondered what became of the luncheon her lady had brought her. Of course, it was days gone, and—"

She raised her hand. Its effect was precisely like muting a trumpet. Montgomery's voice blurped into silence.

"Mrs. Downshire is awake now?"

"Yes. Quite, Mrs.—"

"Doctor," Deliverance corrected coolly. As if her colleagues would have accepted her with any less a pedigree. As if the Bishop would have trusted her, without years of training and careful study informing her every move.

"Doctor Tegura. Yes. She is."

"Then I will see her now."

"I'm afraid I can't actually permit that, Doctor."

She let her arched eyebrow ask the question for her.

"Her guardian hasn't left any instructions indicating you are to be involved in her care or visitation, Doctor," Montgomery explained sheepishly. "Now, perhaps I can offer you a brandy, and then—"

"Her guardian," Deliverance echoed. It was not a question. Her reverend peer shifted uncomfortably under her gaze.

"*Benefactor* might be a better term, actually. There are no instructions leaving her in any specific hands while the benefactor is unavailable."

The Reverend Doctor Deliverance Tegura reached into a small satchel at her hip—tools and notebook and spyglass and reticule all gathered up together—and fetched out a folded letter in an envelope. Doctor Montgomery watched her open its panels, blinking in puzzlement as she pulled out the delicate card of plastine punched with an array of holes down twenty minutely separated rows and forty equally minute columns, each a perfect, tiny oblong, ripe with purpose.

"You have an Engine in this facility, I presume?"

"We have, Madame."

"Read this card in it, then come back and tell me what privileges I do or do not have in regard to Mrs. Downshire."

And with that, Deliverance sat down, hands folded on her lap, back straight as a galleon mast. She waited out Montgomery's absence in precisely that posture. He was back in only ten minutes, all but scrambling in, a tall, dark-haired woman with plaited hair and curious, animal eyes trailing sedately in his wake. Too sedately.

Montgomery had not been gone long enough to make up some fresh tonic for her. *He keeps some on hand*, Deliverance concluded. *For his ladies' visits.* Well. That was one way to ensure the impression of a well-rested, recuperating patient.

"Reverend Doctor Tegura," Doctor Montgomery said, a nervous smile tugging at his lips, "may I present Mrs. Clara Downshire."

Deliverance rose to receive her, and the woman bobbed a curtsy in response. She heard something unfamiliar near the office doorway and looked down. A gray-muzzled hound hop-trotted past Mrs. Downshire's skirts, its collar jingling. It paused a yard short of Deliverance and snuffled the air around her, tail wagging, though from a wary distance.

"*Rab-bit*," Mrs. Downshire chided. She had a musical working-class accent, the sort Deliverance had heard sprinkled liberally among the laborers and the shop-keeps of Oldtemple Down. "Begging your pardon, ma'am. He's a rude imposition on his best days, and this en't been one of them."

Deliverance crouched and put out a hand. The dog called Rabbit snuffled her fingers wetly. It rumbled an assortment of noises—grunts and trills and zuffs—before trotting back to Downshire's side, as if to carry the message that her visitor passed inspection.

Doctor Montgomery cleared his throat altogether too loudly. "So, I'll—ah, I'll leave you ladies to it. Please ring the bell for Miss Merriweather, if you require refreshment. And, erm . . ." He placed the punch card on the edge of his desk, eyeing Deliverance significantly. "I expect you'll want this back, Madame."

"Quite," she answered.

And then the man was gone, as if shot from a gun.

Deliverance turned to offer Mrs. Downshire a seat, but found she was already occupying the settee by the unlit fireplace. The woman sat with her own ramrod straightness. Not, Deliverance noted, the straightness of discipline and study. Mrs. Downshire sat like a woman entirely out of her element—like a small animal in a cage, hoping its utter lack of motion might help it evade a predator.

"So you've come to take me away," Clara Downshire announced.

Deliverance knew herself well enough to bet a hearty sum her surprise hadn't registered on her face. She had known what to expect.

Or, rather, the Bishop had.

"You're not wrong," Deliverance answered. "Can you explain how you knew that, Mrs. Downshire?"

"Some days, I have trouble remembering where I've been and where I've yet to be, but this bit's clear enough. It's Vraska you mean to take me to. Vraska hasn't happened yet. And it's after the Trees on the ship, which is the start of everything else. Since I know you wouldn't come here for just any old reason, it must be Vraska is today. Or near enough."

"You're not at all interested in *why* I've come for you?"

Downshire smiled. The expression cast a pall over her eyes—distant and abstracted. "There's really only two reasons folk have ever taken an interest in me. One, I think, might not be your sort of interest." Deliverance didn't have to think overlong to imagine what Downshire meant. Not after talking to the brute Tucker Pettigrew. She grimaced. The woman continued. "An' the other is the only thing anybody ever seems to want to talk about anymore. I've gotten used to it. At least this trip will give me what I want."

"And what is that?"

Downshire's smile faltered. "They're good men—at least they've tried to be, often as not. But they took my Rowie and she's never coming back. I can't just let that go. But you. You're taking me right to her."

Deliverance reached behind herself, feeling for a chair. The old dog turned three tight circles by Downshire's feet and collapsed upon them. Deliverance's mind ticked through the list of instructions she'd been given, the contingencies she had planned for, or been told to anticipate. Very few avenues of consequence would lead to Mrs. Downshire and her daughter meeting again, if the Bishop's plan unfolded precisely as intended. The pathways were narrow—vanishingly so.

"You're certain of that?" she asked, finding her seat.

"It's a twisting sort of way to reach her, but straighter than any I'd walk on my own."

Deliverance smiled to herself. *What a treasure you've found, Livvy Tegura. Don't let her slip away.*

"It seems I could tell you we must leave on the instant and it wouldn't trouble you."

"I've kept a valise in my chifforobe ever since I settled in months ago. But the dog is new," Downshire added quickly. "He'll need his effects sorted, I expect."

Deliverance blinked. "His—I beg your pardon?"

"He's fourteen years old. He's got plenty of needs. And so he's coming with."

"My travel arrangements included no provisions for an animal."

"Just as well," the woman answered crisply. She rose and patted about herself, as if taking a census of her person and its general order. "He's more people than dog. Who knows how he'd take to a crate in some airship, poor dear. And I promised my Rowie I'd see to all his needs." She smiled wistfully. "She always wanted a puppy, you know. Good of the angel to let her have his."

Deliverance raised an eyebrow. "Angel?"

If Mrs. Downshire heard her or marked the query in her voice, there was no sign. She strode to the sideboard and plucked up the bell, ringing for Merriweather.

Only a few minutes before, the Reverend Doctor Deliverance Tegura had been enjoying Doctor Montgomery's dismay. Now, as she watched Mrs. Downshire rattle off a string of orders as crisp as any housemistress's, she wondered how much she and the Doctor would come to have in common.

She could suffer a bit of confusion, at least in the near term. Soon enough, Bishop Meteron would have a new source of information, and if there was anything she and her mentor did well together, it was impose order on chaos.

16.

Captain Qaar loomed over Anselm Meteron, his knotted face a closed door. The set of the thief's jaw warned Erasmus how close his partner was to kicking that door in.

"I've considered your proposal, Master Meteron," said Qaar.

"And?"

"No."

The Alchemist was half-sure he'd cracked a tooth keeping his own temper down as the Tree captain stonewalled them, but that didn't excuse him from at least attempting to pose as the voice of reason. *Not now or anytime in the last thirty years*, he thought.

"Before anyone says something they are bound to regret," he began, speaking around the stem of his pipe, "we might consider the circumstances that brought us to this moment. Your crew. An ambush."

The Captain's lamp-like eyes trained on Erasmus.

"A certain vigorous application of a spark to one of said crew," he countered. "The scorching of my portside deck and the demolition of its rail." Qaar's voice burned as his crewman had—at least until Erasmus had wrapped his frock coat around his arm to shield it and shoved the flaming creature over the side into the dark waters thousands of feet below.

Anselm raised an accusing finger. The other hand he kept to his side, a little out of view. Qaar was already none too pleased about the stake he held in it and the ampule of picloram installed in its blood-groove.

"And that," Anselm noted, "*might just* have something to do with our being attacked."

"You have no right to keep my crewfolk hostage," Qaar snapped. "Release it."

The Alchemist stood, obliging the Tree captain to edge backward. He put a hand on the table where his field kit lay open, both to keep it from shifting as the ship keeled windward and to keep his own feet steady. The burned lanyani had been Rowena's handiwork, but spilling the creature over the side and hauling Rowena back up using the coiled hemp lines she'd been lucky enough to trip through—that had left him rattled. His temper buzzed like a beehive, all but audible in the closed space of their cabin.

"Your men tried to kill us. I woke with a thorn at my throat in that bed," Erasmus growled, indicating the bunk behind Qaar. "Rowena went over the side. Anselm—"

"I'm fine," he lied.

Usually Erasmus had to touch someone to sense how deep their pain went, but he'd known Anselm too long not to sense the outline of his presence anytime they were in the same room. His side still ached where one of the lanyani's spiked club-limbs had connected. Not hard enough to crack ribs, Erasmus had concluded, but anyone could see his seeping bandage through the linen of his shirt.

"We need an explanation for the attack," Anselm finished, trading overt irritation for icy calm, like a street performer palming a sovereign. "The surviving attacker is the only being likely to have one."

"Unless you're hiding something, Captain?"

Qaar's white stare flicked over to Erasmus, seethingly silent.

"I hired them out of one of the hothouses in Corma," he admitted. "Crystal Hill. My crew from Anchor Pass was deep in wilt and needed time ashore."

"How many of 'em came from Crystal Hill?"

All three turned toward Rowena. The girl had said very little since waking up in the cabin a half-hour before. There'd been more than enough to listen to, certainly. The hiss and rattle of the remaining crew in the gangway outside the cabin. Qaar's efforts to quell them. Erasmus and Anselm's muffled argument, huddled over the field kit, passing glances toward the last of the attacking lanyani: a ponderous piece of lumber with arms like oak trunks, now pinned to the cabin wall by stakes in its shoulders, wrists, ankles, knees—clever contraptions left over from Leyah's machine-working. Each stake had a trigger which opened the tip into a fierce, flat cross of iron, mounting the creature more brutally than a Kneeler crucifixion.

If the theory that the lanyani had no pain receptors was true, it was an excellent work-around. Erasmus had never believed that claim. Pain was an evolutionary benefit—how a being's body signaled distress to itself, discouraging further damage. Still, he preferred the practical limits of force and physics: even if the lanyani captive could endure the pain of tearing itself into kindling to escape, it lacked the leverage to do it. And it was deeply concerned by the poisoned spike Anselm carried.

So was Captain Qaar. Hence the stalemate.

"Five came from the hothouse on the Hill," the captain answered, after a long, uncomfortable hesitation.

Five attackers. One sent to do in Erasmus as he slept—a plan badly fouled when it found him a habitually light sleeper; one set upon Rowena; three gone after Anselm.

"If you took on five and the same five were the ones that jumped us, then your usual crew's probably innocent," Rowena concluded.

"If you mean to keep this news from the Rolands," Anselm said, leaning into the Greatduke's family name with nothing like nonchalance, "you'd better let us have a conversation with the Tree that will clear your good name."

Qaar studied his pinioned cousin, inscrutable and silent. Then he nodded. "Do what you must. When you are done, give it to me. We have ways of disposing of . . . rubbish. And see to it *that*," he nodded toward the poison spike Anselm carried, "does not leave your baggage again before we reach Lemarcke."

Erasmus grimaced. "One day's journey left. Our problems will be much greater than your displeasure if we cannot make it that long without needing it again."

Visibly reluctant, Qaar slipped out of the cabin, letting the door fall shut behind him.

Anselm's eyes flicked over to Rowena, too fast for her to notice as she focused on the tar-paper muzzled lanyani. The Alchemist caught his eye and nodded.

"You should go, girl," he said in his gentlest voice.

From the look she gave in response, he might as well have told her to jump off the stern.

"*No.*"

"There's a chance it could break loose. I won't have you nearly murdered twice in a day."

"But that's just it. They weren't *trying* to murder me. The one I used the sword's shock-end on tried to tie me up. It had that pointy, stabby arm and could've done me in with it any time. But it was binding me, instead. I mean, why bother? I'm smaller'n either of you and I wasn't armed. I'd have been easy to kill, like swatting a fly."

Anselm raised an eyebrow. "Give yourself a little credit, cricket."

"Don't," she snapped. "Don't flatter me just to pretend I'm not on to something. I know I am. After I broke free, it tried to knock me out. I don't think it wanted to kill *me*, but they sure had all their thorns and stickers out for you two."

"Going over the port rail hardly qualifies as not trying to kill you," Erasmus countered.

"I jumped back from the fire and tripped. I'm just lucky I dragged my foot through the ropes doing it."

God save us, she was. The memory of her spilling out into the dark seized Erasmus's heart all over again, closing it in a fist. He had rebuilt his world around her only to see it nearly dashed to pieces by happenstance. The others, he realized, were staring at him. He leaned into the table a little harder than he had a moment before. The ship must have shifted course, the cabin heaving in a way only he had noticed, or—

The fist thrust behind his breastbone bore down again.

He sank down to the bunk and put up a hand to stay Rowena as she swept over to check on him.

"I'm fine," he muttered.

The almost-voice of Anselm's thoughts needled privately. *Your turn to lie, Bear?* Erasmus put his head in his hands, breathing slowly. "I'm *fine*," he repeated. The fist in his chest was hardly a stranger to him. The curare he'd taken to perpetrate their hoax with Regenzi had made sure of that. It had been the *frequency* of its visitation more than its existence he'd hoped to keep from his companions. Rowena had seen him in a spell just once that spring, and her wild, pained look had convinced him to keep his troubles to himself.

"Stay if you must," Erasmus said, fixing Rowena with a hard look. She'd crouched in front of him, eyes wide and searching. He hoped his face looked less drawn than hers. "But if it does anything to threaten you—"

"I'll keep my distance," she vowed.

Erasmus grimaced. *Mind the trigger, Ann*, he thought.

His partner sent a signal back—a wordless pulse of affirmation. Then he drove the stake into the center of the crucified lanyani's chest, precisely where a breastbone would be, if it had one.

The Alchemist had been expecting the blow, but it still rang like a gunshot in the enclosed space, loud enough to make him flinch. Rowena jolted to her feet, staring at the jagged crack where Anselm had smashed the iron wedge through a seam in the lanyani's body. The fissure wept beads of golden sap.

"Thank you," Erasmus murmured. He picked up his pipe, checked its bowl, and struck a lucifer for it.

Rowena scowled. "After that shake-up, I don't think you ought to be doing that."

"I am not," he answered, drawing on the stem twice to encourage the flame. The tobacco plumed dense, gray smoke. He passed the pipe to her. "Set this below its feet, near the wall."

Rowena coughed. "Right. And then I'm to break a porthole or something so the rest of us don't stifle?"

"We need the smoke." The Alchemist levered himself to standing, pausing a moment to assess how much of the sick spin he felt was the ship and how much his unsteady heart. The inventory came back decidedly in arrears. It would have to do.

"Why smoke?"

"They use pollen clouds to communicate with each other from a distance. The particulate matter of the smoke will combine with the pollen, confusing any messages it tries to send through the cracks in the door."

Anselm offered his one-shouldered shrug. "It would be impolite for it to invite anyone else into our private conversation." He donned a pair of leather gauntlets tailored for his missing finger and tore the tar-paper binding from the slash of the lanyani's mouth. With a few, irritable flicks of his hand, he managed to free the paper from the leather, picking at its tarry surface fussily.

"Well, friend," Anselm began. "Seems you've made quite a debacle of this pleasure cruise. Care to explain yourself?"

The lanyani did its best to burn them all under the white heat of its eyes.

The Alchemist examined the contents of his field kit. Having chosen the wrong ampule twice, he sighed and plucked his spectacles from his shirt collar. "Time was," he said, not a little ruefully, "I could conduct a proper interrogation without reading glasses."

"Weakness of the flesh," the creature hissed.

Erasmus saw Rowena shift uncomfortably at the creature's rasping voice.

You wanted this, he thought to her.

I know. I'm fine.

And that makes liars of all of us, he thought, though only to himself. *We might at least have thought of something original.*

"I suppose you're right," Erasmus continued, addressing his captive. "But lanyani fiber isn't entirely impervious, either."

Anselm snapped his fingers, feigning an epiphany. "What's the stuff you've put into this thing, Bear?"

"Picloram."

"*Right*. How does it work again?"

The lanyani's eyes rounded into moons. "You would not."

"Captain Qaar has some misgivings about us using it," Anselm allowed. "And you'd think we'd want to stay on his good side. But honestly, we're two deeply pissed off human savages. Who knows what we're capable of? So in the interests of full disclosure, I will keep this hand here, on this stake and its trigger, and *you* had best keep your mind on the topic at hand."

Erasmus grunted absent affirmation, having found two more phials of picloram. He was glad Anselm had passed his news from Haadi-yaa Gammon along in time for it to influence his packing. He loaded another ampule into a second spike. It wouldn't take more than one dose of the herbicide to kill the lanyani, but two would make it go much, much faster. If the quantity housed in the spike currently seated deep in the Tree's vascular core were released, it would be only moments before the lanyani's hyperactive osmosis passed the toxin along, breaking down its cell membranes, destroying the creature from pith to periderm.

"What do you want to know?" the lanyani asked, its voice piping minor-key from its fissured chest.

The Alchemist could not muster a twin to Anselm's smug smile. He rested against the table instead, turning the spike in his hands. "Why did you try to kill us?"

"You are my people's enemies. You are trying to protect the ones we must undo."

Anselm lifted an eyebrow. "Last I was aware, we had done a magnificent job making enemies of the aigamuxa. I don't recall wronging any lanyani."

"There might be hope for your people, if you showed any sign of understanding what you have done to our world."

Rowena frowned. "Filled it up with cities and railways and factories and such?"

The creature's blank, blocky face tilted. Its eerie voice hummed with pleasure. "It is a shame you are marked, little one. You are not so foolish as your fathers."

The girl opened her mouth to reply. Erasmus rode over the words she had not yet spoken.

"Who sent you?"

The creature's attention snapped his way. "My clan on the Crystal Hill, of course. We learned of your plans to travel from the servers in the Greatduke's house. And we know who you are. *Dor* knew."

"Dor?" Anselm looked to Rowena. "Is that one of the lanyani fences Ivor bought for?"

"No, he worked with Sticks and Sugar Maple and—" She rounded, shaking her head as if to throw off an irrelevancy. "Look, what do you mean I'm *marked?*"

"My people have *allies*," the Tree hissed. "We will find the ones your precious book names, and we will see to it the Experiment ends. We can return the world to what it was, wipe you from its face—"

Ann, Erasmus thought urgently.

Let him go on. We need to know more.

"Why were you trying to capture me?" Rowena demanded.

Ann, please— Erasmus took a step forward, turning his spike into a stabbing grip. If he had to, he could lunge for the Tree and silence it before it spoke the whole truth with Rowena standing right there to hear it. But he could very well move too slowly, and Anselm was already there, his hand on the poisoned spike, holding the lanyani hostage.

"You've gotten in the way," it growled. "You might have been left alone for a time, like all the rest, but you are too deep in the truth and we must make an example of you." The lanyani's craggy face split with a cruel, chipped-bark sneer. "Your fathers were expendable but Dor needed you in Corma to *prove her point.*"

And all at once, the creature seized up, its pinioned body shaking. Long, spidering cracks opened up around the stakes driving it in place, its limbs crumbling into jagged spears.

Watching Anselm's cold, focused face transform into a mask of shock reminded the Alchemist how lucky he was to have a very fine actor for a partner. "Oh, fucksake, Bear, my hand must've slipped—"

Rowena rushed up, heedless of the lanyani's convulsions, and slapped

Anselm's hand away from the poisoned spike. Its thin blood-groove, once capped with black, inky poison, stared back at her, empty.

"You stupid toff! He was about to tell me something!" she cried.

And that's why he had to die. They could have gotten so much more from the Tree, if she hadn't insisted on staying. But some things were worth the world to keep from Rowena Downshire.

The creature was still trying to make some last pronouncement. Half-words juddered forth from the rotting splits in its chest, too close to intelligible to be risked. Too much like agony to be borne.

"Here," Erasmus called, tossing Anselm the second spike. "End it quickly."

He plunged the second stake inches from the first, and a moment after, the room fell silent, apart from the muted crackle of the smoldering pipe.

Rowena stared at the rotten wreck of limbs and fibers hanging from the cabin wall. A piece of the lanyani's ruined head fell away and rolled toward her feet, seesawing in place before settling with the hideous half-moon of an ocular cavity staring up at her. Rowena's eyes flashed with unshed tears, her gaze darting back and forth between Anselm and Erasmus.

"I have to—I—"

Erasmus put out a hand. "Rowena. I did not want you to see—"

"I'm going up for some air," she sobbed, scrubbing at her face as she stormed toward the door. "Stupid smoke is bothering my eyes."

Her shoulder clipped Anselm's as she passed. There had been more than enough room to make it to the gangway without staggering him. But it was the point she had to make.

The cabin door slammed shut. In the darkness beyond, Rowena's bare feet scrambled up the companionway.

"I shouldn't have pushed it that close."

Anselm stood at Erasmus's side. His false shock had fallen away, replaced with something etched between his brows, furrowing the corners of his eyes.

"She shouldn't be alone up there," he added. "And she won't thank me to check on her now."

"I'll go after her," Erasmus murmured. "You did your best. She didn't make it easy."

"When does she ever?" Anselm peeled his gloves off and flung them to the deck, his mouth a hard line. "She's going to figure it out, before long."

"More than likely."

"What then?"

Erasmus closed his eyes. The pain in his chest had subsided, at least for the moment—polite enough to make room for new arrivals, perhaps. He tried to formulate an answer, but it eluded him amid a tumult of variables, too much to weigh and consider at a drop.

For forty years, he had cured, murdered, conspired, freed, tortured, kidnapped, protected, stolen, retrieved, and escaped. He strove to be a good man as often as circumstance allowed, and had been a bad one more than he cared to consider. He had plotted campaigns that were still legends in his field, and achieved a notoriety so great, it had swallowed up his given name and spat him back, stripped of everything but his profession. And yet he had no idea what to do about this single, solitary girl.

No. Not truly solitary. The sixth of nine. A fraction of our future.

"The lanyani was right," he said, at last. "If this Dor has the book, then they'll be able to find Rowena anywhere she goes—track her with a living map. If Gammon is right, too, and the aigamuxa are still in pursuit, it's that much worse. We will keep her from them until we can't anymore, and train her to take care of herself as best we can, in the meantime."

"Not what I meant, Bear."

"I know." The cane in the corner would no longer be ignored. Erasmus limped toward it and hooked it on his arm for the climb up the companionway—to fresh air, and the spreading dawn, and the girl who held a knife turning like a mainspring in his heart. "Let me know when you have a better answer."

17.

Dor felt the prodding of her clansman's consciousness, a woodpecker persistence burrowing like an awl toward heartwood. She unfolded her close-gathered limbs and lifted her head, peering around.

The riot of green and reek of sweet, earthy rot filled the Gathering Grove. Dor was settled past what humans would classify as her waist in the soupy depths of the most recently cured Pit, letting its richness seep in through her ragged roots. As ever, an uncannily precise knowledge of how long she had been sunk in the feeding torpor followed her unfolding. Four days, seven hours. Sunrise hung over the Grove's cut-glass ceiling, raining beams of rusted light.

What do you need, Lir? she asked

Lir stood at the Pit's shore, one limb extended into the mire, his digits twigging outward. *There's something you must see*, he said. The rest of the message came not in words, but in urgent flashes of impulse and hunger.

Uproot me, then.

The twigs that bore Lir's message wove into an arm, encircling her. Dor levered herself free of the mire with a slow, squelching noise, then let Lir drag her up to the surface. She skimmed like a leaf on a pool, and strode to meet him on legs whose outlines blurred with budding and new growth. *The Pits*, she thought, *are finally doing their jobs properly.*

Since her rise to the united clans' command, Dor had made the Pit Masters earn their titles through sacrifice. Each of the Hill's three Pits was now the permanent home to one of the crooked, cantilevered elders who had grown so vast and wild, there was no hope of them passing among Men anymore. Each absorbed the excesses of the Pits, siphoning off moisture, acids, and bases, using their own bodies as sponges to contain the first, imperfect fruits of composting. As the Masters no longer left the Hill or strove to control their bodies' growth, they required far less energy, in a far less refined state, than their smaller, more mobile cousins. In time, a Master would go dormant for lack of perfected nutrients, and when the dormancy turned at last to a true sleep, the Master would themself be broken down to improve the Pits for the good of their clansmen.

Before Dor, the Pit Masters of this sad, coal-choked city had forgotten that power over a Pit made one a living sacrifice, not a petty tyrant. Dor had made sure these ancients *remembered* the cost of their titles.

Each Pit's Master was surrounded by a half-dozen lanyani at any given time, hewing or grinding corpses, adding water, heaving in wood shavings or pine needles or whatever dry matter could make the Pit's balance true. Once, a young treeling had returned from its city prowls with crates of tea, fouled by mice and abandoned beside a neighborhood drop-chute for the moling men who cleared the refuse pits studding the city's underside. The lanyani would take anything for the sake of the Pits, even the pages of a discarded gazette. Tending these oases properly was a nigh-endless task.

Thus, the stillness surrounding the Pit Lir directed Dor toward was very, very strange, indeed.

Look there, Lir urged, gesturing toward one of the blood-slicked boulders where treelings took shifts butchering the bodies they'd claimed.

A lanyani stood beside the stone and, seeing their approach, sidled backward, almost hiding the meat cleaver in its grasp. This clansfolk had not deigned to shape itself to seem male or female, its reedy frame a study in perfectly neutral proportions.

Dor followed its gaze to a butchering stone where a hand, once belonging to a human child, lay quite alone. Out of the corner of her vision, Dor spied a small, dirty body crumpled beside the Pit's edge.

Both hand and body, separate as they were, moved. The hand opened and closed—but not with the spastic movement of death-throes. Dor knew enough of meat-creatures to know whatever powers animated them could linger in the moments after a mortal blow. Mouths opening, hands splaying, eyes blinking. Some birds even careened about after death, running and pecking with headless necks, though she had never seen such an abomination herself.

The hand clenched, the fingers coiling and grasping, riffling the air. The body lurched in place, apparently missing too many pieces already to do more than shift uselessly on the ground made mud by its blood.

Dor tilted her head, curious. *How long has it done this?*

Since last night, the treeling butcher answered.

Dor turned to Lir.

I did not wish to take you from your rest, he explained, his body rustling and thrumming eagerly. *At first, it seemed an ugly mistake of Men's bodies. But then hours passed, then dusk, then dawn, and I knew it must be something worthy of your notice.*

Dor turned a half-circle, looking all around. *Who else has seen such things? Is this the only dead creature that moves?*

No answer. The treelings looked one to another, uncertain, until at last, one stepped forward.

I have seen such things before. Another androgyne, this one broad and many-limbed, like a chokecherry bush. *Indeed, I have made them.*

Lir strode forward, his branches a rattling storm. *Why did you not share this earlier, when we first discovered this?*

This creation was meant for the Leader only to know of.

The ring of lanyani around the Pit's edge burst into a chaos of noise—creaking, snapping, hissing, groaning.

Dor raised a hand, and silence reigned with her.

Explain, she said.

For ten seasons, I have experimented with breeding a fungus that would be useful to us in our conflicts with the Men. There are fungi that make puppets of insects or some that live in plants, but none that could inhabit and command so large and complex a form as Man, until now. One hundred generations of breeding, my Leader. And now, it finally shows signs of working.

Dor's eyes narrowed over the grisly scene.

Inhabit and command, you say.

A variation of cordyceps, the kinfolk answered. *More sophisticated and specialized than others of its kind. Harmless to plants or lanyani flesh, but a bane to the nervous systems of complex mammals. It burrows, influences, shapes. It may even be able to direct the body to complete a simple command.*

Dor laughed—a real sound, like a phrase of music from a cello. *Friend, have you made me something that will turn humans into our minions?*

It could, my Leader. It might.

It will. Her smile was as crooked as a Pit Master's back. *Lir, tell me what has transpired in the book since I took my rest,* Dor demanded, turning toward her lieutenant.

His face seemed to wilt. *You will not be pleased.*

Perhaps not. But I sent five of our kin out on that airship. I must know what became of their mission.

Lir gestured toward the Pit Master nearest to hand. With an agonizing slowness, it reached into its crags and withdrew the book. The tome spiraled toward Dor's outstretched hands, dangling in the Master's vines.

Dor had become so adept at navigating the text, she could turn to the desired place without reading carefully. The book fell open to its latter third, where the cataloging of Subject Six's life took place. Dor had learned Six's human name only after the text's other information— maps of the city, addresses of her lodgings, notations of her activities— made clear her true identity. *Rowena Downshire.* The luxury of lungs and breath gave Men such complicated, musical names. The lanyani could not be bothered to call themselves anything more complicated than a groaning tree branch or whistling breeze could convey. *Rowena Downshire.* So much wind and waste. A profligate's name.

She found the newest entries in Subject Six's section and stared at them in dismay.

All our agents, dead?

Lir bowed his head. *All, and the last most treacherously.*

The book was a thing without bias, without tone. Dor knew little of the practices Men called science and even less of their theology, but she knew they were systems merged into a dispassionate whole, intended to interpret the nature of God through the study of His world. It was a foolish leap, to the lanyani way of thinking. Why study the world and claim it taught you about anything other than the world itself? Was the earth beneath you not enough? Was the sky above not vast enough to contain every meaning, revealed in good time?

But then the book fell into Dor's hands, and she could no longer deny that something more than the earth itself spoke from its bindings. These new pages told her of the journey her five agents had taken aboard the *Lady Lucinda,* of their attempt to complete her orders—*kill the men, take the girl*—and their promise to convert the captain to their way of thinking, once the deed was done.

She was to have been the first offering, Dor hissed, the sound an explosion of leaves in a gale. *Returned to us in triumph. The first we would give to the Pits. How did this happen?*

The story is all there, my leader.

She read, turning the pages, jumping between passages with an ever-deepening scowl. *These men. They have been in the book before, captured sidelong. Little glances of data. They are dangerous. Too dangerous.*

So is the girl.

But the girl we needed to keep. *These others are impediments. And we have no means to call on our brethren abroad to continue the search.*

Lir had been hunched over the book, peering with Dor. Slowly, he straightened.

Perhaps we do, after all, my leader.

Dor was ready to rebuff him, but then she saw the peeling, birch-barked hand he gestured back toward the androgyne lanyani, still presiding over the twitching corpses.

And at last, Dor nodded. *Send a messenger for Rahielma,* she told Lir. *We will need her help in this, and—* she chuckled, the words thrumming in her like a bass string plucked and resonating. *And in another thing, as well.*

Lir's face rippled with uncertainty. *What thing?*

We will need a messenger to go across the waters, and a hunting party to travel our lands here in Amidon. Rowena Downshire is not the only Vautnek we might bring to the Pits. We've waited long enough.

Lir nodded and went to speak to the fungus breeder.

Dor looked back to the Pit Master who had held the book so long. She marked the first signs of wilt in its outmost flourishes. She stepped onto the surface of the Pit, extending her lower limbs into long, spidery stilts, a dozenfold and slender, striding toward the ancient lanyani.

She paused before it. A gash in its bark, very like an eye, shifted a little, the wood crackling and shedding at even that tiny motion.

Dying already, she observed.

Its silence, she knew, was not a sullen thing. It was a sign of its growing weakness. Dor placed a hand against its bark and eased herself into its crevices, watching her hand disappear and waiting for the connection that would let them speak, one to one.

You are a hard mistress, the Pit Master observed.

I should hope you would have no regrets. It is past time you did more to serve your people. Look upon their strength now. Their resolve. We are more now than we have been.

Dor felt the shift within the vast, craggy kinfolk more than saw it. The equivalent of a skeptical snort.

You haven't told them the truth about your book, it said.

Dor smiled. The expression was a lightning scar in her almost-human face. *Couldn't help browsing while you held it, could you?*

I lived before the Men came to this shore and made their city. When I was young and small, as you are now, I lived with the rain pouring down on my head. There are Trees like your Lir who have lived despite being foolish. I have never had that luxury.

Well. You can understand, perhaps, why I would not let him hold the book as I slept, said Dor. *He might . . . think differently of my plans, if he knew not all the Vautneks are the humans we despise. I could not trust his incuriosity to keep my plan safe.*

The ancient one sent her a pulse of assent—grudging, at best. *But they will discover it, eventually.*

Eventually, Dor agreed, caressing the Pit Master's bark with the hand not sunk toward its bole. *And by then, perhaps they will understand that I do not care. Each of the Nine must be cut down—ape and Man and Tree alike.*

If your goal is to prove to the Creator that we are worthy of this world, destroying the ones who represent us makes no sense.

Dor tilted her head. *It does, if we wish to say we do not consent to being judged. That we know ourselves to have been the first of all living things, and that we reject this foolish experiment. These petty observations. These games. We have been given the information, in our own tongue, to make a final choice.*

And that choice is yours to make alone? the Pit Master challenged.

Well . . . see for yourself, Dor murmured aloud.

Understanding dawned on the Pit Master just fast enough for Dor to feel the whip crack of shock moving through its usually staid branches. Her hand, growing hard and intrusive under the Master's many layers, closed around its pith, crushing with all the strength she had saved up in her days rooted in the Pits. Then it exploded outward, shattering the Master's trunk from within.

It was the nearest thing to a broken spine a lanyani could suffer.

All the treelings in the Grove turned at the thunderous crack, watching their leader stride away from the Pit Master who had gone suddenly, alarmingly still. A raw wound gaped at its side. They watched, waiting for the Master's powers to close the injury.

Nothing happened.

Dor reached the Pit's shore, yards of mossy, budding legs winding back up behind her, like a bridal train gathered against her body. She regarded Lir, whose conversation with the cordyceps breeder had died on the vine, and spread her hands.

One of our Masters has fallen, Dor declared in a shimmer of leaves. *May its body bless the ground it made for all of us.*

Lir stared at her, then nodded.

A dozen lanyani emerged from the copses surrounding the Pit, bearing axes and spades, moving with slow, certain reverence. It was not the first time they had prepared one of their own to give back to the ground.

A Master's body presented a challenge all its own.

Dor surveyed her people and wondered who might rise up to replace the Master who knew too much. She watched Lir move among them, gesturing and commanding. He had never been clever, or even very brave, but he was strong. Loyal. Commandable. And a Pit Master, under her rule, was meant to plant its roots forever—bound to her will, and her silence.

It was possible. It could even be a solution.

18.

The final day of Rowena's journey passed peaceably. Clear skies. Good air current. No strange attacks from the remaining crew. No forbiddances or cautions from Master Meteron or the Old Bear beyond what she had grown accustomed to—minding the rails or keeping to center ship when the winds plowed high, the cautions all shared in sidelong comments, awkward and muted.

It was utterly unbearable.

Rowena had done all she could to keep from talking to either of her companions after the lanyani's horrible death. The timing of it had been too precise, too clearly tied to what it had been about to say. It galled her to wonder what that meant—what they were trying so hard to keep from her.

How would I prove Dor's point? It was exactly the kind of question she'd like to have sorted out in company, running her guesses and fears over the sanding stone of someone else's wits. The Old Bear was good for that, more a listener than a talker. And Master Meteron loved torturing truth from speculation, like a cat making a toy of its mice. But Rowena had sworn *not* to make them her confidantes, partly out of petulance, but also practicality. They were clearly keeping things from her. She stood to gain a good deal more playing the game back at them. At least, that's what she told herself, when passing them by with her chin raised and eyes averted changed from feeling righteous to being lonely. How could she be just yards from them and miss them so terribly?

Stupid eejit. You got yourself tamed.

Rowena couldn't reconcile her anger and suspicion with the ache that passed through her when she saw the Old Bear and Meteron nearby and tried to spurn them, just to teach them a lesson. It was teaching someone something, all right. It just wasn't them.

When Lemarcke's anchor yards appeared under the *Lady Lucinda*'s shadow, Rowena's resolve to punish her companions broke like so much driftwood.

"What . . . what *are* they?" Rowena gasped, staring over the starboard rail at the creatures massing around the anchor pad.

Anselm glanced up from rolling a cigarette. He'd parked himself at the rail an hour before, just beyond her arm's reach, wordlessly smoking and squinting at the horizon as the port drew ever nearer.

He sniffed, acting as if there was nothing remarkable in her breaking a full day's stubborn silence. "They call them the Fabricated."

It was an apt name. The mooring area surrounding the *Lady Lucinda* swarmed with stevedores and longshoremen hefting cargo from the ship's unloading chute. Rowena had seen such activity before around Corma's Rotten Row, the work mainly done by groups of aigamuxa and the occassional human overseer or clerk.

These laborers were clockworks. Animals. A veritable zoo of high-gloss brass and ticking flywheels. Gorillas, oxen, dray horses, and bears with human-seeming hands hefted and hauled, without a foreman or gang boss in sight. A few slender young women, all wrapped in what looked to Rowena like dressing gowns bound with sashes stood by, tapping notes into keyed machines slung from harnesses about their necks. Secretaries of some kind? Engineers? Once, a smallish clock-work creature fell still in the midst of scaling a stack of crates the gorillas had made. One of the women plucked the creature up, crack-ing open a panel under its belly. A few adjustments, and the creature— some kind of tamarin, Rowena thought—was back on the tower of crates, marking them with a grease pencil in clear, tidy print. A rope ladder tumbled from the *Lady Lucinda* into the midst of the Fabricated crews, and one of the women mounted it, heading up to meet with Captain Qaar.

"The Fabricated," Rowena repeated. "Holy handcarts, why go to the trouble? I mean, there's enough aiga to man every port in every city and then some. They work cheap enough."

Sometime in the midst of her staring, the Old Bear had arrived at the rail. She smelled the sweet marjoram and fennel of his pipe before she heard him. She tried to keep her back turned, but it was too hard. She missed looking into his eyes.

Stupid girl. Rowena looked his way, silently swearing that she would, at minimum, *not* smile.

"It's more complicated than supply and demand," he said.

"It's more a matter of—" Meteron began.

"Exercising the blessings of Reason to secure ourselves against the threat imposed by lesser species," cut in a new voice.

It was one of the women from the anchor yard, the one climbing the ladder a moment before. She adjusted her odd mechanical device—a box of keys with letters and symbols, all of them unrecognizable—on her hip. Rowena had thought her bright red sash covered in embroidery and floral designs. Seen up close, she saw it was laced with small, gold-threaded pockets and slits through which the glittering heads of tiny watchmaker's tools peeked. She bowed, full from the waist.

"Exercising what?" Rowena blurted.

"You're our employer's representative?" the Old Bear said, smothering Rowena's outburst. She scowled at him, not liking how easily he took to riding over her.

"I am Miyako Kurowa, and I have the honor to be the Logician First Rank assigned to your needs while you make your rendezvous with Reverend Doctor Chalmers. I am also scheduled to accompany you on your journey to Nippon."

Nippon. Rowena studied the woman's face. Her features reminded her of Lady Simone Roland, though this woman's face was carved and angular where the Greatduchess's had been broad and welcoming.

"We are honored by your assistance, Madame," the Old Bear said.

Madame Kurowa bowed again, this time more curtly.

The Alchemist made introductions. Rowena suppressed the urge to put out her hand for a shake or bob a curtsy when she saw how Master

Meteron and the Old Bear returned the Logician's bow, albeit less deeply. Madame Kurowa's eyes burrowed into Rowena, studying her awkward, stiff-backed imitation of their courtesy.

"Rowena Downshire," Kurowa repeated, upon learning her name.

Rowena straightened and tried to muster up something approximating adult dignity. It lasted until a sudden gust threatened to toss her petticoats into view. She bent to stuff her skirts back down, feeling her already-forced smile turn into a grimace.

"Um, h'lo."

"You have arrived forty-nine minutes ahead of schedule, and thus only a portion of the Fabricated we assigned to your debarkation are available. Nevertheless, we should be able to maintain your itinerary."

"Thank you, Madame," the Old Bear said.

Rowena only realized she was gaping when she felt Meteron's elbow jog her arm. Her mouth closed with an audible snap. Madame raised her sculpted brows a perfect millimeter in something that, on a face less rigid, would have scarcely suggested an expression at all. On hers, the look was practically a monologue.

"You seem puzzled, Miss Downshire. It is sacred to my duties as an Emissary of the Logical Righteous to bring an end to the pain of confusion and ignorance. I am ready for your query."

"It's just, you—" Rowena fumbled. "People say things run like clockwork in Lemarcke. I hadn't realized they meant literally."

Madame Kurowa's face yielded to an indulgent smile. Something about it made Rowena wish she'd go back to looking like a shopfront automaton.

"You have heard the metaphor of God being a clockmaker?"

"And a researcher and an engineer and a scholar and a half a hundred things, sure."

"If the lord over all Creation and its Grand Experiment is a clockmaker, we owe it to Him as worthy creations to work with clear intent. We are the beings of greatest knowledge and aptitude ever set upon the earth. We show our gratitude for these gifts by using the tool of the mind to shape as He does." And with this, she gestured toward the anchor yard. The movement took in the dozens of Fabricated lurching and climbing and carrying, ticking like a whole music shop of metronomes clicking in round.

With that, Madame Kurowa bowed to them, left a card with the address of the rooming house awaiting them once the ship was unloaded, and excused herself to her duties.

The Old Bear grunted and leaned against the starboard rail. Rowena wedged herself between him and Master Meteron, watching them roll and stuff their respective vices. A flash of orange fire from the tip of a lucifer, and the air swelled with the smell of the Alchemist's pipe.

"What she doesn't mention," the old man murmured, sidelong, "is the Logicians would rather make their laborers than hire them, because they despise the working man nearly as much as they despise the aigamuxa."

"I was wondering if it was something like that," Rowena admitted. "I en't ever seen a place with so much to haul and hang and no aiga to do a lick of it."

"Inferior species," Meteron noted.

Rowena looked at him.

"According to Logician doctrine," he clarified.

Rowena doubted Meteron had much of an opinion about common workers, but she was quite sure of what he thought of the aigamuxa. Most humans found the eye-heeled ogres unsettling at best. Meteron— and the Old Bear, for that matter—had reason to hate them outright.

Rare. Rowena hadn't gotten a clear look at her battered body down in the Constabulary's basement morgue. Truthfully, she hadn't tried. She'd seen more than enough of it in the collapsing corridors of the Old Bear's mind, not long after.

"Is it," Rowena began. "Um. Is it usual for your employer to have a representative waiting for you, wherever you're bound?"

"In some cases," the Old Bear answered around his pipe stem. "Typically, they're named in the contract."

Rowena frowned. "Bear, I don't read as well as I'd like, but I don't remember seeing her name anywhere in the papers."

"Because you didn't," Meteron agreed.

She straightened in her slouch and peered down into the yard. Madame Kurowa had returned to the Fabricated, using the typing box slung against her hip, one hand flying across its keys as she watched a bear-creature wander past, a crate balanced on its back. Rowena's frown deepened.

"That's why you said 'our employer's representative' instead of naming the Rolands."

The Old Bear grunted affirmation. "I suspect she knows Doctor Chalmers, or knows of him enough that her appearance wouldn't alarm him. But she's still come from another group and for her own purposes."

"The Grand Library, or I'll eat my purse," Meteron said.

"So we don't trust her."

"As a rule, cricket, we don't trust anyone but each other."

Easier said than done, apparently. "So what happens now we're here?"

"Now," the Old Bear answered, teeth clenching the stem of his pipe, "we keep our suspicions quiet. We settle ourselves in our lodgings and go to the Maiden's Honor to rendezvous with the Doctor. After that, we get registered."

"What're we registering for?"

"Campaigning permits and our charter," Meteron said.

Rowena pulled a face. "I thought the whole idea of the work you folk do, these contracts, is that it's *not* permitted?"

"Yes and no," he answered. "A contract binds us to the Rolands' mission. A professional charter and permit make us, in a broad sense, legal. If you have all three, you have the closest thing to a legitimate business operation any campaigner's likely to achieve."

Rowena considered this. "So the charter states who's in the group, stuff like that?"

"Mostly. We have one on record from the old days, but it requires a little—" Meteron shrugged. "Updating."

"It is safer to have you on the charter than off it," the Old Bear said. "It protects you from the worst legal entanglements we might face." He tapped the contents of his pipe over the side. A wind caught the smolder and whisked it away in a cloud of gray flakes. "We'll put Chalmers on, too."

"*Chalmers?*" The thought of the feckless Reverend Doctor winning a place on the same campaign company roster as Rowena squashed flat her sense of accomplishment. "He's no bleeding campaigner!"

Meteron snorted. "You aren't, either."

"But I've learned so much! You've taught me to handle a blade and climb without a kit and load a gun and . . . and even *read*. What's he done? He got kidnapped, gibbered like a spooked monkey-rat, put you both back together with strapping tape and best wishes, and then disappeared to teach weights and measures at some finishing school for dim-witted barristers' daughters!"

"He understands more about this book and where it came from than we do," the Old Bear answered. "And he's demanded this contract between the Rolands and ourselves, which means he feels he's onto something worth being frightened about."

"Like a nit in his knickers?"

Master Meteron smirked. The Alchemist did not.

"Regenzi knew a lot about the book, too," Rowena muttered. "Don't see you offering him a berth."

"Because he's a pile of rotting meat now, and even when he wasn't, he was a puppet," Meteron answered, all the humor draining from him. "Look, cricket. Chalmers is a pint short of passable on his best day, but he's an asset we need to protect. So he gets a promotion, same as you."

For a fleeting moment, Rowena could swear she saw a glance, brief and cutting, pass from the Alchemist to his old partner. She studied them sullenly. They'd known each other longer than she'd been alive. Half the things they said to each other were said without words—and the other half, said without even expressions or gestures. Something like that explained what had happened with the lanyani. Rowena wondered—

She reached out, past the frame of her own mind, feeling for the edges of Meteron's, hoping he was just distracted enough by Captain Qaar coming by to ask about unloading the baggage that maybe, possibly—

Don't, Leyah cautioned.

Not you, too.

He's felt that kind of contact before. You're not going to take him by surprise.

Oh, I'll bet he'd be surprised.

Rowena. Leyah drew out the final syllable of her name, wagging it like a verbal finger. Pouting, Rowena relented. But she did decide to keep an eye out for Master Meteron using his ether. That might just lower his guard enough for her to slip by.

Don't try those tricks here, Leyah begged her. *Not in Lemarcke. They have ways of finding answers for things that don't bend to Reason.*

Reluctantly, Rowena put her plot away.

Slowly, the ship vented its gas. The Fabricated manning the mooring cranks below wound the *Lady Lucinda* ever closer to its docking cradle. Once it had settled, they pushed a rolling staircase up to its gangplank. Beyond the anchor yard's fences, Rowena spied a clockwork carriage.

"That's for us," Meteron announced. He gave the Alchemist a genial swat on the shoulder and strode toward the gangplank. "Mind your leg on the way down, Bear."

19.

Dusk came late that summer evening, bringing with it a cool, seaward breeze. That, at least, gave the Reverend Doctor Phillip Chalmers a little comfort. He felt very much entitled to it, especially as he stood before the sign of the Maiden's Honor, trying to determine through an indignant fog if he was the victim of some tasteless prank.

The longer he considered the evidence at hand, the more certain he became of that assessment.

First there was the seedy establishment itself, and the winking directions the rat-faced woman at the lightning rail station's payment stile had given. "The Maiden's Honor is on Quick Street. You'll have to look *down* to find it, if you know what I mean, sir."

And, sure enough, there was a crooked set of iron steps leading down into a grotto and a rusty sign waving from its arch fashioned like a buckle on an unfastened belt. Add to this the steady stream of clientele passing up and down those stairs to disappear through the tavern's entrance, which was only a tattered curtain frisking in a doorframe, and there could hardly have been a doubt.

The Rolands *must* have been mistaken to send him here. Surely. Of all the places he should be expected to conduct business!

Phillip Chalmers sighed at his chronometer. Quarter past nine already. He would be late to this meeting, whether he was at the right establishment or not.

The grotto was a clot of comings and goings. Chalmers counted passing heads, sizing up the proper opening, and then surged forward, stumbling after a trio of opal-eyed lanyani, their sexless bodies budding with green shoots and leaves. He bumped against one of them and earned a steady, expressionless glare for his sins.

"Sorry! Terribly sorry . . . excuse me!"

He staggered down the little staircase and ducked through the drapery door into the hot, humming space beyond.

Pubs were hardly unknown to Phillip Chalmers. Indeed, there were a few he had frequented in his seminary years. One was called "The Library" by its bookish patrons, a name given so long before, no one remembered its proper name. The Library was as full of its particular patrons as the actual bibliotheques themselves, though (naturally) far less staid and silent. It was the thriving heart of Rimmerston's scholarly youth, and like all places that had captured a particular sort of people, it had *become* like its people.

The Maiden's Honor was that sort of a place, too, though for a very different class of patron.

Campaigners, Chalmers thought, looking around. *All of them.*

The pub was a great ellipse of activity, with a curved bar hugging its back wall, the space behind it barely broad enough for a pot-bellied, gray-faced keep to prowl up and down on bandy legs. The space this design saved did not go toward more seating for the patrons, whose tall, teetering tables with backless stools speckled the room like the edges of a scab lifting from a wound. It was given over to a pit, instead: thirty feet by fifteen, curved like the room itself, and burrowed ten feet into the floor. The pit was floored with sawdust, the better to soak up sweat and blood—and possibly worse. Presently, two men dragged a third from it. They'd hooked the battered man's heels under their arms and hauled him toward the ladder. Given how the man's head bumped along, Chalmers judged he was in no position to protest his treatment. The ruin of his face suggested he wouldn't be protesting much of anything for a long time.

The crowd looming over the pit, dicing at tables or trading murmurs over pints, was as clearly composed of campaigners as Chalmers's pub had been filled with students. He passed men whose coats lay across nearby chairs, showing off the pistols strapped to their thighs. Eyes followed him, and conversations stalled for a syllable or two. His palms had gone sweaty.

The air teemed with tobacco and stale drink, a sweltering heat rising up from the fighting pit, where a new pair—two women armed with glares that tokened some ancient quarrel—dropped from the ladders and dusted their hands, watching one another. Those who gathered around the pit called to have their markers placed on a peg board carried on the hip of a slender, smiling hostess. She gestured to a man on the other side of the crowd, who nodded at her signal and climbed up on the bar to make some obscure notation in chalk on a leaderboard.

Eyes ahead, Chalmers told himself. *Just make for the bar.*

Phillip Chalmers had survived the general rigors of his studies and the more recent trials of his life through main force of concentration. He was capable of focusing on a task so entirely, he could miss the moment of having completed it.

And so, glancing at the man updating the board, thinking of reaching the bar, watching the mill of the crowd so as to avoid stepping on feet or, worse, *being* stepped upon, he achieved his objective three strides earlier than anticipated, and applied his midsection with some force to the bar's brass-railed edge.

"*Ooof.*" Chalmers doubled over, righting himself so hastily, he nearly tipped over a burly Trimeeni's rum.

Both Trimeeni and barman eyed him with cool contempt. Chalmers took some consolation at that. Their scorn suggested he ranked somewhat beneath the effort required for a solid drubbing.

Chalmers waved apologetically to the barkeep. "Sorry . . . Um, sir, I was wondering if you could direct me, to, um . . ." He glanced about conspiratorially, then hooked a finger, beckoning the man closer.

Frowning, the barkeep limped nearer. His single bushy eyebrow climbed toward his hairline.

"I was wondering," Chalmers continued, "if you could direct me to *table forty-nine.*"

He spoke the last words through gritted teeth, eyes wide and nodding significantly.

The barkeep stared at him.

"*Table . . . forty . . . nine,*" Chalmers repeated urgently.

"What, the Corma Company's table?" The barkeep snorted, his voice anything but discreet. He jerked his stubbled chin to Chalmers' left. "S'over there, where it's always been. Tell your friends to see me before they cast off, eh? I've got a tab older than that girl with 'em that needs settling. I could stock the top shelf for a year off the interest alone."

Chalmers blinked. "The—the girl with 'em? Er, them?"

The barkeep shrugged. "Look, mate, I don't have time to gad about much running this place, but I know a girl when I see one. Here." He reached into the pocket of his apron and retrieved an onionskin sheet, torn roughly from a ledger's page. He shoved the paper into Chalmers's hand before turning him toward the table in question and the trio awaiting him. "Tell 'em it's only water from the well until I see the rest of this iron go from their pockets into mine."

Chalmers might have stared at the bill—the figure was markedly higher than the costs for his final year at seminary, including room, board, and examination fees. But given his shock at seeing Rowena Downshire waving cheerily between the Alchemist and Anselm Meteron, it scarcely fazed him.

Sakhida Island might have been the capital of the Logicians' much-vaunted Protectorate, but places like the Maiden's Honor better resembled Corma than the rest of Lemarcke. It was a cancerous place of a sort Chalmers had long avoided. But it was, he supposed, Meteron and the Alchemist's sort of place. When the Rolands relayed this as their rendezvous point, Chalmers had thought the old rogues had lost their wits. Seeing the most singularly precious and dangerous person he'd ever met along for the meeting confirmed that suspicion.

He reached the table and offered one hand in greeting, the other in apology, holding the bill.

"Ivor's doing, most like," the Alchemist concluded after examining the barkeep's scrawl. "All wodke and cigarillos."

Meteron chuckled into his pint. "Well. Seems the old sot got us in the end, after all. How much?"

The Alchemist pushed the page across the table and folded his spectacles, hanging them from his shirt's uppermost button hole.

Meteron whistled at the figure admiringly. He pulled out a cartridge pen and jotted a string of numbers below the total—an exchequer's routing code. His cramped, curving grip left behind a long mark Chalmers would have called "chicken scratch," had that not been a cruel insult to avian literacy. Meteron finished with a flourish that began with an A and terminated in series of waves and curls roughly approximating the syllables of his given name.

Chalmers hugged his satchel, easing onto a stool as if it might at any moment buck him off. It wobbled just enough to make the concern seem reasonable. "When the Rolands told me in their spark that you knew *just the place to meet* here on the island, I had, um . . . rather a different mental image prepared."

Chalmers looked around warily and leaned close. Rowena had slipped away to stand tip-toe at the fighting pit's edge, peering between shoulders and under elbows at the women squaring off below. Chalmers turned a chiding finger on his companions.

"Are you out of your minds bringing her here? Reason's Rood, she's only one of *the most important people alive*, and this is the . . . the . . . *education* you've offered her?"

Meteron smiled wickedly. "She seems to like the place. Said it had . . . what was it, Bear?"

"Atmosphere," the old man answered from behind a fist. His dark gaze trained on the girl with such intensity, Chalmers imagined him counting her breaths. "She's safe here, Doctor. We know how this place works."

"And you assume nothing has changed in a generation?" Again, Chalmers scanned the room. The Alchemist was twice the age of his nearest equivalent among the patronage. There wasn't another gray hair to be seen, apart from those on the barkeep's bristling face.

Meteron shrugged. "They've kept our table, and our tab. God's balls, Doctor. Settling the bill alone will ensure our professional notoriety another ten years, or I'm a Tobagan monkey-rat. Now, tell me something worth opening a new tab. How did you land Greatduke Jonathan Roland as your patron?"

Chalmers smiled nervously. "It was quite the easiest time courting a sponsor I've had. You might say I was all but thrown at them."

Meteron arched an eyebrow. The Alchemist's face gathered a new collection of shadows.

"You don't mean to say that they *kidnapped* you, Doctor," the old man murmured.

"Having had a little experience with a proper kidnapping," Chalmers answered, "no. But there was an unexpected dinner invitation delivered by a very large man and two lanyani valets for which I was asked to drop everything. I was just concluding a lecture at the finishing school where I'd been tutoring, you see, and—"

"Wait." Meteron lifted a four-and-a-half-fingered hand, barring further speech. "Two lanyani. They were from the Roland household as well?"

Chalmers blinked. "Well, yes. Serving staff. They drove the clock carriage back to the Rolands' manor, and there it was—a great feast and Lady Roland quite familiar with my body of research, before and after the Decadal Conference. Their solicitude was something of a relief, given how my services had been secured before."

"Your services."

The Alchemist's bone-dry growl made Chalmers shiver. "Um, yes. The Rolands asked if there were any next steps I might take to continue my research into the Vautneks. They offered to fund the work, provided I gave Lady Roland an author credit on the final papers."

Meteron snorted. "That's one way to make a grand re-entry into the world of theosophical scholarship. I don't suppose you've noticed your tail?"

Chalmers felt suddenly overconscious of how long it was taking him to process the question. He measured it with his finest mental calipers, still uncertain of its dimensions. "My . . . tail? I'm being followed? By whom?"

In his own opinion, Chalmers was now quite a seasoned survivor of intrigues and malefactions. He would have anticipated any number of canny, judgmental looks from Anselm Meteron; a look that bordered on open pity proved far more disconcerting.

"By the Rolands' people, you spectacular toff. If they expect you to achieve something that will springboard Lady Roland back to theosophical prominence, they won't give you a very long lead. And there's this Madame Kurowa, as well. What do you know of her?"

Chalmers's eyes darted back and forth between his interlocutors. "I don't . . . Kurowa? She's from Nippon, I suppose?"

"She claimed to have been sent by our employers to see to our arrangements in Lemarcke," the Alchemist answered.

"Perhaps she's from the Grand Library. I contacted them, but I didn't think . . . Well. As to the Rolands, surely they're trustworthy? They sent you, just as I requested, after I investigated Nora's deposit box. I knew when I saw what was in it that I'd need your help."

"The Rolands have reason to be less than pleased at your choice of assistants," said the Alchemist.

Meteron sighed. "We'll keep our eyes open. There's a limit on what we want filtering back to our benefactors, and when. Now, about that deposit box?"

"Here." Chalmers wrestled with his satchel, fussing with its buckles until he unearthed the thick, red, cloth-bound volume secreted within. He laid it on the table with a proprietary air. "This is it. The start of it all."

The Alchemist leaned forward. Chalmers spun the book round and nudged it toward him. Again, the old man unfolded his spectacles and, donning them, lifted the book's silk-wrapped cover.

The seal of the Grand Library Special Collection stared up from the frontispiece.

Meteron raised an eyebrow. "Some *other* book, then?"

The Alchemist turned the pages slowly. Chalmers watched him handle them with the care of an archivist. Pages crowded with precise, geometric print filed past, studded here and there by graphs and tables, sketches like street maps or land elevations. The deeper into the book the Alchemist turned, the darker both men's faces grew.

"Not some *other* book," corrected Chalmers. "*Another* book. There are dates. Those are the only things uncoded. The latest of them leaves off—"

"Five years ago," the Alchemist murmured. "When did you start working with Doctor Pierce?"

"Around then, more or less."

"You've never seen this book before?"

"No. But I've seen one like it. One I knew very well."

Meteron shook his head. "But this isn't the same thing. We haven't seen the script moving."

"You won't, either. It's done. Used up."

The Alchemist peered at Chalmers over his spectacles. "Used up?"

"Every last page," Chalmers thumbed the pages, snapping through them like a deck of cards. "There's no room anywhere. All the spaces for the entries. Every bit of the margins. All of it, taken up. But the language is the same, and nearly all of the subjects, too, as near as I can tell. Don't you see?" He looked back and forth between his interlocutors, smiling so hard his cheeks ached. "They're only books, after all. They *must* run out of pages someday. I used to wonder with Nora, some nights—after long hours at the ciphers, trying to break the language and translate the datum . . . Well, we'd have a drink and fall to talking, and I'd wonder aloud what would happen to the subjects when the book finally ran out of *pages*. I'd had a rather morbid theory that they'd simply, well, you know." Chalmers made a slitting motion across his throat, accenting it with a protruding tongue, in case his meaning was at all ambiguous. Then he tracked the Alchemist's gaze back toward Rowena.

"Sorry . . . I wasn't thinking about—"

"Carry on," Meteron said.

"It was a silly notion, anyway. I'd muse all sorts of things—that perhaps the book would just wipe itself out and start over again from *tabula rasa*, and all that the time, Nora kept mum. I always thought it was because she was such a humorless drunk. It might still have been that, I suppose, but she also *knew* the answer."

"Lovely," Meteron drawled. "Now tell *us*."

"Do you remember the old book—the book in Corma? It was nothing, an ugly thing. A common laboratory notebook. Nora must have owned half a hundred of them and kept a few blanks for her next project when she traveled. She liked to be prepared. If you look at the dates in *this* book, you'll see it lines up. This was the book she found first; she must have had it on her person, and then, when the pages filled, the particles—" Chalmers laughed, spreading his hands wide and nearly knocking a passing waitress's tray of drinks clean out of her grasp. "Well, that's just it. The particles aren't just *attracted* to the book. They author it, somehow. They're like . . . emissaries of His consciousness. Little observers, ambient scribes. It's brilliant, don't you see? When the book at hand has no room for more material evidence, the particles search for the nearest similar receptacle, and they take it over."

"You mean the book back in Corma wasn't stolen property after all," the Alchemist concluded.

"Ah, but it *was!*" Chalmers crowed. "Nora took this book from the Grand Library, just as her undelivered letters suggested, at the Bishop's urging. But the book she stole was near the end of its lifespan, and it carried on recording by taking over one of her ordinary notebooks. Look. I have a theory," he continued, tapping the open book, its curious writing all the more alien in its stability. "Somewhere in the Grand Library, there's a room *full* of books like this, stretching back Proof even knows how far. As many as have been filled, there must be dozens more just sitting there blank, waiting to form the next volume. It's the story of the entire Experiment, self-sustaining and inviolate."

Anselm Meteron pinched the bridge of his nose. "'Inviolate' my ass."

Chalmers blinked. "I . . . I beg your pardon?"

The Alchemist shook his head. His hands, Chalmers noticed, wrung the neck of his cane.

"We don't *have* the active book anymore," Meteron said, in a tone that suggested his estimation of Chalmers—never quite so high as the doctor felt he deserved—had precipitously dropped. "Nora set it loose in the world, and when she found the data could carry on in another text, she hid the evidence and took the live document away to work with you. Now that it's missing, it can move on to another carrier—not just another person's hands, but into another text entirely."

"How close to being full was that book, Doctor?" the Alchemist pressed.

"I—" Chalmers's mouth opened, but all he managed was a squeak like a door on a bad hinge. "I . . . I can't remember."

"*Try.*"

"Parts of it were nearly done. There were dozens of pages left, though. A hundred, maybe? I don't . . . it would last awhile longer."

"Would it last eight months more?" the Alchemist asked. "From the time you saw it last until now, or beyond?"

Chalmers bit his lip. "Based on the previous speed at which data accumulated, yes . . . barely. Perhaps? It had awhile left. But that must be nearly gone now."

Meteron looked to the Alchemist. "This Dor from Crystal Hill found Rowena. The lanyani on the ship said they can use the book to find the rest."

Chalmers jumped in his seat as if a galvanic current had run up his backside. "I'm sorry, Dor from what can use which?"

"They have the book," the Alchemist continued, quite as if the young doctor were not there at all. "But not for much longer, it seems."

A waitress swept over, ready to refresh the table's drinks. Chalmers watched Meteron wave the girl off, his heart pounding so fiercely his vision blurred.

"What do you mean someone *found Rowena?*" The solemn silence that followed made Chalmers long to call for a bottle of gin. "So some-one—"

"The lanyani," Meteron clarified.

"The *lanyani* have the book, and they've figured out how to use it to track Rowena down?"

The Alchemist nodded. "And presumably the rest of the Nine."

"We're not just running out of time to find the Vautneks and get back the book," Chalmers groaned. "We're running out of time before it moves to a new receptacle entirely."

"And we're on the wrong side of the world to intercept it, when it does," Meteron added.

"But it also means we're on the wrong side of the world to stop whatever the lanyani are planning," Chalmers cried.

The Alchemist pushed the book back to the Reverend Doctor. "See if Keeper will let you use his spark line, Ann. I need you to pass word of this to the Dolly Molls."

Rowena watched the fighters in the sawdust pit dig into each other with elbows and knees, hurling their weight against each other hard as the surf on stones. She'd seen her share of street brawls near Rotten Row and Blackbottom End, but this was something different. Those fights were brutal and artless, and always cost a man more than he won. This, ugly as it was, looked more like some kind of a dance, with bodies closing and weaving together.

The broader of the two women hooked an arm around the other's leg and dropped to her knees. Turning, she flung her opponent like a rag baby. Even the sawdust and the cheers weren't enough to dull the loud report of a shoulder popping and cartilage tearing when the thrown woman struck the ground.

Rowena winced. But she kept watching. The thrown woman kicked her legs up, kipping to her feet, and paced around her opponent warily.

A hand closed on Rowena's shoulder. She flinched, jumping back.

"Our supper's come," the Old Bear said.

Rowena glanced back at their teetering table, its surface crowded with plates and mugs. The room wavered in the smoke and sweat and heat. *Food?* The thought set her stomach on edge.

"I don't—" Rowena shrugged apologetically. "I'm not so hungry."

The Old Bear grimaced. "We should have found some other place to meet."

"No. No, I like it. Sort of." Rowena let herself be guided away from the crowd, though she stopped the Old Bear at a quieter nook where the kitchens curved away from the rest of the Maiden's rowdy floor. "This was an old haunt for you?"

"One of several. The Logicians care about it enough to see it remains open, though not to see what goes on inside. All the best campaigners base their charters here."

Rowena scanned the room, appraising. "Yours, too?"

He grunted in the affirmative. "Ivor always favored it. When it was only the two of us, before Leyah and Anselm, we could use the pits to make coin between contracts."

Rowena's nose wrinkled. "Not hard to picture him knocking folks' heads around." She glanced at the Old Bear. The set of his jaw under his graying beard made her look again, harder.

"What?" he asked.

"*Bloody Reason.* Was it you down there?"

"They wouldn't allow a man with a clockwork limb in the pit. Their only sensible rule. A hand like Ivor's could drive clean through a man's face."

"Were you any good?" Rowena asked, too eagerly. The idea of the Old Bear—*her* Bear—circling and punching and crushing in that pit was at once revolting and fascinating.

"Good enough to keep the bills paid. Some of them, anyway. It was a long time ago."

"Still, though—"

"Don't get any notions of it being romantic. It's nothing but broken noses and split lips, and that's for the lucky ones."

They turned back toward their table, only to bump into a man as big as one of their airship's boilers.

The stranger smiled down at Rowena. His teeth were very white and terribly crooked, like a hand of playing cards badly fanned.

"Sorry," Rowena said. "Didn't see you there."

The Old Bear took her arm, pulling her a little closer.

The boiler took note of that. He raked his smile over the Alchemist—looking up to do it. The Alchemist was a hand taller than the next largest man in the pub.

The next largest man, Rowena judged, was probably this cove.

"Heard you say you've done some rounds below," he said, loud enough to draw the eyes and ears of the folks on the near end of the pit. The boiler looked the Alchemist up and down. His gaze lingered on his cane and the girl at his side. "Must've been a long time ago, grandpa."

"It was. Excuse us."

The boiler put a hand up—waiting to do it so his palm would thump against the Alchemist's chest as he moved to pass him by.

"You any good?" the boiler demanded.

The Old Bear stared at the man's hand, two of its fingers smeared against his folded spectacles. He looked up, his eyes gone flat and hard.

"I've answered that question already tonight. And we've yet to take our supper."

The boiler shrugged a shoulder the size of a holiday ham. "Just making conversation. I like conversation. This yours?" He nodded toward Rowena. An angry flush burned up her neck. "I didn't know the cat dens sold 'em off so young."

"I am afraid you've made the wrong assumption," the Old Bear replied. "Rowena. Go join Ann and the Doctor, please. I'll be along."

Rowena tried to skirt around the boiler's other side, but someone from his table had risen, covering her path like a rolling boulder. She flinched back, realizing it was a woman—broad as a brick wall and hemmed in by something between a corset and a bandolier, pockets of munitions and bladed things stashed here and there like the bows on a proper lady's underthings.

"Oh, hell," Rowena muttered.

"We could use somebody small, you see," the boiler was saying, edging in closer to the Alchemist, his hand still pressed to the taller man's chest. "Got a job that needs an inside touch, and Mayeline and I just aren't suited."

"Name us a price on her," the woman the boiler had called Mayeline said. She had a voice like gravel pouring down a factory chute. "We can have her back to you in one piece. Just need her for a day or two. What d'you say?"

"No."

Mayeline sniffed. She looked honestly hurt. "We'd keep her out of harm. C'mon. We're chartered. Legal. Anybody hereabouts would vouch for us."

Rowena surveyed the room. The concentric circles of observers had grown. The looks Rowena spied passing between them suggested Mayeline might not have had as many backers as she imagined. One skinny man with a hooked nose spat at the floorboards, punctuating some sidelong comment Rowena couldn't hear. His comrades laughed. She had the terrible feeling, as his pinprick stare dragged across her skin, that it wasn't Mayeline he was scoffing at.

"The girl isn't what you suggest," the Old Bear answered, grinding the phrase in his teeth.

The boiler snorted. "What is she, then?"

"I'm his daughter," Rowena blurted out. "He's my da."

For an instant, an expression Rowena couldn't quite read flashed across the Old Bear's face – something warm and unguarded. Then his sober face ordered itself again, before anyone else took note of it.

Mayeline belted out a laugh. The boiler sniggered, shaking his head. "Sorry, grandpa," he said. "Guess I didn't see the family resemblance."

Rowena's hands knotted into fists. She wished she wasn't wearing a skirt and blouse, even if it was a riding skirt and good for moving. The strangers' greasy solicitude was bad enough. Their scorn was a bridge too far.

"Well, he is," she snapped. "And you can piss off with your inside work or whatever it is. C'mon, Da."

The Alchemist raised a hand to brush the boiler's paw away. The brute's fingers closed over his wrist, instead. He leaned close, bare inches from the Alchemist's face.

"She en't your daughter," he snarled. "Any fool can see that. And if she en't on your charter, there's nothing to keep us from having a conversation with her about *incentivized employment.*"

"The hell you will!" Rowena spat.

An arm came down on her shoulder, knocking her off balance. She fell into a wall of humanity. *Mayeline.* Rowena tried to stomp the woman's toes, but Mayeline's boots might have been made of iron, for all the good it did. She snatched Rowena up in an embrace that was decidedly more bear than hug., crushing the breath out of her.

Then a lot of things happened, all at once.

There was movement off to Rowena's left, dark and darting. Master Meteron stealing up behind Mayeline. In the same moment, the Alchemist spun in the boiler's grasp, breaking his hold and snatching his opponent's wrist. He straightened the man's arm, then reversed his grip on the cane in his right hand, palming its handle like a set of boxer's knuckles. In one, sharp motion, the Alchemist drove its brass head into the outside of the boiler's elbow. There was a sickening crack as the whole arm buckled. The boiler howled and sank to his knees, hugging his ruined limb.

Meteron's hand flashed past Rowena's face, plucking a leaf-bladed dagger from one of the pockets in Mayeline's battle-corset. He raked it across Mayeline's forearm as she wrangled Rowena.

Her roar came an instant later, strangely deeper than the boiler's. Blood coursed down her arm as her hand went slack. Rowena scrambled back, bumping against Meteron, who stood near enough to admire his handiwork—and to finish it, if it came to it. The Old Bear loomed over the boiler, his jaw tight.

"Oh, stop it," Meteron said, the screams of the wounded finally subsiding into whimpers. "You're both right-handed. Consider yourselves lucky." He raised an eyebrow at the Alchemist. "You could still invite that one down into the Pit, you know. He seemed interested."

The Alchemist turned his grip on his cane and leaned into it, making his way back to table forty-nine. "I'll pass."

Rowena turned to follow him, then spied someone else darting from behind Meteron toward the curtained exit to the grotto and the street above.

"Hey!" she cried. Master Meteron turned. She snatched the bloodied throwing knife from his unguarded hand, hurling it hard for the running boy's knee.

She missed by nearly a yard, the blade *thunking* into the wooden landing by the door. It was still enough to scare him. When he looked back, wide-eyed, she put her hand up to throw again. He didn't linger long enough to notice it was empty. The bank wallet that had been stowed under Meteron's jacket tumbled from his hands as he scrambled, whimpering, through the curtained door.

Master Meteron smiled at Rowena. "Nicely done. I hadn't been thinking about scavengers."

Rowena imitated his one-shouldered shrug. "I was one. Comes natural."

He took his time sauntering over to fetch his wallet. No one in the pub seemed interested in contesting his ownership of it. By degrees, the Maiden's Honor resumed its usual business. Someone—bouncers of some kind, though Rowena had to wonder where they'd been just half a minute earlier—came by to gather up the boiler and Mayeline. No one said a word about damages, or who would clean up the mess, or if there was some price to be paid for one company attacking another.

Rowena had a feeling this place had worked out its own way of managing moments such as these.

20.

5TH EIGHTMONTH, 277 A.U.
WESTGATE BRIDGE, CORMA

The trouble Bess Earnshaw had with calling on Sugar Maple was she could never be sure which Sugar Maple she was meeting. True to its name, the lanyani fence had sprouted up a dozen or more cuttings over the years, at least two of them uprooted in the last few months. Not all of Sugar Maple was a fence. Some of it was a spy. Some was a burglar. Some a forger. Bess had heard rumors that at least three of it comprised a team of assassins. That last idea had a certain quarter-clink novel appeal, but she couldn't imagine anyone trusting a lanyani killer when there were more than enough humans all too happy for the work.

Today, the trouble was that three of Sugar Maple had agreed to meet with Bess, and worse still, none of it seemed to agree on what information to pass along.

"They're plotting to kill the city," the Sugar Maple standing beside the Stone Scales's ever-blooming lilacs insisted. Early evening shadows pooled around the bushes of the shop's back garden, closing the space between Bess and her interlocutors in a way she didn't much like.

"Liar," hissed a counterpart Sugar Maple.

Bess flinched at the rattlesnake bite in its voice. She turned toward the lanyani, not sure how much attention she could afford to split between it and the one she had contradicted—or how much wariness she ought to keep in reserve for the still-silent Sugar Maple seated amidst a ring of beakers and crates brimming with herbs. That Sugar Maple occupied itself snipping back the blossom ends of basil with scissoring fingers.

I shouldn't have told Rowie to handle all those meets without me, back in the old days.

7

Bess had always been a little unnerved by the lanyani and had left as many deals that involved Sticks or Sugar Maple as possible to Jorrie Downshire. Later, when the girl was old enough to remember a script and stick to it, she liked to shrug the jobs off on his little sister, Rowena. Gentry folks, wealthy merchants, the smalldukes and duchesses—those were clients Bess understood. Besides, they had *always* been ready with a gratuity, provided she smiled prettily or curtsied low enough to display her décolletage. The only tip lanyani ever left you with was your own life, and even that came off as grudging.

"I'm sorry, I don't understand—"

"Neither of them is lying," the Sugar Maple seated among the herbs thrummed. Its cascade of leaves, styled into a dense rope a little like a braid, was almost absurd in its humanity. It tossed its head. Its other selves tossed theirs, too, echoing the first's movement. "But neither of them is right, either," it finished, with a look that bordered eerily on a smile.

"That really doesn't clarify."

"The clans at the Gathering Grove on the Hill want to kill the city *Men* built," the first Sugar Maple said. Its rattling voice still seethed resentment. Bess hoped it was directed toward its counterpart's semantic argument and not Bess herself. The Scales's back door felt much farther away than it used to.

"How is killing what Men built not killing the city?"

That Sugar Maple's splinter-teeth snapped over some comment unmade—a suppressed laugh?

"There are things in this city which should not belong to Men," the Sugar Maple who had called its other self a liar answered. "Things that could belong to us and the aigamuxa again."

Bess turned toward the Sugar Maple seated among the herbs. She liked it—her? God, how to really be sure?—much better than its other selves. It didn't seem as ready to pounce.

She took a slow, composing breath. "*Tell me what you mean.* How do you *kill* a city?"

Sugar Maple of the Herbs lay back. The rest of itself seemed to take that as a signal. The other two abandoned their posts and walked toward the third, lounging against a crooked arm, leaning into a raised knee. They sank against one another, limbs stroking and grasping in positively orgiastic fashion until, finally, Bess realized that the two Sugar Maples who could not agree were merging with the third, twining into a being of many limbs, many faces growing between shoulders or thrust out where a breastbone might have been, on a human.

Together, Sugar Maple spoke as one, its voice an eerie chorus as it rose upright, a centipede of living wood.

Bess stared, frozen in horror.

"Our apologies. We are not of one mind on this issue," Sugar Maple crooned, contralto, like the reed in a clarinet.

Bess made her voice small enough to squeeze past the lump in her throat. "Did . . . did doing that . . . help?"

"It will help us explain more clearly."

One by one, the faces spoke, emerging from the bark of Sugar Maple's monstrous body as if pressing through a layer of silk, then disappearing, drifting away, to emerge again somewhere else.

"They are looking for the ones they must feed to the Pits—

"To prove they have earned this world—

"Hunting—

"Making allies—

"Sending messengers."

Allies. Gammon had said the lanyani and the aigamuxa were up to something. It was why she asked Bess to call up any contact she still knew how to reach.

"I can understand allies," Bess said. "But why messengers? Messengers where?"

"Over the water. Messengers—

"To the other clans.

"The other tribes."

Tribes and clans. Each of the other species had its preferred word. It chilled Bess to hear them used together.

"Sending messengers where?"

Only one of Sugar Maple's faces smiled, but the cruel slash of its mouth bore malice enough for a hundred more.

"Everywhere," it sang, "everywhere, *everywhere*."

Days of slow business at the Scales had left Bess the time to stare at the shop's map-covered walls. *Everywhere?* Surely not. There just wasn't a way—not for a people with no access to the vox boxes or the galvano-graph lines. No post, no courier services. How could trees—even sentient trees such as the lanyani were—hope to speak across the water to their siblings, the remnants of other clans scattered all over the world?

"But what's the *message?*" Bess insisted. "How will it get anywhere?"

"By the same means that will destroy this city for Men—

"By flesh, and blood—

"And bird—

"And it will say—

"Come. Bring the ones we hunt for—

"*Come.*"

The faces stilled, frozen in a moment of shared rapture, until Bess flinched at a sound like gunfire. Sugar Maple reached its six arms across its knotted torso, digging needle-whittled fingertips into its own fissured bark, and pulled until the fibers of its body cracked and split. Pieces of it fell away, new limbs budding out of the exposed greenwood. It gave birth to itself, crawled apart into three separate selves once again, the subtle features that had helped Bess keep a sense of which Sugar Maple was which strangely blended. Flattened. The lanyani stood in a ragged line and swayed, dazed, staring white-eyed through Bess's marrow.

"Why are you telling me this?" she demanded. Bess scanned the three parts of Sugar Maple. It had emerged with new curves and planes—shapes like breasts, but drawn awkwardly, as if by a child, all out of proportion and lopsided, with a mound of moss between its legs like a salad passed off for a sex. It . . . she? . . . looked proud of this transformation.

Sugar Maple smiled, like petals opening into the sun.

"I always liked your friend, back when she worked the streets," said one of her. "The little one with the mouth and no grace. The one they could not bring back to the Pits. It would be a shame if they found her. And I thought, if I liked that one—" A shrug.

"—there was a chance I would like the others they are hunting for, if only I knew them," another fragment agreed, picking up the speech. "So many things we have destroyed, because we do not know what we should."

Bess's mind spun trying to hug the curves of this non-logic. "You said you weren't of one mind on this issue, though."

The last of Sugar Maple's heads tilted, thoughtful. "Men are a waste. I have profited from them but could live just as well in a world without them. But some . . ." Again, that shrug, so close to being human, it turned Bess's stomach. "Some are not as terrible as the rest. They might be spared."

"Is there a way to spare people?"

"Leave the city," Sugar Maple answered, all three speaking in chorus. "It will start with the rats and the birds."

Sugar Maple turned toward the brick wall of a sundry shop framing the north end of the Stone Scales's yard and reached upward. Her bodies sprouted vines and thorns, and she crawled up the mortar, a mossy shadow in the dusk. She gained the roof and disappeared, soundless except for a stirring of leaves in the electric air of a night that would not yet give up its storms.

Bess raked her fingers through her hair and turned toward the machine shed. Julian and Gammon hunkered there, the boy poised behind the crouching woman. Each was armed with a slingshot and fistful of pellets the Alchemist's inventory sheets promised were highly flammable.

"You okay?" Julian leaned into the shed, relaxing his pose and dropping his ammunition—gingerly—into a bin secreted beside them. He looked tired. His mechanical leg was a brilliant contraption, but torture to stand on without an occasional respite.

Bess knew better than to ask after his welfare in return. During Nasrahiel's reconstruction she'd made the mistake of complimenting him for being "tough" and "brave" after a long day's work at his lathe obliged him to spend hours with a spanner adjusting his prosthetic's suspension.

"*I'm not brave for having two working legs any more than I was brave when I had just the one,*" he'd snapped. "*Pass me the quarter-inch, would you?*"

It was the last time she'd spoken of his mechanical limb. That seemed for the best.

"I'm fine," Bess replied. "Happy you were there. I'm glad she didn't notice."

Gammon shook her head, packing up their arsenal. "She had at least six eyes roving around. She knew."

"What do you suppose she meant about the birds and rats? Or sending messengers?" Julian asked.

"The same thing." Gammon looked up to the rooftops crowding around the yard, lips moving slightly as she counted something both Bess and Julian had failed to see.

Julian frowned at Bess. They'd shared that look before, though a few times it had been his mother who had precipitated it. "You'll forgive me for saying I'm getting damned tired of cryptic evasions, Haadi."

"Not being cryptic," Gammon muttered distractedly. "How far do you think he can jump?"

Bess blinked. "How far can who jump?"

Julian clearly knew what she meant. His eyes turned to saucers. "He's not to be out before dark!"

"Well, it's *your* turn to tell him that," Gammon sighed.

Bess looked up. The roofs of buildings in Westgate Bridge shared a common, claustrophobic design, each terminating within three or four yards of the next. Sometimes, when the savoyards servicing the neighborhood's chimneys had too heavy a load of equipment to carry from one job to the next, they would hire an aigamuxa to haul it up to the top for them and leap from gable to gable with the packs and cases strapped to its back. It was enough for aigamuxa on the rooftops in Westgate Bridge to be, while certainly less than commonplace, better than improbable.

Gammon's counting had been her timing Nasrahiel's jumps.

The dark blur of his body descended in a long, punishing arc toward the cobbles. Paving stones exploded upward under the force of his landing, showering Bess and Gammon and Julian with a powdering of limestone and dirt. Bess coughed, swatting at the clouded air.

"Reason's bloody ruin," Julian groaned. "You don't *need* to land on your hands anymore! I spent ages building those legs with enough shock absorption to—"

"The lanyani stepped into the river some time ago," Nasrahiel rumbled, ignoring the boy. He remained as he had landed, hands splayed on the ground before him and between his legs, supporting his body in the pedestal position. However well suited his legs were to a feet-first landing, they were just as suited to bending up along the aigamuxa's back and resting, heels on his shoulders. His cyclopean eye whirred and flickered above his flat nose.

"She was probably headed for the Hill," Gammon agreed. "Hoping to avoid detection. You cleared twelve yards skipping that last roof, you know."

Bess couldn't keep the exasperation from her voice. "I don't understand—is Sugar Maple trying to help us or not? Why would she bother?"

Nasrahiel snorted. "She plays both ends of the game." The aigamuxa unfolded himself, putting his mechanical feet to the ground and rising like a line of scaffolding. Bess didn't know how tall the creature had been before Resurrection Jane and Julian began their work, but he was assuredly the biggest aiga she'd ever seen—nearly twice Gammon's height, even with his shoulders rolled and back hunched.

"If the Men in the city are saved from whatever destruction the Trees have planned," he said, "then they will still be able to hire Sugar Maple, buy her goods, and make her as comfortable as a weed. If they are destroyed and the Trees come to rule this place . . ." Nasrahiel's eye blinked, its shutter *snicking* loudly. Bess flinched. "There is much to be gained there, as well."

"The Trees," Julian said. His voice was flat. Skeptical. "You keep saying that like we haven't seen evidence of the aigamuxa working with them, too. Your people."

Nasrahiel growled something that might have been a word in his language—or something worse.

"I still want an answer to my other question," Bess insisted.

The aigamuxa lumbered past her toward the Stone Scales's stoop, hunkering low, as if he meant to pass through the door. "What other question?"

"Why *birds?*"

The aiga stopped, his hand resting on the lintel. "Birds?"

"Sugar Maple said there would be a message," Gammon explained. "And to look for the birds and the rats as a sign."

Nasrahiel put his head against the lintel, rumbling again. "We must find Rahielma. We have waited for my recovery. It is as complete as our time permits."

Gammon passed the box of incendiaries and slingshots back to Julian. "Will she be in the Aeries?"

"Hopefully."

"And what do you mean to do when you find her?"

Nasrahiel looked down at himself, straightened, sighed. "Explain what I can." He turned to Bess, who had reached his side. In the rising dark, she spied her reflection in the lens of his eye. "The Alchemist did not take all of his things?"

"Proof, no. There's years of stuff in this place," she said. "What do you need?"

"Something," he said, raising his arms and studying them with a crease in his brow Bess found strangely sympathetic. "Something to cover all of this."

She considered the scars and wires crazing his flesh. She grimaced. "I'll need a few minutes."

"Just as well," Gammon said. "We're better off traveling in the dark."

Bess ducked past the aigamuxa into the Scales's back room. Within, she heard the *tikka-tikka-whirrr* of the antique Galvex recorder printing out a line of galvano-graph tape. Bess tossed the dust cover draped over the machine aside and scanned the paper spooling from it with a frown.

To: The Stone Scales
From: ZN
Location: [withheld] 5th Eightmonth

ZIIREVW RM OVNZIXPV HZUVOB. OZMBZMR
ZGGVNKGVW GL XZKGFIV ILDVMZ. ML MVDH
LU HXSLOZI BVG. LYGZRM GSV OLHG YLLP
RNNVWRZGVOB — RMULINZGRLM DROO YV OLHG
KVINZMVMGOB HLLM. IVOZB NVHHZTVH GSILFTS
NZRWVM'H SLMLI GL ZMXSLI HGZGRLM RM MRK-
KLM.

—ZN

"What on earth?" she muttered. *Well. Maybe Julian would know.* He was
good with machines, especially when they were acting up.

Bess found a set of bedsheets large enough to bundle around Nasrahiel and brought them outside, the printed spark balled up in her fist.
The creature took the sheets without comment. She thrust the mangled note to Julian when he emerged from the machine shed, passing
something that looked like a small bundle of tools along to Gammon.

"I don't know how the Alchemist expects me to keep up his business
if he won't keep up his galvano-graph. It's rubbish."

Julian opened the wad of paper and his eyebrows climbed. "Haadi."
He passed it to Gammon, who examined it in turn. "I'm not as good
with Mother's code as you are, but I think this is for you?"

Gammon took only a moment to read it, dark eyes flicking fast across
the page. Only a distant alchemical street lamp offered a golden glow to
read by.

"Birds and messengers," she whispered. "They're on to her already.
Are you ready, Nasrahiel?"

The bundled form on the stoop could not have been mistaken for
anything but an aigamuxa, but at least its shining, hinged legs and peering eye remained hidden in folds of linen. "I am now."

"Good. It's time to find out what your people know about the rats and the birds."

21.

The Reverend Doctor Phillip Chalmers shifted awkwardly from foot to foot, feeling too little the seasoned scholar and too much the restless schoolboy under the notary's disapproving glare. The Alchemist studied the document before them with furrowed brows, his raptor eyes swooping up over the rims of his spectacles as he paused in his reading, punctuating the silence with questions about changes in the law, riders and clauses, and other minutiae that put Chalmers in mind of his first year Apocrypha lectures.

Rowena all but danced in place as she waited. Chalmers steadied himself on the soles of his shoes, hoping that if he did not cut a very convincing pattern for a campaigner, he might at least avoiding looking half so puppyish as she. For his part, Master Meteron looked little more than bored.

"Eight pages now?" he'd complained when the Lemarckian notary passed them the charter update. "God's balls, do they expect a cheek scraping and our marks from Sabberday exams, as well?"

"Don't tempt," the Alchemist murmured over the papers.

"Hmph. Well, best do them the usual way, then."

"What's that?" Rowena asked.

The rogue winked. "Pepper boring honesty with audacious fiction until all the blanks are filled."

That had been nearly a half-hour before. Now, they were down to the signatories' page.

"You'll need the final page notarized, of course. Mind the change to the Ecclesiastical Commission representative line, as well," the hatchet-nosed woman behind the grille cautioned as Meteron produced a cartridge pen.

"What change?" Chalmers asked. He crowded between the Alchemist's tall shoulder and Meteron's much shorter one, jabbing his face as near to the page as he could manage.

"A properly filed charter used to require the signature of a single EC representative to render it valid. Our offices now require two. Far too much graft in the past, Doctor. I'm sure you understand."

Chalmers cast the Alchemist a worried glance. "Two. I—I've met a few deacons and such since I arrived in the spring. Perhaps one of them could—"

From Chalmers's left, a hand with four and a half fingers pressed a ring to the paper in one of the three places where it been chemically conditioned to take on the impression of a seal.

Chalmers bird-necked around to gawk at Anselm Meteron. Meteron's hand disappeared into the inner pocket of his jacket, like a conjuror vanishing a false card.

Chalmers dropped his voice to a theatrical whisper. "Did you steal that from someone in the queue?"

Meteron sighed. "Bloody Reason, Reverend. You can't honestly believe I was born to Allister Meteron and not put through the seminary paces."

Chalmers blinked. "You're a Reverend Doctor?"

"Deacon. Never sat my final examination. Other interests to pursue."

"Err—yes. Of course."

Chalmers affixed his signature and his seal to the page beside Meteron's and passed the document along.

Rowena scratched out her signature in a wobbly, wide-spaced print that more closely resembled the hand of a kinder-student than a girl better than half-grown. Chalmers wondered how often she'd practiced those letters and how many margins of how many account ledgers in the Stone Scales now bore her infant scrawl.

She reached the final letter nearly a minute after beginning and looked up at the Alchemist, beaming.

Phillip Chalmers had grown up the lackluster middle son of a coster-monger, too weak to take up his father's barrow and not brilliant enough to demand an immediate elevation out of the free schools. He'd had to work twice as hard as others to achieve even modest success, but he had done it, all the same. His father and mother's pride had been his chief motivator. Only later had his own pride entered into it.

He imagined he must have looked at his family as Rowena looked at the Alchemist, earnest and hungry for praise. His parents had looked back with pure, uncomplicated admiration. But there was nothing uncomplicated in the look the Alchemist gave his ward.

They returned to the Maiden's Honor that morning, which appeared to have opened for the sole purpose of providing them (now properly the Corma Company and again a member of its preferred patronage) a place to conference over the contents of Nora's safety deposit box. Chalmers unpacked the papers and the now-silent notebook bearing the Grand Library's crest, passing them around to his companions. They read, Rowena sometimes leaning over to point at things in Nora's letters, mur-muring questions to the Alchemist. Chalmers translated Pierce's hen-scratch dutifully. Anselm leaned his chair at a perilous angle, perched against the wall, its two front legs insolently airborne. He flipped pages in Nora's lab book and ground at the stump of his missing finger with a restless thumb.

Chalmers paced. It was a habit to which he had always been prone. A crook-backed old woman made her rounds of the bar floor, shoulder-ing a wash-bin of half-drunk ales. She was probably still working from the night before. Madame Kurowa had departed the rooming house the Rolands had rented them almost an hour earlier, armed with Engine-printed copies of their traveling papers with which to secure their final passage to Nippon. She had *not* had a copy of their campaign charter.

That was, at least in past, what they had come here to discuss.

The sound of a throat clearing brought Chalmers into proper focus.

Meteron tossed the notebook on the table. It would have skidded off its edge, if not for Rowena's hand swatting it back. The girl scowled at him as he stretched, yawned, and laced his hands behind his head.

"So, summing up," Meteron began, "you think there are things in the Grand Library that will help us find the Nine and keep them out of harm's way."

"*Nora* thought that," Chalmers corrected.

Meteron raised an eyebrow. "We've a difficulty to navigate, then, seeing as your partner stole from the Library and meant to give a presentation to the whole of the Ecclesiastical Commission on the very thing they've been keeping secret for generations. I very much doubt they failed to notice."

"But I have a *plan*, you see—"

"He's right, Doc." Rowena alternated between peeking at the letters the Alchemist surveyed and digging a deeper trench with her knife through the butter crock. She gnawed an overtoasted heel of bread, wrestling out words between bites. "I wouldn't let you near any of my stuff if you did me a turn like that. Can't see why the Library would be forgiving."

"They might be, if the trip were intended to make amends," the Alchemist said through a cloud of pipe smoke.

Chalmers pointed to him victoriously. "*Yes*, thank you! Just—look, I understand Nora's work with Bishop Meteron puts me in a very precarious position as a researcher seeking access to their archives, but if I've come with the intention of returning the old book, the one she took, and apologizing for my role in a theft I *did not even know had taken place*, that seems a reasonable plan. It's not having the *current* text to return which poses a problem."

Rowena pulled a face. "Does it? I mean, you were beat up, kidnapped, and had your apartments all busted up. Your stuff got stolen, and once you came here and found this dead book and how it connected to the other one, it was too late to find it again. There's a Constabulary report about your being held captive and everything."

"Even so, what we have to determine is why I need you with me," said Chalmers.

"The public reasons," said the Alchemist.

"And the private ones," finished Meteron.

"Security," Chalmers suggested, pacing again. "That will do for both, though it does very little to explain Rowena's presence."

He tried to keep the irritation out of his voice. He'd been proud of his scheme for begging admittance to the Library and relieved to learn through his research that there was some precedent for reverend doctors and bishop professors traveling under guard. But typically, the Ecclesiastical Commission provided its own staff for the purpose.

"Your hiring private security makes sense," Meteron answered, sounding bored with the preliminaries. "You were held by EC security, though that's been explained away as Regenzi using his wealth to corrupt otherwise reliable servants of the Commission. Now that you're free, they all seem a bit suspicious to you. You were in Corma, so you looked up an out-of-date charter, hunting for some old hands on the cheap. The Rolands took care of the rest."

Rowena snorted. "Why would anybody believe you went back on campaign, let alone *on the cheap?*"

"Anyone who knows me well knows I do rather foolish things when I'm bored. As for explaining your presence, cricket . . ." Meteron shrugged, one-shouldered. "You're Chalmers's secretary."

The girl all but fell out of her chair. Chalmers might have, too, had he been sitting.

"But she's barely literate!"

"I en't a *secretary!*"

"Enough," the Alchemist barked. Chalmers winced. The Alchemist folded his spectacles, hanging them from his shirtfront, and straightened Nora's papers. "It's a passable story. Gammon's report on the events at the Cathedral left our names out, so our prior connections are largely unknown. Now what, Doctor, do you need us *actually* looking for?"

"The Bishop's allies. Whoever has been helping him research the Grand Experiment. Anything connected to the Nine. A way into wherever the librarians keep the completed copies of the book, if I'm forbidden legal access. I must find a pattern in the older texts, something that might allow us to predict how soon the text will choose new subjects, or if there's a distribution pattern to them I've missed."

"That could take years of work," Meteron said.

"If needs must, Master Meteron."

Rowena's eyes had gone wide. "But my mum! She's back in Amidon. I never said I wanted to stay here *forever*."

"I understand your goals, Doctor, but they're impractical," the Alchemist said. "Our first priority is to find the people working for, or with, the Bishop and what they're after."

Chalmers blinked. "Isn't it obvious? They want the names. Of the Nine. The Vautneks."

"But why?" Anselm Meteron's smile could have cut glass.

"I . . . because . . . Regenzi wanted to find them and keep them all?" Chalmers stammered. "In a sort of moral quarantine."

"Lab rats," Rowena muttered. "He didn't mean for those Vautneks to sit pretty like in a zoo. They're lab rats—kept because they're *useful*."

Chalmers grimaced. "I know what experimental creatures are *for*. I also know what Regenzi told me."

"And what did my father tell you?"

Meteron's face was a frozen lake. There was no telling how deep the ice went, or what pressure would break through.

"We never met," Chalmers admitted.

"Then it's possible Regenzi went a little off-script." Meteron slid from his seat and stretched. He winced at a pop in his right shoulder and looked to his hands, working their knuckles, spending more time on his missing forefinger than anything invisible warranted. "His Grace isn't gathering a petting zoo of the divine will as an exercise in conservancy. He has an agenda—something he wants them to do for him. If we can learn who his people are and what they've been researching, we can potentially gum up his agenda without ever finding the Vautneks."

Rowena perked up. "But we're still going to try, aren't we? Since the lanyani are after 'em now, too?"

Chalmers watched Meteron and the Alchemist share a look, indecipherably brief. He looked away, not trusting his own treacherous face.

"We'll try," the Alchemist said.

"To that end, Doctor, I could use your help with something," Meteron said.

"Anything—I mean, well." Chalmers spread his hands. "I'll try."

"Are there any scholars of lanyani culture at the Grand Library?"

Chalmers wasn't sure he'd heard correctly. "Lanyani *culture?*"

Meteron rolled his eyes. "That thing sentient beings do when they all get together and live in places and partner up, yes. Culture. Surely someone's bothered studying it?"

"Um." Chalmers was sickly certain the others could see the color rising on his face. He set about pouring tea, and forgot until he'd nearly turned over every notebook and carbon paper on the table in search of the milk that Lemarckian tea service did without it. He shoveled a desultory spoonful of strawberry jam into the smoky brew, instead. "Well, I know one. We shared a flat back in Rimmerston while I was looking for a post as a lecturer. It was after my doctoral thesis was accepted. They were just doing a few courses at seminary on a lark. They were from some wealthy Vraskan family—coal barons or some such, I think. Last I knew, they were in Nippon, gadding about, making donations to the Library in their family's name to pay for their access."

"They." Meteron paused in rolling a cigarette. "You said you know *one* scholar."

"They're a more complicated person than you're accustomed to, Master Meteron. I'm not entirely convinced you would . . . um . . . work well with them."

The thief looked as though he were prepared to interpret that as a personal challenge. The Alchemist cleared his throat.

"We'll settle the matter of personality differences another time. Let Anselm find your lanyani scholar while I look into Bishop Meteron's contacts."

Rowena looked up from her breakfast quizzically. "But if Master Meteron's got the background in the EC, en't it a waste not to give him that job? I mean, you probably know something about your da's affairs, right?"

Meteron lit his cigarette with a flick of a lucifer against his thumbnail.

"And his people know something about me. It's too obvious. Better to keep me further from those circles. His Grace always kept our family's connection to the Old Bear as quiet as possible."

Chalmers did not have to wonder why. For all its claims of having made men equal in the world through education and science, there were those in the EC who saw in science an excuse to substantiate old biases. So many studies claimed to link the slope of a Leonine native's brow to their native intelligence or celebrated the pedigrees of decorated scholars as a thin gloss on inherited traits. And then there were the whispered alehouse theories linking various women's career growth with certain physical charms. Amidon was a better country than most at putting such petty conjectures aside. But there were other differences Amidonians liked to enlarge upon, whenever possible. Certainly a scientist of trade marrying the daughter of a prominent theosophist was one.

"All right," Rowena said, a little too brightly. "That leaves me in charge of getting into the room with the old books, if nobody will give us a free pass in."

Chalmers dropped his next spoonful of jam into his lap, rather than his cup. "I'm not certain that's a good idea."

"It is if I go with her," Meteron said. He smiled. "Unless you'd like the man with the cane in charge of breaking and entering."

The Alchemist gave his partner a look that could have gutted a fish. "If I did not know better, I'd think you enjoy my being lamed."

"I am always starved for novel entertainments."

"After nearly thirty years, needling me should have gone stale."

Meteron shrugged. "And yet, here we are."

Chalmers leaned toward Rowena, speaking sotto voce. "Are they *always* like this?"

"Pretty much. Pass the jam, would you? This porridge is awful."

He nudged the pot her way, not entirely sure he had found her answer comforting.

"Oh, and . . ." She leaned close, too, a mischievous smile playing on her face. "Tell me about this 'they' of yours, doc."

INTERMEZZO

The Archivist lives in a compound, of sorts, at the heart of the Grand Library's campus. It is a space of several houses and rooms, connected by narrow causeways and paper screens, commanding a flowering corner of the Library's space—a total square footage that would be unseemly, even irrational, had they been dedicated to some lesser cultural light.

But I am ahead of myself.

My escort paid the cabman and sat with me in the open arms of the steam car, chill midday air sliding past us as we drove from the anchorages to the city proper.

And then I saw for the first time in person the phenomenon that has prompted so many scholars and architects and civil engineers to stagger away from Kyo-Tokai, quaking with awe and uncertainty.

I have no skill for sketching. My words must suffice. I will try to make of them something sensible.

Corma, metropolitan queen of Amidon's western coast, began as a river town and grew, swelling toward the sea as it learned how to build up its shoreline with tow-heads of refuse, paving a landscape above it. Now, the city hugs the seashore as if it had always done so, with very little of it recalling its earlier days miles back from the tides and their erosive touch. Westgate Bridge serves as its only reminder. That easternmost neighborhood's baffling name has never been changed.

The building materials of Nippon are not suited to the Amidonian style. Thus, its urban spaces do not spread vertically but laterally. Yew and bamboo and oiled paper, with the blessing of mortar and brick reserved only for structures that must be permanent—the Emperor's palace; the Protectorate's ministries; the Grand Library and its surrounding campus; the Tower of Water.

As we rode into Kyo-Tokai, I had the decided impression of driving deeper and deeper into the core of an onion. The city began as a little sphere of humanity, laced with roads winding aimlessly among its squat boroughs. After the coming of the Logicians and the argument for Unity, the Nipponese saw the wisdom of taming their islands, taking them back from the kitsune and kappa and other genetic oddities that thrived in its isolated spaces. The cities expanded in smooth circles, each layer spoked to the original, ambling center, until those cities, like drops of oil, touched and flowed into one.

I've heard that only three thousand square miles in total of Nippon are not, by law or custom, part of this mega-metropolis today. It seemed an absurd claim but I know now it must be true. Everywhere, humanity presses against itself. The women are most selective about bearing children, for the island can only support so many, and each couple is assigned the duty to bear either son or daughter, as the census of a given period dictates. The orphans of Nippon are more populous in the streets of Indine across the narrow sea than the Indine peoples' own progeny. Once, the Nipponese put those surplus births onto rafts of bamboo and sent them down rivers to the sea, where luck and the tide would bear them to their mainland neighbors. Now, they have the resources to carry on the practice, but with properly kitted galleons.

And so, the Grand Library's campus, without that familiar concentric, ordered style boasted by the rest of Kyo-Tokai, resembles the Emperor's palace more than the city surrounding it. The Logicians scoured the Asiatic continent for its wisdom and, after the treaty that brought Nippon under the Protectorate, enshrined it here, in their nearest expansionist stronghold. Since then, the Nipponese have made their own seminaries and given their own Reverend Doctors their orders. They do as their Logician allies taught them, finding scholarship wherever it shelters and bringing it back to their redoubts. The Grand Library is usually described as more than six million volumes in size. I see now that figure is far too humble. It occupies a compound so vast, three Westgate

Bridges might be settled into it comfortably. And it is a building of three stories. Three! I should hardly be impressed, but in less than a day the image of an urban flatland has so burned itself into my eyes, it takes very little to seem monstrously tall.

But my welcome dinner. I have forgotten the direction of my musings, and time is quickly waning.

The Grand Librarian, Madame Curator, is assisted by one Madame Kurowa, a woman I would be well advised not to—[excerpt ends here with a torn page]

22.

Rowena Downshire glared at the golden monkey perched in the sitting room window. It wasn't a proper monkey, of course. She'd been in Kyo-Tokai and inside the walls of the Grand Library's apartments long enough to know, except for the cherry trees and ginkgoes lining the city's avenues, very little around her was actually *real*. The megacity's riverway, cut at right angles through the metropolis that never seemed to end, was controlled by sewer tributaries and a pumping system that could reverse its flow completely in less than an hour. She knew because the rooming keep of the Grand Library was tall enough at three stories, she could see the rest of the city spread out like a bamboo mat beyond her window. The river current changed nine times a day, Madame Kurowa had said—once every two hours and forty minutes. It kept the waters cleaner and allowed the Fabricated poling barges up and down its length to keep to a schedule suited to commerce.

Rowena hadn't thought she would be left alone in the suite of rooms set aside for the Corma Company long enough to actually keep time by the river-shifts.

"Why aren't they back yet?" Rowena snapped at the monkey.

Its golden mane rippled, copper plates shifting as if it had shrugged.

"It's been *ages*," she continued, pacing.

There wasn't much else to do. Chalmers and the Old Bear and Master Meteron had left to introduce themselves to the Grand Librarian, escorted by Madame Kurowa, hours earlier. One current change complete, and another just cycling up, and still not a word from them.

At first, Rowena didn't mind being left out. Libraries were new to her. She wasn't altogether sure she could pass herself off as a secretary to Doctor Chalmers, but she did know she could unpack their luggage and settle up their rooms. That would seem secretarial. Besides, it would give her a chance to prowl about a little, checking the room for nooks and crannies. If the Grand Library were half as important as it was made out to be, she was certain every room would be full of little hatches and tunnels and hidden nooks, a whole ancient maze, like Master Meteron's secret study off his penthouse dining room writ impossibly large.

Well. Maybe her secret passages theory was right, but so far, Rowena'd found no sign of it. What she did see very clearly was the mechanical golden monkey, with its flourishing mane and faceted quartz eyes. It wasn't there as a decoration. It was most definitely watching her.

Rowena stopped pacing right in front of it. She crouched down, heels to haunches, and peered into the fabricated ape's shining face.

"I'll bet," she said, "if I opened you up you'd be just full of phono-corder bits, wouldn't you? Lucky for you I don't know how."

Unless . . .

Leyah, can you show me?

The sense of her lingered as it always did, if Rowena thought about the ghost long enough to turn a vague inkling into a clear picture. Just over her left shoulder, just behind her—both in and out of sight.

I'm not sure that's wise, the dead woman answered.

Is it booby-trapped? Gonna take off my hand or blow up in my face? Instantly, Rowena winced at her own crassness. The vision of Leyah in her last moments sprang up painfully clear—blast wounds, a mangled body. *Sorry, I didn't mean—*

I think it's safe physically. I'm not sure it's wise practically.

Rowena frowned. *Because there isn't a recording device in there?*

Because there almost certainly is one. Dismantling it won't prove any-thing but your willingness to destroy the Library's property. They would only find other ways of putting Fabricated around you and make them more subtle—or so ubiquitous you'd have no hope of picking out the real spies among them. It's better to keep their surveillance out in the open, not drive it underground.

"Balls," Rowena spat.

She glowered at the monkey, still placidly blinking, and decided to confine further comments to her inner monologue.

Why are they taking so long, Leyah?

No answer for a long time. Too long a time.

Rowena stood—a little too quickly, for the mechanical monkey leaned back to avoid her and nearly lost its balance. One arm pinwheeled and the other clutched at the painted sill. After a hissing of fast-spinning gyros hidden somewhere in its glinting body, it was safely settled again. Spy or no, it was a remarkable creation.

And Rowena hated it.

The creature's faceted eyes spun, refocusing on her.

"Oops," she said.

The Fabricated's head tilted, curious. If it noticed Rowena take a step back toward the changing screen near the window, or had an inkling of what her stepping into it would mean, there was no telling. It did have time enough to look up as the shadow of the toppled screen descended, landing on it with a terrific crack.

The Fabricated monkey fell, spinning ass-over-teakettle down three stories to slam into a tiled awning over one of the building's many entrances.

"Think it survived that?" Rowena wondered aloud.

Not in one piece. That was good thinking.

"Well, thinking's about all I'm in a position to do now, innit?"

For the hundredth time, Rowena scanned the sitting room, then paced to each of its adjoining sleeping chambers and its shared bathroom. The bathroom was a vast affair with drains set all over the floors and tiles running up half the height of the walls, little alcoves for sitting stationed above four separate bathing pools that seemed always full and always set to a very specific temperature. The faucets were shaped like serpents; the tiles shone red and gold. It smelled of something piney or woodsy or, really, she didn't know what, and it was, all of a sudden, more than Rowena could take.

"I'm leaving," she announced.

Leyah's presence loomed nearer. *Where?*

"Anywhere. This building's big, and it's not even the Library proper. Nobody told me I have to stay here forever, so I won't. I'm going."

Rowena strode through the antechamber screen to the solid apartment door, wrestling it open with a rather undignified effort. Someone with an eye for design and not much for physics had put the doorknob at its center. While that lion-faced bit of hardware was nice to look at, it didn't offer much in the way of leverage.

If introductions are taking this long, things aren't as simple as taking up your rooms and being given a pass into the stacks.

Rowena didn't know what "the stacks" were, but supposed they had something to do with library-ish things. Things not being simple, too, was less than a surprise. When was the last time anything had been simple? Madame Kurowa spent nearly the whole debarkation from the anchor yards explaining honorific addresses, appropriate and inappropriate greetings, and reviewing with Rowena the various pieces of the visiting scholar robes she would be given to wear upon arrival. *Everything* was complicated.

Leaving these rooms, however, was not.

The door thudded behind Rowena, leaving her in a wide hall lit by alchemical bulbs gleaming from the mouths of dragons and the eyes of fierce birds. It would be dusk soon, though this space showed no sign of it. There were few windows on this floor, and none at all in the halls linking one suite of rooms to the next. But there was a numbering system beside the suite doors to help her find her way out of the residential building, at least, and across its open-walled, tiled-roofed skyway to the Library proper.

The air of that skyway was as different from the residential quarters as an open market was from a mausoleum. It buzzed with the back-and-forth traffic of passing pages, none of whom seemed much older than Rowena herself. Each carried books or pushed carts or juggled tubes that looked like fat scroll sleeves, capped at either end in brass. From time to time, the pages carrying the tubes would feed them into chutes set under signs painted with a cuneiform Rowena couldn't begin to parse.

A pneumatic message system, Leyah murmured in the back of Rowena's mind. *I had wondered what they did here, without a vox network.*

Rowena angled and sidestepped and turned to keep from clipping the many passers-by. Most seemed headed away from the Grand Library's third-floor entrance at the skyway's terminus. Was the Library closing already? Doubtful. While she'd never had much use for written words until recently, Rowena had passed by enough bookshops and library extensions in Corma to know most stayed open well after dark. Maybe these pages were all messengers or couriers with packages due to staff across the campus at the same time. They kept their heads down, paying no attention whatever to the strange girl in her stranger clothes weaving among them. Intent. Purposeful. Only her mother's debts and Ivor's hawthorn had kept Rowena sharp on the job. What was motivating them to work so hard?

The skyway opened onto the Library's vestibule, an arched entrance flanked by elaborate cranes whose eyes were too lively to be mere statuary. Rowena straightened and strode past them. And all of a sudden, there she was, standing at the top of a staircase, looking down at something all too familiar.

"Holy Fucking Reason," she gasped.

Rowena had traveled a third of the way round the globe, been attacked by her own lanyani crew, been bartered over as a spare sneak thief in a campaigner's watering hole, and enrolled in a mercenary company to infiltrate the secret holdings of the Grand Library, only to find that—somehow—she had already been there once before. In a manner of speaking. It was a place she had once been certain she could never return to.

Shows what you know, Rowena Downshire, she thought.

The shelves of the Grand Library extended outward from a cluster of study desks like the spokes of a wheel, or petals from a flower's heart. The Library floor's black-and-white tiles shone stark and clean, though they remained stubbornly in place, no coal-black winds hurling them up, no vortex below sucking them down. Slowly, gingerly, Rowena slid her boot forward and placed it on the first stairstep.

It held.

Rowena leaned into the balustrade. A slice of her reflection stared up, warped, from its cherrywood finish.

Leyah? Rowena almost forgot to think the words rather than speak them. *It's . . . the same. It's exactly like the Old Bear's memory. Isn't it?*

It is.

Has he been here before?

The response came immediately, emphatically. *Nippon, yes, but not the Grand Library.*

Not even on a job? Maybe one of his jobs from before he met you, one of the ones with Ivor?

No, I'm sure of it. They— A pause. *They would never have let him. The Nipponese don't care much for Leonine people, and the EC wouldn't grant him entry without him having completed at least a year of seminary.*

Moments before, the question of motivation troubled Rowena. Why the Library staff worked so very hard might be a question more about her ignorance than their actions. But motivations mattered, and seeing this space, so jarringly foreign and familiar at once, threw that fact into stark relief. Why had she traveled halfway across the world? Because the Old Bear and Master Meteron took a job from Chalmers and his patrons. Fine. But why had *they* done it? To spare the Nine and save the world? It seemed too vast, too melodramatic to be real. There had to be something real, something specific and intimate driving them. She needed them to have something driving them, because if they didn't—what was *she* doing here? What was she following them for?

Rowena looked out over the floor of the Grand Library—at the tiers of balconies surrounding it, and their many doors to many rooms—and realized that whatever her companions' motivation for coming had been, she had just found hers. There was a mystery inside Erasmus Pardon. She meant to search it out.

Rowena trotted down the staircase. Leyah's specter followed close behind, or beside, or within her. Wherever it was she fitted herself.

What are you going to do?

Rowena smiled. *What we came for. Research.*

23

As a small boy, Anselm Meteron had suffered from a prodigious and problematic lack of fear. He had been talented enough to do well at most tasks with little tutelage, arrogant enough to pretend at talent where he lacked it, and absolutely unconcerned about being called out for his behavior on either account. A Bishop's child, he lived well insulated from the concerns which taught other children to tread lightly. Fortunately, Allister Meteron had not been ignorant of his son's unearned courage. For the boy's sake, and for the sake of his own reputation, he had the good sense to ensure that there would be at least a few things the boy would grow to fear.

Lectures, for one. Allister's were of the highest caliber, sparing no syllable for praise that could profitably be applied to correction. Hand-copying, too, was designed for young Anselm's particular torment. By the age of six, he had cultivated remarkably precise handwriting and a vocabulary sufficient to serve as a stenographer at most of his father's meetings. His missing finger had long since undone that careful script, but Anselm's close-trained attention to detail remained.

Last but never least, the young Anselm had learned to fear old women. Those tedious meetings whose note-taking turned his hand into a cramped claw always involved at least one woman older than the Ecclesiastical Commission's geological findings could possibly account for.

The Grand Librarian of Nippon was just such a woman—small and frail, so bent in upon herself, she was painful to behold. Anselm kept his place at the rear of the audience chamber and let Chalmers do the talking. He examined his manicure with an attention it assuredly did not warrant, barely curbing the urge to crack his nine fingers before settling on rubbing the stump of his missing digit raw, instead. The Old Bear answered when spoken to, brief as always, sliding grudgingly into the position of spokesman for the bodyguards the Reverend Doctor Chalmers had brought to accompany him. Anselm merely waited, feet crossed on a sitting cushion, and did his best not to think how he was sure to fall on his face as soon as he stood up, given how long he'd been sitting on his arse doing not a blessed thing, his legs going numb.

God's balls.

The audience, Chalmers had assured them, could not possibly take more than an hour.

After the first hour, Anselm no longer cared if regular consultation of his chronometer looked in poor taste. Poor taste might just liberate him from the room full of paper screens and bamboo mats and sitting cushions and stark, angular paintings of herons or storks or some other leggy goddamned birds. Through the oiled paper walls of the surprisingly airy room (wasn't it a custom to keep musty old people shut away from draughts? Perhaps those who vied to be the Grand Librarian's successor hoped to off the old biddy with a stiff wind) he could spy the progress of the setting sun, blurring pink along the wooden frames of the open windows. Hours later, and still they were at it.

Madame Kurowa kneeled beside the ornate wheelchair in which the matron Librarian rested, reading from a list of prepared questions and echoing queries the bundle of sticks beside her murmured into her ear. The interview had begun with Chalmers's formal introductions, then his explanation of how he had come to work with Nora Pierce on a research project whose materials were not rightly theirs (a little threadbare, Anselm had thought, but at least delivered without the Reverend's usual stammering). And finally, the presentation of the "finished" book.

That really *should* have been all. But these weren't just EC librarians. These were Nipponese librarians: arch-Logicians, lifelong scholars, and they had *questions*. Tracing back from the group's arrival in Kyo-Tokai to where each had been born and educated, the interview embodied the word "exhaustive" in all its possible applications. A small girl sat in a corner with a broad wooden desk across her knees, typing at a machine that reeled out yards of transcription. Anselm might have felt a pang of sympathetic camaraderie, if the typing machine didn't make her note-taking so damnably much easier than his had been, years before. Still, he did not envy her rolling up the notes and wrestling them down the hall, as they seemed on course to outweigh her before the interview was done.

The whole affair was a ridiculous, useless waste of time, unworthy of these supposedly Logical scholars. Only two things of interest had come of it. First, the knowledge that the self-writing texts—the exhausted copies and, until Nora Pierce's intervention, the "live" one—were kept in a section of the Grand Library called the Amanuensis library. Second, Anselm had finally learned the names of all five of the Old Bear's sisters. Until today, he had been sure there were only four . . .

A tap on Anselm's shoulder broke his reverie.

Phillip Chalmers smiled awkwardly at him. Anselm rose, less wobbly than he had feared, while the Old Bear accepted a hand up from Madame Kurowa, echoing her bow.

"Thank you once again, Madames," Chalmers said, sketching his own overhasty bow that put him at momentary risk of tumbling sideways into Anselm. He put up a hand to ward the Doctor off, scowling. "We are grateful for your assistance in my work."

The old woman muttered something unintelligible, her sunken cheeks wobbling. Madame Kurowa nodded at her, as if absorbing something for translation.

"It is our duty to Reason and the Grand Experiment," she said, after a pause. "We find your applications acceptable and welcome you to make use of these grounds and all of the standard collections at your leisure."

Chalmers blinked. "The . . . standard collections?"

Kurowa's voice crackled with frost. "Madame Curator requires time to consider your application to access the Amanuensis library." She gestured to the red-bound book resting on the low table before her mistress's wheelchair. "We hope you understand."

"We understand," the Old Bear said, riding over some objection Chalmers had been about to voice, "that we have been separated from our baggage, our rooms, and our secretary for many hours. Please inform us of your decision when it is made."

The Old Bear turned himself and the Reverend Doctor toward the door, Anselm ready to fall in behind.

A sound came from the Curator. Madame Kurowa raised a hand.

"Wait, please."

All three turned back and saw the younger woman leaning close to the ancient Librarian, ear pressed almost to her lips. She nodded, glanced up. Her gaze fell on Anselm.

"Master Meteron." Madame Kurowa gestured to the cushion opposite the Grand Librarian's wheelchair, only the squat tea table and formerly stolen book between them. "Please stay. Madame Curator wishes a private audience."

Chalmers's eyebrows lifted, punctuating his unspoken question. *Is this a problem?*

Anselm shrugged, one shouldered.

He frowned as Madame Kurowa ushered his companions through the panel door and past the women standing sentry in the hall. The page with her scrivening machine and yards of printing shuffled after, all her burdens packed neatly on a cart, and slid the screen shut behind her.

From a face like crazed pottery, the Grand Librarian of Nippon's shockingly bright eyes studied Anselm.

"I am afraid I speak very little Nipponese," he began, speaking slowly but not with excessive volume. He had met enough grand-dams and graybeards to understand they preferred not to be treated as if they were half-deaf. They invariably *were*, of course. But they liked to correct others for showing behaviors wanting in thoughtfulness rather than be assumed as wanting in capacity.

The old woman's head tilted, birdlike. She spoke in a voice a little like a singing bowl, high and sonorous and clean. "It is well that I speak a good deal of Amidonian, then. Is it not your custom to sit in the presence of a lady, Master Meteron?"

"If I am so invited, Madame Curator."

A sniff. The invitation, he noted, did not materialize.

Anselm folded his hands behind his back. He trapped his right thumb in his fist to keep it from worrying at his stump any further. It would not do come away from this interview with his hand bloodied.

"I am here at your pleasure," he announced, a little stiffly. "What do you wish me for?"

"You look very much like your father," Madame Curator mused. "Or like he did forty years ago. We met at the Decadal Conference in Aerion, you know. I was there when he interrupted Doctor Bennington's thesis on the Vautneks. Her proposal to revise their number to nine." Her creased face spread into an almost wicked grin. "And you were there, too, weren't you? With your sister."

Had he been there? Anselm had no idea. "I'd have been five years old at best, Madame. I am afraid I do not recall our meeting."

She nodded obligingly. "I suppose you wouldn't. I was much younger then. Only seventy-one."

Anselm's stomach lurched. *One hundred eleven years old, this creature.* He was far too invested in himself not to desire as long a life as he could get, but to envision himself pushed to such a straining limit—to the last instant between twitches of the second hand? Horrific. If he was to die an old man in bed, he wished it to be after making love to a succession of scandalous women, the last of whom would drop an anvil squarely on his head.

The sliding door behind the Curator's wheelchair opened, admitting a startlingly well-coiffed and ribboned serving girl, her shuffling, slippered feet just peeking from the satin hems of her robes. She crouched to set down a tea tray and bow wordlessly away. It took a moment's reflection for Anselm to parse what made her movements so odd.

Her slow, deep bow. A little judder as she straightened. He waited for the screen to close again.

"How many of the Fabricated in the Library are fashioned after humans, Madame?"

"All those made for tending kitchens and bedchambers. We use the animal Fabricated for messages and heavy lifting and such. Every tool suited to its task."

Anselm fixed the old woman with a crooked smile. She laughed, a sharp-edged cackle that ground between his bones.

"I suppose you wish to know what task I have for you? What manner of tool I mean to make of you?"

"I've already answered all your questions. There must be something else you want."

A gnarled finger *tsked* midair. "Your *colleagues* answered the questions. You were most sullen during our conference."

"I hope you can forgive me if I found the length of the questioning absurd."

"I am glad you have the mettle to say as much. It was meant to be so. Visitors must be examined carefully. Ideally, past the point of reasonable endurance." Madame Curator waved her finger, no longer scolding, toward the tea service. "Pour."

Anselm knelt beside the table and prepared two cups. The tea was a striking green, its surface dense and oily. He found himself obliged to put Madame Curator's cup precisely in the bowl of her hands to keep from spilling.

"It seems a little counter to a library's purpose, attempting to deter visitors," he said.

The Curator snorted. "Please, Master Meteron. Do not play coy with me. There was never any question of our allowing you into the main collections of the Library. But we needed to know more about what brought you here—more than Doctor Chalmers's thin excuses. So tell me." She studied him over the rim of her raised cup. "Why *are* you here?"

Anselm set his cup down. He examined its depths, then shrugged, one-shouldered. "Someone I loved died learning His Grace wanted that book. Her death gave us the means to find it, and our reason to come here."

"Ah. You long to make the loss worth something."

Anselm's jaw tightened. He measured his words, clipping them to size. "Nothing will make it worth it. But I intend to make sure the Bishop never gets what he wants."

"A pity." She reached out a trembling hand, no hope of replacing her cup on the table without aid. Anselm took it gingerly and set it as far from his as the table allowed, still examining its color untrustingly.

"You'd prefer my father and I were on good terms?"

The old woman gestured at the spent book. "Reverend Chalmers has apologized for his role in Reverend Pierce's crime. But the silence from your quarter has been most astounding, given that it was your father who employed Pierce as his agent."

Anselm did not try to keep the steel from his tone. "I am not in the habit of apologizing for Allister Meteron's machinations. It would spare me precious little time for anything else."

"I suppose His Grace could say the same in regard to you."

"Very likely he does."

"You are very much the man I had hoped you to be, young Master Meteron."

"I am pleased to be pleasing. I am somewhat less pleased to be travel-worn and unrested. Do you have anything particular requiring my attention, or may I recover myself with my companions?"

"The thing which requires your attention, I do not have, Master Meteron. That is precisely why I require you."

Years working as a campaigner and a lifetime as a gambler had taught Anselm a great deal about how to rule his features. He was by careful practice a lake of glass, rippled now and again by a pebble-drop of irony or scorn. He felt a smile twisting his lips into a wicked line, all the same.

"God's balls. You have a job for us."

"No, young man. I have a job for *you*."

Anselm sat back on his heels. "I'm afraid I'm already bound under contract, Madame. It forbids my taking work not directly connected to the interests for which I was initially hired."

"Well. Perhaps leaving this room will help you appreciate the importance of this opportunity, after all."

The old woman's claw-like hands reached to the braking levers of her wheelchair. She gestured imperiously toward the sliding door at her back. "If you would be so kind, Master Meteron. There is something I would like you to see."

"To the right here," the Grand Librarian said.

Anselm turned her chair around a corner, winding deeper into a hallway entered by way of a crank-operated lift burrowed into the building's ornate walls. The lift itself had required a key for the padlock holding its grated doors shut. A series of switches and dials the old woman operated from her chair selected the floor, and the hallway had begun behind a wall panel disguised to look like a bas-relief.

It was not the most labyrinthine path to a secret room Anselm had seen, but it was well secured and well guarded. He had rolled her past four guards stationed at various points along the way, and none seemed to take Anselm's presence with the Curator as promise enough that he wasn't worth a long, measuring stare.

"You're familiar with the term 'amanuensis,' of course," the Curator said.

"I was my father's amanuensis. I scribed for him through my whole childhood. In this case, it's a clever name for the place where you keep all the old books."

She sniffed. "We are less interested in being clever than being precise."

The hallway ended in a broad, oval-shaped door with an elaborate dragon's-head knob and locking panel at its center. The Curator nodded her white head toward it.

"Go on. Open it."

Anselm paused, setting the brakes on her chair. The Curator's pinprick gaze followed him around from the woman's side to the space between her seated legs and the door.

He reached for the door handle. Only a faint tremor under his hand warned him to pull back.

A high, ringing sound pierced the air. Anselm stared at the needles protruding from the fixture's fangs. The tips, he realized as he bent to squint at them carefully, were baited with tiny beads of hardened rubber.

He raised an eyebrow at her. "Not very welcoming."

The Curator's cracked pottery smile showed a flash of gum and her own monstrous teeth. "Don't be fussy. I asked Madame Kurowa to take the sting off, for the sake of this demonstration. You might, however, wish to wait on this side of the threshold after I open the door. There are a few more nasty things waiting once you pass through."

Anselm unlocked the woman's wheels and moved her close enough to let her nudge the door open. It gave before her weak touch with remarkable ease, the door sighing inward.

The room beyond bore the same ovoid shape, but its walls were tiered three stages high with shelves and its center sliced back and forth with long rows of books held under glass, their spines stamped in foil.

A faint haze of dust drifted through the room's too-still air, illuminated by pale moonlight pouring down from a skylight high above.

"God's balls," Anselm murmured.

"A most useful phrase," the Curator answered. "I imagine it must see a good deal of use in your mouth, young master."

One quick inventory of a shelf only three yards from the door told Anselm there were at least a thousand volumes in this room—likely many more.

"Are they all spent volumes from His collection?" he said.

"Nearly all. A few are indices with historical context for the Library and the Unity during periods corresponding to the listed dates. And many of those," she gestured toward the shelves at ground level, "are blank. Volumes waiting to take up the burden of the record, when the most recent tome is spent."

Volumes that will never see their proper use, Anselm thought.

He looked down at the woman, striving to keep his voice even. "If you don't intend to permit us access to the Amanuensis library, why take me here at all?"

"To make a point, of course," the old woman snapped. "There are traps set just inside the doorway. Security systems installed around the skylight. Even Fabricated designed to prowl the air shafts for vermin— including pests of unusually human proportions. And all that still says nothing of the keys, the guards, the proper code for operating the lift, which is changed at regular intervals. I have not given your company permission to enter this place. But I am not so great a fool as to imagine you would not try to enter unbidden."

Anselm scanned the room, nodding. "Breaking and entering here would be a death trap."

"Most assuredly. I thought you might prefer another means of earning your entry."

"I'm listening."

The Curator smiled. "There's someone whose research could prove quite problematic to the security of the Amanuensis library. I would like you to find them. I imagine you might be quite interested in them for reasons of your own, as well."

"Quite interested in *them?*" Anselm mused.

"Them."

"Some*one* whose research would be problematic?"

"Indeed."

Anselm quirked an eyebrow. "Just how problematic?"

"Enough," the old woman said, "that I must ask for you to do something your father would find most compromising to his reputation. Something I expect you are uniquely qualified to do."

Slowly, a smile sharp as a knife's edge sliced at the corner of Anselm's mouth. "We've been away from your chambers for some time, Madame. I imagine you'd like to be restored to your comfort."

"Indeed."

"Can your Fabricated manage delivering a supper tray?"

"They are more than capable of such things."

Anselm took hold of the Grand Librarian's wheelchair, unlocking its wheels once again, and turned her with the same courtly grace he might apply in a waltz. "I think we'll need time to discuss your proposal. I intend to give it my most careful attention."

She looked up at him, her wizened eyes shining wickedly. "I'm happy to find you so reasonable."

"Oh, I assure you, reasonableness is only one of my many virtues."

24.

Never one to complain overmuch, Erasmus Pardon found he had an ever-growing list of objections to his first day in the Grand Library of Nippon, and nowhere to apply his concerns. Nowhere except his subconscious, which had never been as quiet as other men's. Of late, it had proven particularly restless. And rude.

You don't remember it at all, do you? Rare challenged as he limped down the marble staircase leading to the Grand Library's main floor.

He missed Leyah. She had been an echo, a vague haunting, a feeling of love and regret knotted together. She was a hurt too tender to be touched. But the pain of her reminded him his heart had once had a purpose. He had held the memory of her more than she had held the reality of him. When at last he let her go, something altogether different slipped into the space left behind.

Rare was a wound tearing itself open, one stitch at a time. She strode alongside him, often before him, peeling away his attention in layers. She perched in the background of conversations with a Cheshire smile. Some days were worse than others. Days like today verged on intolerable.

Don't remember what? he thought back to Rare, scanning the long spokes of library shelves for a dark-haired girl in jodhpurs and walking boots. Chalmers hadn't wanted to leave the apartment suite once they'd escaped Madames Curator and Kurowa. Nervous and disconsolate about the interview, he'd thrown himself into rearranging all Rowena's unpacking, making little visible improvement in the order of his temporary study, but succeeding handsomely at redistributing the packing shavings otherwise confined to the crates. Erasmus hadn't liked the look of the broken Fabricated lying stories below the sitting room window in a puddle of moonlight. Two other, larger Fabricated whirred and clacked around it, sweeping up its ruins with funereal solemnity.

Rowena was nowhere to be found. A supper trolley waited in the hall, attended by a mute, glass-eyed Fabricated fashioned to resemble a young woman, its features improbably lush and curves anatomically dubious. The untouched food troubled Erasmus far more than the eerie servant. He didn't think Rowena would enjoy Nipponese cuisine, being unused to its elaborate preparations, sharp tastes, and unexpected textures—but it was still food, and the girl had a ferocious appetite.

He'd left the Reverend Doctor behind, trusting the unpacking to keep him out of trouble. Anselm would return soon enough. Rowena, on the other hand—

This place is exactly like your mind, Rare insisted, her exasperated impertinence clutching at Erasmus's divided attention. *Surely you can see that.*

He responded with the mental equivalent of a grunt. *Libraries are a highly generic landscape.*

He spied a girl rounding a shelf halfway across the reference floor, then noticed her kimono and slippered feet and muttered a curse.

Rare's revenant crouched before him, knocking soundless knuckles against the checkered floor. The tile beneath her was the first in a ring of embossed stone forming an ellipse up and down the wheel-hub floor. Even upside down, he recognized its mark, distinct from the others in the arcs to either side.

Highly generic? Rare's brilliant blue eyes flicked toward Erasmus's right sleeve, half rolled, the deep, black lines of a tattoo matching the mark on the floor nearly lost against his dark skin. *Tell me another one, Father.* She stood, watching him pass her by, cane punctuating his steps. *For all intents and purposes, I live here, you know.*

He knew all too well.

There's no reason not to explain yourself to me, Rare shouted, rising to follow him. Her voice held no echo in the Library's vast space, for it was all contained in his mind. On campaign, he'd mastered the awkward trick of parallel processing snatches of conversations in his mind and his awareness of the outside world, but Rare's presence—even when she chose to conceal it—was as distracting as a dull roar in his ears. Perhaps he would adapt to it, in time. But she seemed uninterested in making that adjustment any easier or more likely.

What is there to explain? he thought back. Two clerks pushed carts of books awaiting reshelving past him, moving down the spokes of shelving with a precision eerily like the library's automatons.

Rare cut in front of him, her timing fortunate. It would have looked to an outsider as if he had stopped to avoid a clash with one of the passing clerks. He knew it was possible to step through her entirely—or for her to pass through him—but it was too much a reminder of the absence at the core of her presence. He scowled at her, hoping it would appear to be at his own cantankerous musings.

You could explain the mark on your arm, Rare demanded. *The similarity between this Library and the innermost landscape of your bloody mind, perhaps? And while we're at it, a host of other things you've never spoken of. What you did before campaigning with mother, or even with Ivor. How you do the things you do. Where you came from.* Any *of it.*

His daughter's face had begun as a storm cloud. Now it was something else, electric with tension and about to break.

You never let me in, she seethed. And then, with a bitter bark, she looked all around. *And now, even on the inside, I can't find my way through to you.*

Her gaze fell on something, then, and she snorted disgust. *And I suppose I'll have to keep waiting.*

Erasmus saw Rowena jogging down another spoke of shelving, turning her shoulders aside to trot narrowly past a clerk carrying an armload of books.

"Bear! Do you recognize it? Isn't it amazing?" she cried, a few decibels louder than any sensible library patron ought to have done.

Rare raised an eyebrow. *Not so dim after all, is she?*

Quiet.

Erasmus stayed the girl with a hand on her shoulder, drawing her up short of some delighted gesture.

"A secretary," he chided, "knows better than to run and shout in a library."

Rowena rolled her eyes, but didn't protest. "But d'you recognize it?"

"Most of what occurred after my fall from the Cathedral is lost to me," he murmured. It was, at least, partly true.

"Talking to the Grand Somebodyorother go well?"

"It went long; whether well remains to be seen."

"But we've got access to the old volumes? The what-do-they-call-thems?"

"The Amanuensis library. And no."

Rowena leaned close, barely suppressing a wicked smile. "When's that sort of thing stopped us before, eh?"

"Come along, girl. There's supper to be had and planning to be done. And Anselm will have something new to share with us, I suspect."

"Why's that?"

"He's still meeting with Madame Curator. He wouldn't have lingered this long without very good reason."

"*Everything*," the Reverend Doctor Chalmers despaired, "is a catastrophe, Miss Downshire. How am I supposed to find anything in this mess?"

He stood at the center of the room he'd chosen with considerable deliberation and a triumphant collapse of baggage hours before. The various bioluminescent plants—drapey ivies bred by the Logicians for their heatless, flameless illumination, well suited to buildings full of paper and bamboo—glowed from their sisal-woven cradles, lending the chamber a warm, ruddy glow. Rowena glowered at him with a gravity well beyond what her small body should have been able to generate. The Alchemist stood behind her. Chalmers couldn't help but suspect the pipe in his teeth masked a subtle amusement.

"Well, *maybe*," the girl countered, "you could have started with unpacking your *own* stupid things and you wouldn't have this problem."

Chalmers had intended his response to sound offended. It did, insofar as any half-coherent splutter might. "You are my *secretary*!"

"Exactly!" Rowena ticked her response off, finger by finger. "Which means I en't your maid, your seamstress, your laundress, your stevedore, your footman, or your mother. 'Sides, things *are* organized."

"Organized! How?"

"Alphabetically."

"*Alphabetically*," Chalmers echoed flatly.

"Alphabetically-*ish*."

Chalmers snatched two books set on a shelf near a sidetable. "The Z's are *before* the A's on this shelf! What kind of alphabetizing is that?"

Rowena's mouth set in a hard line. "It's not by *author*. It's by *topic*."

"*You don't know what these books are about!*"

"But I could read *most* of the titles!"

Chalmers rounded on the old man, who by that moment was indeed sporting an ill-concealed smile. "Alphabetical by *topic*. Honestly, who does that?"

"I do that," Rowena snapped. "Now the supper trays have been sent up, and I'm starving, even if it all smells like pickled dress stockings."

Chalmers did his best not to revisit the topic of his portable study unboxed into chaos. (It would appear Rowena had alphabetized his possessions down to his suit jackets, her only defense being a certain fondness for the alphabet, now that she was learning to read properly.) He ate with chopsticks and thin rice pancakes as his tools, gathering up shreds of pickled cabbage and rolls of dense, raw fish and spicy condiments wrapped in dried seaweed. The native cuisine of Koryu, the mainland arm of the Lemarckian Protectorate, where Chalmers first learned the coordination required to eat in such a manner, bore many similarities to that of Nippon. He even quite liked their various dishes of whipped egg in hot rice porridge. Rowena Downshire seemed markedly less at ease with the food, more poking at it than eating it, despite her bold declarations.

Chalmers served up his view of the meeting with the Grand Librarian and digested Rowena's suspicions of the Fabricated tamarin in return. Her account gave him pause, even though he had anticipated their presence in Nippon would occasion some scrutiny. The hours-long entry interview would have confirmed that by itself, even without his campaigner companions' infectious paranoia creeping past his immunities. Chalmers's concern (one the Alchemist shared, if his more-than-typically-taut silence were any clue) was that the tamarin's destruction would only redouble efforts to spy on them more subtly.

Anselm Meteron did not appear until the supper tray was quite eaten through, the apartments transformed by the deployment of tatami mats, cushions, and a game table over which Rowena and the Alchemist moved tiny, porcelain chits down a system of lines and interstices Chalmers found altogether inscrutable. He looked up at Meteron's arrival from a sheaf of notes he'd been reorganizing, marveling at Rowena's ability to lay waste to an entire logical system.

Chalmers's mother had always liked cats, despite her husband and sons' rampant allergies. The young Reverend saw in Meteron's satisfied grin a look that would have fitted quite nicely between their impertinent whiskers.

"You've missed supper, I'm afraid," said Chalmers.

"I assure you, Doctor, I haven't. Glad to see no one was worried," Meteron replied, shutting the sliding paper screen to the anteroom behind him. The thief arranged himself on an ersatz settee of cushions, just in arm's reach of the game board. He waved a four-and-a-half-fingered hand toward one of its corners. "He's going to have you on your knees with a basic joseki in four turns, cricket."

Rowena pulled a sour face. "I'm doing fine. I've already got a bunch of his pieces."

"Suit yourself."

"What kept you?" the Alchemist murmured. He lifted a black piece and passed it down the line, pinning down another of the girl's chits. She flinched in surprise.

"Dinner. Plotting. Scheming. My irresistible charm."

Chalmers's ears pricked at that. "You've talked her into letting us access the Amanuensis library?"

Before Meteron could answer, the Alchemist tapped a finger by his ear and cast his gaze around the room generally. *Mind your tongues*, the look said. Meteron nodded.

"There's a little errand she'd like me to run before that decision is made."

Chalmers frowned. "What am I to do in the meantime?"

"There are those names of His Grace's likely supporters you could check against the Library's visitor logs. Cross-check their recent research interests. I very much doubt they've sat idle all this time. Some may have been nosing into matters of interest to us."

"En't we going to just, you know?" Rowena gestured in a manner that suggested maneuvering a lockpick.

Meteron sighed. "That, sadly, looks a good deal more impractical than we had hoped. I wouldn't hazard it."

Rowena opened her mouth to ask a question and stopped short, seeing two more of her pieces disappear in the cramped corner she'd found herself herded into. The Alchemist sat back on his cushion, looking satisfied.

"I'll be damned," she muttered at the board. "Well, if Doc can keep busy with all that, good for him. But what about Bear an' me?"

What about, the Alchemist countered mentally, *the security surrounding the Amanuensis library? Describe it.*

Chalmers's nerves had found nothing very soothing in Anselm's report up to that point. Being suddenly looped into a four-way congress of minds, where communication was equal parts words and the kinotrope slides of remembered images and sensations and impressions, did even less to comfort him, even if it guarded against unwanted ears. Meteron's careful enumeration of the hazards, human and otherwise, set between them and the cache of Vautnek texts turned his stomach in knots.

The Alchemist's usual scowl resumed its place. *It seems unlikely the books have always been guarded so well. Ignorance alone would have kept them secure.*

Anselm nodded. *The grease inside the lock still smelled fresh. I'd guess it's been on less than a month.*

So the Library knew we were coming, Chalmers said.

We knew that as soon as Madame Kurowa showed her face in Lemarcke.

The Rolands never hired her as a liaison. They wouldn't have done it without our leave.

Chalmers shivered off the uncanny connection and returned to speaking aloud. "And this, um. This *errand* you've been asked to do, to earn us entry?"

"You let that be my concern. I have a few ideas of how to be about it."

"But *what will Bear and I do*, if we can't get into the Aman-u-whatever library now?" Rowena pressed.

"The Old Bear will be free to work as he sees fit. There are several directions I would advise that to go, pending Doctor Chalmers's findings," Anselm replied. "As for you, cricket, Madame Kurowa wants your help."

"For what?" the Alchemist and the girl spoke in near-unison.

Meteron smiled. "Apparently, there's a project afoot which requires very small hands. I think it will prove quite worth our while for you to carry it out."

25.

Haadiyaa Gammon's early career taught her dealing with lanyani and aigamuxa was a catch-as-catch-can business. The Constabulary had never quite settled on what to teach its coppers about policing them, so Gammon had taught herself. Keep a set of iron cuffs near at hand; their hardness was important in the face of aigamuxa strength and lanyani twigging, often enough to forestall either creature's efforts to strain the metal and tear it apart. Always collar aiga with a partner—one officer walking ahead to guide the creature and one behind to keep it from reaching up to throttle the officer in front. Strip the bulb and safety guard from the end of your magnesium torch and you'll have an improvised (though short-lived) flame stick to hold lanyani at bay. When casing a nest of aiga or following one, keep downwind of them, coming no closer than your monocular's sight lines require.

It was that last piece of advice Haadiyaa Gammon presently relied upon. The previous two nights had been agonizingly still, all of Corma smothered under a sodden blanket of unmoving Eightmonth air. Now, a very light breeze eased down from the quayside, bringing a little relief and a great deal of stench. Gammon was a long time since her last day in Constabulary blues, but the memory of their wool and canvas drinking up perspiration made her glad to have forsworn them. The quayside wouldn't have been the only thing reeking in the heat. Tonight, she wore shirt and waistcoat and trousers only, happy about last month's decision to chop her chin-length hair back to something even tighter. No blocky bangs clinging to her face.

She lowered her monocular and wiped her forehead with the back of her hand. Her vision of the aigamuxa juvenile collapsed back to a distant gray lump the size of her thumb. She put the monocular back to her eye. The aiga's form leaped back to scale, a clear image of a child larger than most full-grown human men doing . . . what? Playing a game?

"What are you on about?" Gammon murmured.

From a vantage point at the mouth of an alley gagged with broken shipping crates and overturned dustbins, she had passed an hour watching what might have passed for a child's game. Without Sugar Maple's cryptic warnings, Gammon would have seen little peculiar in it. The aiga child crept along the quayside, so careful to look all around that it stayed curled in the pedestal position, feet resting on its shoulders and eye-heels forward, walking on its splayed hands. When it drew within a few yards of a rat or paused at the sound of one scuttling out of the shadows, it lunged forward, turning over in midair to land atop the pitiable thing. A few times, the creature had even plucked the squealing rat up, dangling it before a blinking foot and crying "meow meow" in singsong tones.

It was the last step of the game that held Gammon's interest, and concern.

The aigamuxa child pounced along, as it had done five times in the previous hour. Three of the five, it had captured its tiny prey. This leap improved the child's average.

"Meow meow," it chirruped, head tick-tocking back and forth in time with its chant. "Meow meow meow."

Then it plunged the rodent into the Indine rubber bag tied to the rope belt at its waist, slopping it about like a man mopping his plate with a heel of bread. The rat emerged powdered white and thoroughly displeased. The aiga child turned the vermin in its hand, murmured something in its growly native tongue, and then dropped it on the quay's rotting boardwalk. The stunned animal zigzagged away, sneezing.

Whatever that powder was, Gammon was certain it would come to no good. Why else would the aigamuxa wear a pair of clumsy rubber gauntlets on its otherwise nimble hands?

Nasrahiel had been no help solving the mystery, but not for lack of trying. His efforts to confront Rahielma had been frustrated by her days-long absence up at Crystal Hill—an absence that clearly worried him. It was bad enough she had gone inside, presumably to meet with her allies. She was long due to have come out again. Nasrahiel waited for her by occupying himself with Gammon's study of these aiga children. He had seen similar scenes in the trash yards outside butcheries. Sometimes the children played in little teams, giving the rat a name, a title, and a commission. All the names and duties were nonsense-play, things based on the cradle rhymes of his people. Gammon had seen aiga children loitering around the air galleon anchor yards, feeding pigeons and seagulls scraps of food dredged in their powder bags' contents. Human workers would tire of the children lurking about—or "tire of their stench," raising belaying pins and running them off with shouts and curses. But not before a sizable number of birds had dined on the aigamuxa's offerings.

Tonight, this young aiga ran low on whatever substance featured in its bag, the rat-dredging process taking longer, the animals emerging less smeared than before. Gammon didn't relish confronting the child, but felt waiting until it had dispensed the last of whatever proved noxious enough for it to have donned rubber gauntlets was in her best interest.

A crash like a load of copper piping dropped from a height made Gammon whirl around.

Nasrahiel had dropped from the fire escapes and gutterworks of the buildings flanking Gammon's alley ambuscade. His saw-teeth were bared in a wince of frustration, his body poised in a half-crouch. His metal legs had been the culprit, of course. Recovering locomotion had been easy compared to the challenge of recovering the raw, animal stealth he had once enjoyed.

Out on the quayside, the aigamuxa child sprang into the air, like an actual startled cat, and bolted for a rickety tower of freight pallets stacked pell-mell beside a cannery's warehouse doors, scaling them for the safety of the building's shadowed eaves.

"Blessed Reason," Gammon growled. "You've run him off."

"I will see to it," Nasrahiel snapped back. He turned his cyclopean head toward his target, his telescoping eye flicking in and out, its iris focusing, and leapt.

"No no no no no—no!" Gammon cried.

Futilely, stupidly, she reached for one of his passing metal heels, as if she had any chance of pulling him down or forestalling his leap out in the open over the trash that had hidden her. All she got for the effort was one of his legs slicing open her palm.

Gammon hissed and clamped her hand in her armpit. Already the cloth of her shirtwaist dampened with blood. Her monocular clattered to the cobbles, adding to the tumult, spoiling all her patient work. Nasrahiel had sprung well past her alley's rubbish barrier, rebounded off the face of a shuttered gazette shack, and left behind a clapboard door gouged an inch deep by his clawed mechanical feet. He turned midair, hooked a lamppost, and swung off it toward the warehouse roof, landing just in front of the fleeing aiga youth as it gained the copper-sheeted summit.

Whatever Gammon might think of Nasrahiel's gift for spoiling a stakeout, she could not fault his skill at apprehending suspects.

Gammon scrambled over and between the barricade of refuse barring her from the quayside. She reached the base of the building where Nasrahiel had intercepted the young aigamuxa and squinted up into the dark. Two forms moved, grappling. A sharp cry, quickly silenced, told her Nasrahiel had come away on the better end.

He dropped down to the boardwalk, the child creature bundled in his arms. It snapped blindly at the air, never quite finding a piece of its captor to latch onto. Nasrahiel hissed in his people's tongue, and the child slowly settled. Then he dropped it unceremoniously to the ground and whipped himself into the pedestal position before it. Nasrahiel's mechanical eye retracted, its iris spinning wide to take in as much detail as the quayside's alchemical lamps could illuminate.

The child cowered, eye-heels shut tight and toes curled down much like hands smothering some terrible sight. It hugged itself and barked a series of frantic noises.

"Speak Amidonian," Nasrahiel growled. "For the human."

Gammon stood over the child, keeping close enough to unsettle its sense of personal space, and far enough to avoid an impulsive swipe from one of its claws. She nodded an acknowledgement to Nasrahiel, though she knew his demand hadn't been made as a courtesy. He simply found translating tedious.

"You were dead," the aiga child answered. Its voice was ragged. It took a moment for Gammon to recognize the hitches and gulps between its words as sobs. Had she heard an aigamuxa cry before? She looked for signs of tears under its tight-clenched toes and eyelids. Too dark to see anything for certain now.

"I was," Nasrahiel replied. "What are you doing here alone? Where is your beva?"

Gammon looked to him, puzzled. "Beva?"

Nasrahiel grimaced, thinking. "It is . . . like a relative, but not always related by blood. Family. A child-keeper?"

"A nanny?"

"More complicated. The beva is like the chieftain of the young, and also like family."

They could try definitions all night and get nowhere. "Never mind," Gammon said. "Carry on."

"Beva Ramelunma is sick. This was her job; I took it because she was sick."

"What job is this?" Nasrahiel demanded.

The child's toes slowly curled open. It blinked. As if it were being pulled by a string, the young aiga moved into its pedestal position and stared, slack-mouthed, at Nasrahiel.

Whatever awestruck phrase it uttered meant nothing to Gammon. It was enough to earn a clipped answer in Amidonian from Nasrahiel.

"It is of no consequence. Tell us of this job. Since when does your tribe play with vermin for sport?"

The child's eyeless head shook vigorously. "Not sport. Work. The lanyani have paid us."

Gammon and Nasrahiel exchanged a wary look.

The youth's eye-heels blinked nervously and it shifted, hand to hand, cornered like the rats it had captured only minutes before. "Our chief-tain tells us that the tree-people have a plan to rid the city of Men, but they need the vermin to do it. The lanyani cannot do such work."

That much, Gammon suspected, would be true. Lanyani were as natural as the air they breathed, yet animals understood that a tree that walked and acted like men—a thing in which they were meant to nest, or hide, or from which they gathered food—was a fearsome beast, indeed. Lanyani frightened animals far more than the predatory aigamuxa. Prey creatures understood evading predators. It was a skill rooted in their bas-est instincts. But something that was both landscape and fellow-creature required a more subtle understanding than a beast could muster.

Gammon nodded to the young aigamuxa's rubber gauntlets. "Did your beva take sick from this poison?"

"I . . . don't know. But I know it's not a poison."

Gammon's copper instincts warred between putting distance between herself and the offending substance and claiming it for further investiga-tion. The battle must have been plain on her face, for Nasrahiel rumbled his impatience and plucked the sack from the child aiga's rope belt.

He held the bag at arm's length from his scarred face, his telescop-ing eye whirring in and out, iris adjusting, until it reached a perspective Nasrahiel found informative.

"This is some kind of . . . fungus?"

"Don't know." The young aiga's eye-heels had opened so wide, his irises were only faint pink pinpricks in a sea of white. "It came from the lanyani. We're supposed to make sure birds and rats get into it."

"And then what?" Gammon demanded.

The eyeless face and one limber ankle turned her way. "Then find the lanyani who gave it to us and ask for more."

Gammon crouched before the youth. "Which lanyani?"

"Thorn. It keeps a little hole in the wall near Misery Bay. Deals tar and herbs."

"Take us to him."

The ecosystem of Rotten Row conformed to most of the rules governing interspecies survival. One or more species acted as a herd-creature, prey to the stronger ones surrounding it, or as a gatherer species, whose stores and populations alike could be raided at a predator's leisure. Rotten Row, despite its indisputably human character as a shipping port and loading dock for sea- and sky-faring vessels, was home to lanyani predators—scavengers, really—who skimmed from the humans and aiga around them out of convenience when times were good, and by force when they were tough.

A few seasons before, Thorn had been little more trouble for Gammon and her officers than its name suggested, but hard weather and crowded streets made desperate lanyani an offering of easy prey. Nothing Thorn sold was technically illegal. Little analgesics and cough remedies sold at discount from reputable alchemists, supplies of carefully parsed opium distilled into tonics, and bundles of cannabis cut with common tobacco. But all Thorn's customers understood they weren't meant to consume its products in a fashion that would keep them legal. And so Thorn's dank, lean-to hovel dug like a weed into its alley wall, surrounded by a reek of death. Thorn shrugged away inquiries from constables about the suspicious, lingering vapor.

Flesh creatures, its reedy voice would thrum as it spread its twelve-fingered hands, feigning innocence. *So very fragile.*

Gammon had been to Thorn's shanty more than a few times. She strode up to its door with a hand on the blunderbuss pistol she'd found back at the Old Cathedral. *For all the good it might do.*

Thorn answered on the third knock at his doorframe. Letting it go past the first had been sheer audacity, she knew. He was likely twigging all throughout the hovel walls, feeling for passers-by and tasting the wind for trouble.

"What does the lady require?" Thorn rattled.

"Answers."

The door was a hide stretched on a splintered wooden frame. The skin's patch-sewn, poorly shaved exterior suggested it might once have been a den of feral calicoes. A yellowish, irisless eye peered around its frayed edge, and then Thorn's chimney-brush face jutted into view, its namesake cheeks prickling with hostile animation.

Nasrahiel loomed behind Gammon and reached overhead to deposit the aigamuxa child—Naveeqil, she thought she'd heard him call it—and the child's bag in the space between Gammon and Thorn. The aigamuxa youth folded up, hissing like a cat, its blind face keeling forth and back to ensure lanyani and human alike got a share of its ire.

"Not my garbage," Thorn replied, shrugging fit to skewer a whole clutch of quail. "That belongs in the Aerie."

"He says you gave him this." Gammon tapped the toe of her boot beside the sack, but made sure not to actually touch it.

"Is it a crime to hire an errand boy?"

"It's a crime to set him out poisoning in the city."

Thorn tilted its head at the aigamuxa. "I thought I told you to keep to rats and gulls."

"I did," it snapped back.

Thorn lolled its head toward Gammon and spread its arms, an arabesque of insolence.

"No doubt you were motivated to employ him in this fashion out of the goodness of your heart."

Thorn might have sketched the mockery of a bow, but its body was woven deep into the walls of its hovel from what passed for its waist down. Pinned.

Well then.

Gammon reached into the thigh holster opposite her gun. Thorn stared as she withdrew an alchemical flare and a tube of waterproofed lucifers.

"What are you doing?"

Gammon had the wax safety cover off the flare and a lucifer in hand already. She held them before Thorn, turning her wrists slightly, mimicking the flourish she'd seen a street conjuror use to dazzle his marks.

"I'm preparing to pursue your goal of cleaning the streets, Thorn.

There must be at least three building codes your little outpost here violates, to say nothing of how it chokes this alley passage. Dangerous in an emergency. There's hardly anywhere to go, and no time to get there before the whole thing goes up like a box of tinder."

Then she scraped the match up the length of the flare and touched off the top. It roared to life, sending both the aigamuxa shrinking back from its heat and sparks. Thorn hissed, plastering itself to the backside of its hovel. Gammon stepped over the forgotten bag, edging forward slowly. She dragged the flare along a tuft of desiccated fur still clinging to the front door-skin. It singed and smoked, the half-tanned skin curling with char.

"You're mad! What about the buildings around us?" Thorn cried.

"How many of them contain more of that powder?"

"Two. Small supplies. It doesn't take much."

Gammon put her face as near the flare's tip as she dared. "What would happen if I let those *small supplies* burn?"

Thorn's eyes seemed to dart forth and back, even without the benefit of pupils to clarify the expression. "There would still be much to burn. Other caches. Dor has seen to it."

"Well, I've never complained over a job needing time to be done right," Gammon answered. She touched the sparking tip of the signal flare to the splintered wood. The lanyani wailed an anguished oboe-note as it barreled past her to escape the flames consuming the shanty. Gammon kicked the empty sack into the conflagration. She turned in time to see Nasrahiel let the scrambling aigamuxa youth go, pouncing upon the fleeing lanyani instead.

They fell in a tangle of tearing wood and clattering brass. Nasrahiel rose holding one of Thorn's broken limbs like a sportsman's bat, threatening to tear it away entirely with a single twist.

Gammon strode out of the alley into the quayside's sea air, sweating from the flames licking at the sides of the hovel. Nearly all the buildings of Rotten Row were brick and mortar affairs. Thorn's lean-to would take a few dustbins and moldering piles of straw up with it, but that was all. It would still be enough to make her point.

"I'd like to see one of the vermin your aiga gophers have dosed," she said to the writhing Tree.

Thorn surged toward her, its face quilled and barbed and full of hate. It jerked under Nasrahiel's grip, spitting curses as its shoulder splintered.

"Or I could have my friend deposit you back in your home," added Gammon. "It's burning well enough, I'm sure you wouldn't suffer long. Your choice."

Thorn's wild, white gaze fixed on Gammon's placid stare. "You sure you want to see them?"

"Very."

Thorn all but cackled. Its shift from rage to demented glee rocked Gammon back a half-step.

"Check Oldtemple," it cried. "Check the Court and Bar. Outside the Governor's manse. You'll see. Then you might as well give yourself up to Dor. It would be quicker that way."

26.

Madame Kurowa ushered Rowena down the long spokes and aisles of the Grand Library's main collection, guiding her toward who-even-knew-what. Rowena had been collected from her company's apartment suite shortly after breakfast, still groggy from a long, late night sitting up on her roll-bed, thinking through theories of how the Library and the Old Bear's mind connected, sounding them against Leyah's ghostly half-presence.

Kurowa had appeared with the Fabricated sent to tidy up after the meal. After a murmured side-conversation with Chalmers, she hustled Rowena off to do the job Master Meteron had alluded to—the one requiring small hands.

Now the world to Rowena's right and left was a blur of titles etched on spines in gold and silver, half a hundred languages accounted for before she and Madame Kurowa reached the end of the first aisle of shelves. Sometime during the walk, Madame must have started in lecturing. She spoke as if Rowena should recognize the thread of her statements and paused, waiting for some reaction.

Rowena smiled and nodded with perfectly false confidence. "Oh, sure. I know what you mean."

Madame quirked an eyebrow. Rowena winced. *So much for saying the right thing.*

"I hadn't realized a girl your age would have experience cataloging translations already."

"Um—"

At last they reached a pair of doors sporting a lock the size of a fist.

Kurowa produced a ring of keys and set one into the lock. "Executing and cataloging various textual translations," Kurowa explained over her shoulder, "makes up a goodly percentage of our librarians' work. Sadly, we can't always devote as much time to other pursuits as we would like, and so what amounts to busy work is passed along."

Rowena tried hard to keep the scowl she felt coming off her face. "So this job you told Master Meteron and Doc Chalmers you needed me for is just busy work?"

If Kurowa was at all troubled by Rowena's confrontational tone, she gave no sign.

"I imagine you will find it tedious, but it's hardly arranging lucifers all the day."

The door opened. Beyond lay a kind of . . . what? It reminded Rowena uncomfortably of the makeshift study the aigamuxa had designed for Chalmers. Several tables with slanted surfaces and ink blotters made up its general furnishings. A girl around Rowena's age hunched at one of them. She peered back at the door; Rowena had to stifle a bark of laughter.

The girl's eyes were magnified into miniature moons, distorted behind the reticulated lenses of a headlamp strapped to her forehead. The card the girl had been working over dropped from one hand, the ruler and punching tool from the other.

She scrambled up from the chair. There had been some kind of tray full of tiny metal bits balanced on her lap, and another jutting over the table's edge, which she narrowly saved from flying everywhere with two hasty snatches. The girl pushed the trays to safety and managed a hurried bow.

"Madame Kurowa. I didn't know you would be here. I would have made my working surfaces more—"

"It's all right, Umiko. I've brought another pair of hands to carry out today's work."

Umiko considered Rowena a moment, then flipped the headdress of lenses up and away. Rowena had imagined a happy reception. Instead, the girl's upturned nose wrinkled.

"I haven't asked for help," she griped.

It took another battle of will for Rowena to keep her face arranged. She suspected she was losing this one.

"I know that," Madame Kurowa snapped back. "And you wouldn't *bother* asking until the entire project came down around your ears. Don't think I've forgotten what happened to Ieyasu's Cataloguer last spring."

"That *wasn't my fault*. Gichu didn't properly cam the flywheel. He was supposed to check his work with me!"

"And you were supposed to check his work, even when he forgot to ask."

Rowena suppressed a sympathetic wince. Umiko said nothing, taut with anger.

"You will take this girl," Kurowa continued, "and put her to whatever task will see this job done sooner. I need you back where you belong."

Umiko glared down at her hands. A lock of glossy, almost-black hair slipped from behind her ear, curtaining her face. She didn't bother tucking it away.

"Osu," she muttered.

Rowena didn't know the word. It must have indicated assent, given Madame Kurowa's small, satisfied smile.

"Good. Umiko Haroda, Literate Third Order, this is Rowena Downshire." Madame Kurowa gestured at Rowena, then regarded her with an uncomfortably acute interest. "You have . . . no title?"

"Not really, no."

She sniffed. "Well. Things *are* done differently in Corma."

Of all the things Rowena has disliked so far that morning—and she had a good list going, from the stewed apricots over barley porridge that had gone cold by the time she learned the trick for rolling up her tatami to the quarter-hour she'd spent trying to properly fold the collar of her kimono before binding the sash—she liked Madame Kurowa's tone in that moment least of all. She was a heartbeat from cutting into the Logician woman about *just* how differently folk did things at home when Umiko spoke up.

"I will teach her, Madame. Thank you."

And with that, Madame Kurowa offered a tiny bow, hands folded, and swept away, shutting the door behind her. Rowena's ears pricked at the sound of a key scraping the lock.

She whirled to the door, stumbling on her kimono's hem, and jerked at the handle. The elegant crane-shaped lever moved, its wings pumping up and down, but the door itself would not pull inward.

"She locked us in!"

Umiko Haroda walked up to Rowena, standing imperiously close, her hands folded in her broad sleeves. The girl was nearly a hand shorter than Rowena, and Rowena was hardly anyone's definition of tall.

"What do you expect?" Umiko asked bitterly. "Cataloguer repair is miserable work. It's boring, repetitive, and most Literates wander away from it as soon as her back is turned." Rowena must have pulled a face, for Umiko rolled her eyes dramatically. "It's not as if Madame's leaving us here to *die*. She'll be back before supper, and the Fabricated bring a tea cart with a dinner crate around midday."

Umiko returned to her workstation. Seeing little else she could do, Rowena followed.

The rows of desks filling the room were arranged for a variety of purposes. A few were screening tables, with bottles of ink and fountain pens and brushes, with reams of paper set to either side of broad blotters. Other tables held little contraptions that resembled parts of a seamstress's friend or spinning wheel, but instead of spools of thread, they boasted paraffin cylinders and long, rectangular sheets of something white and rigid punched with holes in different shapes and formations. The tables nearest the high, arched windows were all like Umiko's—set with trays of tiny metal pieces, some much smaller than the nail on Rowena's baby finger, with a rack set at the table's head bearing a headdress of lenses, scopes, and other such tools. Umiko all but flopped into her chair, then pulled her awkward goggles back down. She plucked up one pair of pincers, then another, discarding both before finding the tool she wanted.

Rowena fetched a chair from the workstation beside Umiko's and watched her work. A tiny gear. Or maybe a cog? She didn't know the names for these things, or if there was a difference between them. A longish bar, with squared-off edges and saw-teeth. Umiko set the gear over the bar, seating both pieces inside a wooden box like a chronometer with its dial face missing. She pushed the gear forth and back along the bar's teeth. It made a quiet zipping sound, like a bee gliding past Rowena's ear. She carried on, setting more bars and more gear-cog-whatevers in a row, hunched close over her work, saying nothing.

Until she finally said something.

"So is this the help you mean to give me?"

Rowena blinked. "Pardon?"

"Staring at me and doing nothing." Umiko's eyes bugged behind the spectacle glass again; she looked more fierce than funny, this time.

"That en't exactly—" Rowena bit down on a curse before trying again. "That *isn't exactly* fair. I don't even know what work you're doing. If you *told* me, maybe I could help."

The girl leaned over, so close her bespectacled gaze seemed to fill the room. "I'm recamming the main calculating chamber of a Subindexer that belongs in the First Literates' research room, but nobody bothers taking care of their equipment properly anymore and so it's broken and I'm here mending it when I *should* be working with the Aggregator!"

Rowena blinked again. "Oh. That . . . sounds hard."

Umiko yanked her spectacle set off and flung it at the tool rack. It almost managed to catch a hook properly, but the momentum swung the rack down, hurling it onto another tray of supplies at a neighboring station. Glinting clockwork bits scattered like seed, shooting toward every seam in every floorboard, fetching up against the feet of surrounding shelves. Once the clamor of the chaos she'd created faded, Umiko sighed.

"It's not hard. Just dull and stupid."

"And you're being punished."

She looked at Rowena accusingly. "Kurowa shouldn't have told you."

"She didn't. Honest. It's just kind of obvious."

Umiko slid out of her chair and started sweeping the scattered mess of metal up, gathering it in the hems of her robes. "I guess it is," she muttered.

Rowena knelt beside her. They worked in silence awhile, crawling between table and chair legs, fetching bits of brass and copper wire. Rowena shuffled forth and back, dropping her handfuls into Umiko's pouched robe until, at last, they had all the clockworks gathered up. Rowena held a tray in front of the gathered garment.

"Not that one." Umiko pointed to one an arm's reach away. "There. With the sorter."

Rowena switched trays and held the new one before the Third Literate as she shook her robe out into a kind of funnel piece. A mechanism just past its chute ticked along, spitting components left, right, center, and so on, until everything was back where it belonged.

"That thing's really jake," Rowena said.

They stood, Umiko dusting her palms on her sash. "I invented it, based on a chit sorter from a gambling house. Had to. I . . . have a temper."

"That wouldn't be what ended you up here, eh?"

A smile seemed dangerously close to upending the scowl on Umiko's face. "Could be."

Rowena offered her hand. "I'm Rowena."

Umiko looked at the proffered hand as if it smelled a bit off. "I know that already."

"I know you *know*. S'not the point."

Slowly, Umiko took her hand and puzzled over Rowena's pumping it once, twice, in a firm, callused grip. "You're no secretary," Umiko announced.

"Not exactly. And you en't—aren't—"

"En't," Umiko allowed, amused.

"*En't* a librarian."

"Not exactly." Umiko gestured to the seats they'd just abandoned. "Here. You're small and you've got good hands. Madame must think you'll be useful with the code cards."

Rowena frowned. "Code cards?"

"Those things." Umiko waved toward the stacks of pale rectangles near the odd, not-sewing machines bristling with not-needles. "They're part of what got me in trouble."

Rowena considered Umiko. She was maybe a year or two off her own age—older or younger was hard to say. Rowena had done a fair bit of growing since last fall, given a decent place to eat and rest and less to be harried over day in and out, but she was still smaller than most people. Umiko's tongue lacked the hard edges of street talk. Indeed, she spoke with a lady's intonations, though she lacked a lady's composure. Her hands were full of nicks and scars, just like Rowena's—souvenirs of building locksets and cams, not picking them apart. But still. Her face had the familiar, wry twist of a person who was used to putting up a scuff about things. It was a face Rowena knew she could trust. Folks who put up fights over things don't bother not telling you what they're thinking. They'll be for you, or against you, but they'll be square about it.

"If you tell me what got you in trouble," Rowena said slowly, "I bet I can help get you out of here faster."

Umiko snorted. "What makes you so sure of that?"

"I came here with Reverend Doctor Chalmers, from Amidon. He's here by the Rolands' orders."

"That doesn't mean anything to me."

"They're paying the Library money for his time here, I think. A lot of money. And I think they'd pay to make sure he gets all the help he needs." Rowena leaned hard into that last word. "And I can imagine I'd *really need* your help to do the work he expects me to do."

Umiko smiled in earnest. "You might."

"So?"

"Let me show you how to use the puncher on those cards. Then I can tell you all about it while you show Madame Kurowa how useful you're being."

After an hour's work with the puncher and Umiko's damnable pearl cards, Rowena wasn't sure she was proving very useful, though she had proven herself plenty thin-skinned. The pearls—the sheets of some kind of plasticine onto which Umiko was instructed to copy out strange patterns of holes, consulting graphs and charts that meant nothing to Rowena's unschooled eyes—were sharp as razors and nearly as stiff. She broke three just trying to learn the trick of holding them right, then ruined five more feeding them into the punching machines whose dials Umiko had painstakingly set. If they rode through the machine at all off-kilter, tripping awkwardly through the slot grinning at the machine's front, the card would snap or, almost worse, would feed out the back with the holes all jagged round the edges. If the card didn't come out perfect, it was junk and ended up on the embarrassingly tall stack of rejects slouching at the desk's edge.

"Why," Rowena asked through her clenched teeth, "are you doing this, anyway?" She glowered at the card that fell gently from the tray at the punching machine's back—perfect-seeming, until she lifted it in gloved hands and saw a spider web of cracks running between its holes.

"This is stupid," she added, by way of punctuation, before spiking the card in the rejects tray.

Umiko was back at her desk, adding bobbins and whichwhats and thisandthats to another clockwork box. "It's important work."

"Important *how?*"

"Important that someone a lot less skilled than me do it. Stupid to waste my time on that when I'm needed fixing machines. Now come on. I need sixteen of those pearls cut before the end of the day. They belong with these Indexers."

"I'm supposed to be doing something useful," Rowena muttered. She hadn't meant for Umiko to hear it, and was glad when she did that the other girl didn't know she'd been thinking of Chalmers, and the Old Bear, and the books that wrote themselves.

"*Useful,*" Umiko snipped, "is whatever Madame Kurowa decides we should do. People who don't do useful things as they're supposed to—"

"End up here?" Rowena suggested.

Umiko looked at her, expressionless. "For a while. You said you can do something about that."

"And you told me to prove I'm useful." Rowena gestured at the heap of ruined punch cards. "How's this for proof?"

"Maybe you'll have to be useful some other way."

Umiko set the box before her aside, tidied her supplies and workstation, and pushed away from the desk. She dusted at the folds of her kimono fastidiously, putting on an air of practiced, almost performative calm that reminded Rowena of Master Meteron.

The lock outside rattled. A Fabricated in the shape of a young woman—uncomfortably like Umiko herself, in its petite size and plain, orderly features—rolled a cart into the room, a large, boxy affair of many drawers and large doors, clearly meant to hold a host of meals for room service. The faux girl bent to the cart's side doors, opening them in a series of stutter-stop motions. Rowena opened her mouth to thank it for the meal—a stupid instinct, really, but she'd had few enough meals in her life, she wasn't one to let them go without comment. But Umiko silenced her with a sharp, shushing motion.

Frowning, Rowena watched her creep toward the Fabricated as it bent back to its full height, two closed metal boxes with tea flasks balanced atop them in its reticulated hands.

With hands fast as any cutpurse's, Umiko reached up under the figure's sash. Rowena heard the sharp snaps of switches being thrown and all at once, the Fabricated maid jerked to a halt. One of the tea flasks tilted and rolled off its dinner box to the ground, disappearing under nearby desks and benches.

"What are you—?"

Umiko made another chopping motion, across her neck. She pointed at the cart's open belly, then gestured between them.

Rowena gaped at her. *Are you cracked?* she mouthed.

Umiko blinked in confusion. Close to snapping out loud, Rowena stopped, realizing the girl probably didn't know the expression. The Third Literate gestured to the cart again, mouthing, *Get in.*

You'd better know what you're doing, Rowena tried to say back with her narrowed eyes.

She had a fair sense that Umiko understood her, based on the wink offered in return.

When she was small, Rowena played hiding games of every

description with her brother, Jorrie. Bess's old steamer trunk of costumes had been her favorite hiding place. Under the dinner cart wasn't so different—apart from Umiko crowded in beside her, fighting to keep her breath quiet and slow. After a moment, the stalled maid seemed to wake up, resuming its duties as if nothing untoward had happened. The Fabricated maid pushed them along without the slightest hint it cared why the cart, emptied of its meals and supplies, was still so heavy and ungainly. Rowena sat, hugging her knees, bumping up against Umiko. After a time, the cart stopped moving. Rowena craned her head to peer through the slit between the cart doors. Nothing. Or, nothing she could see, anyway.

She put her hand to the inner latch. Umiko smothered it with her own, head shaking hard. A finger to her lips. The wink again. They waited.

Outside, the Fabricated whirred and clattered, doing something that sounded like it involved a door, or a lock. Both? It stopped, and the sound of the Fabricated's movements faded, too.

Rowena counted to herself, reaching a hundred before Umiko took her hand away, letting her open the doors.

Light poured into the cart, and in awkward jerks and starts, the girls spilled out, landing atop each other in a grunting, giggling jumble. Rowena blinked up at a vaulted ceiling, sunlight filtering through a lattice of leaded glass chased with delicately cut dragons and phoenixes.

"Where are we?" she asked.

Umiko shook her foot up and down, trying to untangle her sandal from the hem of Rowena's kimono. "The best place in the whole Library."

"And you ride here in the dinner cart?"

"When the Fabricated stop outside the cataloguers' offices to bring them their correspondence, sure. They come back again and finish their route in reverse a few hours later, to tidy up. I always make it back to the mechanical room before Madame Kurowa comes to collect me."

Rowena puzzled over the room. It didn't seem so very different from the one they'd left—emptier, even. "I don't see what's so interesting here."

"You would," Umiko countered, "if you had a specific set of queries to research. But you must, or you wouldn't have come all this way."

The acid of accusation tinged her tone. Rowena studied Umiko. Did she know what they'd come to the Library for? No. Chalmers wasn't very good at being private but he wasn't an idiot. Or not a complete one, anyway.

"There's something Chalmers is trying to do," Rowena answered carefully. "But there are a few things the Curator has asked us to do before we can get started."

"Ahhh." Umiko grinned in triumph. "He must want to see the Amanuensis library."

Rowena remembered Anselm's critique of her card playing face. She thought hard about not blinking twice. "I'm not really sure."

Umiko rolled her eyes. "There's no point asking for my help if you won't tell me what—"

"Fine. That's what he wants to see. We've just been asked to . . . well. One of us is doing a job for the Curator that should clear the way."

"Doubtful," Umiko sighed. "I can't think of what'll get her to open the place for research again. Not after what happened this spring."

Rowena had been prepared to hear Umiko say "last fall." Her life seemed measured from the first of Elevenmonth, a new calendar unto itself. She couldn't keep the confusion out of her voice.

"The *spring?* This spring? What happened?"

"The whole wing is shut to everyone—everyone but the Curator, Madame Kurowa, and Scholar Cyddra themself, I suppose. It's because of Cyddra's research. Madame Curator hates letting them in, but there's nothing much to be done about it."

Rowena frowned. "Why's that? If the Curator wants some part of the Library closed, shouldn't that just be it? Whoever made trouble—this Cyddra—aren't they the one who ought to be shut out?"

"It's hard to close a special collections wing to the last scion of the family that paid to build it, and pays for its maintenance still. Besides, shutting Cyddra out would just make more of a fuss out of whatever they did or found out." Umiko gestured dismissively, clearly bored by the topic. "I don't ask questions. It's the sort of thing I don't want to get caught asking questions *about*."

Rowena went back to scanning the room. "So . . . you said this is a place for researching serious questions?"

Now, the Third Literate girl seemed to come finally, properly alive. "Here, have a look!"

The room was only a little larger than Rowena's bedroom in the Grand Library's guest wing, apart from its generous ceiling. It was empty save for a roll top desk and a long bank of glass-fronted cabinets sitting behind it. And yet, as she studied that wall, Rowena saw how full the room really was—full in a way she had only heard of before.

Rowena stared at the cabinetry, running her eyes up and down the maze of cogs and levers and casters and pins jutting from its surface. The far wall was a series of panels and doors, falling-over-full of so much clickety-clacking EC tech, it was a wonder the latched glass doors didn't rattle to pieces when the machine was running.

Umiko smiled at the cabinet, breathing in its none-too-faint machine-grease smells. Rowena mimicked her smile uncertainly.

"Isn't it amazing?" Umiko blurted.

"It's . . . sure something."

"The Aggregator." Umiko rushed toward a block of rattling cabinetry different from the rest. The roll top desk sat before it. She scrolled its cover away, revealing a spool with some kind of film or fiber wound up on it on its work surface. A long instrument rested beside it, its grooves and arms reminding Rowena of the inside of a piano.

Umiko's fingers flew over the device, which began spooling sections of the ecru-colored material over the instrument of grooves and arms. The keys she tapped set little, oblong-ended hammers punching into the card over and over, darting up and down its length. The punched-up film was, Rowena realized, a continuous, spooling sheet of a material not unlike the pearl cards—but vastly longer, holding a much deeper complexity of information, and apparently able to input changes to that information with simple, direct signals from this workstation.

"This looks kind of like those what-do-you-call-'ems you were working on back in the indexing room."

Umiko shook her head, her eyes tracking the lightning movements of her fingers punching keys. Each key bore an inscrutable mark. She flew through them as fast as a Fabricated running a player pianoforte. "Indexers are only cammed to read certain types of operations off certain types of cards," she explained. "They're stupid machines. You can use them for small inventories or to sort small information sets, but that's it. The Aggregator is so much *better*."

"So what are you doing?"

"I'm asking the Aggregator a question. Have you a question?"

"That depends. What's an aggregator?"

Umiko laughed. It was a sharp, musical noise, provided you liked the sound of wind chimes tossed down a flight of stairs. "It keeps information. Everything worth knowing."

"You're kidding."

Umiko's hands stopped, hovering over the keys. She could hardly have looked more scandalized if Rowena had thrown open her kimono and used an antique volume as a privy seat. "I don't *kid* about the Aggregator."

"But why have a library all full of books and such if you have a machine that has all the answers to all your questions?"

At this, Umiko's face smoothed back to a knowing calm. She raised a finger, pointing down to the machine whose keys froze in midair, waiting for another strike. "If you ask it what there is to know about cherry trees, it'll print volumes about cherry trees." Here, she gestured toward a kind of miniature printing press crowded onto an inky-black varnished credenza. "But having information isn't the same as knowing actual answers. Answers require Reason and intelligence. The Aggregator is a tool we have made to serve His work. It can't do by itself what *we* were made to do."

Rowena fought hard not to point out that Umiko's notion of the Creator's will and favored people and such sounded more like Kneeler preaching than something a Logician should say.

"I'll show you," Umiko said, punching three last keys with a flourish.

Umiko slipped on a pair of gauze gloves from a little cedar box beside the punching machine. With painstaking care, she sliced the length of fresh-punched sheeting free from the spool and fed it into a slit in the cabinet before them. It reminded Rowena of a mail slot, or of the tape-feeder from a galvano-gram machine, but wider and thinner, meant to take just one thing very precisely.

Something inside the slit whispered, almost politely, as it gobbled up the long, papery card. And then, the wall full of machines shuddered to new life in a hailstorm of percussion. Rowena stepped back, wincing, as Umiko watched the progress of her card and its question—whatever it was—through the glass-fronted innards of the Aggregator.

Just when Rowena was sure her nerves couldn't take the racket any longer, the card reappeared at the end of a long circuit, emerging with a sister card full of different marks and notations beside it. Umiko retrieved both and, examining them quickly for some kind of flaw or concern, fed them into the printing press and gave it four hard cranks to wake its mechanisms. Together, they watched as a spool of paper tickety-tacked upward, like a little lick of white flame, translating the query card and the sheets of punches representing a response into a printed answer.

Umiko tore the paper away and passed it to Rowena. Rowena tried to hide how slowly she read by pretending to survey the whole page at once. Really, she was looking for shorter sentences, pieces that jumped out more legibly than the rest.

150 leagues west by north-west.

5,000 hectares arable land.

Population estimated in excess of 1 billion (human census only)

Rowena had the wherewithal, at least, to scrape the frown off her face before Umiko took note of it.

"It's a lot of, um, facts," she observed, truthfully. The blandness of the comment made her cringe.

Umiko smiled winningly. "But that's what the Aggregator is for! It can't answer a question so much as tell you all it knows that might help you answer it."

Rowena quirked an eyebrow. "So, what did you ask it?"

"The probability of Vraska's EC membership breaking with the Lemarckian Protectorate before the next Decadal Conference."

"So, wait." Rowena looked around for a place to sit and, seeing only the corner of the little printing machine's stand, perched a hip there. "You wanted to know the answer to something really complicated—something involving politics and trade and all sorts of things—and the Aggregator pulls up all the facts it has about Vraska, like its land mass and stuff?"

Umiko pointed further down the page, near its end. "Also data relating to tax rates in and outside the Protectorate for commercial enterprises, rates of immigration and emigration, numbers of prominent members of the Council Bishopric whose studies either rely upon Vraskan resources or who are themselves Vraskan. Everything that so much as brushes on the idea of Vraska." She stopped, shrugging apologetically. "This isn't even as impressive as it could be. I requested an abbreviated report. We'd still be waiting for the press to finish printing at breakfast tomorrow, if I had asked for a complete output."

Rowena's eyes widened. "But if it can find all that information without you having to look for it by hand . . . that's still pretty fast!"

"It *is*."

"But how do you know what information is relevant? Like, it can't all be good and useful stuff. There's got to be a lot of junk floating around in a full report."

"That's why people are so important. The Literates in charge of the Aggregator's engineering would like to build an Algebraic Engine that can interpret information, too, but that's much, much more complicated than one that holds it and retrieves it when you ask."

Rowena shrugged. "This is already so big and complicated. How much worse could it be?"

Umiko's earnest excitement slowly turned grave.

"Rowena," she said, "the most amazing part of the Grand Experiment is its thinking creatures—the lanyani, and aigamuxa, and us. They're our lesser cousins, but we know that they think. And there is so much more to thinking than simply having information. Only part of it is pulling the good information from the bad. Or, maybe just the useful from the not-useful. Thinking turns yards and yards of these reports into ideas. Thinking takes information and tells a *story* with it. We have made many things by our persistent study of the Creator's world—buildings and engines and galvano-graphs and Fabricated. But we have never made another thinking creature. Not of flesh or bone and certainly not of brass and steel. It's the greatest mystery, apart from what the Creator means for us to do with His wisdom, when we unlock it."

Rowena imagined the clockworks of her own mind turning until, finally, a little out-of-the-way gear that had been slipping caught hold of an inference and turned, opening a door.

"But *you've* tried to make something that thinks," Rowena concluded. "That's why Madame Kurowa stuck you fixing broken Indexers. You did something with the Aggregator, didn't you?"

Umiko's pale, moon-shaped face turned hot and red, as fast as if she had plunged into a steam bath. "I didn't do it with the Aggregator itself," she admitted, looking down at her hands. "But I used some of the same theories. Copied some of the mechanisms. She thought I was . . . overstepping. That if the Creator was going to guide someone to that kind of a breakthrough, it wouldn't be me."

Or shouldn't be you, Rowena thought. The look she shared with Umiko—an instant of quiet, knowing solemnity—told her she'd reached the same conclusion on her own.

"I think that's pretty jake," Rowena said, instead. "It'd be great if you could do it. I can't imagine there's anyone smart enough to go through even this short thing here." She rattled the dangling print-sheet for emphasis. It hardly seemed short to her. "How do you begin to make sense of it?"

"With smaller questions, simpler issues with less data, I can construct answers. Anybody with a little practice could. But you're right. Very few people could take even this much of the Aggregator's report and give us an answer that would make sense."

Very few. Rowena squinted at the paper. "How few?"

The girl's brow furrowed. "I only know of one for sure, but there must be more than that. No one that well trained or wise would have failed to teach at least one apprentice."

The numbers and notations hardly seemed to make sense, even as separate pieces of data. To make a narrative of them? Rowena frowned. That would take a very particular kind of mind.

"Bishop Professor Allister Meteron?" she suggested.

Umiko blinked in surprise. "How did you know?"

"Lucky guess." Rowena slid from the table and handed the paper back to Umiko. She hoped it didn't look as much like handing off a hissing viper as it felt. "So, this kind of thing, it's the data he likes to work with?"

"Yes. Using data dumps like these, he predicted the conditions that would give rise to the Coal Wars forty years ago, its casualties, and the terms required for a stable armistice. He overestimated the human toll by only six hundred thirty-nine fatalities and one thousand ninety-one maimings. His armistice guide accelerated the peace negotiations considerably."

Rowena frowned. "En't being about seventeen hundred off of any number a pretty bad estimate?"

"There were more than two million soldiers killed in the Coal Wars over its nine-year period, and better than five million crippled. In that context, it's a remarkably *accurate* prediction."

"You sound like you're an admirer."

Umiko nodded vigorously. "His Grace's work has saved countless lives. He predicted a hurricane in Jakarane that resulted in a sea-wall tsunami, but gave his report ten days before the storm hit. The Indine states were able to set up refugee camps and mobile physicking stations far enough in advance that less than ten percent of the regional populace was still in the most endangered zones by the time the storm made landfall. His mathematical projections prevented an economic recession in northern Europa from deepening into a full-scale depression. He helped their banking syndicates invest in markets whose profits could pull the region out of crisis a decade sooner than if the economic collapse simply ran its course. Bishop Professor Meteron is the nearest thing to a human extension of the Aggregator's functions we have."

Years before, between running Ivor's packages and dodging his truncheon swings, Rowena had learned how to smell an opportunity coming on the wind. There were never enough good opportunities to go around. Never enough pockets to pick, or careless shopkeeps to fleece, or other couriers to shake down. Too often, Rowena had been downwind of trouble, with luck trailing far off.

Today looked to be different.

"I don't suppose," she asked, "His Grace ever uses the Aggregator—maybe sparks a question down for the Literates to run?"

"Regularly. We hear from him several times a month. Why?"

Rowena smiled. "I'm sort of an admirer of his work, too. It would be really instructive to see what someone of Bishop Meteron's abilities has been looking into lately."

Umiko's face lit up—happy to have a chance to play with her beloved machine, happy to have a partner in a new crime. *Genuinely* happy. "It would be my pleasure to help you understand his good works."

Rowena nodded. *You have no idea, friend*, she thought.

27.

Bathed in the dim glow of lamp-film projectors, Deliverance Tegura looked faintly sepulchral. Her scowl only added to the effect.

"This," she declared, "makes not a whit of sense."

She was speaking more to the room at large than any specific other person, but everyone in the laboratory straightened as if she had denounced them personally. Livvy Tegura had that effect on people, second only to Bishop Meteron himself. Everyone knew that when His Grace was absent and his second, Deacon Fredericks, was off seeing to business for him, the Reverend Doctor Deliverance Tegura was the nearest thing to a direct line to Meteron's mind anyone was likely to get.

A rather queasy-looking seminary student, eyes smeary from lack of sleep and perhaps a little nearer tears than was altogether seemly for a functional adult, cleared her throat bravely. Tegura turned her eyes on the girl.

The student quailed, but the Deacon standing at her back had the sense to speak up in her stead. "If you take a look at this reading here," he began, lifting up a spool of printed paper crazed with graphing lines, "the data might be clearer to you, Doctor."

Tegura's head tilted, like a bird of prey realizing whatever stirred in the bush was nothing worth swooping down upon. "You misunderstand me, Master . . . what was your name again, sir?"

"Savery."

"And what is your particular duty, in this research group?"

"I primarily maintain the clockworks and steam power, Doctor."

"Primarily." Her voice had the heat of the desert in it. It could bake you down to bone, if you stayed under it overlong.

". . . Primarily. Yes. And you said I . . . misunderstood you?"

"Quite. The readings are quite clear to me. This does not prevent them from being utterly nonsensical."

"We checked the figures three times," the young seminary student blurted. Again, Deliverance examined her. This time, to her credit, the girl remained her own master. "I agree they're very odd, Doctor, but odd findings aren't necessarily impossible."

Tegura felt a tug at her lips that threatened to become a smile. She smoothed it down and stepped closer to the panel of tiny pins dotting the wall before her.

It was very much like looking at the inside of a wool-pulling brush. An endless-seeming array of thin spikes, each pointing out, but instead of being arrayed in a tiny, even mat, these shifted up and down like the surface of a topographical map transmuted into reality. The tips of many pins glowed—a single, bright filament of tungsten flaring at a perfectly controlled temperature. Raised and lowered into peaks and valleys the length of Deliverance's arm, the landscape puncturing the wall looked like nothing so much as a deserted mountain range left to burnish in the sun.

That description was not so far from the truth. There were doubtless whole tracks of Clara Downshire's brain more barren than any desert.

"The brightest zones experience the most frequent, or at least the most erratic, activity," the seminary student continued. "Then there are the medium and cool zones, which have either very little activity, or prolonged activity of low intensity followed by long periods of inactivity. This gives us a very accurate projection of how the subject's brain works."

"So it does. It also suggests that her cerebral cortex is the least active part of her brain overall, which is entirely inconsistent with what we know of any human brain outside of a coma patient."

"That's true, Doctor," Deacon Savery agreed. The seminary student eyed him warily as he slid into the conversation's narrow gap. *How often has he ridden over her like this?* Tegura wondered. "But Mrs. Downshire is far from either state," he continued, "at least in the broader biological sense."

"Also true. Now, how do you mean to explain this anomaly?"

It was the young woman who burst in. "She experiences time-states not as a process of ordered events, but as a simultaneity."

Deliverance Tegura stared at her, then smiled her slow serpent's grin. "Please. Continue."

"We know less about the brain than we would like," the woman began. She drew closer to the wall, gesturing at the smoldering pins demonstratively. "But we know enough to say that the medulla controls much of our basic neurological functions related to respiration, motor activity, and so forth, which is why it's also closely connected to adrenaline and emotional registers. The frontal and prefrontal zones handle most memory function, but also put our sense of the world around us into reference with memory, giving us a conceptual sense of what past, present, and future are."

"Her turnkey from Oldtemple seemed to think she had inexplicable knowledge. Does that come from what she isn't processing? Her lack of time-order?"

"It's . . . complicated." The young woman's brow creased in concentration. "Her brain doesn't divide time into different states. All time is just all time, to her."

"We've informed the Bishop already," Deacon Savery added.

Tegura frowned. "And his response?"

"He went to his offices," the student said. "To work."

Tegura nodded, brushing past Savery. He extended his hand, perhaps to detain her—she didn't know or care. Instead, she touched the student on the shoulder as she passed toward the door.

"I'm sorry, but I didn't get your name."

"Ana Cortes."

"We are always looking for permanent staff. You've done excellent work here. When you've completed your exams at seminary, please contact my offices. The Bishop's secretary, Deacon Fredericks, can give you my details."

Ana Cortes's eyes opened wide as portholes. That she saw a whole new future through them now, Deliverance had no doubt.

"Yes, Doctor."

Deliverance never quite made out what Deacon Savery sputtered in protest as she left the room. She was far too busy sorting the questions she would have to ask her mentor.

Bishop Professor Allister Meteron's study was pitch black, as it always was after sunset. Deliverance was more than accustomed to this peculiarity. She was grateful, at least, that he was equally habitual in the placement of all his furniture and his belongings. She had navigated the room when daylight poured through the windows. The superfluous dark held no hazard for her long legs. A hand out to feel for the edges of tables and chairs where she expected them—where they would always, reliably, be found—and that was all.

"Ana Cortes," she announced to the general darkness, "is a brilliant analyst who could do her job a deal better without that sponge Savery leeching at her least word, Your Grace."

His voice rattled out a chuckle, some yards away. "You've invited her onto your staff, I should hope?"

"Just now."

"Wisely done. I've an opening coming in mine and had meant to fill it with her, betimes."

Deliverance could hear the smile warming his voice—the slightly reedy tenor of a man long past his prime. It came from her left, where his favorite chair sat angled before an unlit hearth.

"And who will be losing their post under you, Your Grace?"

"Savery, of course. There are technicians who can mind the clockworks just as well as he, and they have much more . . . agreeable habits." There was a pause and a rustling as the old man resettled himself, drawing forward in his chair. Deliverance lowered herself into the seat across from his, two paces back. Just like always. "So," he sighed, "Miss Cortes has shown you her chart on Mrs. Downshire. And you've come with an entire ledger of questions based on her files at the Mercy Commission Home you'd like properly accounted."

"Yes, Your Grace."

"It might be better to do this as the old philosophers did. Let me question *you*, my dear. The chart. Miss Cortes's theory, and its similarities to Doctor Wyndham's notes. What does it suggest to you?"

"As a set of data alone, it would suggest there is no way Mrs. Downshire should be able to function properly in daily life. And yet, she manages well enough, apart from certain bursts of . . . eccentricity."

"And how do you account for that discrepancy?"

"In all probability, her head injury led to this unusual state of being. That injury is better than thirteen years old now. She has had time to adapt to its impact on her perceptions—to learn how to manage her behaviors in a more acceptable manner, and draw less specific attention to comments or observations that regard her knowledge of time."

"Ahh." The sound came from someplace deep in the old man's thin frame, both musing and amused. "You said 'knowledge' of time rather than 'experience' or 'perception.' Why is that?"

"Because," Deliverance answered, hearing a strange flutter in her own voice. She took a steadying breath. "It's true. She knows things. And you know it's true, or you would not have sent me to collect her."

"You'll want to review my notes before we meet again tomorrow."

She felt a packet of papers pass into her hands and almost fumbled them. She unwound the twine that looped the thick envelope shut, and grazed a hand over the first page of the ream held within it. A series of bumps and divots, smooth planes and clusters of pinprick-fine impressions, greeted her fingertips.

"I hope it is not a problem that I've used my usual format?"

"I've kept in practice reading it, Your Grace. I am always at your disposal."

"Good. After you've read the model, come see me over breakfast. Fredericks has some information for you."

Deliverance opened her mouth to ask, but the darkness and the silence were filled by his answer:

"Names. Locations. We're not far from one of them. I'll need you to hunt very quickly, Livvy. Mrs. Downshire's state of mind is very fragile. It demands a guiding hand. Something more particular than we can furnish ourselves. Some recent correspondence from Nippon suggests we may soon enjoy a solution to that problem."

"Will I know the people connected with these names?"

"Personally? No. But I do. I know them very, very well."

Deliverance folded her hands, knotting her fingers together. She had learned to school her tongue against sharing the first fruits of her imagination. This time, though, not speaking her fear seemed more unwise than keeping it close.

"Your Grace, if this is in regards to your son or his partner, the Alchemist—"

She paused. At times like these, the darkness of the Bishop's chambers worried her. Her imagination was too distracted by the effort of inventing his invisible expression. She read into the silence whole volumes of condemnation.

"Continue, Livvy," he said. His voice was so gentle, he might have been someone's grandfather nursing a skinned knee.

"I'm concerned about the personal toll this operation is likely to take on you, Your Grace."

"*Tch.* You are a fine scholar and a good woman. I am very fortunate to have you taking care of me." Deliverance felt him pat the bundle of papers in her lap. "See to the plan here. Contact the Grand Library. Put a spark out to my solicitors and bank-men in Corma, and wire them the necessary details. If you can see to these matters, I will manage the business of my own heart."

Very few would have heard the rebuke in that cozening croon, but Deliverance Tegura did. She rose, cursing herself. She ought to have known better than to doubt her mentor. In close to thirty years' time, he had done little to settle accounts against the son and son-in-law who had so long ago humiliated him. But that didn't mean he had let the matter go.

He was a master of statistics and data, after all. Playing the long game was in his nature.

"Of course, Your Grace. I will see it done."

"Thank you, Livvy. Is Mrs. Downshire settling comfortably?"

"Yes. Shall I send for her?"

The smile crackled at the edges of his words. "When you have a moment. It is well past time for a proper introduction. I owe her an explanation of what is at stake."

28.

It was nearly suppertime when Rowena finally made her way back to
the apartment suite. Master Meteron was settled down beside the low
dining table, surrounded by a spread of something that looked like maps
or building sketches, with the Old Bear across from him, his furrowed
brow directed at a book in his lap.

She could no more have held her news in than plugged a burst dike
with her bare hands.

"I know what he's been researching," Rowena blurted. "Bishop
Meteron. Umiko showed me."

The Alchemist looked up over the rims of his spectacles. The tick-
tapping of Meteron's chopsticks plucking up savories from a charger on
the table paused.

"Who in blazes is Umiko?" he asked.

Rowena opened her mouth to fire back, but the Alchemist's hand
flicked once, fast, over the book. Rowena knew that gesture. She glanced
over her shoulder at the sliding panel door to the anteroom and the hall
beyond. A shadow moved down the passageway, its step oddly measured.
One of the Fabricated servitors. The tamarin had had some kind of pho-
nocorder in it. Why not every Fabricated?

Mind yourself, girl, the Old Bear's voice warned in her mind. Meteron's chin moved slightly, indicating he had heard the same words.

"I was concerned you'd miss your supper," the Old Bear said, almost
in time with the message of his mind. Rowena had learned to expect
that—a sentence spoken aloud as cover for the reactions his unspoken
words might create.

"Wouldn't dream of it," she said.

Rowena flounced onto her cushion at the table's near end and surveyed the meal awaiting her. Plates of pickled plums. Rice cooked with scallions and some brown, salty broth not made from any meat she'd tasted before. Some kind of fish, steamed in cabbage leaves. She grabbed a pair of chopsticks from the stand beside her plate and began shoving bits of this and that together. The quiet whirring on the other side of the thin door receded down the hall.

Rowena stuffed a plum in her mouth, chewing sullenly. "Could sure go for some real walls around this place."

"You'd feel different if you had to sleep between them in this heat," the Old Bear answered. He folded his spectacles and set his book—something that looked at least half-written in Nipponese—to one side. "You were speaking of His Grace."

Rowena nodded vigorously, gesturing for his patience as she wrestled a spicy slice of vegetable matter down her throat and chased it with an unladylike guzzle of cooled tea. "Whew," she gasped, fanning at her mouth. "Whatever that was played for keeps. Now look at this."

She offered a rolled-up length of report to Master Meteron, since his eating seemed more a performance than a sincere effort. He scanned the figures, dates, words, his mouth drawn in a hard line.

"This is data about Corma, all from the last eight months," he said.

"Nine months," Rowena corrected. "Everything since the Cathedral. Or, I s'pose everything he thinks matters."

Meteron passed the papers on to the Old Bear, who resumed his spectacles with sober automaticity. The thief returned to his study of the schematics spread around him, focusing on one of the Tower of Water, according to the title in the papers' carefully inked legends. He'd been scarce around the Grand Library campus the last two days, planning whatever job the Curator had requested of him in payment for access to the Amanuensis library. Rowena craned her neck a little, hoping to get a better sense of what in the Tower held his interest so. Meteron shifted slightly, almost casually, and the schematics fell out of view. *Cagey bastard.*

"I figured he was trying to get a bead on something important in the city," she explained to the Old Bear. "Lookit all that stuff about imports and exports and neighborhood census figures and—"

"And releases from Oldtemple and the prison hulks."

"What?"

"You didn't notice those?" Meteron scoffed. "He's trying to nail down where to find the Vautneks."

Rowena blinked. "I—well, I mean, there's a lot of stuff there, and—Wait, what would that have to do with the Vautneks, anyway?"

The two men shared a look that was all sharp angles and walled-off corners.

It was Meteron who answered, offering one of his half-shrugs. "Data points on a map. Some of Chalmers's notes for Regenzi suggested he was tracking someone who'd been such places before."

Rowena considered. "Wouldn't really narrow things down much, would it? I mean, gotta be thousands in the city who've done a turn behind bars."

"You're not wrong," the Alchemist agreed. "But how did this Umiko help you learn this?"

Rowena leaned in with a conspiratorial air. "You're going to love this Aggregator thing, Bear. It's jake. The best damned piece of crankwork I've ever seen."

"Wait." Meteron raised a hand. "First, who's this Umiko, and how much have you told her?"

Only too happy to share, Rowena leaped into the story with both feet. Before her companions finished their plates, they'd learned all Rowena knew of Third Literate Umiko Haroda. It wasn't much, she supposed, but holy Reason, was it *perfect* for what they needed.

"She knows how to run the Aggregator better'n anybody. Uses it *all* the time, or used to before she got caught doing some engineering stuff Kurowa didn't like. If we ask her to run us some questions, poke around a bit, nobody would think anything about it. She's always sneaking off to visit the Aggregator anyway."

The Alchemist's raptor eyes looked especially sharp. "I wouldn't gamble on what people you barely know judge as strange."

Rowena sighed. "Okay, fine, I can see that, but maybe we don't even have to ask her to run any special queries at all? She's taken a bunch of the Bishop's orders via spark to run different searches. We could just ask her for a copy of anything she gets for him, and then—"

"And then, because you've such a knack for jumping to cute, stupid conclusions anyway," Meteron interrupted, "we could save the Logician Guard the trouble and take turns tying each other up for arrest. I'm sure one of the Fabricated could do for whichever one of us draws the last lot."

"Come on," Rowena groaned. "The Bishop can't actually know *everything* that happens *everywhere*. He en't some kind of kinotrope villain or the Creator or whatever."

"You're right. He's worse."

"*Now* who's jumping to stupid conclusions?"

"Rowena—"

"No, I mean it, Bear. It en't like his da has got eyes in every damned orifice evolution saw fit to stuff into a human body. And even if he did, he's got to blink sometime, right?"

The printout from the Aggregator's press lay on the table before Master Meteron, practically radiating the promise of new leads and better understandings. Why couldn't he see it?

"Would you like me to tell you about His Grace, cricket?" he said. His voice, always cool, all but shivered with ice.

Rowena felt the Old Bear's mind pressing wordlessly against hers. *Let it go*, it seemed to say. She turned her back on it.

"You mean your *da*," Rowena enunciated each word, as if plucking strings deliberately off-key. "Bishop. Professor. Allister. Meteron. You've got his name, whether you like it or not."

Meteron's eyes held hers. For a moment, it was too much like standing at the edge of the Old Cathedral's crenellations. There was a precipice before her. When he spoke, it was if he'd taken her by the collar and pulled her face to its very edge.

"Allister Meteron isn't a slideshow villain or messiah or even a devil, cricket. We're not fortunate enough to have a label for what he is. But he is my father, and you know me better than most. I didn't become who I am by accident. Nothing that comes from him has *ever* been an accident."

Rowena studied Anselm Meteron's face. Whatever was there, beneath the anger, was written in a language she hadn't yet learned to read. She hoped she never would.

"What did he do to you?" she whispered.

Meteron sat back, shrugged one shoulder. Usually, the movement seemed nonchalant. This time, Rowena saw the gesture for what it was—an effort to buck a spider from his back. He sold it so well and so often, she'd never thought to be skeptical of it. Now, though, the tic had its context. She grimaced, shamed to have pressed the issue. She tried to shuffle that feeling to another drawer or cubby in her mind, and found every promising place unaccountably full.

"Nothing that matters to you," he said, finally.

Rowena looked to the Old Bear. "If this is about Leyah—"

"Some other time, Rowena."

She looked between them, frowning. "It's always *some other time* with you two, innit?"

"Let's have another look at that printing, girl."

Rowena passed the Alchemist the unfurled document and resumed her meal just in time for the apartment door to slide open again.

The Reverend Doctor Phillip Chalmers entered, muttering apologies for his tardiness. "I was on my way up," he explained, "when a page brought me this message, forwarded from the galvano-graph station at the anchor yards. It's addressed to me, but I can't make out a word of it."

Meteron and the Old Bear exchanged a look. The former raised his four-and-a-half-fingered hand, beckoning. "Let's have a look."

The Old Bear rolled up the printing and passed it to Chalmers after he gave Meteron the spark. "And tell us what you think of this, Doctor."

Chalmers took the document and his cushioned seat at the table, opposite Rowena. Rowena studied Meteron, who followed the garbled characters of the spark slowly, his lips moving soundlessly. Figures. Numbers. There was some kind of substitution code he was counting his way through. Reaching the end of the process did nothing to smooth the furrow of his brow.

"Well, fuck," he announced, just as Chalmers looked up brightly from Rowena's Engine printing.

The Reverend Doctor turned his head, quizzical. "Beg pardon?"

Meteron thrust the spark at the Old Bear. "There's some kind of plague going around Corma."

"A plague?" Rowena jumped up from her cushion to peer at the crumpled message. She couldn't make out anything, apart from dates and routing codes. "What's that got to do with us?"

"With the lanyani," the Old Bear corrected. "A fungus of some kind. Jane Ardai's taken some samples from bodies found in the lower districts."

At the mention of "fungus" and "plague," Chalmers's hand wandered to his shirt collar, scratching as if a flea had shimmied under his cravat. "When did it, um . . . are we, perhaps . . . ?"

"It presented after our departure. Gammon claims the aigamuxa have been helping to spread it."

"But *why?*"

Rowena rolled her eyes. "I dunno, doc. To *kill humans*, maybe? Because they hate us?"

Chalmers grimaced. "Inspector Gammon's search for someone with robust knowledge of the Trees seems a little less strange now."

"And a little more essential," Meteron murmured. "They're trying to wipe the city out."

"So, what can we do when we're all the way over here?" Rowena asked.

"We follow the plan," answered the Old Bear. "I will pass on what I know of treating fungal agents, though I doubt it is anything more than what Jane herself would already have tried. There are some supplies back at the Scales Gammon might use for protection; she can distribute them to the Dolly Molls, and they can take them where the need is greatest. If the aigamuxa and lanyani are destroying the city in the hopes of destroying the Vautneks with it, our best chance of helping lies in learning what the Bishop knows and acting on it. Your discovery much improves that process."

His response did little to loosen the sick knot binding Rowena's stomach. *A plague.* The Mercy Commission Home was at least a good distance from Corma proper, most of its staff living in the boroughs outside the city. There was a chance her mother was still safe. Maybe not even a bad chance, at least for now.

"This information," Chalmers cried hopefully, tapping Rowena's printout. "Is it from the Aggregator?"

"You know about it?" she asked.

"Nora told me about it, early on in our work together. I imagine she first encountered it when she came here to . . . you know." Chalmers made some elaborate, totally arcane series of gestures meant to conceal his conversation from possible mechanical eavesdropping. Rowena supposed they were meant to say something like "came here to steal the book," but could have just as easily been read as "came here to row a canoe upstairs."

"This is quite remarkable. Why did you pose it this query, though, about Corma?"

"We'd spend a good deal less time repeating ourselves if you could be bothered to make supper on time," Meteron murmured over his schematics.

Chalmers flushed. "You'll pardon me if I am inclined to devote myself to our work with particular rigor, Master Meteron."

Meteron grunted. Rowena retold her meeting Umiko and discovering her connections to the Bishop. Chalmers's eyebrows climbed until they seemed likely to be lost in the receding thicket of his hair for good.

"You don't happen to know how often Umiko processes a query from the Bishop?" he asked.

Rowena frowned, thinking. "Before she got reassigned, every few tendays. She said she's run dozens of 'em since she started tending the Aggregator a year or two back."

"And is there a log of queries?"

"Probably. That seems like something the Literates would be keen to keep up on."

"If that's true," the Old Bear added, "these records I copied out could prove very useful."

He cleared dishes, stacking and organizing them, and set down a diary where his careful, close writing recorded columns of dates and names. Meteron craned his head nearer, frowning.

"Is that some kind of visitor's log?"

"Customs reports. While you've been planning your job for the Curator, I've stopped by the anchor yards and spoken to a customs supervisor about EC agents coming and going from Nippon in the last year."

Meteron raised an eyebrow. "And you managed to pry this intelligence loose how?"

"He was under the very strong impression I was an EC financial auditor—or that is how he'll remember our meeting, should anyone think to ask him."

If it had been Master Meteron pulling that trick, Rowena would have expected money to be the thing that paid for such an impression. With the Old Bear, though . . . He could shape things a certain way, if he really wanted to.

Chalmers frowned. "This is all very lovely, but I don't understand what it has to do with records of the Bishop's queries."

Meteron wagged a finger at the Reverend Doctor. "Not thinking carefully enough. If His Grace uses the Aggregator to pull data about places he thinks he'll find the subjects of the Experiment, and if he finds something in that data—say, a promising pattern or researchable anomaly—he'd pursue that something with more than just another Algebraic Engine query."

"He'd send an agent with the data and instructions to look into things in person," Rowena completed.

Chalmers looked at the Alchemist, Rowena, Meteron, and back to the diary of names and dates.

"Blessed Reason. We might be looking at a register of his agents and their movements here, if the declared destinations match places he'd queried about. Surely they'd have moved through Nippon as a waypoint, to gather whatever datum the Bishop felt was critical from the

Aggregator search, and to use the Logician's resources. He's been a favorite of their faction for years now."

Rowena stared. Two pages, side by side, were full of names and dates
and locales. The Old Bear's handwriting was not wasteful. She knew all
too well how much he could fit into an account ledger, or on a shipping
order.

"This is going to take awhile to sort through," she murmured.

"Well." Meteron chuckled. "Good thing for us you've made a boon
companion with an interest in rattletrap computing, cricket."

She passed him a sour look. "And what'll *you* be up to while I'm sneaking around the Aggregator with Umiko and risking both our hides?"

"I?" He smiled and closed his atlas with a dramatic thump. "I shall be
going to a dinner party."

29.

Anselm consulted his chronometer. He had timed his arrival almost perfectly, down to hiring a riverboat whose lanyani pilot—a drooping, tentacular creature—was just laden enough with other finely bedecked passengers to ensure a leisurely voyage. His refusal of the ritual robes and sashes Madame Kurowa had suggested for the excursion had been utterly tactical. People loved a bit of the exotic sliding sideways into the everyday. All that changed, really, was how the exotic was defined: whose gaze offered judgment and applied standards. Anselm's jacquard vest and tailcoat would have been de rigeur for an evening soiree in Corma, but in Nippon, they were strange and usefully disarming. Drawing attention to oneself on the job had its risks, but attempting to adopt local dress and doing it poorly hazarded far more.

"Let the leopard wear its spots, Madame," he had told Kurowa. "It's more natural than putting him in bearskin."

He mounted a staircase leading up from the boardwalk, shrugging past other pedestrians too well-mannered to let their gazes linger on him overlong. The street toward which he bore translated, more or less, to "Ring of Fishes," a kind of roundabout for clockwork carriages and Fabricated-drawn sedan chairs, with people in fine, summer-weight silks slipping along the lanes like fish down a river's tributaries. At the center of the Ring of Fishes lay the Tower of Water. The sight of it stopped Anselm at the final stair's edge. Someone behind him muttered an urgent, perhaps not altogether polite comment in Nipponese. He murmured an apology and sidled out of the main path, pausing beside a flower stall being boarded up for the night by a distractingly curvaceous girl.

Anselm had heard of the Tower of Water even before practical need set him to a careful study of its design. He'd been told to expect it would be magnificent—one of Nippon's first and oldest architectural innovations, the centerpiece of the city's elaborate design. He had not been prepared to be so entirely underwhelmed.

The wheel-like outer rim of the River of Fishes offered paths down toward a sunken-looking building. The pavement around it showed gaps where the walls seemed to have dropped down into a sheer sinkhole and then a few spare yards—three stories, no more—reached up from that crevasse to a pinnacle that looked better suited to the crown of a spire than a vaguely ovoid structure collapsed into the heart of Kyo-Tokai.

Anselm puzzled over it. He wondered if the mechanism still worked as the diagrams had described. Nippon fell victim to earthquakes and tsunamis in various seasons. Over the years, they had proven brutal enough to scour the sprawling nation-city off the coasts, scraping it back until mighty bulwarks had been built off its most vulnerable tracts of shoreline. Very little of Kyo-Tokai touched the open ocean anymore. The Logicians specialized in astronomy and meteorology, engineering and mathematics, more out of necessity than natural love, and this had led to dozens of meters and graphs and other devices meant to detect natural disturbances and build substructures of support against them. It was why so little of the city was even slightly elevated, instead sprawling like a rhizomatic plant to cover the ground and root into it for safety.

The Tower of Water looked like nothing more than a collapsed relic. Surely, its peculiar design would have made it vulnerable to such a calamity? How could the catastrophe have escaped news, and how could it not have changed the purported venue of the event the Grand Librarian had asked him to infiltrate, with one deadly objective in mind?

Slowly, as if raised by a magnet's field, the hairs of Anselm's neck rose. Behind him, the flower stall girl continued her packing, unperturbed. The ground began to shake. Slow, at first, then insistent rumbling, with a doggedness that made his instincts crack like a whip.

The flower girl smiled and nodded toward the fallen Tower. "Every day. It's okay," she said, in uncertain Amidonian. "You'll see."

And Anselm did see. The schematics had seemed impossible—but they had not lied.

Somewhere far underground, a mechanism rumbled, and out of the groove and the darkness into which the tower seemed to have tumbled, it rose, level by level, turning like a screw, sections sliding apart like the bands of the Old Bear's telescoping blade. The upper three levels of the Tower of Water were, indeed, its only true habitable area, but not because the rest had fallen in some disaster.

The rest was a machine. A piece of art. Anselm did not realize he was staring until he felt his chin pulled upward, tied on a marionette string, his gaze tracking the long pipes and runnels, the curves of gleaming metal and planes of sparkling glass turning upward in the moonlight. It took fully ten minutes for the Tower of Water to rise up to its proper height, all the architecture of its long lifts and staircases revealed like pearly bones. And then, the tower made good on its name.

High above—twenty stories, Anselm's burglaring eyes counted—the metal spouts shimmered, suggesting some unseen movement, and then a mist began to fall. The Tower of Water's sluices opened, the pneumatic press used to deploy the structure pumping down its great confection of pipework a trio of waterfalls, spiraling around its outer edges and gathering like a moat over the crevice in the plaza below.

"God's balls," Anselm murmured.

The water channeled back to its natural runnels just around the tower's base. Other people—elaborately silked and brushed, pinned and adorned, no doubt bound for this soiree, too—gathered around the River of Fishes. Women stepped down from sedans borne by Fabricated chairmen. Men handed one another down from rolling steam ricks and clockwork crank-carts, removing driving gloves and goggles and testing that the pins that set their hair in the traditional arrangements were right. The shining silver doors at the Tower's base, crafted to resemble carp caught in mid-leap, parted, and a footman within bowed to the assembled.

Anselm eyed the proper place to slide into the crowd and studied those around him, sizing up the money and titles both implied and overt in their dress. The misty air left women's pale, painted faces sparkling, though it did their silks no favors. He felt the dagger in his left sleeve and the pistol tucked under his right arm, both well out of sight with his jacket properly buttoned.

He passed his invitation to the waiting servant, who studied its cuneiform and the nine-fingered man who had offered it with unconcealed skepticism.

"Our families are old friends," Anselm said, smiling. It was not even a lie—or not entirely one.

With a curt nod, the servant passed him up the line. For quite the first time since arriving at the Rolands' ball, Anselm Meteron felt utterly at his ease.

Cyddra disliked many things. It was what made them difficult company. Their friends were forever worrying over offending their temperament. It wasn't that these friends put much concern into Cyd's well-being or happiness. Cyd's money made keeping them contented a matter of crude, practical survival for those naturally ambitious sycophants, and everyone knew it, few more than Cyd themself. On the occasion of a substantial parcel of grants being awarded in the Tsuneteva family's name and celebrated in Kyo-Tokai's celebrated Tower of Water, Cyddra felt more scrutinized and catered to than ever.

It was awful.

And so, they stood on the balcony that wound round the ellipse crowning the Tower of Water, sullen and bored and thoroughly resenting their guests, their duties to their mother's fortune, and most of all, their chaperone. They had stepped out into the open after the building's ascent was complete, though that hesitation had only come at their chaperone's insistence. Mother dictated they were to have a chaperone until they were properly married, or until they took ordination with the Ecclesiastical Commission, whichever came sooner. Neither event struck Cyddra as particularly likely. Still, they supposed it wasn't an entirely unwise imposition after the debacle they had made in lower Vraska the year before. "Swanning about," Mother had called it. She'd had no problem with Cyd's going when the ostensible purpose had been to court a match. Sadly, though Cyd had mastered the fine art of dissembling to their mother, their friends did not share the same talents, and all too quickly revealed what Cyd had *actually* been doing in the courts and libraries of Old Mongolia. It was around that time that these these same friends discovered that among the many things Cyd disliked, they disliked *meddling* most of all.

No wonder the friends Cyddra still had in Nippon had taken one look at the young scholar's sour, imperious face spurning their escort's guidance and steered well away from a scene that was only minutes from dissolving into a proper row. Madame Tsuneteva's choice of a chaperone for her only child, a spinster aunt with the instincts of a goshawk, was sure to provide some entertainment for the party—but only if one observed it from a safe distance.

The fact that Cyd had delayed stepping out onto the balcony so long—had missed the entire glorious cascade's beginning—was, in their mind, a most generous concession to their mother's intentions.

It was also absolutely the last concession Cyd meant to afford anyone that night.

"Tell me," Cyd said, stifling a yawn with their woodcut fan, "who I am looking at."

Auntie Suki peered down at the line of people, barely more than beetles without her opera spectacles. "Hard to say."

Cyd plucked the spectacles from the bangle at the old woman's wrist. Two quick flicks and the lenses were at Cyd's eyes.

"Madame Gorsky. Master Hanzo. At least three of the Ong-ba clan, though I can never tell them apart." Cyd sighed, lowering the glasses. "*Nobody.*"

"There are nearly two hundred guests," Suki protested. "All the finest—"

She had been about to say dignitaries, or scholars of the city, perhaps. Cyd rode over her, seething. "The finest xenophobic, close-minded, doctrinaire idiots Kyo-Tokai has to offer. I told Mother I would have been further along hosting a gathering in Hwarang, but she never listens. In Hwarang, at least, there are *actual trees* in places."

"We have Fog Island," Auntie Suki said.

Cyd scowled. The tone Suki had used—as if mentioning that place would score some positive mark in the conversation—rankled them.

"Don't," they answered.

Suki wasn't cowed. Very little cowed her, an absolute necessity with Cyd as her charge for the night. But she did have the decency to look a little subdued.

The old woman glanced back at the lines of guests entering, the golden lift carriages spinning them upward. "Foreigners aplenty," she observed. "I think I have spotted four already. Suits and cravats and other things."

"And a taffeta gown, too," Cyd agreed. "Stupidly hot, those. I tried a few back in Rimmerston, but the look never became me."

"I suppose it wouldn't."

Cyd chose to ignore that. They were surprised how easy ignoring Suki proved to be. Hopefully, for the old woman's sake, she would not be paid for her services based on her effectiveness. Everyone had to eat, and Cyd did not resent their auntie enough to be spiteful. Or at least, they didn't resent her that deeply *yet*.

Something occurred to them.

"Four foreigners, you said?"

"Yes, four for certain."

"I invited three."

"Someone local must have passed their invitation on."

"Possible. Well." Cyd deposited the fan and spectacles behind the broad sash of their kimono. "I think it's time to meet the guests and mingle. The sooner I know who isn't expected, the sooner I will know whether to be pleased by the surprise."

Anselm had perfected the art of appearing to mingle with a crowd while dwelling largely at its periphery during his boyhood's Sabberday lessons. It had been an exceedingly useful way of abandoning tours of historical sites, with lectures given by docents and deacons, and returning at odd moments without the least notice of his comings and goings. The key was to make just enough conversation in passing with congenial-seeming people, and to find opportune moments to disengage from them and travel the floor to some other innocuous-seeming location, that everyone would remember having seen him somewhere, at some point. That impression of ubiquity led to an easy assumption of actual presence. If he spread his movements about properly, he could disappear for ten minutes for every one he spent in clear view.

At the present moment, he was exercising the liberties of a five-minute disappearance, assessing the tiered cocktail hall that comprised the Tower of Water's usable space. For a building created by Logician technology, it was a beautiful, majestic, appalling monument to inefficiency. The hall could hold only a little better than two hundred guests comfortably, by Anselm's estimates, and all for want of more actual floors beneath it. Whatever bulwarks had been built in the substructures of the city to protect the tower when it was not deployed were deep, complex—and capable of hiding many more things. If Anselm could be done with his task involving the ingénue the Grand Librarian so resented in good time, he had a mind to investigate what else lay below the Kyo-Tokai the people around him took for granted.

The benefit of a vast structure with a very small practical gathering space, though, was that keeping an eye on his target's comings and goings became very easy.

Chalmers had been more than a little squeamish about Anselm's plans when the thief pumped the Reverend Doctor for information about his former friend. Then again, Chalmers was capable of seeming squeamish about everything from breakfast menus to library catalogs. Now that Anselm had a look at the tall, rangy youth who was to meet with certain dire plans, he could understand Chalmers's concerns.

"Cyddra isn't what I would call your type of *person*," he had warned. "You might find them difficult to charm."

And Anselm had snorted, checking the edge of his knife against his thumbnail. "I think you underestimate me."

The Reverend Doctor Chalmers, as it turned out, had not underestimated Anselm Meteron. Anselm Meteron had altogether misjudged his target.

A man of about Anselm's age—an Amidonian, by the look of his coat and spats—indicated the host scholar with a tip of his champagne flute. He must have noticed Anselm watching Cyddra Tsuneteva's descent of the spiral stair from the Tower's outer rail, their kimono lifted slightly to prevent a most unfortunate tumble.

"Pretty, aren't they?" the man said. Anselm pretended not to notice his solicitous smirk. "A friend of mine and I have a pool going about them. About what's under those skirts, I mean. Ante's a hundred marks, if you're keen."

Anselm studied the man, taking careful inventory of his ill-fitting waistcoat and overbrushed side-whiskers. The eastern Amidonian drawl was all affectation, far too little north coaster and too much southern bay to pass as authentic. A midlander, hoping to come off as old money.

Anselm eyed him grimly. "It's not a skirt, you nit."

Anselm followed Cyddra's passage down the stairs, tracking which guests came forward to greet them at its foot and which hung back, murmuring like pigeons among themselves. A henpecked-looking older woman trailed after Scholar Cyddra, taking offered tokens cast in metal and carefully enameled with icons and inscriptions. The Nipponese equivalent of calling cards, to be displayed in a place of honor in the Tsuneteva household. Anselm had no such token. Certainly Madame Kurowa, bearing the Curator's instructions, would not have wished him to carry something so material and traceable.

It was a shame their plans and his converged only so far. Differences of opinion about a job's outcome tended to resolve badly. Then again, sometimes, it was just such matters of nuance that made a job really worth one's while.

He moved around the room, quiet and conspicuous, and kept track of who spoke to the scholar and what tokens they passed. He waited for signs of the host making their escape.

30.

Parties need last only as long as hosts are of a mind to sustain them. At a certain critical mass, however, they create their own sustenance out of thin air. Cyddra had learned they were best off to retreat in those later, tiresome stages of celebration, leaving behind the hanafuta and karuta tables, the Fabricated servers tick-tocking cordials up and down the undanced ballroom floor, and simply find a place to set roots. The party was three hours gone and seemed in danger of carrying itself on longer still. And so, Cyd had retreated to their balcony to watch the waters fall and to sift through the satchel of tokens Auntie Suki had gathered from various guests. But their interest in that pursuit had long since evaporated. Suki wandered off to slake a gambling habit she'd had to keep well concealed to earn her place as a chaperone. Pity. Still, Cyd was happy to see their Auntie fall to vice if it meant a few moments of real privacy.

That privacy seemed on the verge of ending now.

They studied the man entering the balcony behind them, his shape bent in the reflection of their wineglass. A hand shorter than themself, with a shadow of a carefully groomed goatee just growing in, pale against his skin.

Cyd turned the glass in their hand, watching the man's shape twist and blur. He had stopped a few paces back—near the door to the balcony but not within it. He seemed a moment from attempting to depart unnoticed, until he put his heel to the corner of the balcony door, closing it without a sound.

Cyd straightened and turned.

The man offered a nod that was just a shade short of a bow. Or was it the other way around? He smiled, and a surge of interest at the wicked curve of his lip warred with the unrest working its way up Cyd's spine.

"This isn't a private veranda, is it?" the stranger inquired.

Cyd's ears pricked at that. *Veranda.* Amidonian, then. From somewhere in the continent's southern climes. They hadn't heard the term since their semester touring seminaries, and that had been—

"Rimmerston," they said.

The man raised an eyebrow. It was, given the lines his face produced to accommodate it, his most natural expression. "I don't know that I've ever been identified so keenly by a single sentence."

"I can tell where you're *from*. That's quite a different thing than knowing who you are."

"All of a piece, really." The stranger from Rimmerston gestured at the railing beside Cyd. "Do you mind?" He produced an engraved cigarette case with an apologetic expression. "If I don't take some bad air soon, my nerves will drive me to a killing spree."

Cyddra couldn't help it. They laughed. They eased back against the railing and let their wineglass dangle, cupped lazily in their palm. "None for me, please. I gave it up. Yellows the screens and walls here so easily. But you are more than welcome if the alternative is homicide."

"My thanks."

The stranger settled a few feet from Cyd, just beyond arm's reach, which gave them some comfort. They surveyed him again, up and down, and made no effort to conceal the inspection. It was useful to see how others responded to their open engagement. At times, it spurred interest. And, just as often, confusion, revulsion. Dismissal. It was better to force an interlocutor to reveal such prejudices outright than dance about them.

"It's barely after midnight. If murder seems reasonable, the soiree has deteriorated more quickly than I am accustomed to," they said.

"You come to these gatherings often?"

"It's a matter of course when one is the host."

The stranger had lit his cigarette and dropped the spent lucifer into a gust of wind. It tumbled toward one of the cascades pouring down the tower face, disappearing in a white cloud of mist.

The stranger chuckled. "When I make myself scarce at my own events, I am told I am rude."

"Well." Cyd sniffed. "That's Amidon for you. Rimmerston would never tolerate such behaviors."

"I think Rimmerston would rather forget me, given the chance. I made my fortune elsewhere."

"What a loss for them. You seem charming." Cyd made a point of holding the stranger's flinty gaze a moment longer than could be read as purely incidental. The man, they decided, would be quite excellent at cards.

"I don't believe I've had the pleasure of your name," they said, very slowly.

"Anselm Meteron," he replied. "At your service."

Cyd arched an eyebrow. "Meteron. Not, by any chance—"

"By that very chance."

"Most interesting."

Meteron ashed his cigarette into the mists below. "You're a student of my father's philosophies, I suppose."

"Proof save me, no. I couldn't give a mouse's turd for applied social economics. Well, not as they apply to humans, in any case."

If Cyd's practiced irreverence had any effect on their interlocutor, Meteron's card player face forbade telling it. "My focus is on the lanyani," they added, by way of explanation. They raised their glass, swirling its dregs with a theatrical interest. The wine was particularly keen that night—sharp on the tongue and light-fingered with the senses. It blurred the edges of Cyd's judgment in a most delightful way. "I study their culture."

"Do you really."

Some part of Cyd registered, through a warm and comfortable haze, that Meteron's voice lacked the terminal rise natural to a query. They sidled closer. The man did not retreat. The night air, damp with the rising mist of the tower's falls, sparkled all around. They were seized by a curious desire to kiss this Anselm Meteron—to taste if the bitter drawl in his voice lingered on his tongue.

Meteron's face was very close now, the brackets of his wicked mouth provocatively clear. Cyd leaned, feeling their breath meet his, lips parted. They closed their eyes only a little, smiling.

"The lanyani have no gender, you know," Cyd murmured. "No fixed definition of that social construct, and no need for it. They evolve as they please. Some never put on the ornaments of gender at all."

"Fascinating."

His hand wound round Cyd's hip, drawing their body gently against his. They felt the pressure of Meteron's grip, strange and imbalanced, something missing in it. The drink, they thought. It was their third of the night, and it was making them feel things that weren't real.

Well. *Some* things that weren't real.

"I learned a lot from studying them," Cyd continued, tracing a hand along Meteron's jaw. "A lot about myself. About making choices."

Meteron's face dipped, mouth pressed to Cyd's throat and working upward, searching and slow. Cyd hummed with pleasure, sagging against the rail. Meteron's body met Cyd's planes and curves, his other arm wrapped around their body.

"And what did you choose?" Meteron murmured into the thumbprint of Cyd's collarbone.

"That in some things, it's more natural not to choose."

They reached to take Meteron's face in their hands, to guide that wicked mouth toward hungry lips, but their hands hung heavy, stubbornly unresponsive. Cyd's heart pounded, and their fingers slipped, unbidden, away from Meteron's cheeks. They blinked to clear a fog that was more than the wine, more than—

Wait. *No.*

A very small voice, blurry with more than drink, protested from some half-forgotten corner of Cyd's brain: *Run.*

But Meteron had them against the railing, and his mouth was no longer warm and sensual against their flesh. It turned into a hard line, sharp as a knife's edge.

"Well," he purred. "I am sorry to say, sooner or later, everyone has to make at least one choice they can never go back on."

Cyd blinked. A nimbus of pale light surrounded Anselm Meteron's face. It rotated slowly, and it was all they could do to keep from feeling they would fall, spinning helpless and limp, from the Tower of Water itself.

"What do you want?" they said thickly.

"Quite a lot, actually. First, I need to know this: how badly do you want to live, Cyddra Tsuneteva?"

Meteron's words were almost enough to dispel the fog gathering around Cyd's wits. Almost. Their heart thundered for entirely new reasons.

"You're going to kill me?"

"Technically, I'm already killing you. You must drink a good deal of that Samoan white to have needed three doses of the toxin in it before feeling any effects. Your liver and mine would make admirable companions."

Cyd realized the sudden listing of the Tower was their own gradual slump. Meteron gathered them up, lounging on the intricate tiles of the balcony with Cyd's head in his lap, toying gently with their hair. To anyone passing by the closed balcony doors, it would look like a lover's tryst—a moment of foreplay elegantly framed by the swirling mist and the lamps of the river below. It would not have been the first time Cyd had lain in the arms of a beautiful man or woman, where anyone might see.

And Meteron must have known it.

"You should know," he said amicably, "I've no desire to kill you, though it's been requested of me in the most specific and urgent of terms."

Cyd licked their lips. Why was their mouth so dry? "Who?"

"The Curator. The Grand Librarian herself."

What little order remained in Cyd's mind rallied itself to this puzzle. "But . . . the Tsuneteva wing . . . named for my family. Donors."

"Fabulously wealthy dilettante scholars, the lot of you. Loyal to the EC in vague, broad gesticulations of money, but not *so* loyal that studying something as déclassé as xenoculture got you disowned. Your family's money was very useful to the Grand Library and a fine excuse to give you all the access to the collections you wished. But it's your *research* that's made the old woman rather . . . uncertain of your value going forward."

"Why?"

Meteron smiled. "Why, indeed?"

Cyd managed to shake their head. The nimbus of light was fading now, a burning blackness like the charring edges of paper touched to flame taking its place. They did not want to think what would happen after their vision burned through.

"No, why . . . why *you?*" Cyd asked.

"Because I am very good at killing people, and she trusted me not to make a botch of it. Because she's holding back something I want very badly. And because whatever you know or can do scares her, which means I want it as badly as she wants it to go away."

Meteron leaned close. For a delirious instant, Cyd thought this might be the longed-for kiss, some fatal mockery of what had almost happened moments before. Instead, his breath brushed their ear in a whisper, delicious and sinister, smelling of cinders.

"Remember what I said about choices?" His lips grazed Cyd's ear, murmuring into their hair. "You have less than two minutes to make yours."

Cyd's eyes didn't want to work right. They tried to blink. Only a flicker of response came, instead. The stars were stingingly bright in the burning tunnel of their vision. Hot tears spilled down their cheeks, trying to ease the pain. Something pressed down on their chest, the heaviest weight they'd ever felt.

"Here are your possible elections, Cyddra. Option one: after tonight, you are, as far as anyone else knows, dead. I'll take you from this place by a route I've planned in advance. You see to the details of disappearing in the long term, but you stay close. I'll have a job for you. It's what you'll do to repay me for not letting the poison take its course. As a bonus, it's work that might save humankind from its ultimate destruction, so there's even a delightful moral frisson thrown in the bargain. When the work is done, you get back whatever life you care to buy with your fortune, as far from that mad, ancient harridan as you can get. Or, option two: you politely decline and find yourself well and truly dead. The kind of dead where other people see to the details. Now close your mouth and swallow if you elect option one."

Cyd feared for an instant that they couldn't do it. Their lips buzzed with an almost painful numbness. But then, by an effort of will, they forced their mouth closed over their tongue and choked down the dry stone sitting in their throat.

Anselm Meteron turned his wrist like a street conjuror producing a sleeved card and a small phial appeared in his hand. He pressed it into the taut corner of Cyd's mouth. A powder sifted over their gums and between their teeth, slowly coating their tongue. The warm, strange numbness was still gathering all around, wrapping Cyd like a blanket.

They had a vague sense of Meteron casting about for something— picking up and tossing aside the cup with Cyd's poisoned drink before finally muttering a resigned curse.

All at once, he kissed them, his urgent mouth probing theirs. The dry powder—the antidote, Cyd realized—softened with the kiss and finally took hold, their rigid body going slack in his arms. A gasp of relief rose in Cyddra's throat. Meteron seemed to take it for a moan of pleasure. The kiss deepened, if only for a moment.

Meteron eased Cyd down again, laying them again in his lap. He fished about his coat, producing a handkerchief to dab at the tears running unchecked down their throat.

"I hate to have been a tease before, but I had to help the poison get started," he explained, in the same tone with which he might have given the rules of a card game to a novice. "After three doses and no real effects, I couldn't just follow a server and drug your cup again. That would risk the toxin being stronger than the antidote could counter. Had to get your heart going to make it take. But that was good for me, too. There's so little left in the world I can really call novel."

Cyd glared up at him, trying—and failing—to sit up and shove him away.

"No, don't," Meteron advised. "The Old Bear tells me you'll be a half-hour or better shedding the ill effects. Best not to rush it. The antidote already needed a little help getting moist enough to process."

"Bastard," Cyd spat.

"Undoubtedly. Now, friend. How about you lay here awhile and tell me all about what you've learned that makes Madame Curator so very ill at her ease?"

"And when I finish?"

"When you finish, we start the exciting process of convincing the world you really have died. But that will involve our secret, torrid affair and your precipitous leap from this remarkable tower."

Cyd's eyes went wide. "No one will believe that."

Meteron quirked an eyebrow. "In our affair? I assure you, I've cultivated a reputation which ensures people believe me capable of damned near anything." And he smiled. "Besides, who's to say there isn't something to it? I do love exploring the unknown."

"Fuck you."

"Not here. It's wet and we'd take a chill. Now about your scholarship. There are people dying in Corma because the lanyani are working with the aigamuxa."

"What does that have to do with me?"

"The Trees are your pet subject, no? Why would they be taking orders from the apes?"

Cyddra snorted. "Don't be so sure you haven't got that backwards."

Meteron's face closed like a door. "Interesting. While you're shifting that world view, try me another one: what on earth would learning to translate the lanyani language have to do with the woman charged to maintain the Amanuensis library?"

It was Cyd's turn to smile. "I think," they croaked, "you've just answered your own question."

31.

The Reverend Doctor Phillip Chalmers lacked the endurance for late nights unless he had a specific project in hand—a kind of mental wheel and grindstone. Absent that encouragement, he was keen for bedtime followed by a lie-in as early as he might possibly find an excuse. As dawn crept nearer that 10th of Eightmonth, his task—self-appointed and long-suffering—was waiting. It seemed unlikely to be rewarded before the breakfast cart came along.

Chalmers paced the common area of their company's apartments. He straightened books piled on the low dining table and sorted through his notations on the research patterns of various members of the EC he had deemed suspicious following their sudden departure the morning of his escape from Regenzi's captivity. Various historians and philosophers. Curiously few invested in the hard sciences. Certainly, Cyddra Tsune-teva's name was nowhere on the list. Accomplished as they were, they had only dabbled at EC studies, staying in Rimmerston long enough to satisfy a few narrow curiosities before moving on to other universities and libraries the world over.

Chalmers had spent very little of his post-seminary years thinking about the foreigner who had found him amusing and paid for their shared apartment for a year on lark. Now, he feared Cyddra was dead, and someone he was supposed to call an ally was at fault.

The hall door opened, and Chalmers turned to see Anselm Meteron enter.

Meteron's hair was darkened and plastered by water still dribbling down his neck. His jacquard vest and silk cravat were altogether ruined, and an audible squishing in Meteron's dress shoes suggested the sartorial losses might indeed be total. Strangest of all, the man looked—though very tired and completely sodden—thoroughly pleased.

"Good heavens," said Chalmers. "Did you fall in the river?"

"I jumped, and it wasn't in the river you're thinking of."

Chalmers watched Meteron squelch past, bearing for the bathroom. He paused at its door to kick off his shoes, pushed aside the screen, and walked straight for the broad, pool-like basin forever filled with piping bath water. He fell into it fully clothed, plunged below its surface, and breached nearly a minute after, gasping and mopping his hands down his face.

Uncertain if this was intended to mark the end of conversation, Chalmers followed, lingering in the door. "Do, um," he began. "Do I assume wrongly in thinking this means your mission didn't turn out as planned?"

Meteron sat up, unbuttoning his suit pieces, peeling off layers and throwing them on the tiled floor like so many rags. "You do. Everything's well in hand. Also, you might check my shoe. The left. There's a note from your friend that's probably survived my escapades. I don't think they like me at all. Pity."

Chalmers grimaced, recalling the vial of toxin, the antidote, the Alchemist's careful instructions before Meteron's departure, all given when Rowena was off investigating the Aggregator with her Literate friend.

"*Really*. Can't fathom why," Chalmers murmured.

He picked up the sodden shoe and fished about below its insole until he found a slender folded paper wrapped in a sheet of waxing apparently stolen off a caterer's cart. He shook the beaded moisture from it, found its closed seams, and unfolded it for reading. At his back, Meteron splashed out of the bath, humming tunefully. Chalmers read and felt himself turn a positively chameleonic range of colors.

"Holy Reason, what did you do to them?"

Meteron shouldered past him, more soap-scented than river-sopped, a towel wrapped around his waist.

"Well, I didn't kill them, for one thing, so whatever they have to say about me is thoroughly unjust."

"Only that you're a seducer, a liar, and a fink."

Meteron shrugged and opened the liquor cabinet. "Actually, that's quite fair. Carry on." He squinted at a brandy, seemed to find it acceptable, and poured himself a generous helping.

"*Send a packet for translation via a Fabricated. Master Meteron will know to whence it should be bound,*" Chalmers recited. He waved the paper incredulously. "What are they talking about? I thought you wanted to keep Cyddra near at hand because Gammon wanted access to a scholar of lanyani culture."

"I did," Meteron agreed. He winced at the brandy's bite, recoiling from the glass to sniff it mournfully. "Oh, this is horrible. Probably been airing since before the cricket was born."

Chalmers stepped round the liquor cabinet's sideboard, still flapping the note. "Focus, please. What did you ask them to *translate?*"

He patted Chalmers with a four-and-a-half-fingered hand, speaking for a moment like a tolerant father. "*Phillip. Think.* I went out tonight to commit murder and ruin my very best traveling formals to give us access to a *whole roomful of books.* Books that, I recall, you have seen the like of before and needed to translate. Books that are quite time-consuming to work through."

Chalmers swatted Meteron's hand away, glowering. "Of *course* I remember the books in the Amanuen—" He hesitated. "—sis library. Wait. Does Cyddra know the Enochian code?"

Meteron rolled his eyes, dumped his brandy in a potted bamboo, and strode for his bedroom door. "They don't know *the Enochian code.* They know *lanyani.* And that's what your precious books turn out to be written in."

More than a few times, Phillip Chalmers had heard the colloquial saying that a man, issued the right kind of shock, might be knocked over with a feather. At that moment, he felt quite certain it was more than a mere turn of phrase.

"Wait—"

"I'll explain to the lot of you in the morning. We'll need the facts straight before we spark Gammon. I've a date with my ether now. Be a good lad and order up something that *isn't* pickled for breakfast, would you?"

Chalmers stared at the door panel as it snapped shut, half hoping it could furnish answers—or perhaps a share of Meteron's ether. His own sleep seemed further off than ever.

32.

The corpse that was not a corpse lay before Rahielma in a heap, its limbs tumbled like a marionette fallen from its puppeteer's hand. She shifted forward in her pedestal position, splaying her fingers for better balance, and craned her slitted nose closer to the lifeless thing.

Lifeless?

No. *Almost* lifeless. Rahielma had seen death many times before—more than she could count without a long and careful reflection. It was the almost-ness of the creature's lifelessness that troubled her.

As she pulled back, the smell of something earthy and rich and other than putrescence tickling her senses, the corpse-thing twitched.

Sunbelma recoiled. She walked backward on her hands, eye-heels wide and boggling on her shoulders.

You are the chieftain, Rahielma reminded herself. *You cannot flinch.*

But she wanted to. Oh, how she longed to.

"What is it?" Sunbelma hissed.

Rahielma's eye-heels narrowed in thought. Then she folded upward, feet to the ground, the world gone dark.

"It is our doing, somehow. I smell the powder the lanyani asked us to put in the rats' dens and on the pigeons' wings. It's alive. Growing."

"Things always grow in corpses."

"This is different."

Rahielma reached up and grasped the cargo net that linked the rows of alley and fire escapes across open air. She climbed fast, her eyes staring down at the ground as it raced ever farther away, her body swinging upward. Sunbelma took to the nets in her wake. Rahielma stretched a leg out, eye closed to keep from dizzying herself with a split gaze, and hooked it, ankle and foot, through a neighboring net. She flipped down and around to the wide balcony formed by an old warehouse's split facade. She landed, hands planted, and bent her legs around to take in the sight of her sons, wrestling with their cousins around the cooking fire. Nasievan, withered as an old root, sat with his legs folded, one atop the other, his eyes gazing from atop his knees—too stiffened by his years to bend fully back. Decades past his warrior prime, he took pride in playing the children's beva.

"You saw the dead thing, then," he called to the chieftain and her bond-sister.

Rahielma lifted one hand to caress her youngest son's back as he tumbled past. She settled beside Nasievan and, out of deference to his age, folded her legs as he did. She would not shame him by holding her gaze higher than his.

"How long has it been there?" she asked, keeping her voice low.

"Since dawn. Nassunbel found it and covered it with a tarp so the children would not see."

Sunbelma settled on the other side of the fire. It seemed to grow up between her knees, her eyes flanking the blaze. She tended a kettle nestled beside it and turned a piece of meat roasting over in the high flames.

"I smell something like the powder we used to treat the vermin for the lanyani. The powder they said would destroy the city," said Rahielma.

"A fungus," Nasievan said. "Cordyceps, most likely."

Rahielma frowned. There was a certainty in his voice. Cordyceps? Had she even heard that word before?

Yes . . . Yes, she had. Dor had used it, once, when explaining her plan—the same night Rahielma herself had dosed the sea terns Dor had asked for with the powder (*to strengthen them for the voyage ahead*, Dor had claimed). The lanyani leader had orders for the birds, coded in the pollen they bore—instructions to her kinfolk far abroad, where one of the Nine lay just out of reach.

For now. Only for now.

"Dor asked us to help her make the humans submit." Rahielma's brow furrowed. She longed for Nasrahiel. He never struggled to find the right words. "To . . . break their city. Will the cordyceps not do this?"

"It will," the elder sighed. "All too well, I think. It rides within the body and sometimes moves it like a puppet."

Rahielma remembered the fallen creature, the vision of a marionette with cut strings somehow still twitching. She shivered.

"What would make it stop?"

A shrug. "All creatures need nourishment. If the cordyceps has consumed enough of the host that contains it, perhaps it would die, as well. The thing below, it twitches. But less now than when Nassunbel first found it."

"Why would the lanyani do such a thing? Why not simply poison men and kill them?" Sunbelma's voice, subdued with horror, sounded much farther away than the other side of the fire.

Rahielma considered the question. Creatures containing the cordyceps could be used. Directed, perhaps. But so could the lanyani's own cuttings and seedlings. The lanyani had rallied, so many copse clans and volunteer groups massing about the Hill, it was a wonder any of the humans in the north of the city could sleep soundly in their beds. She wondered if any did, anymore.

"You've seen these things before, these cordyceps?" Rahielma asked Nasievan.

"Mostly in lesser creatures. Dogs and rats. Insects."

"How do such creatures behave? Is there a pattern, a purpose?"

"The cordyceps drives its host to seek out conditions in which it can flourish. But if the lanyani have created this cordyceps, then it could do much more than that."

Rahielma did not think of herself as imaginative, but she had imagination enough to fear her elder's words were true. She nodded grimly. A distant whoop sounded over the crackling fire—the calls of aigamuxa coming home to their food and fellows, ready to turn in to their burrows and sleep out the day. The wrestling children's shadows tangled in the glow of firelight.

"Could these fungi enter us, Nasievan?" Rahielma wondered aloud.

His head turned, wrinkled brow raised as if surprised at her ignorance. "Of course. We may be the chosen people, but we are all made of the same flesh."

"I must speak with Dor," Rahielma resolved aloud. "She has not dealt plainly with us."

Sunbelma's face contorted with worry. "And what will you do, chieftain?"

Rahielma stared at her sons through the flickering flames. They had spent themselves in roughhousing and lay in a panting heap. The shabby warehouse floor below filled with aigamuxa meeting—touching hands, bowing eye-heels to one another, making spaces by their fires to spread plates and cups and whatever food forage and felony had provided. She had put too much faith in the Trees and the power of a shared enemy to make them . . . what? Trustworthy? No. Even that was too much to have hoped for. The enemy of her enemy was not a friend; it might even be something worse than an enemy. One look around her ragged people turned the truth like a knife in her heart.

"I don't know," Rahielma answered at last. "But I will not go alone. I will go armed with answers of my own."

33.

Bess Earnshaw padded down the steps from Rowena's bedroom into the Stone Scales's back-room kitchen, muffling a yawn. She still hadn't quite gotten used to thinking of Rowena having a bedroom or a place of her own, least of all this place. Bess most certainly didn't sit comfortably with having a room there all to herself. The Stone Scales was every bit as intimidating from the back of its sales counter as it had been from the front, full of things she wasn't meant to be in charge of. Customers seemed resigned to her limited competence. They got their prescriptions and standing orders filled, and most didn't ask when the Alchemist would return. It was simply a given that he would. The people of Westgate Bridge could imagine him disappearing without a word of explanation. He was, to their way of thinking, some sort of wizard, and that was what all the old stories said wizards were prone to doing. His equally sudden return was as inevitable and guaranteed as the sunrise.

And so Bess Earnshaw began her day before dawn, stoking the fire in the pot-bellied stove and putting a kettle on for her breakfast, unlocking the yard door and pulling the milk bottles in before the hot summer's morning could turn them. Then she attended to the front door, whose traps stood watch all night, armed and ready.

Disarming their mechanisms was the part of the daily routine she liked least, but the Alchemist had been resolute in his instructions: she was to set the safeguard bulbs each night and secure them again during the day. If the worst that happened was a daily ritual that came to nothing, she should count herself lucky.

Bess was in the middle of counting herself tired when, one hand still stoppering the bulb at the door's right-hand cornice and detaching the tubing connecting it to the shop's lamp-sparker, she heard the back door slam.

Bess froze, listening. A noise she might have mistaken for the pre-dawn breeze panting at the kitchen curtains. A scratching sound. Foot-steps.

She unstoppered the bulb again and reattached the tubing. Too soon to turn off her security measures, after all.

"H'lo?" she called. An umbrella rested in a stand near the door. She took it, holding it like a sword, and paced the room's perimeter, eyes focused on the curtained doorway behind the shop counter. She stood perfectly still, listening, but heard only her heart thudding between her ears.

The air split with a groan, then a snap. Metal giving way a moment before wood. The door to the storage closet? Or the cellar? Bess shifted the umbrella in her grip and checked its nickel-pointed end, as if it had by some miracle turned into a proper weapon.

It hadn't.

She had crept to the counter's edge and could slip into the kitchen fast as a mouse. But what would she do then? Lure the intruder to the front? Try to make them leave by the main door and hope the acid-spilling mechanism was as effective triggered from the inside as it was from outside? Possible. But Bess had too low an opinion of her luck to trust in that plan.

She rushed through the curtain, instead, hollering and brandishing the umbrella, and found—no one. The small, shabby room sat empty, after all. Bess frowned. She couldn't have imagined the disturbance, all that noise. The door to the cellar—

She turned to check it and a huge, many-knuckled hand clapped over her nose and mouth, stifling a scream. Two powerful arms hauled her back against a looming body. It had been crowded into the corner near the coal scuttle, its animal odor masked by the oily fire and air gone dusty with splintered wood. Bess managed to look straight up, her eyes half-covered by long, clawed fingers.

An eyeless face loomed near her own. Bess's screams were choked off by the aigamuxa's barbed fingers plugging her mouth.

"Take me to where the old man keeps the things that kill plants," the creature rumbled.

Part of Bess's mind screamed that she should struggle—should lash out, and bite, and kick. But it was such a small part, smothered by the rest of her, which had fled from the terror, cornering itself like a rabbit. She tried to answer. Even without the aiga muffling her, nothing intelligible would come.

The aigamuxa's hands and arms relaxed, inch by inch, a python easing its crushed prey loose. Bess struggled to keep from sliding down its body, her knees jellied by fear.

"Show me," the creature repeated. "Please."

Bess tasted copper. She put her fingers to her mouth and felt the ragged sting where her lip had been gashed by the aigamuxa's lobstered fingers. *Please.* It had said, *Please.*

"I don't really know what's in this shop," she protested. "I'm sorry, but it's true."

Anger twisted the aiga's eyeless face. "Who does know?"

Bess had been about to answer—to try, at least, though she couldn't imagine what she could say to calm the creature. The scrape of a boot on the shop's back step snapped the silent tension. Through the slice of the door hanging open (*Stupid, stupid, why didn't you lock the door after you brought in the milk?*) Bess saw a figure picking its way through the thicket of plants overtaking the yard.

The aigamuxa's face tilted toward the sound, orienting its ears. It sniffed. Bess felt the creature's growl through her back.

"Gammon," it snarled.

The aigamuxa whirled toward to the yard door, Bess still hugged to its chest, and covered the threshold to the shop counter with its broad body. Bess yelped in terror. Her cry alerted the former City Inspector, who spun through the door with her monstrous pistol drawn, finger resting against the trigger guard.

Its barrel all but stared through Bess's chest. She stifled a whimper.

"Let go of the girl," said Gammon. "Very slowly. I won't shoot you."

The aigamuxa snorted. "I will not release the only thing keeping you from shooting me. I know that gun, Inspector. I've smelled its powder before. I tended my kin who survived its wounds."

"You can't see if I'm about to pull the trigger when you're on your feet. She's no good as a hostage against it."

"I disagree."

The aigamuxa reached around Bess's face and wrenched her chin around, turning her head as if she might bottle-twist her body open. Her vision exploded with comets and stars, white-hot with pain.

"I can hear if you've dropped the gun," growled the aiga. "You have until I reach ten to do so."

Another sharp, twisting pressure brought tears to Bess's eyes.

"One . . . two . . ."

Baubles of color and light swam before her. Her legs, she realized, weren't holding her up anymore—

"Three . . ."

The room erupted in a thunderclap. The floor surged up to meet Bess's face. The aigamuxa's roar of pain and rage was muted, as if it came from the other side of a bad vox line, a smell like ozone hanging in the air. Bess rolled over, pushing herself away from the pool of blood spreading near her dressing gown. *Had she been shot?*

She reached something hard that jangled loudly enough to reset the muffled buzzing in her ears. The coal scuttle. The whole room was a cacophony now, the aigamuxa staunching the blood from its grazed shoulder with the same clawed, four-jointed hand that had threatened to tear Bess apart moments before. The wound looked like someone had taken a melon baller and scooped out half the joint.

A hand closed on Bess's shoulder, hauling her away from the wounded aigamuxa. Gammon never took the gun, or her eyes, off her target, even as she tugged and prodded Bess toward the back door.

"Bitch! Traitor!" the aigamuxa wailed. Bess stared, suddenly realizing it was female—there was a definite high-toned register of distress in its cries. Beneath the knotted muscle of the chest Bess had been clutched against lay her bare, now bloodied, breasts.

"Tell me who you are and why you came here and I won't shoot again," Gammon shouted over the aiga's cries.

She folded downward, more a crouch than a proper pedestal position, and put her right leg over her shoulder, kneeling on the left and letting that side's wounded arm hang limp. The bloody milk-eye was shot through with veins of pain and anger and . . . Bess frowned. Grief?

"I want a poison to keep the lanyani at bay," she gasped. "I want something that will cleanse the cordyceps before it can harm my people."

Gammon's jaw tightened. "I met a child of your tribe tainting vermin by the south river quays. The poison is called cordyceps?"

"Perhaps. One of my elders believes so."

"This child of yours—"

"Not mine," the aigamuxa snapped. "Perhaps some other chieftain's child. I told Dor I would send my people out to spread her poison but never sent children. Other tribes chose differently."

"This child said his beva had done the dosing, until she took sick."

The aiga nodded, panting, and gave up keeping a foot aloft so she could close a hand over her wound. "I sent our poisoners away until they completed all their duties to the lanyani, so that if they suffered ill effects they might recover before returning to us." Her head bowed. "None have yet returned. I had hoped it was because the task was such a large one. But I have hoped in vain. I saw a human body taken with the sickness. It might have been dead. Should have been."

Gammon grimaced in something that might have been sympathy. She put out her left wrist to brace the muzzle of the heavy gun, now shaking in her grasp.

She did not lower it.

"I knew the Alchemist was gone. I have watched him ever since my chief fell, waiting. Hoping . . ." Whatever the aiga might have finished that thought with never came. "Dor said she would use her book to follow him and the girl he kept. I had hoped to steal from this place some protection for my people."

"Wait." Gammon did move the blunderbuss a little now, lifting her finger from the trigger. "You're Rahielma. Nasrahiel's mate."

"And you are the creature who betrayed him when he destroyed Regenzi."

Gammon ignored that. "Bess, spark Jane at her workshop. We need her to send Julian—and Nasrahiel."

A sound escaped the wounded Rahielma, something between a gasp and a bark. It might have been a word in her language. Bess thought she had heard Nasrahiel make just such a sound before.

"He's with Jane Ardai getting an adjustment," Gammon explained.

"An adjustment," Rahielma echoed, uncomprehending.

Bess turned toward the nook with the vox line and galvano-graph box, then hesitated. "Haadiyaa, I don't think this is a good—"

"He lives?" Rahielma demanded.

"He does. But you won't, losing all that blood. If you can keep from killing me, I think that table might hold your weight. There are bandages aplenty here. Can I trust you to let me use them?"

The aiga's brow furrowed with more than pain. "Can I trust you to stow your weapon?"

Slowly, Gammon set the oversized pistol down on a driftwood chair, careful to let Rahielma's one raised pink eye follow her movements.

"Your move," she said.

"Actually," Bess said, tearing a spark from the galvano-gram printer. "I think it may be ours. There's news from Nippon."

34.

A key in a lock, a turn, and the door opened.

Though the rest of his party were all too ready to cross the threshold into the Grand Library's long-withheld Amanuensis collection, the Alchemist stood to the side to consider the space and let others pass. Madame Kurowa swept a hand over the chamber, not with the élan of a cabaret maestra unveiling a prized performer, but as a monarch introducing a favored subject. The ovoid chamber's three levels rose upward, bathed in sunlight from the peaked confection of glass and brass adorning the ceiling above. Anselm strode in, hands folded behind his back, looking unapologetically smug. Phillip Chalmers nearly bowled Rowena over, and then retreated a step, mastering his eagerness long enough to remember to be a gentleman and let her pass. The girl rewarded his gallantry with a confused stare and a shrug, which the Reverend Doctor's durable obliviousness permitted him to survive without embarrassment. Comfortable at the rear, the Alchemist came through last, only half-listening to Madame Kurowa's instructions to Chalmers.

His mind was, as it had been for the last several days, deeply divided.

". . . freedom of entry day or night. We have lifted the hall guards for the remainder of your stay and installed a lock on the door with a key only your party possesses," Kurowa explained as she watched the visitors walk the center space and its glass-shielded cabinets of identical-seeming texts.

"Our party and you," Anselm noted.

She smiled. There was nothing pleasant in the expression. "Your party and I, yes, Master Meteron. The lift access code will be changed to a sequence of your choosing. That, too, will be shared with me. For the sake of the collection's well-being, you understand."

Books, Rare called from a corner, where her phantom self perched sidesaddle on a long cabinet, *don't* have *well-being*.

It was precisely the kind of petty side-commentary Erasmus had been working to filter out—the kind that, if Rare pushed hard enough, he was in real danger of responding to aloud.

But the comment did provoke a question.

"It seems strange to put a skylight in a room of books you are eager to preserve against damage," he said.

Kurowa nodded. "This was once the private meditation chamber of the monastic order that constructed this building, ages ago—long before the Library became a part of the Protectorate. It was sufficiently remote from the rest of the complex to suit the Amanuensis collection's . . . necessary exclusivity. The glass is treated to filter out the wavelengths of light that do the worst damage to the books. Ultimately, natural light still poses less of a risk of destruction than gas lamps, arc lamps, or even bioluminescent plants, which can molder over time."

She likes that you asked that, Rare observed. *Was that the point of asking?*

The point of asking, Erasmus thought back, *was determining how unusual the glass is, should we find ourselves needing to breach it.*

Ann must be so proud of you, thinking of the next sideline.

I'm sure he's thought of that already.

"We ask that you handle the texts with the archive kits provided," Kurowa continued. She opened a low cabinet near the entrance where prepared trays of magnifying glasses, book props, lead weights, and pencils waited. "Leave anything you've used on top of this sideboard. It will be properly cleaned and treated before the next day."

Kurowa said her goodbyes, leaving the four companions—or the four that could see one another—alone in the strange, layered room.

Rowena peeked out from behind a long, glass bookcase, smiling mischief at Anselm. "Race you to the top?"

Ann's answer was to wink and bolt around the bookcase, peeling for the nearest set of stairs.

"Not fair!" Rowena wailed. "You didn't say 'go' you cheat, you arse, come back!"

Rare watched the girl disappear up the staircase, leaping the steps two at a time. Her features creased unhappily. Then she looked toward Chalmers, who was already pulling an archive kit and bringing it back to a shelf on the main floor.

Erasmus stood just behind Chalmers as he carefully selected a book—one of the last in the sequence whose spines were marked with arcane notations likely indicating dates. Chalmers glanced at him, gesturing to the volume, as if to say, "After you?"

"Carry on," Erasmus said.

Chalmers opened the book and stared down at the page. The Reverend Doctor's brow creased. Rare's revenant passed her father a skeptical look. He shook his head, very slightly. *Not now.*

"Do you believe it's true?" Chalmers blurted. He froze, looking up at the top tier of the chamber, where Rowena seemed to have just beaten Anselm to the final step, based on her unladylike gloating. He continued, more quietly. "That all of this is written in the lanyani's language, I mean?"

Erasmus donned his spectacles. He considered the blocky, serif-heavy shapes crowding the page. "Why would you rather it was not?"

"I never said that!" The young man paused, as if suddenly remembering to whom he spoke. He grimanced. "Very well. I would rather it were not true."

The Alchemist waited.

Rare smiled. *You know, I always hated when you did this 'patience while the student teaches themself' thing to me, but it's really quite delightful to watch with this idiot. I've seen kinotrope shows with less drama.*

Hush, the Alchemist replied.

"I'm not sure what the worst part is," Chalmers admitted. "The fact that, if this is true, it confirms our denial of the lanyani's civility as specious nonsense. Or that it renders the years I spent working what I thought was a cipher into an embarrassing waste of time. Or . . ." He looked to Erasmus uncertainly, as if hoping to read in the older man's features an understanding of what he was unwilling to say aloud.

"Or that it calls into question the actual purpose of this Grand Experiment," Erasmus completed.

Rare peered at the topmost balcony, the rise and fall of Anselm and Rowena's voices in conversation plainly audible. *Or who it's really about,* she added.

"Do you always try to trip people in the last leg of a race?" Master Meteron demanded, scowling at Rowena as she paced up and down the long rows of books lining the walls of the third balcony.

"If I want to win, sure."

Rowena ran her fingertips along the glass, counting bookcases under her breath. The shelves curved like the ribs of some great beast. She puzzled over the books' curious spines. She had seen sets of books in identical binding before. The Stone Scales boasted more than a few encyclopedias, and she'd seen bookshop windows with dainty sets of research diaries and philosophical arguments by Lucan or Dideraut or Chatterjee-Bhalla. But Rowena Downshire had never seen whole shelves—no, a whole library within a library—with books so identical in every respect. Each was bright red, with a seal on the spine featuring the Ecclesiastical Commission's insignia, and a range of numbers that meant nothing to her. More than that, the books were the same height, the same thickness, even the same in their degree of dusty disuse.

"These are . . . weird," she decided.

Meteron plucked a tome from the shelf. After a moment, he slid it back and continued pacing after her. "Looks like these each cover a period of a few years, based on the dates."

"You can read the dates?"

"They're from the old calendar, before the Unity. We started counting over from zero after the Ecclesiastical Commission formed."

"So, it's 277 in the EC calendar."

"And 1794 in the old calendar," Master Meteron finished.

Rowena walked down the curve of another aisle, calling over her shoulder, "How far back d'you suppose the record goes?"

"If the books average, say, five years apiece, and each of these cabinets holds around fifty volumes—"

Rowena paused in rolling aside a glass panel. "Wait. That's—that's *hundreds* and *hundreds* of years. Way before the Unity. Way before the EC."

"This used to be a monastery, in the old days."

Rowena frowned. "Kneeler?"

"Not in the sense you mean. Anti-attachment pagans. Naturalists. Meditation masters."

"But they were still keeping records."

"Seems that way." Meteron opened the cabinet Rowena had stepped away from and brushed a thumb over the seal on a book's spine. "These could have been added at any time. Easy enough to standardize the collection after the fact."

"So, now that we know how far back this really goes . . . what do we *actually* know?"

"We know more about what we *need* to know."

"I don't follow."

Meteron peered up and down the row of shelving, gestured to the curve where it passed out of clear view. "The math doesn't add up, even if one takes the old monastic orders into consideration. There are thousands of years recorded here. Bear ever told you how long mankind has kept written records?"

"No."

"A really fucking long time. And this lot—the Grand Library, and the EC, and the monastics before them—haven't been organized long enough to account for all of it. These texts came from somewhere else first."

Rowena followed him down the aisle, then paused as he followed the bend toward the opposite side of the balcony, wrapping behind another wall of shelving.

1794, he'd said.

Rowena scanned the spines nearest by. The oldest volumes must be kept at the top of the chamber, based on these dates. One stared at her through the glass, its dulled numbers barely legible: *11m380–2m384*. The m's, she decided, were likely markers of months, which meant the short number after was a year. She had to work at remembering that if what Anselm had said was true, these weren't dates for the future, but of the distant past.

The rogue had wound away some distance, finally stopping centuries away. She walked after him, scanning the shelves, and noticed one book in particular had grabbed his attention. *Xm519–Xm521*(*), it read.

He opened the glass, pulled the volume, and turned it over in his hands.

"What's the little star about, d'you suppose?" Rowena asked.

"An asterisk."

"A what?"

"That's what it's called. Notates some exception or detail peculiar to this volume. Most of the volumes in this block seem to have it. The month notation is an X, which suggests—" he shrugged.

"The date's just a guess?" Rowena finished.

"Likely. Notice anything else?"

Meteron turned to a page at random. Rowena had seen the active book—the active Amanuensis, she guessed she should call it—back in the Old Cathedral's bowels, even watched some of the text swimming to the surface of its pages. At first, she thought it was just the stillness of the blocky, serif-heavy markings Chalmers had called "Enochian" that seemed strange. But then, she looked closer and noticed some shapes, totally meaningless to her, but familiar for their frequency, and they were . . . wrong. Or—no. Not wrong, but—

"The writing isn't shaped the same as the others," she announced. "This is a copy."

Meteron nodded. "So it seems, cricket. These ancient volumes came from somewhere else, from some other medium, and were transferred here."

"And then, sometime or other, the library must have had an active book here at the same time as a blank text when the old book filled up, and then—boom."

"Boom," Meteron murmured.

Rowena studied his cagey face, frowning. "You say there's somebody who can translate these for us, fast?"

"Faster than Chalmers fooling with ciphers."

"I suppose," she continued, "it's too much to hope you can, y'know, just bring them up here to have a look-see?"

"From what I've pieced together, it's their having come here and had a *look-see* before that makes it impossible now."

"So how're we going to get the information we need out of these books?"

"Simple, cricket. We'll make our own copies."

"How?"

Meteron smiled wickedly. "I thought you'd never ask."

35.

owena had always been talented in at least three things, in no particular order: reading people, sneaking about, and being persistent. Master Meteron's plan seemed to her a good one, especially since she had been so sure she had a solid read on Third Literate Umiko Haroda and the perfect lever to encourage her help.

That self-assurance didn't seem well-placed, anymore.

Umiko glared at Rowena through her clockmaker's lenses. "I'm not doing it, so you can just stop asking."

"Oh, come *on*. Why not? You're always keen to nick out of here when Kurowa's not crawling down your kimono. And I even have permission to go *into* the Amanuensis library and everything now. I've a key! Did I show you the key?"

Umiko's glass-magnified eyes rolled dramatically. "Is it *really* your key?"

Rowena pouted. "Fine. Master Meteron gave me his, because the Old Bear wouldn't let Kurowa give me my own copy. But it's a *real* key and it actually works, and now that I'm supposed to be doing secretarial things for Doctor Chalmers, there's no reason I have to stay in here and help mend Indexers."

"You mean 'no reason to stay in here, sneak out with Umiko, and make her run logs of the Bishop's questions to the Aggregator.'" Umiko pulled the goggles off and dropped them in a clattering heap on the Indexer she'd been recamming. "So fine. *Go.* Do your stupid plan and snatch a Fabricated and just see how it goes over. I *dare* you."

"Umiko," Rowena snapped. And then she stopped. The other girl

334

looked honestly hurt. "Umiko," she repeated, more gently. "I'm . . . I'm sorry. I didn't mean it like that. I just . . . I need your help. I've needed your help for days, and you've been there for me. The Old Bear has been looking into the results you pulled up, and he's . . ." She hesitated. Rowena knew all too well how much Umiko admired Bishop Meteron's skill with data. She hadn't shared just why following his trail of inquiries was so important, fearing Umiko would catch on that she wasn't actually an admirer of the Bishop's work, let alone a student of his methods.

Bishop Meteron had been at the head of a conspiracy that, not so long ago, wanted her dead. If she was safe now, it was only because he hadn't yet tried to find her. It wouldn't last. She knew that.

"Bear's been doing a lot of important work with it," Rowena finished.

It wasn't a lie. Using Umiko's reports, Chalmers's list of suspicious names had been pared, honed, and focused. That very day, the Old Bear was off looking into records of a certain Reverend Doctor Deliverance Tegura, who had come to the Library some months before to collect a parcel of data from the Aggregator on the Bishop's behalf, and then set out again. To Corma. Strangely, she hadn't been on the list of attendees suddenly disappeared from the Decadal Conference, so the Alchemist felt her case merited special attention.

Umiko sighed. "That's true?"

"That's really, *really* true."

"Fine. Explain what you want me to do again."

Rowena had to suppress a yelp of delight at her success. She pointed at the Indexer on which Umiko had been working. "How close are you to fixing that?"

"Not very. It'll take me hours more to—hey!"

Rowena snatched the Indexer and dumped all its unfastened gears and levers and keys and card-wheels into a heap on the floor. She thumped at its wooden frame, banging the errant bits out, leaving a hollow frame like an empty drawer.

"I was working on that!"

"Oh, hush, you said it wasn't near fixed anyhow. I'll help you sort it out once we're done, I promise."

Laying the box at her feet, Rowena crouched over the secretary's satchel she'd been carrying of late, full of spare ink pens, notebooks, sheaves of paper—and two books of a certain size in red binding with bright, gold-leaf stamping.

Umiko had been stunned by the abuse of her Indexer; now she looked positively horrified. "Wait, you've taken two books already?"

"Not yet. These are dummies. We need to go into the library and switch these out for two of the more recent volumes."

"Two?" Umiko frowned. "Isn't that a lot to work with, all at once?"

"Not more'n we can handle."

That was a lie. Rowena had sat up late into morning the night before last, following Master Meteron's lead as he guided her through making a credible forgery of an Amanuensis text using one of Chalmers's more disposable notebooks. It featured many pages of scrawl where the Reverend Doctor had attempted imitations of Enochian script—perhaps enough that a cursory inspection would not attract undue attention. She had crept into her own rooms the night after that, armed with most of the same tools and one of Chalmers's unused notebooks. The first hour of work had been nothing but the hand-cramping business of writing out nonsense imitations of Enochian, over and over, and adding in little sketches and graphs here and there for effect. The rest of the night had been occupied in cutting ersatz gold leaf, and re-clothing the cover, and so on. Rowena had every confidence their translator—whoever they were, wherever Master Meteron had secreted them away—could manage with one text. The second one wouldn't be a particular problem for them.

The second text was for her.

"We're going into the Amanuensis library and pulling two books, see? But we can't be seen taking books *out*. So we'll go in with this Indexer box, you coming along to help me run some numbers through it, since I don't know how to do it."

"And the box will just be a dummy with the two books in it?"

Rowena grinned. "Exactly! And it'll be how we sneak the two books we want out, out."

Umiko chewed her lip and crouched beside Rowena, squaring the two books inside the Indexer, trying to make them fit on the level. "How long before the real books come back?"

"Coupla days, I think."

"And you *will* bring them back?"

"I swear on the Proof, honest. They'll be safe as houses."

Umiko blinked. "Safe as . . . what does that mean?"

"It's an Amidonian thing. It means really, super safe."

Rowena's friend sighed. "I believe you. I don't know why I should."

She smiled back. "S'cause I have such an honest face."

One of them broke first, though Rowena couldn't say who for sure. By the time the Fabricated pushing the dinner bento came through, they were laughing themselves silly, unable to do more than wave the mechanical servitor off as it stood awaiting further orders, two meals stacked between its hands.

The girls ate, Umiko complimenting Rowena on her technique with chopsticks. Rowena wasn't altogether sure she deserved the praise, having dropped two fish rolls already in the space of the meal and chasing them all over a desktop that would need a good mopping-up after. But she was happy to see Umiko happy.

"I borrowed an old book of Engine code from the maintenance library night before last," Umiko volunteered through a mouth half-full of roe. "It's not hard to use. Most of the smaller Fabricated still take pearl cards punched for that system, if you want to use it."

Rowena nodded. "How big a Fabricated could I get without the coding being too hard?"

Umiko shrugged. "A tamarin or stork, maybe. But the flying Fabricated tend not to be able to carry much weight beyond themselves. So I'd stick to something like a tamarin model. Plus there are dozens and dozens of them all over the Library campus, to say nothing of the rest of the prefecture. One could go missing for weeks without being noticed."

"So we get the books when you come to help me research, and I can snag a machine sometime before dawn and program it to go to our translator."

"Are you sure you don't just want me to do it?" Umiko asked.

"To—to program the Fabricated?"

"I've got to be better at it than you would be. I've seen you trying to copy out pearl cards."

Rowena poked at the contents of her bento. Umiko was right, of course. Rowena knew nothing about programming, really, apart from how to foul it up.

"You said it was trying to program a better Engine—a thinking Engine—that got you in trouble with Madame Kurowa."

Umiko poured them both tea. "More or less."

"If the directions the Fabricated has to follow are complicated, is that a problem for me doing it right?"

"Depends on what you mean by complicated."

"Pretty complicated."

"Then it could be a problem."

Rowena nodded. "I think I could use your help again."

Umiko's voice dropped half an octave. "Only if you tell me what you're really doing here with Anselm Meteron, digging into his father's research, and snatching books from the Amanuensis library. And, while we're at it, why you asked me to run a report through the Aggregator for every mention of someone called Erasmus Pardon in connection with the Grand Library."

"I probably really shouldn't—"

"Do *you* really know why you're here?" Umiko pressed. "Because I'm not sure you do. Or if you do, it's not for the same reason as Doctor Chalmers."

"I'm here with the Old Bear and Master Meteron."

Umiko raised an eyebrow. "And you're helping Master Meteron spy on his father while *you* spy on the Alchemist?"

Put that way, it seemed absurd to Rowena, too. Her ankles hurt, she realized—her feet nervously rubbing together out of sight, under the desk. "It's complicated."

"That's why I'm worried about what you're asking me to do."

Rowena stole a glance at the Indexer box, credibly topped with its spool of paper and printing arm and wired to nothing particular inside. *A box of one thing, full of something else*, she thought.

Rowena, Leyah urged her silently. *Be careful.*

I've been *careful*, Rowena snapped back in her mind. *All I ever get for it is less answers and more trouble.*

"If I tell you some things about why we're here," she said aloud to Umiko, measuring her words, "can you promise not to tell *anyone?*"

"I swear on the Proof."

"Not on the Proof. On . . . on your mother. On anything. Everything. It's that big a deal."

Umiko frowned. "On my mother, then. On everything. Will you tell me?"

Rowena, don't, Leyah begged.

Rowena pressed her hands against her ears, as if it could mute the voice that carried no sound. She hoped it only looked like battling off a headache. She would be, soon enough.

Rowena mustered herself with a slow, even breath. "All right. It's about these books in your special collection. I've seen one like them before—the one that's gone missing."

36.

Rowena had gotten the knack of reading under the covers back at the Stone Scales. She'd had to, if she meant to stagger through the pages the Old Bear assigned most nights. None were so long or so far from reasonable reading for a girl her age, but she'd had no schooling worth speaking of. Every syllable she could make sense of confessed itself only after a royal drubbing, beaten into sense under the shadows of her patchwork quilt. Before long, Rowena learned to enjoy reading, though she did it less than half as fast as she had any business doing, and would probably never recite aloud in anything more than a dull monotone, all the punctuation plowed under into a flattened veldt.

Rowena prowled the page before her with the eyes of a hungry lioness. The tent she'd made over her head was a dressing gown, as Nipponese beds boasted little more than thin sheets, and the bed itself was a long, unrolled cushion. But apart from those details, she was back in her element, propped up on elbows and digging through line after line of impossible script, a magnesium torch tucked between her wrists.

Chalmers liked to call it "Enochian," though he always swallowed the word like a bitter seed. Probably some fusty old Kneeler legacy in the term. If Rowena had a quarter-clink for every time mentions of the Kneeler days made the scholar squirm, she could've bought herself a whole wing of the Grand Library. Whatever you called it, the book was chock-a-block with lines and wriggles that rudely defied comprehension.

"What on earth even are you?" she whispered at its pages.

No telling. There were the oddly familiar blocky letters, but Aramite numerals, too, and even some graphs and charts with arcs spilling off the axes.

The numerals in many places resembled dates. As Chalmers requested, she had stolen the volume dated immediately before the text Nora Pierce had stolen and passed that on for the Reverend to append notes and questions to. The book in her hands—her secret theft—was dated 1m1777–4m1780. Her logic in taking a book whose recording began better than fifteen years ago was simple. First, it was far enough removed from the other stolen and dummy-replaced book that she thought it unlikely both would be pulled and examined at the same time—or at least, not straight away. Second, its timeline began right at the end of the Old Bear's campaigning days, before Leyah's death and his retirement.

It was, therefore, the perfect book to test her theory: that the reason his mind so closely mimicked the format of this Grand Library, and the reason some of the seals on its entrance floor were copied in the tattoo he'd never let her see too closely, was that he was a subject of the book itself. One of the Nine. Why else would such a material link exist between them? Surely, at such an active, chaotic time in his life, the book would show signs of him she could recognize—clear, definitive proof.

The blocky symbols all looked the same, at first. Hours into scanning the pages, her vision blurring, Rowena noticed a few that seemed familiar—not just as part of the endless march of close-printed text, but because they were the same, familiar pieces of text, regularly repeated. Labels? Or names? Yes. Likely so. Every time the date would change, or a map would appear, and she felt the dawning warmth of a new day in the record, a new point of focus, those naming symbols would repeat, as early in the document as possible. Sometimes even as a header, or as part of marginalia.

Rowena was somewhere deep in the text, between two seasons and a host of scrawled-out notes, when she saw a map of intersecting streets she recognized as Westgate Bridge, and a caret mark above a cramped space in the highstreets she knew very well. *The Stone Scales!* Could she have found her proof so quickly? She plowed onward, finding shifts in maps and positions, long, painfully obscure paragraphs of illegible text—shifts to different subjects and different perspectives. Even what looked like a navigational chart plotting an arc over the Western Sea, with a blot hovering midway between Vraska and the western coast of Amidon, a string of frantic-seeming notations in formation around it. The notes terminated with a date—2m13d1780.

Rowena sat up, her dressing gown sliding off her head, spreading her torch's light on the room's paper walls.

Her birthday was the 13th of Twomonth, 263. What was it Master Meteron had said? They started counting over from zero after the Unification? And the year now—in the old calendar way, the way it used to be—was . . . she tried to remember. 1794? She tried counting back, but she was so tired, and the numbers had turned into a jumble. Yet the blot over the Western Sea looked strangely familiar.

Rowena, Leyah's voice urged in the darkness. *You need to stop.*

She turned the page, and there was a jump—a break in the text formed by a clearly hand-drawn line, and a symbol in the margin. A header. And a new sketch. Rowena drew back from the page, blinking at what she saw.

Every cell in Oldtemple prison looked more or less the same. Rowena had spent the first five years of her life there. She'd taken her first steps down its moldering hallways, played in the sawdust of its tumble-down exercise yard. Yet for all that sameness, long familiarity gave her a penetrating awareness of her family cell's tiniest details. If there was anything the author of this text was good at, it was capturing tiny details.

Mama always kept a little laundry line strung up in a corner, a kind of blind to slip behind when she used the privy pot. Other inmates on her floor—the sickest, sorriest lot in the whole sorry prison—didn't bother to screen themselves. They changed their ragged dresses with shrunken, half-starved breasts in full view and did their morning business glaring at their turnkeys.

"Even when things is hard, Rowie, love," Mama had always said, "a lady must be a lady."

Rowena squinted at the page. The image refused to dissolve into something more sensible.

If anything, it grew clearer that the cell was the one she had grown up in—the one her mother had only recently left behind. A rag bundle in the corner for Jorrie to sleep in. A rough-framed, tiny rectangle for the old linen drawer requisitioned as baby Rowena's cradle. More marks, more arrows pointing to objects, and to all-too-familiar-looking cuneiform.

One of the marks floated just above the sketch of her drawer.

Rowena slammed the book shut and twisted her magnesium light off, too hard and too fast. She heard a snap, then a tinkle of broken filament. Darkness. All that remained to fill it was the hot glass in her hands and the pounding between her ears.

INTERMEZZO

If the arctic tern understood itself the way the ornithologists of the Ecclesiastical Commission did, it would be more than a little proud.

It would know itself to be a hardy, temperature-durable, far-ranging bird, capable of a migration of more than five thousand leagues each season. It would recognize the virtue of its sophisticated communication habits, its close-knit familial arrangements, and its adaptability over time.

It would not appreciate how these very virtues had recommended it to Dor as the ideal bearer of an order driven into its consciousness by the cordyceps rooted in its brain stem. The tern—one of seven sent forth by Rahielma's own hand, infected with an urge to find the farthest shores of Nippon, its body imprinted with pollen that carried layers of news for Dor's far-flung lanyani brethren—knows only that it must fly.

It is the last of seven sent out across the Western Sea many days before. Two of its brothers perished in a hard-driving storm. One was snapped up by a hungry whale when it chose the wrong place to dive for smelt. The other three succumbed after the cordyceps seduced them into forgetting food, forgoing rest. One by one, they had dropped from the skies, leaving a single sister plunging toward a small island miles off the shores of Kyushu, a narrow strip of land the Nipponese call "Fog Island."

Names mean nothing to the tern, but the fog is very real, wrapping around the steamy summer island, weighing down the bird's weary wings.

It does not land so much as plummet to the rocky beach. A plume of its feathers confettis the air.

The lanyani have no sense of smell, but they know the weight of wind and what rides upon it. Rot and ruin and a pollen-based report rise up from the tern's flapping body. These are what draw the lanyani from the forest beyond the shoals—mandrake-like kandelias, shrubby gampi, and broad-backed dogwoods each giving inspiration to their wild forms. They have never shaped themselves to look like Men or pruned themselves to keep their size in check. Each of them could be a Master in a hothouse's Pits. The lanyani of the cities are sick, stunted things compared to the creatures of Fog Island.

Their home here has its own, special name. The Forest of Suicides. When the prisoners abandoned on Fog Island can no longer bear its horrors—the choice between brutal savageries or slow, wasting death—they walk into the lanyani's lair and are never heard from again.

The tern stares, blind and glass-eyed, into the sun. It does not blink as the lanyani's shadows eclipse it in shade. Their craggy chests expand and contract, taking in the last, faint traces of the message Dor sent, too complicated and important for their written word.

In the island city, one lanyani shaped like a riot of juniper hums. *That is far. Many miles through waters too deep for the sunlight to pass through. We would not survive the walk.*

We would not, one of its thorny kin agrees. *But we are not the only ones of our kind.*

True, the mandrake says.

The longest-limbed of all, it gathers up the tern—dead now, though still beating its wings, an automaton coming slowly unwound. It wades into the water and plunges the bird beneath the low tide's faint waves. Many yards from shore, where the water climbs around the mandrake's uppermost blossoms, a shadow of color rises up from the deep.

The lanyani of Amidon know nothing of their kin below the waves. It is too massive a continent for them to have need of the sea, whose waters would rot them from within. But the lanyani of Nippon are island creatures, pushed to ever-smaller scraps of land by a city so large it has joined with another, then another, and finally consumed the archipelago entire. Nippon's lanyani are docile boatmen or brutalized, stupefied glowplant lamps. Only Fog Island offers them space to live as they were meant to. But islands are too small for their limits not to be tested and, eventually, outgrown.

The blotch of color that surrounds the mandrake-shaped lanyani making an offering of the tern is a tangle of seaweed and plankton. It is a hundred thousand entities bound into a single, conscious form. Sailors used to fear creatures of the deep that looked like creatures of the land, telling stories of serpents beneath the waves. Those legends came from the ones who survived to tell a tale and make it fanciful.

The ones who die never get to share the truth: that the deep holds lanyani the size of an anchor yard which attach to ships' hulls and crush them like rotting walnuts. No one hears their horror at seeing a mass of creatures ooze up the pilings of a pier, suffocating what walks above.

Ordinary lanyani can walk the waters, provided they aren't so deep as to go without sunlight overlong. The distance from Fog Island to Kyushu and Kyo-Tokai is much too far, the pressures of the ocean floor too intense, for lanyani to simply stride along them. But nature adapts.

The lanyani of the Forest of Suicides adapt Dor's request in kind. They are not without their own resources, after all.

The mandrake wades ashore again, the tern gone, devoured: feather and flesh and bone and the burden of its message, all passed on to a willing servant. A hound on the scent, the planktonous lanyani surges toward the mainland, in search of its quarry.

32.

You seem out of sorts."

Rowena flinched at the sound of the Old Bear's voice. She realized she'd stopped walking dead in the middle of the canal barge's boarding platform. Muttering apologies in her best Nipponese, she let the other passengers shoulder past, taking their seats under the painted canopy. The old man's raptor eyes studied her until her cheeks flushed.

"S'fine," she answered, "I just didn't sleep well last night." *Or the night before, or the night before that.* "Thanks for taking me out of the Library today. I needed to get some air."

Rowena stepped into the boat first and put a hand back to help the Old Bear keep steady as the craft keeled under them. He nodded his thanks, unhooking his cane from his arm. They claimed an empty bench at the back. Rowena surveyed the distance between them and the other passengers—shoppers and social callers and servants sent across the vast, state-sized city on some errand or other. They were near enough the rest not to seem suspicious and far enough away to converse privately. At the front of the boat, the drooping, tentacular lanyani that manned the craft lurched forward, stretching down into the waters. The barge drifted from the quay, the locks holding it in place falling away, triggered by some unseen mechanical cue.

"We've more than enough information from the Aggregator to parse through. I am glad to have your help," the Old Bear said. He stretched out his bad leg as far as the seating permitted. "Now what's troubling you?"

Rowena hesitated. He could just reach into her mind and poke around for the answer. But he wouldn't. He'd done it once when she was a stranger and a liar. She was still a liar, but one he had decided to trust. She was sure of that. Her certainty of his faith hurt, when she thought of the second book she was not meant to have, secreted in her steamer trunk under a panel she'd made herself before they'd left Corma. Still full of secrets, after all this time.

The Alchemist would let her keep her own counsel. But she didn't want to. She didn't know how to explain the shuddering panic the stolen text had sent through her, or how deeply it still gripped her.

She tried, all the same. "You ever seen something for even just a second that made you feel . . . really small and sort of big, all at once? Like the whole world isn't sized the right way, and you're in some kind of dollhouse where if you turn too fast, you'll knock everything down?"

The old man frowned.

"I can't explain it right," Rowena continued. "But it's kind of like that. I thought, maybe just going out with you—looking for answers to questions that are simpler, like 'where was so-and-so going?' or 'what data did they ask for?' . . . maybe that would make the feeling go away."

And she had wanted to be with him. Their tasks—hers, earning Umiko's confidence and using her tools to investigate the Bishop's next moves, and his, taking her findings and probing the weary minds of disaffected functionaries for answers—had kept them on separate schedules, working separate places, for days on end. She had missed him. Rowena was not accustomed to missing people. She'd been a whole unto herself ever since her brother, Jorrie, died. Missing him had hurt so badly, she'd turned that part of herself off, burying it under her quest to pay down Mama's debt. She'd thought she didn't need people. But she needed the Old Bear. Not having him by her side ached in ways she couldn't explain. He'd tamed her. Or she had tamed him. Maybe both. Even without trying, she felt his relief rising off him, a cool breeze amid the city's swelter.

He'd missed her, too.

"Never mind. It doesn't matter," she said. "Who are we looking into today?"

"I visited the offices of the Nipponese Anchor Authority and pulled the travel records of the Reverend Doctor Deliverance Tegura, who came to the Grand Library several months ago to retrieve a parcel of data printed by the Aggregator. They are under the impression I'm an inspector representing the grant commission which has been funding Doctor Tegura's work for the last several years."

Rowena frowned. "Why's that a useful cover?"

"Grant inspectors check into the progress of scholars awarded their institution's monies. The Logicians would not dare dispute their authority."

"That's jake. And so you don't have to worry about not being EC or being a foreigner, then."

"Just so."

"So, how much of them being under this impression is campaign craft, and how much is . . . other stuff?"

The Old Bear eyed her disapprovingly. "An admixture we'd be better served not to discuss openly."

Their barge had paused at another quay head, letting off passengers who paused to drop their coins in the machine tiller set beside the sloe-eyed lanyani. Rowena studied the scene in puzzlement. "Is everybody dropping a different kind of coin?"

The Old Bear looked up from lighting his pipe, squinted, and nodded, shaking a scorched lucifer into the canal. "Nippon, Lemarcke, and the other countries in the Protectorate use a currency called 'marks.' It's a system where certain shapes of coin and their images are tied to certain economic castes, and in some cases, to specific families and businesses. Each mark coin represents a small percentage of income from the owner of its design, and so a single mark to transport a passenger through the canals might represent a very small expenditure for a lower-class household, and a considerably greater one for the wealthy. It's a frightfully complicated accounting process to redeem the actual value of a transaction, but the Logicians swear by it."

Rowena considered. She was no wizard at maths, but one piece of that plan made sense to her. "So, everybody pays the same part of their value for a thing, but people who can afford a lot pay more for it? Reason's Rood, that is a mess. But I guess it makes sure rich folks pay for keeping up streets and shops and such, doesn't it?"

"It certainly does. Now hush awhile."

Rowena saw why straight away. A group of soldiers was taking the place of the disembarking passengers, boarding two by two, six of them total. They wore banded mail shirts, glossy as enameled tea sets. Rowena was a little too used to Corma's plump coppers, easily winded. The sight of proper security—military, really—chilled her. The Logicians who ruled Nippon liked nothing done in half-measures. She resisted the urge to rub her feet and ankles together. "Cricket," Anselm called her. At least the nickname had made her aware of the nervous habit. Rowena gauged the soldiers warily, studying the long, single-edged blades stowed at the backs of their belts and the arquebuses that reminded her a little too much of the gun the Old Bear had never had the chance to shoot last fall.

"What're they doing here?" Rowena whispered. "What's their thing?"

"Their thing," the Old Bear answered, in a voice that lingered around the second word as if prodding it with a scalpel, "is protecting order and Reason. An Argument is always six soldiers strong, and they cover the prefectures of Kyo-Tokai in shifts. These are probably coming on duty now."

"And what happens if you're caught disturbing peace and order and Reason and whatnot?"

"Fog Island happens."

Rowena sewed her lips tight as a deaconess's drawers, at that. She didn't know what Fog Island was, precisely, but the name reminded her of the prison hulks on Misery Bay.

Rowena scanned the river banks, taking in a clearer, more complete vision of Kyo-Tokai than she had been able to previously, despite gazing out the high windows of the Grand Library compound every night. The sprawling city of two-tiered buildings, bowed roofs, tiled porticos, and everblooming cherry trees was little more than a busy blur from that vantage point. Here, she could truly see things.

The barge sailed downriver, angling toward an elaborate loch system. Rowena's boat sat in a kind of purgatory between one space and another, waiting for the reservoirs from the pumping station to finish leveling off before the barrier itself finally opened, letting them pass through.

Rowena and the Alchemist dropped two marks into the till beside the lanyani boatman as they disembarked. Each of the coins bore a symbol Rowena didn't recognize.

"Those didn't come from the Rolands, did they?" she asked as the barge slipped away, taking the staring, stoic Argument along with it.

"I traded a little of the credit they put away for us in Lemarcke for some marks Keeper had put aside at the Maiden's Honor. He sells off false marks stamped for various corporations and interests. What the Logician economic system gains in social equity it loses badly in graft."

"I s'pose it'd take ages to track all the marks from a day of business back to their owners and pass on the charges. By the time anybody figured out they were phony, you'd be gone. I kind of like this system."

"Don't get light-fingered," the old man cautioned. They walked a cherry tree-shadowed lane rising toward a gate and a vast, open yard beyond, air galleons anchored above. "The easiest way to end up in trouble here is to be caught using a mark you've no right to carry. Most of the people on Fog Island go there for just such petty theft."

"So it *is* a prison."

"In a manner of speaking. The Logicians don't believe in wasting resources running a prison, in the usual sense."

"How's it *un*usual?"

"It's an island far from the mainland, a rocky place with bad weather on the land and worse things lurking in its waters. They take the prisoners there by steamship and leave them."

Rowena froze, her sandals rooted to the spot. "What d'you mean, *leave* them?" Slowly, the answer dawned on her. "They don't waste resources," she repeated, "because there en't shelters or meals or guards or anything. They just leave folk there to die."

"Or to live, however they can," the Old Bear confirmed.

Rowena shook herself at the horror of it, then trotted a few steps ahead of him, trying to put the thought of Fog Island from her mind.

"Remember," he cautioned, "you are my secretary, so you ought to take notes during our visit to the Anchor Authority."

"Right. But en't you going to be talking in Nipponese?"

"Your notes can be nonsense. Shorthand looks different in every language, and people tend to see what they think they should. All you need is cover." He smiled at her, so brief Rowena wondered if she'd imagined it. "You'll actually be checking their galvano-graph transmission record, to see who has been relaying messages to Doctor Tegura since her departure, and what about."

Rowena pulled a face. "I can't just sneak off in the middle of your talking without somebody noticing."

"Oh, but they will notice you," he said. "They have to."

Rowena was so accustomed to thinking of Master Meteron as the deceiver of their company, it was easy to forget how comfortably the Alchemist could slip into an adequately tailored lie. The Nipponese Anchor Authority offices were staffed by a combination of Fabricated automata, feeding pearl cards one after another into an Engine that looked like a much-simplified version of the Aggregator. These were in turn managed by businesslike young women who resembled younger, more harried versions of Madame Kurowa. The Alchemist's lie fit their expectations perfectly: an older gentleman, Army retired and likely wounded in action, judging from his cane, carrying out his duty to proper research and enlightenment by protecting the investment of his employers against scholars inclined to sloth, or fraud, or both. The Alchemist cut a figure their training taught them to respect, and so if his secretary were a little young and perhaps a little slapdash in her note-taking, it was an oddity they were prepared to forgive. They had been apprentices once, too. Thus, while the Old Bear ran through what the rhythms of language suggested was a rote list of questions, Rowena waited for the right moment to disappear into her real work.

She didn't have to wait long. After a few minutes of conversation, the Old Bear produced a blank sheet of paper from an inner pocket of his frock coat. Rowena watched, dumbfounded, as he spread it on the counter between himself and the station manager, pointing to it with mute confidence.

"Osu," the woman replied. She turned to Rowena and spoke slowly, her Amidonian meticulous. "Your warrant is in good order. Please be careful of the machines."

Rowena looked to the Old Bear, hoping to convey her bafflement beneath a smile.

"Off you go." He nodded toward the galvano-graph station outside the main office.

"Of course," she said.

What, Rowena asked Leyah as she went, *was that about?*

An old trick. Sometimes, he can make people see things that aren't there—especially things they expect to see.

A warrant, Rowena mused. *Sneaky Old Bear.*

Most of Rowena's trickiest drops for Ivor Ruenichnov had involved acting like she belonged in a place that was actually none of her business. The galvano-graph station was no exception. Though the Old Bear's mind trick had given her leave to run off, she decided to treat it like a job from the old days. You could get away with delivering a parcel, and say, and nicking an extra something along the way, provided you acted natural. Then nobody would look twice. Various mechanics, stewards, and secretaries walked past her. She arrived at the signal station with her head high, returning their courteous nods.

The galvano-graph station's door was a split affair that could open at top, leaving the bottom behind as a sort of counter. She opened the lower half and edged past the lemur-shaped Fabricated perched atop the transmission box. Inside, shelves and drawers and sticking-pins bursting with messages pending or sent studded the walls. Rowena checked one of the very few real dates in her notebook—from the start of Eight-month, when Deliverance Tegura was to have arrived in Corma. She started fishing through the catalogs by recipient, happy Amidonian was the standard language of galvano-graph transmissions. Then she narrowed her search by dates.

There were indeed messages sent to Tegura, each coded from Vladivostoy. Rowena frowned, trying to call a map of the Lemarckian Protectorate to mind. Vladivostoy was at the outmost eastern edge of Vraska, hundreds of miles to the north. Some of the messages were received in Corma, and responded to. All spoke of a package—*package will be needed within the month; package departing with me by steamer, expect delays;* and so on. The signatories varied—L. Fredericks outbound, or sometimes A. Cortes, and D. Tegura inbound. Fredericks was a name she knew already, as close to a confirmation of the orders coming from Bishop Meteron as she was likely to see in print.

It was the messages sent from Corma to Tegura some days later that gave Rowena pause. Each was marked "*to be held at waystation.*"

5th Eightmonth
0800
To: Anchor Authority Station 1, Nippon, Attn: Rev. Dr. D. Tegura
From: Mercy Commission Home, Southeby, Amidon

Returned from holiday to find my assistant relinquished Mrs. Downshire to your care pursuant to a request from His Grace. No medications accepted for the journey; no notice from Mrs. D's benefactor. Please confirm your receipt of this message and Mrs. D's well-being.

I eagerly await your prompt response.

Rev. Dr. M. Wyndham,
Lead Physician

Mrs. D. Rowena scattered the messages around her, scavenging for the requested response. Wyndham's spark had arrived eleven days earlier. Eleven days! She found nothing in response—only a tiny paper slip indicating the system had pinged to confirm the message's arrival. Other messages from Wyndham—each a little more urgent and clipped than the last—confirmed he had never received Tegura's response. Nothing in the little galvano-graph office suggested there had ever been one. Rowena's eyes stung with hot, furious tears.

Why had she ever left Corma? Why had she believed she needed to go? To save the world on an adventure? Adventure had found her, after all. It had found her mother. But why would the Bishop want her? What could she possibly have to offer him?

And then, like an avalanche of snow and twice as cold, the memory of the book and its charts and its all-too-clear markings of Mama's cell reared up in Rowena's mind.

"Rowena?"

She whirled around, still clutching the message from Dr. Wyndham. The Old Bear stood under the galvano-graph station's awning, mopping his brow in the heat.

"They've taken her," she blurted. "By steamship, ages ago. To Vraska, I think. He's figured it out, Bear. I read it all wrong, but he didn't. He knows she's one of them."

The Old Bear stepped through the half-door, a thunderous scowl rumbling in his voice. "What do you mean?"

"My mother. I saw it in one of the books, Bear, and it's true. It's got to be. And now he's got her, and—"

The Alchemist dropped his stick and bent to look her in the eyes, holding her shaking shoulders. "*Slowly.* You're not making sense."

Rowena shoved a fistful of printed sparks against his chest. "*It's all here.* Just look at it. Why else would he take her?"

The old man gathered up the papers spilling off his waistcoat, donned his spectacles, and scanned the crumpled messages. Rowena backed away, feeling for a stool. She found the wall instead and slid down it, breathing hard between sobs that only now registered in her ears.

The Alchemist folded the sparks with three fast, brutal strokes and tucked them inside his coat. "Come along, girl. We have to leave."

"For the Library?"

"For Vraska."

38.

Umiko Haroda petted the macaque Fabricated perched beside her, wanting more than anything to get off the roof of the Grand Library and back to her bed. But she'd made a promise to Rowena Downshire—a promise that made no sense, had been demanded through a note delivered through the vacuum tubes to the Indexer room, and required her to forgo her sleeping mat long after dark.

But it was a promise, all the same.

"Did you bring it?"

Rowena clambered up the fire stairs lacing the side of the building.

Umiko rolled her eyes. "'Bring the messenger we've been using,' your note said, so yes. *I brought it.* I thought Reverend Chalmers wouldn't have another packet for your translator before—"

Rowena dashed up to the macaque and opened the cylinder in its right forearm—or tried to, jabbing at its seams, poking and cursing.

"Wait, you're going to break it," Umiko complained. She batted Rowena's hands aside, then put out her own. "What's that note? Give it to me."

"I don't want—"

"To trust me? Too late for that. Or don't you want me to help you?" She wagged her empty hand again. "What's gotten into you? You look like you're about to come out of your skin."

The edge of the roof was a picture frame of bioluminescent vines. In their wan, green light, Rowena's face had turned to ash.

"We're leaving in two days," she blurted. "I tried to get them to leave tonight, but they said that's too suspicious and they need time to sort things properly here."

356

Umiko blinked. "Leaving? Why? Where?"

"Vladivostoy. I just . . . I have to let somebody know we en't forgotten her, in the meantime."

Umiko had been about to object again, but Rowena silenced her with the note. She unrolled the paper and scanned its hasty, childish scrawl.

16th Eightmonth
To: Dr. Wyndham, Mercy Commission Home, Southeby, Amidon
From: R. Downshire, Kyo-Tokai, Nippon
Re: Mrs. Downshire

Found your messages to D.T. and we're coming after her because nobody said she could take her and don't worry about anything because once we're done Bishop Meteron will wish he never—

It went on in a blur of poorly spelled, only loosely grammatical phrases. Umiko stopped reading. "Rowena, what is this?"

"The Bishop took my mother. Her doctor's losing his mind with worry and stupid Bear and Ann and Doc say we can't just go now but I have to *tell someone* we're going to fix this. I need *somebody* to know I'm trying."

"You want to use the Fabricated you've been sending packets to your translator with to take this to a galvano-graph station?"

"You can do that, can't you? Reprogram it?"

"Rowena, this spark isn't even coded. Anybody could read it."

She threw her hands up in wild frustration. "*Of course it isn't coded!* Wyndham's just some stupid medical doc trying to take care of cracked old ladies! He's not a spy or a campaigner or anything like we are!"

The moment the last of the words came out, Rowena's mouth snapped shut, her teeth clicking so hard, Umiko herself winced. They stared at each other in silence for a long, awkward moment.

"You told me enough already," Umiko whispered. "I kind of figured that part out for myself."

"I can't wait two days," moaned Rowena. "We're already such a long way from Vladivostoy. Anything could be happening to her!"

And then she was up and pacing, hugging herself, teeth chattering. It wasn't cold. Umiko sweated beneath her sash and skirts. Rowena's useless, cornered animal energy ran her like a clockwork.

"If you could be just a little patient, I'm sure—"

"I was patient for *seven years*," Rowena cried. "I worked and stole and begged for every clink I could get, just to get her free, just to know she'd be *safe*, and then finally she was! And now that's gone and I don't even know for sure how to find her."

Umiko stuffed the aborted spark into a pocket of her sash and stood. If only she could get Rowena to calm down, to stop looking at her as if she'd seen something terrifying.

A chill poured down Umiko's spine, running like ice water. The roof seemed darker than it had a moment before. Rowena's eyes fixed on her, then trailed past. Umiko turned, certain of something wrong in the bleeding darkness behind her.

The vines outlining the roof's gabled edges had shriveled, coiling into blackened snakes, leaves hissing. Something was coming up the building, not from the fire stairs, but from its very face, rising like a wall of green flame. It smelled dank and briny, like the lanyani boatmen on the canals.

But so much *bigger*.

Umiko screamed.

Rowena rushed forward, stepping between the monstrous tangle of greenery and Umiko. One hand disappeared into her kimono, and then flashed out, the bright tip of a sword arcing through the moonlight.

A long, mossy beard of greenery fell from the thing, sliced clean through. It reared up, flailing, screeching. Umiko scrambled back, covering her ears. Rowena shouted something at her. She pointed to the fire ladder, but Umiko couldn't hear, and the roof was so dark, and what would she do if something else rose up from its shadows?

The monster—some kind of lanyani, impossibly vast and formless—braided itself into a many-legged thing, a centipede's nightmare. It skittered forward. Rowena rolled to the side, luring its mandibled jaws away as they snapped and oozed. It crashed through the Fabricated monkey, trampling it in pursuit of her.

Umiko didn't know when she'd stopped screaming. She stood rooted to the spot, watching Rowena dart and dive, slashing and sparking at the creature, crisping its limbs with jolts of electricity from her sword's curious tip. Then it surged over her, a wave of kelp and rot, wrapping around Rowena until she disappeared like a mouse down an adder's belly.

Umiko snatched a broken copper plate off the twisted Fabricated's body, hurling it at the horrible thing. The scrap veered wide, but what passed for the lanyani's face still turned toward her, a dozen blank, fathomless eyes glaring murder.

Then the creature spasmed. A long, metal point appeared in its belly, tearing a ragged hole. The lanyani shrieked, bucking, and Rowena spilled forth in a gush of salty ooze. Gasping for air, she had barely gained her feet before the beast spun on its many legs again, its underside already knitting in a long, withered scar.

Rowena swiped at the two coiled limbs lashing toward her, slicing off the one bound for her neck. Another hooked in her kimono sleeve. She pulled the knot of her sash and shrugged free, scampering back, stripped of everything but her juban undershirt. The lanyani shredded the abandoned kimono, chittering rage.

"Run!" Rowena shouted, waving Umiko away. "Go!"

Umiko turned and collided with someone twice her size.

The Alchemist—the one Rowena called the Old Bear—stood barechested in his britches, a strange pistol in his right hand. He shoved Umiko aside. "Rowena!"

Her eyes found his. She leaped away in time to avoid the creature's next lunge, and the Alchemist's flare fired into its face.

The lanyani must have come from the waters, sodden as it was, and yet it burned, a gel spreading across its fibrous, braided body. A choking black cloud plumed from it, spitting like a grease fire, until the beast finally crumpled in on itself, twitching and burning under something other than flame.

Rowena stood a few yards from Umiko, panting with her hands braced on her knees. Her saber lay at her feet. It looked strangely shorter than it had only moments before. She looked up to say something, but Umiko never caught the words.

The Alchemist moved between them, taking Umiko's chin and forcing her to meet his gaze.

He said something then, in his deep, urgent voice—something about remembering. No, about . . . *not* remembering. About going to bed. About Umiko needing her rest.

He was right, of course. Creator only knew how late it was. And repairing her Fabricated was no small task, come morning.

Umiko gathered the monkey up, glad it was still in three mostly solid bits, and strode for the fire stairs. The city smog seemed far worse than usual, reeking and oily in a way she associated more with Amidon than pure, intellectual Nippon. She thought she heard a shrill voice calling after her. Then again, it might have been the wind.

When dawn finally came, Umiko awoke in her own bedroll, rested and unconcerned.

She might have gone the whole day like that if, while preparing for her bath, she hadn't found a crumpled galvano-graph message stuffed behind her sash.

The memories came flooding back with it.

39.

Haadiyaa Gammon paced the Stone Scales's overgrown yard, pausing every few passes to glare at the night sky. Barely a wink of starlight peeked through the smog scrolling lazily across a sliver of moon. She wasn't one to pout and stare at her boots. That was a sign of weakness. At least, that was how her men back at the Constabulary read it. They believed effective commanders kept their chins up.

She'd been trying to do that for the better part of an hour, with little success.

"This is a terrible plan," she announced, not for the first time.

"So you have said," Nasrahiel answered, not for the first time, either.

The aigamuxa sat on the shop's back stoop—on his rear, like a human, looking all the more awkward and out of place for it. Gammon focused on his mechanical eye, its lens glinting in the dark.

"And you're going to do it anyway," she concluded.

"She is my mate. My love. What choice do I have?"

Gammon growled something in an Indine dialect her mother would have considered unforgivably rude. She slumped onto the shop stoop, a step below Nasrahiel. He didn't care if she looked at her boots, or drooped her shoulders, or cursed, or even if she cried. He had made his decision. Put in his place, she wasn't sure she'd have done differently.

Seven days earlier, Rahielma had invaded the Stone Scales, desperate for some solution to the fungal plague she'd helped release on the city. Shocking her with news of Nasrahiel's survival had been enough to get her to listen and, finally, to meet her mate again.

She had paced around him, smelling, touching, recoiling, and he had stood there in the Scales' yard, cyclopean eye shut tight, silent under her inspection. For long minutes, no one had known whether she would tear into him, run from him, curse him. Perhaps even she hadn't known.

Julian had stood by, shifting nervously. He would have to follow his brief surgery on Rahielma's shoulder with a reconstruction of nearly a year's work in medicine and engineering, if she attacked Nasrahiel.

In the end, the two had spoken in a language of purrs and chitters not meant for human ears, and folded down together so Rahielma's eyes could look at what her husband had become. She wept. She still had the means to do it. She gave him a hand, and he pressed it to his eye, and she went still as it whirred in and out, surveying her every scar, every muscle, every inch and angle. And then, without a word to the humans surrounding them, they had bounded to the rooftops and fire ladders above, disappearing into the city beyond Westgate Bridge.

For days, Gammon worried over what had become of . . . she felt presumptuous thinking of Nasrahiel as a partner, and certainly he would not permit being called her friend. Her companion. Her counterpart. They had found nests of staggering, hollowed-out vermin and burned them together. They had found caches like Thorn's and sunk them in dinghies run through with holes, pushed as far off Corma's coast as the tide would take them. She had watched him linger in sight of the Aeries where the survivors of his tribe sheltered in their shanty kingdom— stood by and read the war on his face, trapped between living as the horror he had become and killing who he had been by returning to his people as something else. Gammon had sat beside him, watching the dawn crest the horizon, pink and orange against the oily river's waters. She never said a word. Every line of his body, skin and steel, begged for her silence.

He deserved that much.

For days, she had worried over his return, wondered if she could carry on her mission without him. And then he had returned, no longer alone.

The rooftops surrounding the Stone Scales's yard quilled with the shapes of watching, waiting aigamuxa. Pale pink eyes winked all around. The aiga made no sound. They seemed content to wait for the chieftain's signal. Rahielma perched atop the machine shed, nearest of all, the focus of their attention. She was chieftain, regardless of Nasrahiel's return.

It would be unjust to take from her what she has striven so hard to carry, he had explained.

"If you give me two days—even one day—to make contact with the Alchemist again, he might know something we could do to mitigate the damage," Gammon urged. "His first ideas worked, for a time. The Dolly Molls kept back the plague in every neighborhood they could supply with his formula."

"Until it stopped working," Nasrahiel noted.

"Jane thinks it might have adapted. But that doesn't mean we're out of options. Attacking Crystal Hill will only earn you a quick death. There are hundreds of lanyani there now."

Nasrahiel's scarred shoulders shrugged. "That is possible. I admire your wisdom, Haadiyaa Gammon. You have been a good chief, in your way. But this is not your decision to make. We are not your people to rule. And I cannot wait for the old man to bother responding to your messages."

"I know they've gotten as far as the Maiden's Honor in Lemarcke, and the pingback tells me they've been sent on to Nippon. There must be something blocking them reaching him."

"Just as it has blocked whatever response you may have been sent from this lanyani scholar of Meteron's," Nasrahiel agreed. "Waiting serves us no longer."

Gammon looked at the machine shed. The chieftain's eyes narrowed at her. Gammon refused to look away.

"And what of your children? You've said before you have sons together. Surely you can't fling yourselves into harm's way with their welfare at stake."

Nasrahiel sighed. "Waiting will not help the children. It has done harm already. The lanyani have taken aigamuxa young. Three."

Gammon tensed. "Yours?"

"Children of another tribe, used to spread the cordyceps."

"Were they ill?"

"They were taken because they were well and too small to resist." Nasrahiel's head tilted, as it so often did when he considered a problem—as if turning his body would turn an idea over in his mind. "With as many lanyani as have come into the city, their Pits must be strained to the limit. They're growing a new Master for them, and Masters have . . . needs."

"No, that's madness." Gammon shook her head. "They've needed your people's cooperation. There are dogs aplenty they could butcher for the Pits."

"There were, once. When did you see a cur roaming free last?"

"Merciful Reason," Gammon murmured. She ran her fingers through her hair, though she was tempted to simply pull it out.

Ever since finding Thorn's cache of cordyceps, she had done her utmost to steer Julian, Jane, and Bess indoors, and to keep her own excursions short and direct. The vermin surrounding Oldtemple had taken ill quickly. Its doors had been barred for better than a week, with supplies for the staff and debtors inside dropped at the gutter-head near the top of the hill. Two page boys were sent to fetch the packs and boxes in, then one, and then, one day, the doors had not opened at all. The food lay abandoned on the hill, baking in the sun, drawing rats enough that even the poorest souls wandering the street paid it no mind.

Most of those people were gone now, too, if the eerie silence of Black-bottom End were any proof.

Gammon shook her head again. "The lanyani are fighting us with weapons they understand. Attacking on their ground gives up the last advantage you might hope for."

"And not attacking," Rahielma called, "gives up what we would not sacrifice at any price."

The aigamuxa chieftain prowled down from the machine shed roof. She paced toward Gammon, menace written in her toothy snarl.

Gammon took to her feet, but Nasrahiel pushed her aside, looming in the space between his mate and the former City Inspector.

"*Enough*," he snapped. "Have I not told you the lanyani mean to end us all? *They* are our only enemies."

Rahielma's brow furrowed. "You have told me. The book. The Nine. But I only know what I see before me, and around me. I will believe in this book when I see its power for myself, just as I told you when Regenzi asked for your help."

Nasrahiel rumbled a sound like distant thunder. "I have loved you in all things but your faith."

Rahielma snorted. Her eyeless face turned upward, as if it could regard Nasrahiel's with the same clarity his mechanical eye gave him. He put his clawed hand to her chin, and she turned her thin lips to its palm, kissing. "My foolish prophet," she murmured. "Your eyes always turned to the clouds when they should have bent to the earth."

Gammon coughed, all too aware of playing an audience to a moment not meant for her.

"I will never make that mistake again," said Nasrahiel. "Tonight, we will see to it."

Rahielma nodded. Her eyeless face turned toward Gammon. "Do as you will, Haadiyaa Gammon. I am done waiting and begging. We are aigamuxa. This world is ours, always in our sight. We will take it back tonight."

She sprang toward the plastered walls of the Stone Scales, gouging her way up its facade and hurtling to the roof. At its peak, she threw back her head and made a long, rallying call, equal parts wolf's howl and gorilla's bellow. The night air thrummed with the whoops and growls of her tribe's response. The clouds over the blade of bare moon thinned, bathing the night in a steamy, silvery light.

"That's your cue," Gammon sighed.

Two legs sharp as scissor blades bent and in one leap Nasrahiel lunged to the roof, landing beside his mate. They hurtled across the gap to the haberdashery and dropped out of sight to the awnings and lampposts in the lowstreets below, a line of aigamuxa swarming after them like a spider's nest broken open.

Rahielma's people closed in on the hothouse on Crystal Hill in their twos and threes, dropping down from neighboring buildings' fire ladders and rain gutters into the shadows of a midsummer night. The crescent moon rode high above the city, its slender face blurred by a heat-haze that had, for days, refused to dissipate.

The chieftain paused in the trees ringing the hothouse's perimeter, branches scraping its steamy glass face. Nasrahiel dropped to the base of her tree's trunk. The human bonesaw's work had bound his bones with metal. A giant even before his fall, Nasrahiel was far too heavy now to share a branch or even a balcony with her. Nassunbel flung himself along the rusted iron gutterworks of a neighboring building, stopping in the tree beside Rahielma's.

"My chief, you should not be here," he growled through saw-teeth. "Let the rest of the tribe bring battle to our enemies. Let Nasrahiel finish off the Trees. We will need a leader alive when dawn comes."

"Our people have not survived this long taking cowards for their leaders," she countered.

"Nasrahiel was no coward," Nassunbel agreed. "And yet look upon him now. Would you lose so much without need?"

Rahielma turned an ankle toward Nassunbel so one eye could bore into him.

Nasrahiel would not have had this problem, Rahielma thought bitterly. *He would have known how to put his lieutenant to right.* She looked down the tree with her other eye-heel. Her mate's strange, single-eyed face turned toward her. Despite its scars, she could read its expression.

Settle this, it said. *You are the chief.*

Perhaps Nassunbel wasn't wrong after all. The problem was not that she was at Crystal Hill, about to lead her people in an attack. It was not even that there would be blood and bark falling, soon enough. It was that she was not meant to be the leader. She was a stopgap, a stitch in a torn seam. Nothing more. Nasrahiel's return sat restless within her, both a joy that made her light and a weight that dragged down her authority.

Perhaps Nassunbel sensed his words had gone too far. Rahielma climbed down and he followed, lowering himself beside Nasrahiel's silent shadow. Crouched on all fours, he touched his forehead to his outstretched claws.

"If I have misspoken, your judgment upon me, chief."

"If we are both alive later to speak of this, you will answer for your words." She let her voice crackle with ice. Nassunbel's shoulders tensed. He knew what this would mean. Perhaps his feelings about how important it was for the chieftain to remain safe during the sortie at Crystal Hill had just changed.

"Yes, my chief. It is always thus."

Fine words our people use, Rahielma mused. "It is always thus." They were punctuation to an order. A gesture of acceptance. A declaration of obedience. A weary welcome to further proof that the world was, for all its layers and angles, a flat plane stretching ever onward, vaster than the creatures crawling upon its surface.

Rahielma turned her eye-heels, surveying her assembled warriors. They gathered in their dozens around the hothouse's perimeter, counting on the dense foliage within to conceal them. Others in the pedestal position turned their eyes toward the chieftain, waiting.

"They are ready," Nasrahiel assured her.

Rahielma gave the orders.

Humans believed aigamuxa to be savages, but they were wrong. The aigamuxa were tool-builders, law-givers, child-rearers. Warriors, tacticians, politicians, builders, merchants. Their ways differed from those of Men (and that was a point of deepest pride) but they were not beastly, warped shadows cast by aboriginal campfires. They were organized, lawful, and most of all, driven by duty. Tonight, duty called on them to act.

In an instant, the walls of the hothouse swarmed with aigamuxa, pouring up its cut-glass sides like ants boiling from an overturned hill. Rahielma took the front of the pack while Nasrahiel paced the rear group. Her eye-heels touched against the glass over and over again, offering glimpses of an inverted world below, dense with green and loam. The Pits buzzed with movement, full of lanyani wading into and out of the deep, bearing grisly loads. A lanyani loped on dry land, too, gathering what seemed to be tools. She cause the scene only in snatches, for almost as fast as her eyes could blink themselves clear of the dust and grime coating the Hill's domed surface, they were fouled again. Lanyani paradise or no, the Hill still rose up out of Corma's streets into Corma's horizon. Nothing in this city was ever truly clean.

At the hothouse's apex, three aiga crowded around a glass-cutter arm pegged to the roof by a suction cup. They turned the arm quickly, guiding its diamond-hard tip around and around until the cut disc tilted sharply, only a moment's friction slowing its fall enough for Rahielma to catch it.

She passed the disc, heavy as a manhole cover, to one of her kinsmen. It disappeared down the line of warriors gathering at the portal, to be cast away in silence.

One by one, the aigamuxa dropped through the hole, collapsing their broad, flexible shoulders in on themselves in a hunch so improbably tight, it might have passed for a stage illusion. They tucked, rolled, caught branches and limbs, and brachiated to various perches among the trees. Rahielma stayed by the portal's edge, waiting for Nassunbel's people to take up their places at the building's interior perimeter, their haunting shard-of-spinel eyes winking suspicion in the dark. Nasrahiel joined her at the hole in the ceiling, his metal legs moving slowly as he climbed. His head-mounted eye meant he could see where he was bound, Rahielma supposed, but his prosthetic legs were no advantage for scaling the structure silently.

"Wait here," Rahielma murmured.

"I did not come with you to do nothing."

Rahielma turned an eye on her mate, and he bowed his cyclopean head in deference. "I have a plan for when I will need you, husband," she said. "It is always thus."

"It is always thus. Be careful."

She nodded.

If a final need for a strong warrior came, Nasrahiel would be there. But he was a card Rahielma did not wish to play early.

By the time Rahielma swung down into a tree of her own, the

handful of treelings moving nearby—scraggly, gangling things that resembled stick bugs more than plant people—had gone still.

The aigamuxa kept to their ambuscade in the canopy, watching for some sign of what had stalled the lanyani tending the Pits. They were lanyani, after all. There was a chance they had all gone dormant amid their work, rooting down to draw nutrients and rest. It would be convenient. Convenient and, Rahielma was sure, totally improbable.

Rahielma concentrated, trying to remember. The lanyani had a sense of hearing, of a sort, but no sense of smell. She willed her pheromone stores to release slowly, to better reach her tribespeople spread across so many stations, eyes winking downward where hand signals could do them no good, even if their hands were free of the tree limbs themselves. She concentrated, letting her scent carry the broad strokes of her message.

Caution. Danger? Wait.

Two answers, roughly mingled, drifted toward her. The scent-markers of the speakers let her tease them apart.

Attack. End danger. This, from Nassunbel's brother, Nasrenavv.

Idiot, Rahielma thought.

Leave. Return later. This, Nassunbel.

When had the old lieutenant grown so reticent? He had been fierce, dominant—would have been a candidate to replace her fallen Nasrahiel, if she had been of a mind to bear children again and he were not so far past his prime. He had been among those who escaped from the Old Cathedral. Whether it was the battle that had killed his courage or the sight of his young chief tumbling into the darkness, Rahielma could not say. Nasrahiel's return had warmed Nassunbel's anger, if not his courage.

But Rahielma was chieftain now.

No, she answered. *We watch.*

The treelings moved again, once again carrying bundles of grisly, butchered things to a Pit. The jagged arms of a dead Master stretched up from its oozy depths. One by one, the treelings came ashore. Planted near the broken Master, Rahielma saw another lanyani, its limbs already twining into the dead thing, wrapping around it like kudzu consuming a lightning-felled tree. She thought she recognized the color of its bark, the leathery thickness of its leaves. *Lir? Had Dor made a Master of her Lir?* Rahielma shook the idea away—an irrelevance for another time—and watched the lanyani gathering around a new pit.

It was far too small to be part of the network of composting pits tended by the lanyani Masters. The treelings bent and looked down into it. Their rustling leaves stilled. Rahielma listened. She heard the sobbing rise up from the pit, at last.

Prey? Nasrenavv's scent asked.

Rahielma sniffed the air. From the pit, she smelled sweat and shit and salt-tears.

No. Children, Rahielma answered.

Two stories about the lanyani circulated among the aigamuxa, both older than earth itself. One claimed no lanyani could lie, for it would sunder them forever, shattering their heartwood. That was a favorite of the old ones, speaking to children. The other story ran quite the opposite.

It claimed the lanyani could *only* lie, because everything about them was pliable, prunable. Carved and shaped and trained. To be a lanyani was to grow yourself to convenience. They lied without knowing it—lied because it was in their nature to see everything as brittle and passing like leaves in the seasons. Everything except themselves.

That second story would not leave Rahielma's mind. Dor had promised no harm would come to her tribe. She had been true to her word, insofar as no harm had been visited on Rahielma's tribe specifically. Rahielma had done her part to earn Dor's good faith. But Dor thought too much like a tree to be trusted. Trees had no true allies, even among their own kind. Their roots were grasping, hungry, always reaching for more and never truly satisfied.

And so the three aigamuxa children had gone missing in the space of a week. Rahielma knew little of the tribe from which they'd come, but that didn't matter. Eventually, the lanyani would come after her children.

Trees could root through damned near anything—soil and clay and stone and bone—if survival was at stake. They were indifferent and implacable. The aigamuxa could afford to be no less dogged.

Attack, Rahielma ordered with a puff of pheromone.

The hothouse's canopy exploded, aigamuxa roaring forth like shot from a cannon. They fell, earth churning up in tracks under their claws, long bounds giving enough time in the air for eyes to be thrown forward for a fast glimpse at the target before surging backward again.

The dash toward the pit and its guardians looked, to Rahielma's heel-set eyes, like a ride on a child's swing set, jerking nearer and farther. Aigamuxa were not made for running, but there was a clearing, and not enough overhang in the canopy to brachiate in range for attack. So they surged forward, a howling wall of hunched backs and saw-toothed faces, rage-scent steaming in the mud-caked air.

None of them expected the circle of ground around the pit to open beneath them.

Their howls of fury tumbled down with them. The ragged earth at the pit's bottom crashed up to meet the aigamuxa. Rahielma's jaw snapped shut, her saw-teeth clacking, narrowly missing clipping off her own tongue. Her side was a white fire of pain. Her feet, tangled amid her tribesfolk's limbs, saw nothing, and she closed her eyes to protect them as she wrestled herself free.

Soon nearly two dozen aiga, bruised and fuming, crouched in the pedestal position on the pit floor, looking up some twenty feet to the strange pillar of earth dotting the center of their prison. Rahielma stared in confusion. The lanyani should have fallen in, too, but there they stood at the top of a high pillar of undisturbed earth, its edge laced with exposed roots stretched nearly within Rahielma's reach.

And then, she understood.

"They hollowed out the ground around the children's pit and used their roots to keep from falling after us," growled Rahielma.

Worst of all, the pillar at center was not truly solid. It contained its own narrow, deep-running pit, its prisoners mewling desperately. They were no closer to reaching the kidnapped children.

"They knew we were coming," Nassunbel said.

Very little moonlight came down through the high glass ceilings of Crystal Hill, but there was enough to frame Dor's figure. She stood at the outer ring of the deeper pit, looking down.

"Of course we knew," the lanyani answered. Her voice was a throaty reed. "That was the point."

Rahielma tilted her head, sniffing. Her ankles turned, eye-heels surveying. She snorted the bitterest of laughs.

"So you meant to lure us here? To finish us off? We have been your *allies.*"

"*Your* allies, yes. Not these little creatures'. I swore protection only to your people."

"All the aigamuxa are my people!"

Dor's head tilted, too, though she was too much in darkness for Rahielma to mark if her carefully planed face held anything like an expression. "That must be very taxing."

Rahielma set her teeth. Her jaw ached. "It is less taxing than letting Men whittle us down."

Nassunbel hissed beside her in warning.

Rahielma rattled her displeasure back, a sound half a bear growl, half a rattlesnake's tail.

I will speak, she told him with an acrid stench.

He did not answer.

"So what do you want from us now?" Rahielma demanded.

Dor ignored the question, gesturing to the treelings standing atop the narrow prison-pillar holding the aiga children. They turned with their limbs raised and twigged outward, their roots reaching the outer lip of the pit. *A bridge*, Rahielma realized. Each climbing over the next, they passed to the outer edge, until only one remained at the prison-pillar's top, its roots still dug deep. Rahielma saw the structure's sides beginning to crumble. Her tribesmen edged away from the little cascades of dirt, understanding too well that when that final lanyani left its post, both the shaft holding the children and the pit containing them would collapse, smothering all.

"What I want," Dor finally answered, her woodwind voice weary, "is to be your friend. But you insist upon such foolish loyalties. Such . . . needless *bonds*. I had hoped to draw these striplings' clan here to finish them off. So many had taken ill from the cordyceps, and I have no use for aigamuxa hollowed out in that way. I had to prune away the dying matter. I had not thought you would be so foolish—" She heaved in a breath, exhaled it as a long, mournful coda. "—as to fight to keep your festering limb."

"You want to reclaim this world for your people," Rahielma spat. "Just as I stand for all my people."

Dor watched the last of the treelings disappear, twigging itself deeper into the culvert that held the sobbing aiga children.

Then the screams began anew, high and piping.

Dor shook her leafy mane. "Actually, I don't understand."

Rahielma turned her eye-heels toward the hole in the glass ceiling far above and sent a message with her deepest distress.

Nasrahiel. Children. Save them.

She saw a shadow glinting with steel and brass drop from the darkness. Rahielma's lip curled over a fierce snarl.

"Not to worry," she snarled. "We can teach you."

40.

Madame Miyako Kurowa dismissed her two Under-Artificers, her Third Literate secretary, and even the Fabricated ravens awaiting messages from her offices. She meant to give Umiko Haroda her full attention.

Umiko sat in seiza at Kurowa's tea table.

"An attack on our premises. By a lanyani?" Kurowa purred. "Please elaborate."

Umiko stared down at her lap, twisting the hem of her kimono between nervous fingers. "I don't know why the lanyani attacked, or where it even came from. It wasn't like the barge pilots."

"It came after both of you?"

"Not exactly. I think . . . it's all a little confused. I think it was trying to kill Rowena. It didn't notice me at all until I threw something at it."

Kurowa nodded. "Why," she wondered, "were you meeting her there in the first place, with one of our messenger Fabricated?"

The girl put an admirable effort toward keeping her face neutral. It was not to last. "It's to do with Rowena's mother. But that's not why Rowena wanted the Fabricated in the first place. They're taking the Amanuenses away and, I think, having copies made of parts. Having them translated. They mean to bring them back."

Kurowa's eyes narrowed. "*Of course* they do."

The girl flinched as if she'd been struck. *Good.* Given the rest she had confessed—sneaking off to take the Downshire girl to the Aggregator room, airing the Bishop's research readouts—she had much to fear from Kurowa. There was no need for her to know her crimes had only been what the First Literate had allowed to happen.

Entrapment was a slow game, but its payout, Kurowa had learned, was most generous.

"I suppose you consider this girl a friend," she said. There was no hint of musing in her voice. It carved in a brutal, unanesthetized surgery.

Umiko nodded.

"A pity she would use you this way."

"It wasn't until she wanted the Fabricated and the translations that I worried over that. But even then . . ."

Kurowa poured the tea, passing Umiko a cup. The girl took it in both hands. She waited until after Kurowa drank to refresh herself.

"It's not the stealing that bothered me, or using the Fabricated. After last night . . . it's *them.*"

Madame Kurowa raised an inquisitive eyebrow.

"The old man did something in my head, trying to make me forget what happened. I know that sounds mad, but it's true. I knew they had secrets, Madame. But it keeps getting worse and worse. They think Bishop Meteron wants to do something mad with the Nine—gather them up, or use them in some experiment of his own. It doesn't make sense. Rowena claims Madame Curator demanded Master Meteron do something for her before they could see the Amanuensis library, something so terrible, he wouldn't tell Rowena what it was."

Kurowa shrugged. "She commanded Master Meteron to kill Scholar Cyddra."

Umiko's eyes went wide as flywheels.

"That can't be."

"Umiko," said Kurowa, "I have punished you in the past for overstepping your duties, delving into things you were not meant to know or do. And yet, I have turned a blind eye to your stubborn disobedience. Did you not think I could tell by how little you accomplished in the Indexer room, and how frequently the Aggregator ran the same reports over and over again, that you were slipping away every chance you had?"

The girl's face burned with shame. "I didn't." To her credit, her voice did not quaver.

A brave girl. Dutiful, in her way. Kurowa did like her. She hoped to make use of her, one last time.

"Following the Creator's wisdom sometimes requires what seems like rash action. Scholar Cyddra suggested a heresy to the Curator and wished to publish it to the world. We have a duty to keep and curate truth—and to keep closest the truths that would do humanity harm. Do you understand?"

Umiko nodded again. "I think so."

"Passing the Amanuensis on to an unknown translator, for an unknown purpose, puts those secret truths at risk. We gave Chalmers and his people leave to read the texts because it would keep them close, and asked for their help in ending a threat to those texts. It was a test of their intentions. Clearly, they have failed. Their presence has even brought new dangers to our very door."

"And now?"

"Now we must change how we protect the truths that form our future. Thank you for coming to me, Umiko."

The girl rose, bowed, and backed toward the chamber door. She paused with one hand upon its crane-shaped handle.

"Rowena won't be harmed?"

Kurowa frowned.

"That depends on what she chooses. I hope she is as clever as you seem to think her, Third Literate."

Clearly unhappy with that response, Umiko bowed away. Kurowa watched her shadow disappear through the parchment wall, trailing down the hallway glowing pale green in the light of draping spider vines.

Madame Kurowa rose, dusted at the hems of her kimono, and walked to her rolltop writing desk. She pulled the sequence of smaller drawers that unlatched the broad, center drawer under the blotter and drew out a sheaf of papers and an ink brush.

Kurowa's office never boasted much in the way of natural light. Though it was only past breakfast, she paused to prune the glowplants hanging here and there, adjusting the light to suit the message she must write.

Kurowa had been a child when the first EC researchers bred the glowplants—could hardly remember what it was to walk into a Nipponese home and smell lamp oil or see an alchemist's globe suspended in a hurricane glass. The plants brought an end to whole city blocks going up in flames, wood and oilpaper homes burning like brands. Only the oldest structures of the old Shogunate and the Grand Library were built to survive such disasters. So much the EC had given her people. So much it had taken.

Kurowa's eyes narrowed at the thought.

Nora Pierce. She had come to the Grand Library years ago with a writ from the Council Bishopric and orders to research the oldest corners of the archives. No one thought to ask why a physicist would have been sent to do the work of an historian. The writ was enough, the Grand Library's belief in its own protocol sacrosanct.

When three months' searching brought the woman to the portion of the archive that contained the Amanuenses, it was too late to play at the place being meaningless, some old storage room left out of the public catalog. Pierce had insinuated herself into the Curator's trust, and whatever the old woman was willing to permit, the Library's servants were bound to obey.

Less than a week later, Pierce was gone, and the living book—the Amanuensis in progress—was removed from its proper home. Kurowa herself had written a letter of protest to the Council Bishopric, but received only one response, from Bishop Professor Allister Meteron.

Reverend Doctor Pierce, Meteron's letter explained, had been completing research on his behalf that his age and health did not permit him to travel for. She'd had very specific instructions—had been chosen by the Bishop personally for her particular aptitude in the subfield crucial to his work. Was it possible that the good Literates and Artificers of the Grand Library had conflated his agent's sudden departure with a theft that could well have happened at an earlier time? How often was the room in question actually visited by the staff at large, and were there not other scholars known to reference its contents? Had the Curator herself even been to that room in recent memory, given the state of her health?

It was a brilliant piece of scrivening, that letter. Within three days of its receipt, the Library's Literates were nodding in solemn agreement. *Yes, it had been a very long time since the Curator's health had permitted her to study the Amanuenses.* "Study" was a generous word, for where the Amanuensis collection was concerned, the Curator maintained that these books were present only for their historical value. Only the bothersome Tsuneteva clan, entitled by their wealth and patronage, dabbled in their actual contents, and never in a manner anyone had taken seriously. At least, not until much later.

Within a week, the Grand Library's denizens had all but convinced themselves they had drawn an unfair connection between Nora Pierce and the missing book. They sent out staff to inquire after rare book agents, arts dealers, visitors from recent decades, scholars of a time when less complete records of the Library's clientele were kept, and polled these, looking for signs of their lost text. All thought of Pierce's disappearance had fallen away, a perfect, amnesiac spell.

Or it had, until a handful of years after the disappearance, the Decadal Conference program was featured in the gazettes, translated by linguistic algorithms applied to galvano-gram transmissions. *God Is With Us*, the keynote address was to be called, given by Nora Pierce and some jumped-up physicist dabbling in meteorology.

Kurowa fingered a glowplant blossom as it flexed slowly open, its delicate petals waving like the lashes of a coquettish eye. She returned to her desk and surveyed the documents beside the blank paper, a skeletal understanding of the case drawn in retrospect.

The Council Bishopric had sent Pierce. Pierce was the wrong sort of person for the job—a job she pursued like a woman *literally* pursued. And when she disappeared, and the book, too, only Bishop Meteron responded to Kurowa's protest. In all likelihood, the missive from the Council Bishopric had been his work from the start.

He had wanted the book. He had nearly gotten it—nearly, Kurowa knew, because he would not have taken such eager advantage of the newly minted Aggregator in the last few years had he finally had the book in hand. Too much work gathering information, sorting for clues. It was not the work one needed to do if one already had the raw data.

A single document written in Kurowa's hand sat beside the list of direct and circumstantial evidence. It was the lever she must use to crack the Bishop open: a single page of hard-won facts and conjectures.

A converted Hasid (or Tzadikim?)

Daughter, deceased; son, estranged (in Corma, a dissolute); granddaughter—current disposition unclear.

The rest of the record comprised key votes in EC chamber politics. Governors across the globe who fell under his influence. Revolutions in EC teachings whose genesis lay in his work. Toward the bottom, Kurowa spied the gem in her hoard: a notation about a criminal case in Rimmerston, better than twenty years old. An accustion of rape, the villain some Coal War army deserter. His departure had coincided with a prisoner of war camp being inexplicably liberated of its Vraskan captives. The accused rapist had been sentenced to hang, and yet the case was overturned by the supposedly violated woman's own testimony. He was, she swore under the book and scales, her lawful husband, wed abroad, in a match roundly disapproved of by her father. The conviction was expunged. The records were void of any finer details, including the accused's full name, which lingered only as initials in the previously sealed court records: *Defendant E.P.*

Madame Kurowa did not believe in coincidences. She believed in evidence. Her evidence lined up quite nicely now: signs of the Bishop's search for the lost book; a suggestion of Erasmus Pardon's entanglement in His Grace's affairs, and an old grudge between them; evidence of Pardon and the younger Meteron's pursuit of the Bishop; evidence of their willingness to do unlawful things—never mind the Curator's urging, which was immaterial to the point; and further proof they were disseminating the information of the Amanuensis library without the Curator's express leave. All of these things, compounded with Umiko's claims of Pardon commanding unnatural influence over others' minds, meant there was more than enough information to act on.

She wondered what Bishop Meteron would give in exchange for Erasmus Pardon.

There was only one way to find out.

Your Most Esteemed Grace,

She began the letter.

Yes. That would do nicely.

41.

17TH EIGHTMONTH, 277 A.U.
VLADIVOSTOY, VRASKA

The room was dark, but Clara Downshire had expected that. The Reverend Doctor Deliverance Tegura had been quite clear on that point. Too serious by half, that woman, but then again, what did Clara know of the pressures of working for the EC, let alone for someone so important as the Bishop Professor Meteron?

She found a chair, half-visible in the light stretching from the open door. The room gave her no sense of the Bishop being nearby. No surprise there. For days, she'd been accepting his apologies for the delayed introduction, every one of them noting the pressures of current research dividing his time. Clara wasn't offended. Doctor Tegura and her new assistant, Ana Cortes, had occupied her time in the most curious ways, with little card games and drawing challenges. They were supposed to prove something about her—or test it. It was all the same to her.

And so, Clara sat, smoothed her skirts, and didn't fuss over whether what little she knew of the Bishop Professor really mattered, or was even really true. She was used to knowing things when she needed to. It might be a jumble most of the time, but when it truly mattered, her mind never led her astray.

Her husband, Jerrol, rest his soul, always said she had a good head on her shoulders. The fact of her having a head at all after their dray horse bucked her square in her skull was a matter worth a little vanity.

Eyes finally adjusted, Clara considered the broad room full of the vague outlines of furnishings. She hummed. The nurses at the home had given her a reticule of little lady-things, full of pins and needles and darning thread. She passed the time threading pins through her apron, in-out-up-down, and finally through.

"I suppose," she called, "you might well be in here already, Your Grace, and me none the wiser. That would be a fine trick."

No answer. The vagueness that crept over Clara parted for half a moment. In the clear eye of its passing, she remembered the wrist chronometer Master Meteron—the *other* Master Meteron—had given her that spring and wondered if she had come at the wrong time. Livvy Tegura had said ten of nine . . . Or had it been nine of ten?

She examined her wrist, but found the room too dark, and suddenly, a crashing certainty fell over her. She must be late. She had at last been called to receive the Bishop, and had missed him. Clara choked back a sob and staggered up from the chair, hunting for something that could shed light around her, tell her the time, tell her if she was wrong again, again—why was she always *wrong*, so *wrong*. The warm fog of confidence that surrounded her a few moments before was long gone, like steam pouring off a pump engine.

You thought you knew because you always know but you're always wrong. You shouldn't have come here, stupid Clara. Stupid Clara with a hoof in your head.

What had Tegura promised? That coming here, halfway across the world to Vladivostoy, would be good for Rowena, somehow? Why had she believed it? Where was her darling, dirty girl?

Clara blundered into a sideboard and felt the tall, fluted neck of a lamp. She fumbled about it, searching for a wick dial, or a chamber switch, or—

There.

Her hand closed on the slider that separated the lamp's alchemical vats, mingling them so they burned in a single pillar of light.

Clara looked to her timepiece. Its delicate hands flickered. Quarter to nine. She was not late.

On the other side of the room, near a bay of windows shrouded by long, heavy curtains, a door opened. Bishop Meteron entered, his arm tucked carefully in a portly, red-faced man's grasp. The man guiding him wore the marks of a deacon on his banded collar. The Bishop wore a dressing gown over something plainer, an ordinary set of nightclothes.

Clara almost knocked the lamp to the floor, so great was her haste to curtsy.

The Deacon froze, looking like a horse on the verge of a balk. His widening eyes brought back a memory that made her rear up in turn.

"I'm sorry," she cried. "I was told to be here—I came early. I thought—I thought—"

"Mrs. Downshire, please."

The rest of her words sat in her mouth, heavy as stones. *God almighty, they have the same voice.*

Age had roughened the edges of the Bishop Professor's tenor as much as smoke and poor decisions had his son's. It was a voice she had felt brush against her ear, a voice that pulled her close and murmured into her hair—a voice all ashes and the grave, because the horse's hoof had kicked open every door in Clara's mind, and she knew *everything*, knew *all* of it, knew the things no one wanted to know or hear or see.

She must have started crying, for the Deacon was beside her, gathering her up from the floor, ushering her back to her chair. The old Meteron—not her Meteron—had taken a seat on a divan across from Clara's chair. The Deacon placed a folded handkerchief in her hands. Clara mopped at her face, muttering things that were meant to be thanks, but came out jumbled.

Stupid Clara. Stupid, stupid.

"The fault is mine," the old man said, in a voice so perfectly even, so light in its touch, it soothed her even through her sobs. "I should have had the room better prepared for you. It is my habit to do most of my business in the dark." He smiled, the expression as lopsided as the one she already knew, but its knife-edge was sheathed. "I prefer not to waste resources."

Clara blinked the last of her tears away. The old man's pale eyes had fixed just past her, somewhere above her shoulder and several degrees to the right. The eyes glinted in the lamp light, turning back the illumination like flashes of quicksilver.

Cataracts. He was blind, or very near to it.

"S'no matter," Clara said. "I'm a big girl, Your Gracefulness."

The old man clucked his tongue, a chiding sound—and one, based on his rueful headshake, directed entirely at himself. "I have been so long at my studies, I am practically a brute. Please, forgive me." He offered his hand, more in the general direction of Clara's body than at an angle quite suited to her taking it. She reached out, crossing her body to take his cool, paper-skinned hand in hers and guide it back toward the midline.

He smiled, nodding his thanks. The gesture stung her with its familiarity. Was she looking at the ghost of who Anselm Meteron might have become, had his life not carried him toward back rooms and back deals and blades driven into the backs that occupied them? Bishop Meteron's hair was sparse, his face unbearded and deeply lined, casting all his years in sharp relief.

"I am Allister Meteron," he said, releasing her hand.

"*Bishop Professor* Meteron," Clara corrected. She had been a dithering idiot when he came in a few moments ago, but she would prove now she wasn't the fool she must seem. She *knew* things. She was *useful*.

"The title is a formality," the old man sighed. "I am all but retired from the Commission."

"Miss Livvy—Doctor Tegura, I mean—she says you're doing a project. That your work called for me and she had to see if I was suited to it."

"Oh, yes. Yes, it does. A vanity project, some have called it. You know the term?"

Clara's nose wrinkled. "Sounds beneath you, Your Grace. Somethin' for pride."

"Pride goeth before a fall."

Clara had a prickling notion he was quoting something. She had never been much of a reader.

"It's no matter," he continued. "But this project requires so much more than one man's vanity."

Clara blinked. "Like what, Your Gracefulness?"

"Wisdom. Patience. Forbearance. Courage." He paused, clouded eyes settling almost upon her. "It takes your cooperation and the love of a mother for her child."

Clara had borne many pains in her life. Filth and darkness. Freezing cold and stifling heat. Illness, thirst, and hunger. She could count Oldtemple's little deaths and endless taxes off on fingers and toes and still needed another set of hands to tally what it had taken from her. But first in every accounting came Maggie, and Jorrie, and Proof help her, little Rowie, too. Still with her, that child, but somehow always gone. Clara felt her turn to water, running through her fingers every time they embraced.

"It is gauche of me to call upon that bond when we are still strangers," the Bishop allowed in his measured voice. "But I know something of being a father to lost children."

His words turned a key in Clara's mind. Her eyes went blurry. It started at the center of her vision, the way it always did, pieces of the world slipping out of joint, the kinotrope slides shuffling out of order. Light poured through. She blinked into its glare, her cheeks wet from tears shed to save her sight from the press of all time in a single moment. Allister Meteron—still milky-eyed and blind, but a thousand years younger. A little girl with hair like polished copper, a squalling infant in her arms, crawls awkwardly into his embrace. Then the children are grown. There are trees climbed, pianofortes practiced, playrooms full of tools and gears—all the glittering clockworks that formed a history.

All those visions, yet never the mother. Whatever had become of her? Just a blackened space where she once had fit, like a bit of film burned through.

Clara blinked and shook herself back to the present, where she saw Bishop Professor Meteron and a piece of something that might have been his son sitting unquiet on the divan before her. It lurked, as shadowy as the burned-away mother.

"Are you well, Madame?"

Clara raised her chin, defying her brain, defying time, daring it all to have a go at her again. "So you want me to do some job for you?"

"You have, in a sense, already been doing an important job for me."

"All those tests and such."

"I hope you can forgive my curiosity, but Doctor Wyndham's reports . . ." He trailed off, his rutted brow furrowing all the deeper. "They were most peculiar. I had to be certain of what he'd claimed about you. Reverend Tegura tells me you were able to make some very interesting predictions, based on limited evidence."

Clara sighed. *Oh. That.*

"Begging your pardon, Your Gracefulness, but it en't predictions."

He raised an eyebrow. The expression lanced through her. She had seen it before on a different face, the one that kept creeping around the corners of her mind. Yet the sick, sweet smell of death and lilies rose from them both.

"Predictions," she whispered, "are things that en't happened yet. This has all happened. Just nobody's seen the details right."

A pause. Clara dangled from it. She stared at her slippers, knowing they, at least, weren't likely to turn into ghosts or start talking back to her.

The old Meteron's voice cut the silent thread holding her. "Might you provide me an example?"

"The librarian has your letter and all she needs from it. She's well pleased with the deal you've struck. It doesn't go all to plan, of course, but nothing ever does." Clara held the rest for a time. The words tasted sour and oily, like milk that had taken a turn. "Really," she blurted, stabbing the pin back through her apron again, "you've been expecting things to go this way a long, long time. He's all but dead to you, anyway."

She looked up from her apron and found Bishop Meteron's face sorting curiosity and puzzlement.

"I haven't written a librarian a letter," he said, at last.

"That's as may be. You say you need my help? And that my help will see to Rowie's needs?"

"After a fashion."

"Then tell me what you need me to do."

He pointed to the sideboard. Clara went to it and brought the map waiting there back.

"I'm jake for reading maps," she boasted. "I helped Mr. Downshire, rest his soul, when we ran the carting business. Nearly ten years. If I couldn't read maps to help him make routes, I wouldn't have been much good to him."

"You'll find this map is quite special."

It was, clearly. Apart from the little bumps and shapes punched almost-but-not-quite through the paper's edges, like pockmarks running up and down the margins, it was also hand-drawn. Someone who knew their craft had been at it with a square and protractor and stylus. She'd marked streets in her husband's map that way, once upon a time. This map was of land spaces—big ones. The scale was only fine enough to dot cities and thread rivers, but it was a map all the same, and she had always liked them. Clara squinted over the print, trying out words, turning them on her tongue.

"Nippon . . . What's there?"

"Secrets."

Clara's vision blurred again. She let go of the map, pressing the heels of her hands into her eyes until everything was sunbursts and stars and stars and stars.

A tap at the study door. Clara looked up, seeing Meteron's abstracted gaze turned in its direction. "Come," he called.

Deliverance Tegura entered. "Your Grace, there's been a spark. More of a letter, given its length."

"Has there," he murmured. No questioning note curled that last word.

"I've had Leopold punch a copy out for you." She carried a tablet with a sheet of paper clipped to its surface. It looked blank until Clara's squint picked out an array of nubs raised along its surface.

"You are both so good to me," Meteron said. He seemed to mean it.

Tegura stepped to him, placing the tablet in his outstretched hand, then retreated to await his reading. The old man set the tablet in his lap, the fingers of his left hand running over the bumps and nubs, angling up and down, pausing before leaping onward. His face passed through a succession of unguarded expressions—flickers of eyebrows, tightenings of his lips, a brief smile of satisfaction. Clara couldn't fathom how he read whatever his copy of the letter said, but it was plainly of great interest.

Finally, he straightened in his chair, hands steepled.

"Shall I take down a response for you, Your Grace?" Tegura asked.

"Tell Madame Kurowa . . ." He paused. Clara felt his attention drift in her direction, inexact in its landing. "Tell her I would be pleased to give her the support she requires, provided my conditions are met."

That answer tightened Tegura like a noose. "The same conditions as before?"

"I require her to honor my agreement with the Curator. And to surrender her visitors."

"How many of them?"

"All."

Tegura nodded crisply. "Yes, Your Grace."

Clara watched the woman go. Her own fingers tingled, as if they'd been the ones running over the strange, bumpy script the Bishop had deciphered. *All the guests.* Clara looked at the map spread before her. She knew enough about Nippon to know it had a library, and that it was a monstrous big one. And that it was a long way off. Her Rowie and Anselm had been bound somewhere to do research . . .

Well then.

Clara traced the borders of Kyo-Tokai, a city that swelled over most of the long chain of Nipponese islands. Its inky shape blurred and twisted in her vision, fraying into line drawings little better than stick figures, moving herky-jerky in the space between the present moment and a memory. Something happening. Happened already. Time settled in her like a stone, its weight drawing her down into her chair.

"You remember what I said about your letter to the librarian," she murmured.

"I do, Mrs. Downshire."

"You say you want all of this Madame's visitors. Well. You should know you en't getting 'em. They'll only scare up two."

"Which?"

"Depends what you want most."

Bishop Meteron smiled bitterly. "You might be surprised how accomplished I am at getting all I need from only half of what I wanted."

Clara nodded. "As you say." The stick figures crawling on the map blinked in and out of her vision. She wiped away a tear, hoping it might smear them away, too. Still, they chased on, or were chased. There was a room, and a glass roof, and something tiny and tick-tockily moving, no bigger than a monkey. "Just . . . mind you be gentle with him," she added. "The Alchemist. He's always been good to my Rowie. A positive angel."

"Your angel is better described as a monster. But he is a monster we will need—here, where we can use him."

"For what?"

"To find those like Rowena. And to do that, I will need your help as much as his. You're a good mother and a decent woman. You have the sense to give your help freely. He, though . . . He will require some persuasion."

That seemed wrong. Backwards. "He's always helped my Rowie. If you just asked him, he would help you, too, for her sake. A monster wouldn't do that."

"A monster will do a great many things, where its own needs are concerned." Allister Meteron's mouth flattened into a pale, merciless line. "First among them is to keep from being caught out as what they are. It's finally too late for that."

42.

Anselm Meteron saw the Old Bear's shadow pass the sliding door of his room, limping toward his own chamber further down the hall. It was all the invitation he needed to dispense with manners.

He had closed his chamber door by the time Anselm reached him, carrying two tiny, glazed clay cups stacked in one hand and a sake bottle in the other. He tapped the bottle against the door frame and nudged the panel open with his heel.

"You look in need of a dastardly drink," Anselm announced.

The Old Bear sat on his tatami, boots removed, the leg of his trousers bunched over his knee. A medic's roll lay open beside him. He met Anselm's gaze, a capped syringe gritted between his teeth.

"You might've waited for an answer," he growled around it.

"And I'd have had a time of it, trying to make you out with that thing in your mouth. God's balls, Bear." Anselm crouched beside the bedroll, balanced on the balls of his feet. "What the hell are you doing to yourself now?"

"Cortisone." The Old Bear uncapped the needle.

Anselm studied his old friend's leg with a revolted concern he didn't bother to police. Erasmus's knee was badly swollen, the dark flesh shiny and tight around its web of scars like the veins of shattered glass. Mercifully, he had been unconscious when the physick Anselm hired to assist Reverend Doctor Chalmers opened his shattered leg and tried to make sense of the wreckage. Bone fragments grinding into cartilage, tendons wrenched from muscles and bones, the whole structure orbited well off its proper course from hip to ankle. Hours after spent under a layer of

390

ether and morphine. God only knew how many pins and bolts held him together now.

And for what? In the day since the Old Bear brought Rowena back from the Anchor Authority, the girl hadn't stopped chirruping over her missing mother, and the Alchemist had barely stopped moving. Only a vow that they'd leave for Vraska to find the woman kept Rowena from packing up a satchel, stealing a purse, and running for the nearest air galleon that would take her on for scullery work. Even that hadn't been enough to keep her from begging Umiko to send some pointless message back to the Mercy Commission Home, and nearly being killed by a lanyani monster doing it. Anselm had wanted to finish the sea-tree's work when he learned of the incident, and to throttle the Old Bear for good measure. Using his powers to block Umiko's memory of the incident might have been the fastest solution, but if it didn't work, the consquences would be far, far worse for all of them.

In his agitation, Chalmers had all but suggested that they should tie the cricket up and put her in a trunk until their departure. Anselm would sooner have trussed up the Doctor, whose urgent trips forth and back from the Amanuensis library had become all the more frenzied and suspicious, driven by their vanishing timetable. Meantime, chasing after Chalmers and Rowena and working double-time on their leads into Allister Meteron's network of supporters had taken a toll on Erasmus. And that was before they had reason to worry about a lanyani attack. Their final day in Kyo-Tokai could not come fast enough to spell the Old Bear.

He pushed the needle into the heart of his damaged knee, as if probing the rottenest part of a long-turned fruit. The plunger sank down. The Old Bear's face hardened, jaw tight, and then it was done.

He set the syringe aside and took the gauze and lister Anselm had silently prepared.

"That help?" Anselm asked.

"For a few days."

"And how long until it doesn't anymore?"

The Old Bear's eyes glinted in the crawling light of the room's bioluminescent ivy. "Ann."

"Come off it, Bear. I've had too close a relationship with too many substances over too long a time. I know how it goes."

Erasmus's expression was unreadable. "A few months more. Until the spring, if I go easy on myself."

"You've already hit your limit. I can see it all over you."

"Ann," Erasmus sighed, letting the trouser leg fall back into place, and then himself, groaning as he lay flat on the tatami. "We've work to do, now more than ever. It's in the nature of the job."

"*The job* was to help Chalmers follow his leads on the book and the Bishop. Not this nonsense of going to Vraska." Anselm snatched his sake rather too roughly, splashing some on his hand.

A long pause. Erasmus studied him silently, and though his expression didn't change, Anselm knew he had just put the pieces together. *God's balls.* No amount of hunching his back and snarling had ever put the Old Bear off his scent, the bastard. He lingered over pouring himself another cup, hoping to buck him and knowing it wouldn't work.

Erasmus spoke with the patience of a surgeon. "The last time we had a conversation like this, you were looking for someone to kill for the sake of someone you couldn't save. This is different."

He was right, damn him. Fucking obnoxious habit, and rude, too. Anselm had spent his entire life being comfortable in knowing he was always right—right up until he met Erasmus Pardon.

"It should be," Ann agreed. He finished his sake, shivered against it, and filled the cup again. "It is."

"How long have you and Mrs. Downshire been lovers?"

Anselm shrugged, one-shouldered. "Not the term I'd use. We've never exactly made love, mostly for lack of opportunity—"

"*Ann.*"

"Since a few weeks after Clara came to the Mercy Commission Home. Months now. Cricket has no idea."

A humorless sound Anselm only half-recognized as a laugh escaped the Old Bear. "Of course she doesn't. She'd have killed you twice now, if she had." He grimaced and tried to bend his knee. It moved with an audible grinding. Anselm winced, watching his friend's color drain at the pain.

"You gather that trivia picking around my head?"

"It was all over your face when Rowena told you Mrs. Downshire had been taken."

Anselm raised an eyebrow. "Really?" He passed a cup of sake to Erasmus. He set it beside his pillow, untouched. "I thought I had a very good bluffing face."

"You've never played cards against me, Ann. I wouldn't recommend it."

"I care about Clara," Anselm admitted. "But there's every likelihood His Grace took her to draw us off some other scent."

The Old Bear shook his head. "This Reverend Doctor Tegura had been receiving information from Doctor Wyndham about Mrs. Downshire's anomalous perceptions. However much taking her is a distraction, it may also be of material benefit to your father's plan. Another means of finding the Nine, with the current book missing. That makes her disappearance part of the job."

"Which means shutting up operations here and dashing off to Vraska, right into the lion's den. His patrons keep him in Vladivostoy. He'll be there waiting. Expecting us."

Erasmus sat up awkwardly, balanced on one elbow. "Are you afraid of confronting His Grace?"

"He can wander off a cliff's edge for all I care."

"Not what I asked."

"That stuff you shot in your leg very fussy about what else goes into you?"

"Not at all. It's localized."

"Good." Anselm nudged Erasmus's neglected cup. "Help me finish this off, or I'll be useless in the morning."

Erasmus took the drink and finished it in two draws. He didn't pursue his question. He didn't need to. They both knew Anselm's answer.

"Look, Bear," he said, after fetching Erasmus's pipe following a wordless gesture of request. "I can't sit by and watch you ruin yourself jumping at shadows. We're lucky Rowena's snooping led her to the wrong conclusion about Clara. We can go with the lie and carry on the job. But it's thinking we could just do the job the way we used to that made me get you in this mess."

Erasmus scowled. "*Made you* get *me* into what?"

"The Cathedral. That idiocy with the curare. All of it."

"I didn't have to agree to it."

"I didn't listen to your alternatives."

"That's as may be. You also didn't make me climb up after Nasrahiel. And you didn't make me jump."

Anselm had put his cup to his lips, but the gesture stalled there, the sake's sharp, acid smell making his eyes water. Slowly, his hand fell—slowly enough to keep the drink from spilling this time.

With a grunt, Erasmus pushed to a seated pose and began tamping his pipe.

Anselm said nothing, the clockworks of his mind winding back the better part of a year, past the bruises of battle and the stabbing pain of a dislocated shoulder, reaching for Erasmus's words that night. He'd asked Anselm to arrange the shot, told him just where Gammon's sharpshooter should fire. He'd been ready to take his own shot, for insurance—to pin the creature down and finish it off, if needs be.

Or that was what he'd wanted Anselm to think.

"You grandstanding, suicidal bastard," he whispered. "You *meant* to jump. You meant to take the creature out yourself *the whole. Fucking. Time.*"

Erasmus's hands stilled for a moment over his pipe. He resumed, touching a struck lucifer to its bowl and drawing slowly on it, a cloud of marjoram and fennel rising around him. At last, he answered.

"The sharpshooter's best angle still wasn't a killing shot, even after I lured Nasrahiel into the clear. I only had one bullet. And all that movement, in high wind . . ." He trailed off. "The shooter couldn't have taken another clear shot before the aiga attacked me, or killed Chalmers, or both. It would have turned into a tangled mess without a target. But if I took the aiga over the edge with me, well." Erasmus's raptor eyes found Anselm's. "It was my job. *My* job. I had to be sure."

Anselm regarded his empty cup. "*She* was your job, you mean."

"Still is."

The Old Bear edged backward, bracing his back against the wall. His pipe clenched in his teeth, he busied himself again with his wounded leg, gentling it into a ninety-degree bend, then flexing, his hands searching the joint with clinical care, as if the limb belonged to someone else.

"So this is what you've decided," Anselm said. "To run yourself ragged chasing leads from the Aggregator and the Library's notes and the customs reports. Find every angle my father's using to catch cricket and all the rest. Pack all of it up and run to find her mother. And then what?" Silence. Anselm's right hand screamed in phantom pain. He closed his fist, capped the stump of his index finger with his thumb and pressed as hard as he could bear. "Say you think of a way to get Clara free without His Grace getting ahold of you. Say you find some pattern to his search, and a way to stay just ahead of it, running with the girl from place to place. Because that's what's going to happen. There's nothing to go back to in Corma. When was the last time we had a report from Gammon? For all we know, she and Jane and all the rest are dead, filled up with that fucking murderous fungus. How long can you live with Rowena on the run before you're well and truly worn out? Before the lanyani find her again, or the aigamuxa? You're rattling yourself to pieces."

"What would you have me do?"

"I seem to remember buying you a God-fucking-damned *island* not so long ago."

"We've talked about this already."

"I don't think you getting sentimental about gardening and keeping up a steady visiting schedule to Mama at the asylum counts as a conversation," Anselm spat.

Erasmus's gaze shifted like the counterweights on a scale, squaring over Anselm. "And what would *you* do?"

Anselm opened his mouth, a breath away from saying, *I would run to that island with you.* And yet, he knew that gaze— felt it reading what must surely be written in every line of his face.

"God's balls," he growled, raking his hands through his hair. "For the record, it's both a pain in my arse and an injustice that *you* can lie to *me* and I can't lie to you."

"I believe you've mentioned that a few times, in recent decades." Erasmus's baritone was so gentle, it raised a lump in Anselm's throat. Anselm looked away. "You didn't answer me."

"I'd use what we've learned to go after my father."

"Then you know why I can't go to your island. This is my job. Her. And you. Leyah would never forgive me—"

"Shut your fucking mouth." The lump in Anselm's throat fairly choked him. He drowned it with a swig straight from the sake bottle. "You don't get to play that card. Not with me."

Silence. The ghost of a smile haunted the Old Bear's mouth.

"That was always what worried Leyah about you. Playing cards. You've always acted as though life is a game and people the stakes thrown in. You'll gamble with anything, even yourself."

"Pot calling the kettle black, that."

"I'm the only thing I've ever gambled with." A pause. The smile had left Erasmus's voice. "The only thing I ever *intended* to gamble," he corrected.

He didn't need to explain. They both knew too well. *Rare.*

"This is my job, Ann. My last. If I work it very hard and turn out very lucky, it will come out right." The Old Bear watched Anselm put the bottle to his lips again. "Not that I will be able to count on you for much. You're on your way to being useless tomorrow."

"So drink more of your share."

Erasmus's brow furrowed. "Better to have us both *half* useless?"

"There's always Chalmers to make up the difference."

A pause.

"Half the bottle between us, and no more," Erasmus said gravely.

"Right. Good point."

They were nearly at the end of their appointed shares of sake, discussing the Rolands' response (nonplussed) to their communique about an early departure and the arrangements made for flying out the following afternoon (haphazard, and overcharged in the extreme) when Anselm spied from beneath a comfortably alcoholic haze a small figure climbing onto Erasmus's window sill.

Anselm rose, only a little unsteadily, to meet the Fabricated monkey Umiko had helped Rowena prepare. It lifted its tail—mended with a band of tin, he noticed; the girl had managed the repairs, after all. The tail snickked open halfway down its length, revealing a chamber filled with a rolled note.

Anselm pulled out the Fabricated messenger's pearl card, turned it around to reverse the program, and inserted it again. It bounded away, to a location set for standby long before that evening.

Anselm waved the scrolled note rudely close to Erasmus's nose, to be buffeted away by a hot pipe.

"You read it, Bear," he yawned. "I'm too drunk to manage the cipher now."

The Old Bear rumbled assent, fetching his spectacles from the physick's roll at his bedside. He peered at the message, his drink-smoothed face passing through several weeks of stone cold sobriety in the space of two minutes' reading.

Anselm frowned. "What've we got?"

"Cyd has made a breakthrough translating the sections Chalmers sent along. They've identified another of the Nine, one of the humans."

The warmth of sake left, turning Anselm's stomach sour. "Not Rowena?"

"Subject One, and where to find her."

Erasmus passed Anselm the note, grave as a tombstone. He tapped the relevant passage with a tobacco-stained forefinger.

It had been nearly a year since Anselm had felt the galvanizing shock of standing too close to the ligtning strike of truth. Half a world away in a dank cellar with a mad scholar and a scrawny girl and a book plotting the path to the heart of the world open before him, the knowledge had seared itself into his bones. That feeling returned, throbbing in his missing finger.

"God's balls," he murmured. "We've been played, Bear."

"Wake the Doctor, Ann. I'll see to rousing Rowena."

43.

It was a haze of pain, scented with blood and earth, which told Rahielma she was still alive. She opened her eyes, relieved to find herself curled tight, knees to her forehead, ankles tucked together to protect her eyeheels. That she had taken that position meant nothing was broken—or at least, nothing beyond mending. Stretching slowly, she worked her way into the pedestal position and found, as her clawed hands reached and made purchase below her, the limits of her cage.

We can teach you, she had threatened Dor.

Creator save me, what a fool I've been.

Dor and her clan of many clans had been good enough to let the aigamuxa chieftain share her prison—a culvert of dirt and rootwork dug into Crystal Hill's mossy hillocks—with her mate. And they had been cruel enough to transform him into the cage itself.

"Oh, my love, what beasts they are," she whispered, her heels gone damp with tears.

Nasrahiel was still alive. Rahielma could smell the heat in his blood. He hung upside down, head and shoulders and dangling arms swinging like a chandelier in her chamber's center. His mechanical eye was cracked, its glass spidered and its iris jammed half-open by an errant shard. The intricate pistons and cables and rods of his man-made legs, though . . .

Rahielma turned her feet to the earth, murmuring prayers neglected since childhood.

They had made their raid, and when all seemed lost, Nasrahiel had shot from the hothouse ceiling like a monstrous arrow, lancing into the earth, claws and teeth and arms swinging. Rahielma remembered his attack as a blur of blood and bark and brass darting past the narrow field of vision provided her at the bottom of her prison pit. The column of dirt and roots coming up from its center trembled with the screams of kidnapped young, mid-slaughter. The lanyani did not themselves scream, but their bodies did, fibers shredding and limbs popping, as if a threshing machine had broken loose in their midst.

Rahielma and her warriors had whooped for joy, cheered Nasrahiel with lines of old poems and songs, pounded their fists on the dirt, scrabbled up the crumbling walls of their prison, stepping on one another's heads and shoulders in a mad rush to join him and pull the treacherous weeds up from the very earth of their stronghold. She had given her body as a ladder to others and accepted the same in return. In the lanyani's fury to slay the children and destroy Nasrahiel, they had neglected to keep their captives contained.

She had expected the sight on the surface to bring her joy. Instead, she only saw the dozens—no, hundreds—of tendrils shooting up from the hothouse's pine-needled floor, binding Nasrahiel and tearing through his scarred flesh with vines wreathed in thorns and burrs. Two lanyani crawled out of the center pit, caked with gore, the second of them carrying the dead aiga children in a bulging sack.

A sack, Rahielma saw to her horror, made of one their bodies, broken and gutted and turned into a sling.

Nasrahiel had done what he could to free Rahielma and her warriors and had still been choked on the spot before he could reach the children. It was not the aigamuxa who gave lessons, after all.

The howling aigamuxa, their pink eyes streaming tears and jagged mouths foaming rage, could scarcely react as a lanyani yards away plunged into the earth as they might have plunged into water, disappearing without a ripple or splash. Four more followed suit. An instant later, they breached the earth on which the invading aiga stood, behind and below, their bodies spears and arrows, quilling the warriors like shrike's prey.

All the while, Dor stood on the Pit's seeping surface. The smallest Pit

Master, the one who had once been Lir, convulsed behind her in something that might have been laughter.

After that, there had been pain and blood and darkness.

And now, Nasrahiel.

Though the lanyani had no use for Men's machines, they knew more than enough about how to dismantle them. Nasrahiel's mechanical legs had been peeled like a fruit, divided into parts and splayed in all directions, bent and warped into a dome of bars and cables over Rahielma's prison. His torso still attached, its spines twisted by the Trees' handiwork, he swung like a piece of meat from a tendon, the metalwork suspending him groaning at his pendulous weight.

A lattice of ruddy sunset passed through the weave of Nasrahiel's body and the canopy of trees. Rahielma saw Dor approach her cell.

One corner of a mouth like a lightning gash turned in mockery.

Rahielma put her heels to the ground, shutting the world away. Her skin itched. She scratched at her throat, scouring as if it had wronged her. Something under her nails made her pause.

She touched it to her nose and sniffed. She recognized the smell.

Cordyceps. Rahielma struggled to smear the offending powder from her hand, plunging it into the dirt. But the smell was everywhere, especially her face and hands. A strange taste lingered in her throat, heavy as wet mulch.

"You didn't imagine I was finished with you, did you?"

Dor's words drifted down like dead leaves. Snarling, Rahielma curled into the pedestal position and glared at her through burning tears.

"What have you done to me?"

Dor paced the perimeter of the prison hole, appearing and disapppearing behind the broken pieces of Nasrahiel.

"Nothing you did not force me to do. I had little interest in keeping aigamuxa touched by the cordyceps before, but your boldness persuaded me you still had use." She drew in another breath, played a slow measure of answer, a sinister pianissimo. "I require obedience, chieftain. I will have it from you however I must." She gestured to the tangle of metal capping Rahielma's prison. "Your mate fought bravely. He would never have survived in even this many pieces without the human doctor's work making him so strong. Most interesting. I fear, though, that the cordyceps will not take for him. Too much inorganic material in his nervous system. Nothing for it to . . ." She paused, considering. ". . . grab on to. It won't matter. We have no gift for rebuilding in the manner his body now requires. Death will be a release for him. I am sure you will look forward to it yourself, before long."

"I will be released," Rahielma hissed. "But not by my death."

"By your tribe, you suppose? Soon enough, they all will serve me, too. You will walk out of this city with my scouts to hunt down each and every one of the Nine. You will raze them from the earth. That is the way of life in the wild. The way things are meant to be. Fire burns the forest down so it may rise up stronger. Rains wash out the weakest roots. We must purge. We will begin by showing the Creator that we are above judgment, His first and final survivors."

Dor's shadow turned like a cloak, covering the ruddy sunset. She strode away, leaving Rahielma to the darkness, staring up into her husband's broken face and reaching for his eye that would not see.

Dor crossed the surface of the Pits, stepping past the dry, flaking shards of the dead Pit Master and toward Lir.

It had been only a few days since he rooted and already he swelled with new life, covered in buds that winked like countless eyes, spying from all directions. His limbs had widened, split, and stretched outward in long, willow-like whips. They caressed Dor, countless lovers' hands, as she passed between them, trailing whispers of devotion in their pale yellow pollen.

It is such ecstasy, my leader, he sighed through the earth. The mud all around him teemed with the sharp tang of blood. *I wish you could join me.*

As do I, Dor lied. She stroked his trunk, pregnant with possibility, touching with hands above the earth and her long, reaching roots below. She had no desire to sink herself to one place until the end of her days, perfecting the soil for her people in exchange for own slow demise. True, the Pit Masters grew vast and mighty. But eventually, they would benefit all they could from the first fruits of the best soil, becoming sponges, filters, canaries in a cave of acids and bases. There was much Lir had not understood of the honor offered to him. He would have many, many years now to reflect on it—years that would teach him to accept his fate, or regret it. They were years Dor was happy to leave him to.

I am needed here, she continued. That was not a lie. *Tell me of our progress.*

All the aigamuxa who lived have been given the cordyceps. I sense it will root well in them. The message you sent over the waters to Fog Island has been received.

Dor straightened, as if drawn up in a wind. *How do you know this?*

There is so much the Pit Masters never tell us, my leader, my love. That made Dor worry, until he continued. *The ocean touches the earth which touches even the stones of this city. If I draw down deep, I can feel their answer to your call, even from so far away.*

Dor's body prickled, a wave of burrs and bark that smoothed like a fur settling back into place. *And their answer?*

The hunt has already begun. The girl is in Nippon, as the book has said. There was an attack, an effort to claim her alone. It has failed, but it was only a first sally. Our kin will still claim the child and the ones who protect her. Have no doubt.

You were my best choice to succeed the fallen master, Lir. You do not disappoint.

Something like a face broke through the surface of Lir's peeling-paper bark. It smiled, toothless and euphoric, opened to speak in words—

Then a ring of eyes opened amid the buds surrounding it. Then another. And another.

Dor recoiled.

The ends of Lir's willow-whip branches rose, each a fusillade of budding eyes, their pistols and stamens wildly rolling irises.

INTRUDERRSSSSS, Lir hissed, the soil rippling with his call.

The lanyani crouched amid the hothouse's shadows and branches emerged, bristling saw-edged leaves and wicked spurs.

Dor pressed a hand to the bundle of branches growing from her hip, clutching the book and its secrets. She turned in the direction Lir's branches had pointed and saw for herself.

Just inside the hothouse's great glass doors, the cordyceps-hollowed housekeeper aiga lying dead at their feet, stood four humans—three women and one man.

Dor reached into the Pit's earth for purchase and strode to its shore. She spread her arms in mock welcome.

"Strangers! To what do we owe the honor?"

A copper-faced woman, slim as a riding crop, stepped to the side, clearing a path for a short woman, round-cheeked and heavyset, to step to the fore. The young man plucked at the girl's sleeve, tugging her backward, though she seemed to need little encouragement. She disappeared behind the spindly youth, eyeing the large, cylindrical object the fat woman held.

Dor examined the woman's burden more carefully. The fat woman tossed her head to clear away a kink of dark hair, and raised the object to her shoulder.

It was Lir who understood first. *You cannot let them! No one brings fire to the Gathering Grove!*

Dor's face collapsed in fury. "No!"

The young man looked to the copper-faced woman. "Actually," he said, "I'm thinking yes?" He rolled his shoulder, shrugging the fire-thrower strung across his own back into view.

"I'm looking for the one called Dor," the slender, darker-skinned woman called. Their leader. She walked forward slowly, hands raised for parley. "My name is Haadiyaa Gammon. We need to talk."

"You," Dor snarled, "need to leave."

"Not without the book or the aiga."

Dor looked down at her hands. They splintered into scissoring knives. "Then you will be disappointed."

Gammon nodded toward the girl who had cowered behind the young man just a moment before. Then she was gone, the brush just to the side of the entrance path rustling with her passage.

"That," Gammon said, unbothered by the girl's disappearance, "is a terrible shame."

Lir rustled like a swarm of locusts at Dor's back. "Whyyy?" his limbs ground out, the word barely recognizable as speech.

"Because we didn't only bring fire-throwers," Gammon said.

She reached into a trouser pocket, withdrawing a handful of tiny, pill-like objects threatening to spill over her cupped palm.

Dor had no heart to skip a beat and no blood to run cold. But the sight of loosestrife seed made every lanyani creeping forward with fury written in their tangled faces draw up short.

"Very well, Haadiyaa Gammon," Dor snarled, "We are listening."

44.

Rowena bounced on her heels, restless as a puppy, watching Umiko leaf through the Amanuensis lifted from the Indexer box. The other girl's mouth was screwed up in a scowl.

"I put a few leaves of my own notes in," Rowena explained, hoping her chatter would distract her friend from her funk. "Her name and where she was born and all that. Subject Six. It's my mother, Umiko, I just know it, and we're going to Vraska to get her back."

The Third Literate was seated at one of the smaller desks near the Aggregator's card punching station. "You've said that. Probably a hundred times."

"Today," Rowena confirmed, not really listening. She gestured at her clothes—her usual Cormarran dress, riding skirt and shirtwaist buttoned for easy movement, with a little panel of ruching one pull of a ribbon away from revealing the weaponette in easy reach on her thigh. She'd kept the weapon oiled and ready; the attack on the roof the night before last only confirmed the wisdom of that decision. It felt good to be in her own clothes again, the Grand Library's kimonos and sandals shed like ill-fitting skins.

Something twitched in Umiko's face, too fast for Rowena to read it properly.

"Today," Umiko echoed. "And you want me to use the Aggregator with this to do what?"

Rowena frowned. Her friend was only an arm's length away, but she might as well have been on the other side of the earth, for all the distance Rowena felt between them.

"To find out what else the Aggregator knows about her, I guess?" Rowena suggested, embarrassed at the uncertainty in her own voice. "I know the report would take a bit, so I can make arrangements with Master Meteron to have your data sent along somehow. He's good at that sort of thing. I'm sure there's a way."

Umiko shook her head. "You don't understand the first thing about this machine."

"Come again?"

Umiko spoke in a rush, the threads of her voice unraveling. "The Aggregator doesn't *know* anything. It can't just access any kind of datum about anything you can think of. It only pulls data that's being gathered for a purpose, transmitted into its logs through programming. Important things." Umiko sighed. "You asked me to meet you here at the break of dawn for nothing, Rowena. It'll have nothing on your mother, because she's just a single, tiny data point, not a person. Not as far as the Aggregator is concerned."

A fist closed in Rowena's belly. She forced it open, peeling at its fingers. "You don't know that for sure. She's one of the Nine, and the books about her have been here forever. Surely that means something about her is in data the Aggregator pulls up. Surely there's something that would help us figure exactly where they've taken her?" She swallowed. "Vraska's a big place. Even just Vladivostoy. It's my *mother*, Umiko. I need to do *something*."

"Or you could stay here."

All at once, Umiko Haroda was on her feet, the book tumbling from her lap. She clutched her friend's hands so hard, Rowena yelped in surprise. "Stay. I'll talk to Madame Kurowa. I'm sure she'll let you. None of this is your fault, anyway."

Rowena blinked. "What are you talking about?"

Umiko's hands lowered, Rowena's still tangled between them. She looked away, scanning the cabinets of the silent Aggregator, her eyes wandering, as if in search of the switch or dial that would churn out an answer. "It's not your fault," she murmured, more to herself than Rowena. "Surely Madame knows it. She'll understand."

Slowly, Rowena unknotted their hands. "Umiko. What are you talking about?"

The girl's eyes brimmed with tears. "I told her."

Rowena wasn't aware of having stepped back. The distance between her friend and herself had simply . . . grown. "You told Kurowa *what?*"

Umiko blinked. Tears trailed down her round cheeks.

"Holy fucking Proof," Rowena whispered. "*What* did you tell her?"

"Everything."

"Everything?"

"About the reports on the Bishop's studies, and the stolen Amanuenses, and the translator, and the lanyani attacking you, and what Master Pardon did in my . . ." Umiko shook her head, sobbing. "They're coming today. They might even be here now, gathering them up."

"Everything," Rowena repeated. She felt herself breathing, sawing air in and out, painful and strange. "*Everything.*"

Umiko nodded. "The book, and the Cathedral, and Master Pardon's evil magic—"

Rowena leaped back, stung. "That was just part of the story! It wasn't any of your business, and it doesn't matter for us being here, I just needed you to understand who they are. What they're really here *to do.*"

"I *did* understand!" Umiko shouted. "I thought you were making that story about him and his magic up. But after the lanyani attacked, he went inside my head and told me to go to bed and just forget. That's when I knew I had to tell her."

"But *you* programmed the Fabricated we used to send the messages! You helped us!"

"I needed to see how far you'd go," she protested. "If you were really after what you claimed to be. It might have all been a silly little girl's story, some mad fancy, but then you kept telling me things, and I just couldn't . . . I couldn't allow it. And I couldn't allow Master Pardon's wrongness here any longer."

Rowena covered her mouth with her hands. A heave in her stomach nearly doubled her over. She remembered a cold, wrecked loft in the dark of night and the Old Bear calling to her from the ruined warehouse floor below. She had threatened him—promised to find a Logician and serve him up to their experiments. And here they were now, in the heart of the Logicians' territory, and she had tried to win herself an ally by telling the truth. Telling *the whole* truth. *His* truth.

"There's nothing wrong with him," Rowena spat. She straightened like a viper, hissing rage. It took all her will to keep from drawing the weaponette. "*Nothing.*"

"I don't think Madame Curator agrees, or the Argument that's been sent to take them in."

Oh, God, Rowena. The voice that wasn't quite Leyah's beat inside her like hands on an iron-shod door. *Get out of here. Warn them. Find them.*

She had already been running, by then. Umiko's cries chased after her, and the girl with them, but they stood no chance of heading her off.

If there was anything Rowena Downshire did well, it was run.

Rowena tore across the surface of the Grand Library's seal, its half-familiar sigils taunting her with questions she'd never properly answered. The staircase came next, and she plowed up it, shoving through clerks and Literates trying to make their way down with armloads of books and scrolls. Each fell in an explosion of paper, tripping out of her way. Rowena ducked through the chaos, spun and scrambled and gained the landing, then the skyway, then the corridors to the residences, their windows trading the glow of lamp-plants for the rising dawn.

The door to her company's apartment was open. A crowd of people swelled out from it. She heard voices, shouts, Nipponese and Amidonian clashing like cymbals.

Rowena ducked her head and crashed into the knot of soldiers—a whole Argument's worth—shoving her way through.

"Leave them alone!" she shrilled. "Get out of here!"

Hands jerked Rowena from her feet, then shoved her past the threshold, where a second Argument stood in positions around the apartment's common room, covering each door with a flintlock rifle, their bayonetted ends glinting. Rowena staggered into Chalmers. He caught her shoulders and tried to set her right. She sprang away from him and took in the scene.

Most of the luggage—meager for Master Meteron and Rowena, more ample for the Old Bear and his supplies, and embarrassingly voluminous for Chalmers—sat at the center of the room. Chalmers was dressed, though his waistcoat was only half-buttoned and his hair embarrassingly untidy. He seemed content to be held at bay by the angry stares of the Argument. Meteron had clearly been caught at the end of his shaving, barefoot with a towel thrown over his shoulder and a little foam still at his jawline. One of the soldiers of the Argument kept him in place with the edge of his bayonet, ready to take a vicious bite from his spine.

The Old Bear had been fully dressed—at least before it had been undone.

He was held on his knees by two young men only half his size, their grip of his arms behind his back making up the difference. His face was a knot of pain. Something in Rowena that was half herself and half Leyah quailed as the soldiers leaned forward, lifting his arms and ducking his head, grinding the Alchemist's wounded knee into the floor. His shirt lay in tatters beside him, cut away and discarded.

The guard holding the Old Bear's right arm turned it to reveal the faded tattoo barely visible against his dark skin.

Madame Kurowa glided forward, hands in her sleeves, and leaned close, peering at the markings. She clucked her tongue. "Master Pardon, you have not been entirely forthcoming with us."

Chalmers bristled. "We don't know what you're—" A nearby guard hissed and made a jabbing motion with his bayonet. Chalmers's mouth snapped shut.

"It is no matter now," Kurowa continued. She looked up at Rowena, as if only just noticing the girl. "Fortunately, someone in your party has been most thoroughly helpful."

The weight of a dozen stares piled on Rowena. The Old Bear couldn't lift his head to look at her, thank the Proof. But Master Meteron's eyes carved to the bone. She looked to him, grasping for the words to make him sheathe the daggers in his eyes.

"I'm sorry," she stammered. "I thought the more Umiko knew, the better she'd understand. The more likely she'd be to help."

Meteron's mouth curled in a sneer. "*You thought*." The words came out slowly, tortured on a rack. Then he looked toward the apartment door.

Rowena followed his gaze.

Umiko pushed the Grand Librarian's wheelchair through a widening gap in the Argument's blockade. They bowed, and she nodded in turn, her white head dipping and rising like some ancient bird. Umiko stared at the chair's handlebars as if she never wanted to meet a human eye again.

"Is this how you treat all your guests, Madame Curator?" Meteron called. "A ritual for our departure, perhaps?"

"Sadly," she answered, "no. Though I do wish I had been apprised of your intention to leave."

Chalmers cleared his throat. "An oversight on my part, Madame. You have my sincerest apologies."

Perhaps the old woman lacked the strength for a cackle. She gave series of creaks, instead, grinding as hinges of bone. "Apology accepted, Doctor. You are in no personal danger, I assure you."

"Funny . . . It, ah. It doesn't seem that way from this end of a pointed thing."

"You are, in fact, most fortunate," the Curator continued. "Bishop Professor Meteron extends an invitation to you and to your secretary, Miss Downshire. He would very much like you to join him in Vraska. There is excellent work to be had on his staff." Her fathomless eyes turned upon Rowena. "Even for one as young as yourself, I am told."

Rowena shook her head. "Sorry, I had other plans."

"If you mean plans with Masters Meteron and Pardon," Madame Kurowa interjected, "consider your calendar cleared."

Rowena looked in panic from Meteron to the Old Bear, then back to Kurowa. "What does that mean? What are you on about?"

Kurowa smiled. "Perhaps you should explain, Umiko."

The girl stood silent as a stone, her hands turning knots in the hems of her sleeves.

"Umiko," Kurowa pressed. Her voice crackled with a galvanizing charge.

Umiko flinched. It was as if she were herself an Algebraic Engine, fed a card and spouting back data. "To serve Reason properly, we must live in an orderly world. Logic gives us a system for speaking rationally. Laws give us a system for living rationally. As Logicians, we know that Reason is our path to wisdom, and that it requires an end to all disorder. We take the beings that unsettle the natural order and put them in a place to be of use to Reason, or to be ended."

It was like watching a demagnetized compass needle wander, twitching and spinning, only to find true north at last. All at once, Rowena understood Nippon and the Logicians as she had never done before. No aigamuxa. Creatures of brawn with will of their own were a liability to their order, and so they made the Fabricated to take their place. No lanyani, apart from the stupid, senseless creatures they had bred into boatmen or light fixtures—or the wild horrors risen up from who-knew-where, the ones that had evaded the Logicians' efforts at control. Truly wild things had no home in a city whose very rivers had been turned to streets—a city that teemed over the mass of a whole nation. In such a place, creatures Reason could not explain would be snuffed out. That included creatures like Erasmus Pardon.

Creatures like Rowena herself, if she'd taken her honesty with Umiko even one sentence further. How close had she been to confessing she carried the ghost of a dead woman in her mind, or that she longed to reach out and touch the Old Bear's thoughts, to sit within them again? What would have happened to her, if she dared speak that truth?

"His Grace," the Curator croaked, "has asked our help in acquiring Master Pardon. It seems his most unusual faculties are of some value to his present research."

"My father overestimates him," Meteron cut in sharply. "Parlor tricks. Inferences and innuendoes. His mind games are useful only for amusing the foolish and superstitious. I will be more than happy to explain as much to His Grace when we meet."

The Curator sighed. "That, I am afraid, will not happen."

"Continue, Umiko," Madame Kurowa purred.

Umiko's shoulders sagged. "When disorder comes in the form of lawlessness, we must take other measures. Fog Island is our solution for such disorder."

Kurowa seemed to enjoy the almost measurable drop in the room's temperature. She stood before Meteron, paused, and took the towel off his shoulder to wipe the shaving foam away. "It seems," she mused, "you kidnapped a scholar familiar with the Amanuensis library, secreted them away, and extorted them for aid in your partners' research. For all we know, you've actually killed them by now, to clean up after yourself before leaving the city. A very nasty business. You could hardly expect your father to ignore it."

Meteron's eyes had remained on the Curator during Kurowa's speech. "I don't suppose His Grace has been told how Scholar Tsuneteva's connection with me began."

"I doubt it very much," Kurowa said, smiling.

The Old Bear growled through his teeth. "I would wager he already knows a great deal about you, Madame Curator."

The old woman's birdlike head perked toward him, genuine interest in her eyes. "Would you?"

"There's the fact of your being Subject One," Meteron said.

"Ah. Yes. There is that." She nodded wearily. "We have an arrangement in regards to that, and to his studies. I have promised him something. Soon, he will have the tools he needs to make use of it."

Rowena caught a look, tense and momentary, between Madame Kurowa and the Curator.

"In the meantime, we had best gather you up for your voyage," the Curator said. "It is convenient that you have packed so well, though I am afraid only half the baggage is likely to be relevant."

Kurowa turned to a member of the Argument blocking the door to the hall. "Call up Fabricated to see after the baggage. Leave the trunks belonging to Masters Pardon and Meteron. Everything else goes on the air galleon."

"And what of the prisoners?" One woman—perhaps some kind of captain, by her larger insignia—nodded toward the disheveled remains of the Corma Company.

"The same cart can take them all. We'll separate them at the quays before we reach the anchor yard." Kurowa looked Rowena up and down, her face curiously sympathetic. "You might as well use the ride to say your good-byes. You won't need your hands free to do it, though."

Rowena opened her mouth to shout the foulest words of Nipponese Umiko had taught her, but one of the Argument put an arm over her throat, cinching it tight, as another cuffed her hands at her back.

Phillip Chalmers kept a sort of timeline of his life's calamities, punctuated with various incidents great and small. A broken ankle playing tag with his brothers. His cousin Marjory's sudden death from a vicious cancer, and his mother's declaration that, as a newly minted student seminarian, he should give the eulogy. His first failed examination. His father's passing a year before completing his thesis. And then, meeting Nora Pierce, and everything after.

His journey in a prison cart through Kyo-Tokai earned an entry all its own in that vast space of "after."

The clockwork cart rattled furiously, obliged by the canals to take a long and uncomfortably circuitous route through the city, pausing at lever-bridges to permit various barges' passage. At these intersections, the winding men would leap up from their seats and crank madly with their huge keys, the iron-bound cart needing constant minding to manage a load of four passengers.

Chalmers's wrists screamed in pain, trapped behind his back and banging between spine and steel wall with every jounce. Meteron sat with his head against the wall, a thoughtful squint writing lines at the corners of his eyes. Rowena huddled as near to the Alchemist as their bonds allowed, murmuring apologies in an endless, breathless stream. The old man's usually grave face looked positively sepulchral, though from time to time he answered the girl's urgent voice with a hush or hum Chalmers couldn't make out. He had not been restored the dignity of his shirt, though the Argument's officer had been good enough to throw his frock coat over his shoulders, obscuring his bare skin and its shocking map of scars.

The captain had also been sensible enough to see the coat stripped bare, all its pockets turned out, emptied of hope.

"Three times," Meteron announced.

Chalmers rattled back into the present as best he could. "Beg pardon?"

"We've been carted off to be hanged together three times," Meteron explained, though he was clearly speaking to the Alchemist.

"Four," he answered automatically.

Meteron frowned. "If you're thinking of Rimmerston, you were the only one standing at the gallows."

"Malay."

A look Chalmers thought more fitting to a child opening a holiday present than a man bound for an island of abandoned criminals dawned on Meteron's face. "I'll be damned. I forgot that one."

"Never made it as far as the gallows cart."

"*Psh*. Doesn't count, then."

Chalmers gaped at them. "Perhaps we would be better served by considering the unique features of our present predicament?"

"Technically, your only predicament will be remembering which fork you're to eat your salad with when you take supper with His Grace," Meteron answered. "You've nothing to worry over."

"Except, perhaps, a madman's plot that could lead to the dissolution of life on earth, your imminent banishment to a place of certain death, and Master Pardon's probable dissection as a curiosity of modern—" Chalmers flinched away from Rowena's thrashing foot, narrowly missing a solid kneecapping. "I say, what are you on about?"

The girl had slid off the bench beside the Alchemist and begun writhing on the cart's dusty floor, thrusting her legs in a most unseemly manner. Chalmers spied more than a little of her underslip and looked away, flushing.

"And now Miss Downshire's having some kind of fit," he cried miserably.

"Miss Downshire," the Alchemist said, "is seeing to your freedom."

Chalmers was about to suggest that perhaps attending the young lady's welfare would be a more appropriate response than rash optimism when Rowena gasped in triumph, managing to hook her feet through a hoop made of her bound hands stretched out as far behind her back as they could go. Red-faced and panting, she closed up in a ball, easing her arms up and around her legs, past her knees, and, at last, had her hands in front of her.

Meteron grinned. "There may be hope for you yet, cricket."

"Maybe," she murmured sullenly, then started pulling pins from her hair. "Give anything for a proper set of picks now."

"Two hairpins wound together and hooked at the end are a close match for a size one," Meteron suggested. "Most handcuffs take ones or fives."

Rowena raised the cuffs to her eyes, squinting through each keyhole in turn. She even, to Chalmers's horror, prodded at them with her tongue. "Nhhhh. Feels like a five. Can't see anything for sure without a torch." Muttering curses, she began twisting two pins together. "It's a one or nothing, then."

In the kinotrope films Chalmers had seen, picking locks was a matter of a screwed-up-tight expression, a well-applied tie pin, and a bit of flourish. In reality, it was a boring agony of curses and bent pins and near misses, ending long, long minutes later with Rowena Downshire's freed hands, her wrists ringed with red bracelets of torn skin. She lunged for Meteron's hands next, despite a shake of manacles from Chalmers and what he had hoped was a most encouraging smile and waggle of eyebrows.

It turned out to have been the right choice. Once free and given a moment to rub at the shoulder he had dislocated the previous fall, Meteron moved quickly to the Alchemist and Chalmers in succession, finishing the jailbreak with the last brutalized pins.

Chalmers winced over his chafed wrists, though he began amending his record of calamities to account for this positive turn.

"So now what? We open the back of the cart, overpower the guards?" he suggested.

"Cart's locked," Rowena answered. "We're still stuck."

Meteron and the Alchemist shared a look, long and unfathomable.

"When they open the cart at the quay head," the Alchemist said, "all of you need to run. I'll cover for you."

Rowena blinked. "How?"

To his credit, Chalmers managed to keep from flinching. The plan they had silently formed unfolded in pictures, faster than thought, more complete than words. Chalmers readied himself for Rowena's screech of objection, but none came. He saw in her agonizingly young face not the least understanding of what he'd just been shown. Apparently she'd been left out of the mental discourse. It wasn't hard to understand why.

The Alchemist fixed him with a sober stare.

"It's . . ." Chalmers hesitated, his voice gone brittle. "It's a very good plan, I think."

45.

The Reverend Doctor Phillip Chalmers sat with his knees hugged to his chest, staring down the mouth of the alley and striving to be as small as possible. *Hide and seek.* He'd played it with his brothers and even been good at it, naturally nervous and furtive. Temperament alone hadn't been enough to salvage his winning record at the game after a growth spurt sent him gangling in all directions. He'd never quite been able to fold in on himself in the necessary way after.

He wished he could now.

The plan had worked, in its broadest strokes. They had waited until the prison cart reached the quay head where they were to be separated. They had listened for its brakes being thrown and its winding keys removed. The cart clicked in place, a ticking heart, the four of them tucked in its ventricles. Two members of the Argument assigned as their escort unlatched the cell doors, spilling in summer sunshine, and found—

Nothing. They gaped, cried alarum, and turned to the rest of their troop, which split in all directions, hunting for the prisoners that had somehow evaporated entirely.

Chalmers had held his breath, balled up tight as a hedgehog, eyes darting to each of his companions. Meteron crouched in the frame of the door, still barefoot. Rowena crept up beside him, opening and rebuttoning the panels of her riding skirt to transform them into a pair of broad-legged trousers. She looked over her shoulder, sharing a thought with the rest of them through the eerie link that itched at the nape of Chalmers's neck.

They're gone.

The Alchemist nodded, his usual raptor gaze looking more drugged than dire. Chalmers couldn't begin to fathom what made it possible for him to slink through the minds of others, let alone make them see what he wanted, rather than what was plainly there. Surely he couldn't hold this illusion for long. His grip of the guards' vision would give out and then they'd be done for.

Head for the Tower of Water, he instructed.

Meteron sent a flurry of images—river and tower and tunnel and . . . Oh. So that was what had become of Cyddra Tsuneteva.

We'll meet you there, Rowena promised. *C'mon, Doc!*

She leaped from the cart to the ground and scrambled to an alley off the quayside. Rowena had her orders, too: *keep the Doctor out of trouble*.

Chalmers struggled with a knot of shame to see how easily his incompetence could be used as a cover. He slid to the ground, then looked back at Meteron and the Alchemist. The smaller man had been shrugging into the Alchemist's coat, dusting at its sleeves.

"She's going to realize what you're really about," Chalmers protested. "Soon. What do I do then?"

Meteron looked up to reply but stopped when the Alchemist's hand fell on his shoulder.

"Keep. Her," the old man said, each word a struggle, "From. Coming. Back."

Chalmers swallowed that offending knot. He nodded.

"I'll do it. And you?" He had looked to Master Meteron, hoping to hear he'd be along just a moment after. That he wouldn't be left alone, carrying a ninth of the world with him.

Meteron's smile had been a razor's edge, brutally unfunny. "I'll be having one last hurrah."

A swat on Chalmers's shoulder rattled him back to the present. The girl glared at him.

"We're supposed to be *moving*. The Tower of Water goes down from the night before at noon, and it's a good hump off yet."

Chalmers nodded. He looked back on the tangle of alleys and streets already crossed in their mad dash from the quay head. The Argument had raised the general alarum already, huge gongs sounding from the squat rooftops all around. How long would the first phase of the plan work? How long could the Alchemist sustain it?

Rowena hauled at his arm, then, and Chalmers found himself running, half-towed behind her, crammed against the sides of buildings and between their compactor bins, two mice threading their way through a city-sized maze.

"He's brilliant," Rowena puffed as they tucked into another shallow alcove, this one marked by an inscription of formulae—a shrine to geometrical theory.

Chalmers blinked. "Who?"

"Bear." She beamed. "It's like the trick with warrant at the Anchor Authority, but he's doing it with everybody, making them see what he wants. Their eyes are just . . . just slipping off us like we're a waxed floor. How he can do this and leg it for the Tower, too, I'll never know."

The Reverend Doctor attempted a smile he hoped looked markedly less anemic than it felt. "Brilliant, yes."

The girl had sense enough not to strain the spell's limits by walking in plain sight. Finding a gap in a group of passengers boarding a water taxi, she lunged ahead, tugging Chalmers through with her, and made for the Ring of Fishes several blocks on.

The plan had three stages. They were still in the first. Chalmers hoped it would last longest of all.

Concealment. By glazing the minds of those in proximity to the friends with whom he had linked his consciousness, the Alchemist gave them a clean break from their captors. Sooner or later, though, that would slip, and they'd be forced on to the next stage. Sooner looked likeliest, as the rising chorus of gongs set the citizens on the streets on alert, more and more stepping out of doors to spy for anything suspicious. One careless move, and Chalmers and Rowena would tear whatever veil concealed them, revealing themselves to hundreds of watchful eyes.

They heard the Tower of Water long before they reached it. Its cascades were a thunder rolling over Kyo-Tokai's mercantile center, the streets surrounding it misty and rainbowed in the summer sun. The Ring of Fishes was flooded, a torrential river catching the tower's waterfalls. The barristers and merchants who kept their offices all around its circumference were stepping out into the mist to look for the cause of the alarum. Chalmers and Rowena reached that crowd, still unseen, just in time to see the Tower itself begin its slow, juddering descent back into the ground.

Rowena cursed. Chalmers gripped her hand tighter.

"The others en't here yet," she shouted over the roaring water. "Master Meteron said it takes a long time for it to collapse all the way."

"It does, but we're not to wait—we're meeting below, where Cyddra—"

Between the falling water and the tooth-rattling gongs chorusing, Chalmers couldn't hear Rowena's answer. But he could read the string of obscenities and imprecations on her lips.

Before he could respond, a hand closed on his shoulder like a vise.

Chalmers looked. A broad-shouldered man formally attired in belt and sash jerked him away from Rowena.

Concealment, it seemed, was no longer sustainable. Next in the plan was misdirection, and Chalmers knew it would work. He knew also it wouldn't help him one bit, at the present moment.

He flailed with his fists, hoping to land a lucky blow and scurry free. Rowena's weaponette sprang out of nowhere. She darted forward, slashed at the big man's forearm, and opened up a bloody line well past his elbow. His mouth spread in a howl drowned by the rushing waters. The rest of the citizenry flew into action.

"Come on!" Rowena screamed, ducking under more grabbing hands. She had Chalmers's hand again, pulling, and this time, he needed no encouragement to keep the pace.

The Tower was already several yards shorter than it had been. The river winding at its base thinned, slowly dilating into nothingness.

No time to question if it was already too late, or wonder if the clockworks below the water's surface would chew them into chum. They dove. The river met Chalmers like a fist, smashing his face and chest. The waterfalls crashed down, driving the air from his body. He opened his eyes. Amid the chaos of froth and his own thrashing limbs, he saw Rowena shedding her buttoned skirts entirely, kicking hard, then her hands on his lapels, then the depths of the false river, then nothing.

The soldiers of the Third Logician Argument had fanned all across the district of Nippon surrounding the prison cart, scanning every low, tiled roof and every shadowed alley for signs of their missing captives. Most especially, they scanned for a long frock coat at least half as infamous as the man known to wear it.

Bishop Meteron's report, corroborated by Umiko Haroda's claims, proved that whatever the Alchemist might be in Corma—something between a folk hero and a warlock, shunned and relied upon in equal measures—he was only a monster to the Logicians, and rightfully so. How many of the stories surrounding him were fiction and how many fact, Sergeant Ito, now jogging between the gong stations supervising the alarum, couldn't say. But even the simplest tales of the Alchemist had been enough to curdle Ito's blood. Finding the prison cart empty of its criminal freight had been enough to transform even the darkest stories into undisputed truth.

The coat featured prominently in the various reports the Argument had been sent. Some claimed it could make the mysterious man invisible. It could disguise him—transform him from an old Leonine to a pale, red-headed youth, into a cronish matron, into a seductress, into a wolfhound. Into Proof-could-say what. None of it was even remotely Rational. That was the best reason to put the the old man down. Even if he were nothing more than a chemist with a gift for cultivating notoriety and an escape artist of exceptional skill, he was enough to cast doubt on Reason. Nothing could be more dangerous or heretical.

And so, Sergeant Ito marked it as both his good and bad fortune to whip around a corner in time to see the broad-backed man scramble up a teahouse's drainpipe.

"Up there!" Ito bellowed. If any of his fellow officers were near, they would mass every Argument in the prefecture, closing on the Alchemist like an iron trap.

He bounded for the drain pipe and climbed up after his quarry. The

Alchemist had made it up safely, but the scramble had been ill-footed. And hadn't the old man needed a walking stick before? Perhaps it had only been for show.

Ito more than half-hoped he could make the arrest alone. To capture a stubborn mysticism and stamp it out! To destroy this danger to dogma! He was only a few strides from making his world a safer, more Rational place.

He pounced onto the roof just as the Alchemist reached the opposite corner. The old man had stalled just short of taking a leap for a roof one story lower, perhaps balking at the distance to the next roof's edge.

"Stop!" Ito cried.

But he need not have bothered. He saw why the Alchemist had not made his jump: two other officers of Ito's own Argument scaled the building's edge, flanked by clockwork centipedes armored with blades, mortar flecking off their reticulating legs. The Alchemist hovered between Ito and his fellow soldiers, pinned. The Fabricated insects sliced at the air, drawing closer.

Ito thought he heard some kind of oath from the Alchemist—something both anatomical and theological. Ito smiled as he caught his breath, gloating over the capture that was soon to be.

Scanning the roof tiles to his right and left, the Alchemist paced back from the edge and the new figures bearing down on him. Ito approached from what would be the man's five o'clock position and rounded up toward his seven, trying to complete the circle around him.

The Alchemist wasn't so very large, up this close. Stripped to his skin and forced to his knees in the apartment hours before, the man had seemed a mass of old scars and gnawed-down muscle, even in his humiliation a seasoned soldier with the marks to prove it. Perhaps the chase had worn him out. He was supposed to be crippled, after all (though Holy Proof, he had given Ito a run he would not soon forget). Or perhaps the sweetness of capture simply made Ito feel bigger. In either case, it was clear now that his opponent was no larger than he was—might, indeed, even be smaller.

"You're not leaving here," one of Ito's fellows called. Akane. Good.

She was fast and dogged. He would not mind sharing this coup with her.

"If that is a request, I'm afraid I'll have to disappoint you," the Alchemist answered, a cold merriment in his tone.

The clockwork centipedes skitter-clacked forward, rearing and chattering their horrible, almost-live sounds. One snapped at the Alchemist, more like a snake than an insect. He sprang back. But in evading the clockwork creature, the Alchemist had put himself in range of Ito's waiting grapple. He leaped on his opponent, stuck like burning pitch. Ito threw a forearm around his face and hauled back so his knee drove home to a kidney. A grunt of pain, then a twisting, and suddenly Ito's sky was below him, the roof above, and his wind blasted out of him as he struck the ridged roof tiles with a great woof of pain.

Before the Alchemist could do whatever he meant to next, the centipedes closed with him, and the two other officers fell upon him like a wave. It was all Ito could do to drag himself away from the fracas, wheezing and coughing, narrowly avoiding a slicing mandible in the face.

Curses. Fists. A snarl, and then, a fist connecting with bone, and the yelp of pain that followed—not from the victim of the punch, but its deliverer.

Akane crouched over the fallen man, shaking out her fist. This was usually the moment when she would share a quip. Instead, she shook her head as if she'd been the one who took a blow to the jaw and staggered back.

It had been the right coat. Ito had been so sure it had been the right man—the right *shape* of a man, or at least the right color, or . . . He didn't know anymore.

Akane's partner, Uemi, nudged the clockworks aside, flicking their kill-switches with his heel, and scowled at the Alchemist. The man lying unconscious at their feet was a pale blonde with sharp features, not more than eleven stone and a half-hand shorter than Ito. Anselm Meteron.

"What . . . what on earth?" Akane blurted.

"It was the right coat," Ito offered dazedly.

◿◺

From her vantage point inside Erasmus Pardon's mind, Rare Juells watched, and waited. He walked through a vast chamber of people, each frozen in the moment of action where they had spotted Chalmers and Rowena and Anselm running. He needed no cane in this space and trotted swiftly from one person to the next, passing a hand over their eyes, murmuring in their ears. A woman holding a basket of fruit, captured in the instant of placing it on a scale, turned her head back down to her work, humming contentedly. Two schoolchildren trading notes outside their tutor's home took a deeper interest in debating the minutiae of her last lecture. Erasmus's hand guided a seamstress's eyes back toward her tape, suddenly certain she had misread its measurement.

All the while, Rare kept a part of herself tuned to the world outside. She could hear the Argument's boots hammering, heard the emergency gongs ringing. They weren't far off. They would find him, before long, and then . . .

Then he would be captured. The Logicians would tear him apart, piece by piece. And she would die all over again, trapped inside him.

Rare had thought she could simply wait for the old man to tire, but he danced through the mass of distracted people, their phantoms winking out as they lost sense of what they had almost seen, to be replaced a moment later by someone new. On and on the process went as the others ran through the city, attracting attention that he must break. He stopped by the soldiers and pointed far off, toward a flickering shade shaped like himself, coat and all, and they, too, disappeared, charging off into abstraction.

A swell of pride took hold of Rare, if only for an instant. Her father was many things she had loved, and just as many she had hated, but there was no denying he was remarkable at his work.

Rare had no intention of allowing him to be captured. But on the other side of Erasmus's mindscape, he lay helpless, crumpled on the floor of the Argument's prison cart.

The others could fend for themselves. *He* needed to run, if she was going to survive.

Rare stormed up behind the Old Bear, and just as he reached to turn a burly man's gaze away from Reverend Chalmers's back, she snatched her father's shoulder and spun him around.

"Not today, Bear."

Her punch took him square between the eyes. Rare's own vision burst open in light, then a tunneling dark, as the phantoms surrounding them winked out of sight.

Erasmus Pardon's mind was a stone tumbling downhill. It crashed back inside him, smashing through his sense of self, rolling pell-mell. He found himself fallen in a heap on the cart's dusty floor. He could see through it, somehow. Transparent. He stared at his own hand, thinned and chiseled and callused by time, and could see its bones beneath skin that looked like a shadow on lamp-film, barely there at all. He still felt the power, more solid and real that he was. Why had it broken so suddenly?

A ghostly hand touched his. He saw Rare crouching before him, her ice-blue eyes full of something he had not seen there in years.

The Bishop's going to kill you, if you don't finish the job for him first. Now get up!

He opened his mouth, but all his words seemed wrong. He thought to her, instead. *What have you done?*

Made it so you can run. You have to get up!

Erasmus reached for the walls of the cart, struggling to steady himself. He staggered forward, all but fell through the open doors, and lurched toward the mouth of the alley. He collapsed in its shade, the world gone blindingly white.

Running wasn't the point for us, he thought, feeling Rare still with him, still pushing and needling him on. *I could have gone on. Could have gotten them all to safety. Might have concealed Anselm a few moments longer.*

Rare spat a curse at the ground. *What was the point, then?*

To buy time.

You and Ann, she seethed, *are worth* more *than buying fucking* time.

I could never have outrun them.

Rare's face crumpled.

If they take you, we're both done for. You don't get to decide that for me.

She was right, of course. Erasmus reached for her. His hand passed through air, though he could swear something electric whispered over his fingers as he traced Rare's cheek.

I am sorry.

She buried her face in his hand, pressed it to herself. Strange. His fingers even seemed wet now.

He smiled. A stabbing pain in his chest doubled him up, choking him. The alley swam in his vision as the fist behind his breastbone tightened. But it didn't matter anymore.

He had won. If Rowena could keep her head, she would be safe. He had told Chalmers to protect her because the poor man needed *something* to do. It was Rowena who had the strength to keep them both alive. In the end, there in the cart, Erasmus Pardon had trusted her. She was a child and had made a child's missteps, hungry for friends. Chalmers would have to mind that in her. Better him than nothing. For all her mistakes, Erasmus believed in Rowena's utter temerity. He believed she would understand what he'd done, given time. He hoped she would forgive him.

Painfully, he pulled himself upright. He couldn't run. The strength for that was long since spent, even if he were not lamed. But he had the strength to check his work.

Erasmus focused and found the mind of someone called Ito trussing Anselm up for the barge out to Fog Island. Five minutes, that caper had bought. Just enough for Rowena and Chalmers to slip beyond reach.

He should have just run, Rare said bitterly. Erasmus knew who his daughter meant. *He could have made it.*

"Insurance," he answered thickly. His head throbbed and his tongue moved wrong, slurring syllables. "They would have hunted him, even if he escaped. A liability. The others could disappear without him more easily. Forever, even."

To that island he bought?

"Yes."

Rare looked away, her face drawn in bitterness. *But now he's bound for his own island.*

Erasmus could say nothing to that. Distant through the hum of his consciousness, still twined with Ito's, and through Rare's pressing grief, he heard boots and cocking rifles. The Argument had returned to the cart.

"Ann's a survivor . . . he'll find a way. He always finds a way."

And you?

The first soldier of the Argument plunged into the alley. They must have thought him mad, talking to the open air.

Erasmus smiled. "I can't run any longer."

Rare nodded. They both knew he didn't mean the leg.

The soldiers filled the space around him, slicing through Rare's image. Erasmus flinched. She jerked at their passage, as if she were the one being touched by ghosts. A snarl drew the bow of her mouth.

You know what they'll do to you! she cried, lashing out at the soldiers. Her hands passed through them like smoke. They hauled Erasmus to his knees, shouted in his face, and Rare sobbed in rage.

Of course he knew what awaited him. A jagged reel of lamp-film images staggered past his mind's eye. Operating tables and scalpels and ampules of drugs. Of course he knew. He had always known.

He could only hear Rare's voice. It was all he wanted to hear. The soldiers shook him, demanding a response, and he smiled, deaf to their words. He longed to speak to her alone, just a moment longer, so he might say what she had always needed to hear. That he loved her. That he was sorry for what he'd done. That she had deserved a better father.

He painted Rare a picture, instead. The garden behind the Scales. He put her there, flesh and blood, watching him and Anselm plant the rose-of-Sharon at dusk. She'd had a favorite dress, but the memory of it was gone, so he clothed her in sunlight and the scent of jasmine.

Rare's hands closed over his. He was so sure he could feel them. There were other hands, too, but they didn't matter.

Amid the chaos of the Argument's shackles and shouts, Rare's words rang clear. *I can make it so they can't hurt you, if you let me. I've figured out how.*

Erasmus Pardon opened his mouth to answer, but one of the soldiers pressed a needle into his throat. A flush of heat rushed over his brain. Then the darkness unfolded, smothering his daughter's voice as it called his given name for the first time.

46.

I t had become immediately clear to Chalmers and Rowena why Anselm Meteron had returned from his mission to kill Cyddra Tsuneteva dripping like a drowned rat. They lay gasping on the cement bank of the underground canal feeding the Ring of Fishes, freshly flushed from a drainage pipe leading to the quiet dark below.

Rowena lurched onto her side, heaving up a bellyful of water and that morning's tea. Her throat burned. Chalmers curled in a ball, mouth working like a guppy, hiccupping air and spitting up water by turns.

"You okay?" she gasped.

He nodded. He looked a shade of green that reminded Rowena more of moss than well-being. It would have to do.

She had been about to stand, then remembered her legs, naked apart from her soggy underthings. "Fucksake," she muttered.

She did it, anyway.

The sight of Rowena absent nearly all clothing from the waist down sent Chalmers scuttling to his feet as if trying to avoid something venomous slinking uncomfortably near. "Here," he stammered, wrestling free of his sodden jacket. He dangled it in a confused tangle of sleeves and torn linings, trying both to smile encouragingly and avert his eyes.

Rowena scowled at the ruined garment. "They're legs, Doc. Everybody's got two of 'em, last I looked." She checked for the weaponette in the sheath at her right hip. Still there, though the fasteners were coming loose. She bent to tighten them, though she made sure not to point her wet bloomers at the Reverend Doctor. The last thing she needed was him collapsing in a pearl-clutching swoon.

"Master Meteron said once we were down here, we'd have to look for Cyddra. How'll we know we've found them?"

"If you really need to narrow the field, you might consider that most people don't spend their odd hours in the drain system beneath the city," a voice further down the corridor called.

Rowena turned. At the vanishing point of her sight, a bluish light bloomed, drawing closer.

"Oh," she said. "Hi."

They stood taller than Chalmers, with the sort of grace that only seemed natural to people of good breeding, and they were stunningly beautiful. They wore a loop of braided glowplant around their neck, casting pale shadows over their face. It was a face from everywhere, a perfect arrangement of features Rowena might have used to pick out places on a map—Indine and Europan and Mongol and even, perhaps, a roundness in the lips and breadth in the nose suggestive of Leonine blood. Rowena felt her cheeks run hot under their calculating gaze.

Chalmers straightened at once. "Cyddra." He smiled awkwardly. "It's . . . been a long time."

Rowena puzzled over the crack in his voice. The confusion must have been written in her face, for Cyddra answered with a yawn and a shrug.

"We knew each other in seminary. Roommates, at least for a time."

"Oh," she said. A piece of social mathematics presented itself, squared and divided. Rowena sorted it, then blinked, considering the remainder. "You mean the two of you . . . ohhh. Oh. Yeah. Pleased to meet you. Master Meteron said we could get your help leaving Kyo-Tokai?"

Cyddra's mouth hardened into a line. They tossed Rowena and Chalmers their own ropes of glowplant and turned, striding back the way they'd come. The two followed, slinging the plants over their shoulders and walking double-time to keep up the Scholar's pace.

"If I had my druthers, Anselm Meteron would perish by inches, dissolved by a lanyani pit's flesh-stripping bacteria," they announced, as casually as they might declare their opinion of the weather. "But as he's backed me into a corner where my continued survival is concerned, I don't see that I have any choice."

Rowena trotted up the rest of the distance, pacing Cyddra. "So, you've just spent weeks down in the canal drains, getting things from the books to fuss over and waiting to smuggle us out of the city?"

They snorted. "Certainly not. I've spent weeks on the *Posidonia* taking messages from you to fuss over and been waiting down in the canals for the last two hours."

Shoving aside the question of what the *Posidonia* was, Rowena focused on the timeline. "Two hours? But we were captured by the Argument and taken away just this morning. How did you know we'd be meeting you here?"

Cyddra stopped walking and shot Chalmers a querulous look over Rowena's head. "The Argument? You've been compromised?"

"It's my fault," Rowena admitted. "I needed help making the Fabricated that would bring you our messages. I went too far with what I told our engineer."

"Hm. Did you now?"

Rowena shook off Cyddra's measuring look. "You didn't answer *my* question. A few hours ago, we were still planning to take an air galleon out to Koryu and then up to Vladivostoy. We had it all sorted."

Then Rowena caught Chalmers's eye. He looked guiltily away, this time in a fashion that had nothing to do with her general state of undress.

"Master Meteron said he'd made the arrangements with the Rolands," Rowena insisted.

"He . . . did say that," Chalmers allowed. "Miss Downshire. We suspected something in our communications with the Rolands had been compromised. How else would Madame Kurowa know to expect us and intercept us in Lemarcke? We needed a plan for our departure on record that the Grand Library and the Bishop's agents would find credible, if it were discovered. Cyd's ship has been waiting for us since dawn. We were leaving for our rendezvous as soon as you returned from the meeting with Umiko you said couldn't be spared."

All morning long, Rowena had been avoiding thinking too much of the pit she'd opened up under all their feet. She swallowed. Its edge seemed nearer now. Wider.

"And the baggage we packed?"

"A ruse, to make an afternoon departure look credible. Everything we truly needed was packed away in Master Meteron's wallet,

Master Pardon's coat, and in my study satchel. We meant to leave the rest behind."

Rowena rounded on Cyddra. "Fine. Then you know we're not leaving anyone behind. Did Ann and the Bear get here before us? Are they already on this *Posidonia* thing?"

Cyddra said nothing. They looked to Chalmers, expectant.

The Reverend Doctor cleared his throat. "They're not coming with us, Miss Downshire. After the Argument took us, and Master Pardon came up with his plan—" He trailed off. "They were never meant to make it this far."

The canal was quiet compared to the world above, a place of echoes and shadows and long pauses between the splashes of swimming carp. Rowena heard her heart, stuffed tight between her ears. It hurt. Her eyes pricked and she scrubbed the tears away.

"I'm going back for them."

"No!" Chalmers snatched her shoulders as she swept past him, spinning her back around. "Listen. Please. Pardon hid us as long as he could. When that gave out, Anselm drew them off us. I promised I would keep you with me."

Rowena swatted his hands away. "Bear told *me* to keep an eye on *you*."

"That still means you. Here. With me." The young Reverend's voice bent under the weight of his plea. "*Stay*. Please."

"You're not the boss of—"

"I am now!"

Silence. They stared at each other. Chalmers's eyes looked wet, too.

"This is *my fault*," Rowena insisted. "I have to fix it."

"Some things can't be fixed," Cyddra murmured. "Only . . . managed."

Rowena bulled past them both, cursing. She closed her eyes and *reached* with her thoughts, strained with everything she had. Feeling nothing, she pulled inward. She listened, but only Leyah's voice whispered in answer.

It's true. They're gone, Rowena.

"Why didn't he leave a message?" she croaked.

Footsteps. A man's shoes, squelching wet. They paused behind her. "I don't know what you mean," Chalmers said.

She glowered at him, wanting so badly for something to be someone else's fault. "The Old Bear," she snapped. Letting the anger loose cost too much of her composure. She gritted her teeth, speaking between sobs. "He left a message in me before, after the Cathedral, telling me he would be all right. That Ann was all right. Why didn't he do it this time?"

But she knew. And Chalmers knew. He looked down at his knotted hands, shrugging helplessly.

"This . . . *Posidonia*," he said to Cyddra, after a time. "Is it very far?"

"Just at the canal head, a quarter-mile on." They tilted their head, trying to catch Rowena's tear-stained eyes, and smiled. "I think you'll find it quite a remarkable escape."

The canal ended under a concrete overhang, its shallows shadowed from the sun. It widened into a rocky pool, flecked with golden carp snapping up water bugs and tall, fronding plants standing still in an afternoon without a whisper of breeze. The city was a shadow up a hill, not so far away. Chalmers stumbled between river rocks, heedless of his ruined shoes. Cyddra lifted their kimono's hem and walked ahead. They took something secreted inside their sash, a tiny object like a snuff box, and pressed it thrice in quick succession. It clicked, *one two three, one two three*, and before the third set of calls, a Fabricated monkey Rowena recognized all too well—mended tail and arm and all—emerged from a thicket of water plants. Cyddra followed it toward the smell of seawater. Chalmers fell into step after, slowing when he noticed Rowena lagging behind.

The Reverend Doctor's face creased with sympathy. "Rowena, I know you—"

"Shut up," she said.

He turned and waited for her to pass him by so he might bring up the rear. At last, Rowena saw where the Fabricated was leading them, and what *Posidonia* was.

"Is that a ship?" she asked.

Posidonia hugged the rocks near Nippon's coast, abutting a long, natural pier that vanished into the surf. The ship was almost entirely invisible, its hull submerged with a kind of gangplank running from a little tower bobbing above the waterline. The Fabricated hunkered at the gangplank's end, its lantern eyes winking.

"But that's impossible," Rowena continued. "You can't keep a ship underwater. It's just . . . sunk, then, innit?"

"*Posidonia* is a triumph of research in both engineering and xenobiology," Cyddra called over their shoulder as they marched ahead. "The only mobile observatory in the world specializing in subaquatic lanyani life forms."

Even Chalmers looked baffled at that. "Subaquatic *lanyani?*"

"I've been waiting to take her out for the better part of a year, but could never find the opportunity. I would never have guessed feigning death and ferrying felons would prove so convenient for my calendar."

Cyddra raised an eyebrow at the Reverend Doctor's blank face. "Come along, Phillip," they sighed. "I'll explain below."

Cyddra reached the gangplank, then the tower, then disappeared through a hatch to whatever lay below.

Chalmers stumbled after straight away, but Rowena lingered.

She gazed at the outline of Kyo-Tokai. It swelled on the horizon, shadowing the land from north to south. The ship was pointed east, back toward the open waters of the Western Sea. Toward Amidon, and its sooty jewel of the west, Corma. It had been home, not long ago. Rowena had gone to sleep on her mat in the Grand Library's guest apartments wanting nothing more than her old mattress above the Stone Scales, and Rabbit's ragged ears, and the sound of her mother's laughter on a Sabberday visit to the Mercy Home. Corma had been the lightning rails, and trips to the theater with Master Meteron, and the Shipman's Bazaar full of perfumes and mince pies and old women's junk sold off as antiques.

It was nothing to her now. Rowena could go back, if it survived the fungus and the aigamuxa and the lanyani, but she would take no joy in it. Corma was a collection of places gutted of their people, the spaces where they belonged echoing inside her.

Rowena looked down the ladder into the darkness of the ship below. Chalmers waited at the the ladder's foot, offering her his hand. Something hot burned inside her—something that wasn't anger, or grief, or even fear.

He probably thought, when Rowena took that proffered hand, that *she* was agreeing to go with *him*—that she'd accepted whatever plan he imagined they should follow.

Well. It surely wasn't the first time the Doctor had been wrong.

42.

Surrounded by lanyani eyes shining white as struck lucifers, Haadiyaa Gammon did what came to her most naturally. She squared her shoulders and set her jaw. *It's no different than a meeting with the Governor's cabinet,* she thought. Surely those gentry had wished their hawkish City Inspector would kindly disappear into a shallow grave, given how often she'd caught them with their hands in a pot, sticky with graft. *It's no different,* she thought, trying to force herself to believe it was true.

Dor's voice cut the murderous silence.

"Monster," she hissed.

Gammon shrugged. The lanyani gathered around recoiled as one, their irisless eyes fixed on her palm, terrified of her movement making even a single seed fall. She took a slow, composing breath.

"One thing I've learned recently is that aigamuxa and humans have an equal capacity for acting rashly when provoked. I came very near to following Nasrahiel here when his people attacked, but I held back. We needed better weapons." She nodded toward Jane and Julian, tense beside her with their fire-throwers held ready. "Better even than these, which a competent engineer can put together in a few hours. We needed something that would do lasting harm."

Dor's bark flesh quilled with rage. "It is illegal even to possess those seeds. Impossible to find."

"Fortunately," Haadiyaa continued, "my colleagues have been minding shop for a certain alchemist with shockingly little regard for what violates international environmental regulations. Imagine my surprise when I found this loosestrife seed in his storeroom. A whole shipping crate of it. One of the very last orders fulfilled by New Vraska Imports. I assume it requires no introduction."

Finding the crate in the Stone Scales's basement had been a miracle they had nearly overlooked. Bess's search for useful supplies had turned up little more than an array of incendiaries, which posed as great a risk to Gammon and her allies as the lanyani. It was luck alone that made Haadiyaa look twice at the label her torch-beam revealed.

She had learned of loosestrife years before. The story had made an indelible impression. A farmer in the Midlands north of Longmeadow had asked his local grocer for a type of seed that would discourage volunteer tribes of lanyani from making groves of seedlings on his property—essentially, for an environmental prophylactic against nomadic lanyani reproduction. The grocer, perhaps confusing one plant's biological name with another, placed an order on the farmer's behalf from a supplier curiously slow about filling the request. It had taken weeks longer than expected because it was so unusual. What middle-western farmer needed five stone of a ground-adaptable pond planting? It seemed an absurd request. But, as it was a very profitable one, the supplier made no effort to double-check the order.

Less than a year later, ten thousand acres of land once teeming with good planting and hemmed in by healthy forest was choked out by a sea of purple loosestrife, waving in the plains-driven winds. Nothing else would grow there now, and every effort to pull, tear, or cut the loosestrife away only dispersed more of its pernicious seeds. They would germinate in hours, grow to maturity in days, and cover a field before the moon turned a full cycle. Only flash-burning solved the problem, and even then, the soil where loosestrife once had grown couldn't be trusted not to burst open later with a generation of dormant seed.

A bag of loosestrife scattered in the dirt of a lanyani hothouse—or worse, in its Pits—was as certain a doom as a shot of bodkin to a man's heart.

"I don't want to throw what's in my hand," Gammon called. "But I will, if I must."

She meant it, too. Gammon wasn't fool enough to release something that could kill what little other plant life thrived in Corma's coal-choked haze.

The newest Pit Master, a tentacular tree like a willow gone mad, whipped its branches in fury, slicing out sounds almost like words. "*Where is the girl who came with you?*"

Gammon smiled thinly. "I promise she carries no loosestrife. She's coming round to check on your captives."

It wasn't a lie. Or at least, not entirely.

A lanyani some yards away from Jane snapped a hefty branch from its body, oozing sap. It held the severed limb like a club, thorned and brutal.

Jane adjusted the fire-thrower on her hip and clucked her tongue. "No, I think you should just stay where you are."

For a time, nothing moved. Gammon held her breath, hoping things had not gone so still that Bess's movements would be easily heard. She had wanted to send Julian or Jane along for protection in case a lanyani found her creeping close to the caged aigamuxa. But Jane was no small woman. The kerosene pack loaded on her back did little to improve her chances of moving easily through the close-grown hothouse foliage. Julian was slender enough, but as well made as it was, his false leg tended to stumble over uneven ground. Between that and the awkward counterbalance of his own fuel tank, it was clear Bess had to go it alone.

At last, slow as a creeping vine, Dor moved. She hovered a scissoring hand over the bundle of twigs hugging the book to her side. The fingers rounded, shortened, posing less of a threat to the pages as her body passed the book to her hand, riding up a fusillade of fingers growing and disappearing as quickly as thought. Dor regarded the book coldly, turning it in her hand.

"You may take the book," she hummed, "or the aigamuxa. Not both."

Gammon closed her fist a little tighter. "You're sure of that?"

"Quite."

Gammon turned her hand so her closed palm faced the ground, her fingers dusted with seed. Two tiny loosestrife specks drifted from her grip, disappearing in the pine-needled floor.

The hothouse exploded with the roar of clattering branches and hissing leaves, a shimmer of greens and grays and browns and sudden wind trembling everywhere. A cloud of dirt swirled around the three humans.

Gammon looked back at Jane and Julian. "Trigger discipline, please."

"Sure. Discipline." The boy offered her a strained smile.

Jane's eyes narrowed. She panned the mouth of her weapon across the clamoring field of lanyani, but kept her finger resting over the trigger guard. "Haadi, you and I," she sighed, "have a very different idea of when discipline is a desirable character trait."

"It's desirable until Bess makes it back to us in one piece."

"Well," said Julian. "Hopefully she'll be about that soon."

Bess suppressed a yelp as another prickling juniper swatted her face, blurring her vision with tears. She'd been bullied and cajoled into giving up one of the lovely skirts she'd taken to wearing since starting on as the Stone Scales's minder—leftovers from some other girl of around her height and size, though the Alchemist had been mum about whom. Now she was grateful she'd accepted a pair of Gammon's trousers. They had become a pelt of briars and branches during her adventure, but she at least didn't have to worry about getting tangled in the brush.

Beyond the narrow, winding path she followed near the hothouse's glass wall, Crystal Hill buzzed like a hornet's nest. Bess froze, waiting for the sound to pass. It only built, layers of rage rolling in upon itself, thickening into a palpable mass.

Keep going, Bess.

She shoveled fear aside and crept on, faster as the explosion of noise gave her cover enough to risk crashing through tighter spaces. At last, the far edge of the composting pits came into view, its shore hillocked with dugouts capped by lattices of broken, bleached bone, or—

Bess blinked, squinted, and recoiled.

She knew those lengths of metal and cable too well—had spent weeks wheedling and grandstanding to get them.

Getting Gammon her pet monster back was one thing. Getting it back when it had been woven into the framework of a cage, though . . .

Bess scrambled toward the dugouts.

Nasrahiel's body nearly occluded her view of what lay at the prison pit's bottom. She made a guess.

"Rahielma?" she called.

Something stirred, shifting position. The pinpricks of two bloody, milky eyes gleamed in the darkness below.

"You're the girl from the Scales."

"I'm here to check you're still alive," Bess whispered. "And to give you this."

She lay on her belly and passed a hand through the web of warped metal, trying and failing to thread her hand through so it made no contact with Nasrahiel's bloodied body. A small sack, no larger than a pincushion, dangled from her fingers. The eyes below disappeared, turned to the ground, and a long, clawed arm reached up, snatching the parcel away.

Snuffling sounds. A snort, and a cough.

"What do I need this foul thing for?"

"It's a gift we're leaving for the lanyani. Just put it at the bottom of your cell. How many of the others are still alive?"

"A few. They have been given the cordyceps, though. They will not be themselves for long."

Bess said nothing. Gammon had warned her that might be the case. And she had orders about what to do if it proved to be true.

"What about you?" Bess demanded.

A long pause. Too long. She heard a shuffle below, Rahielma positioning herself again, eyes pointing through the ruin of her fallen husband's body.

"Not me," the chieftain said.

Bess looked to the other hillocks, one after another. She rose, dusting at herself, feeling with nerveless fingers for her other pouch. Seven little spheres of tempered glass, two chambers inside, thin-walled but separate until sufficient impact shattered them. They were intended to refill the security system installed above the Stone Scales's front door. Not fatal, if one could escape the fumes . . .

If one could escape the fumes.

"We'll have you out soon," Bess said, though she had already wandered too far from Rahielma's prison for there to be any hope of her words carrying back.

She stopped over each of the prison dugouts, crouching only long enough to drop a glass sphere and dart away to the next. In less than a minute, a pale, yellow gas plumed through the bleached-bone cages above the pits, sizzling faintly. Another eruption of enraged lanyani covered the coughs, raw and bloody, of a half-dozen dying aiga. A suspension of mercury in something else, something that accelerated its rising temperature and conversion to a mist. Bess didn't know. She didn't want to know.

She spun away, meaning to run. Out of the corner of her eye, she spied something, turned her head for a better look, and felt her stomach flip.

The fingers of a submerged hand peeked from the shallows of the Pit. One of them curled slowly. Almost beckoning.

Bess staggered backward, her back slamming into a linden.

"What is happening? Where are you going?" Rahielma demanded, her voice deadened by the earth.

"I have . . . I have to go," Bess shuddered.

She scrambled back the way she'd come, making no effort to be careful.

"Remind me," Jane shouted over another wave of lanyani fury, "why I let you talk me into coming here?"

Gammon reached into her coat, unholstering the huge pistol that resembled nothing so much as a hornet reimagined by an armorer. She checked its magazine as well as she could without dropping more seed.

"I asked for Julian's help. After he'd agreed, I used your mother's instincts to strong-arm you into coming, too."

"When this is done, I'm going to make love to you, then kill you."

"At least that's the right order."

"Before you do too much planning," shouted Julian, "we've got Bess."

Gammon peered through the tangle of trees, sentient and otherwise, and spied Bess running at the Pit's far edge. She waved her arms, throwing signals that filled in grim details.

"Shit," Gammon said. "Only Rahielma and Nasrahiel. And I think Nasrahiel is going to be complicated."

Julian shrugged one shoulder. "Then it's time to get their attention again."

Jane whirled on him. "Julian, *no!*"

He pulled the trigger just once. Flame knifed through the canopy overhead. A thicket of acacia crackled and blackened, its branches curling like a swatted spider.

The lanyani fell silent as stones.

"That worked pretty well," Julian observed cheerfully.

Dor's irisless eyes opened wide, fathomless holes in the sky of her face. Then the clouds rolled in.

She looked to the book spread open in her hands and seemed an instant away from tearing it asunder. Something stayed her, though. The lanyani nearest her turned, staring, pulling closer to her.

Dor turned a page—the final page of the book—and her face rippled like water.

"You may have the book," she announced. "And the aigamuxa. They are yours, much good may they do you."

Julian blinked. "What just happened?"

"I'm not sure," Gammon answered. "Nothing good."

A knot of lanyani turned toward Bess. The girl jerked to a halt, trembling, a hart under the hunter's gaze. Dor nodded to her people and they disappeared into the earth, the dirt rippling in their wake. They appeared again on the opposite shore, surrounding Bess.

The girl screamed. Gammon raised the wasp and trained it on Dor's head, knowing it would do little good but hoping a sizeable hole would deter something untoward happening.

Whatever harm she meant to prevent, it didn't happen. The lanyani surrounding Bess peeled away, moving from place to place near her, just out of view, as if surveying something buried in the earth.

"Dead!" one called, all vibrato. "All but the chieftain and the metal one. The cordyceps must have killed them."

Gammon exchanged a look with Jane. For now, at least, it seemed they had gambled right. If the aiga had been wounded beyond healing, or infected with the cordyceps, Bess was to finish them off. A gas was ideal, as the lanyani had no sense of smell. Soon, though, the gas's residues would settle as particulate in the greenery around them and the Trees would sense the truth.

Dor turned back toward Gammon. The book was still in her hands, bending under her grip.

"Let the chieftain take what is left of her monster mate," she thrummed. "Perhaps you can put it together again, humans. It will be like one of your nursery rhymes. You may build him of stick or stone or brick next. It is no matter to us. Now put the seeds away."

Gammon put the hand in her pocket. She did not release the tiny seeds thorning into her palm. Not yet.

"I'll put them away properly once the girl is here with me."

Dor smiled. "That can be arranged."

Three lanyani were busy prying a ruin of metal and cables from a hole just at the edge of Pit, nearly out of Gammon's vision. Two others closed in on Bess, clamping her between them. She howled, kicking, and threw her head up to gasp for breath only a moment before they disappeared into the ground, hauling her with them.

A path scored like lightning across the surface of the earth, slashing through the Pits, crashing across its margins and into the clearing beyond. Dor let her hands fall as it stormed between her spread legs. She dropped the book into the furrowed earth to be swept along with the rest, as casually as Gammon might drop a smoldered lucifer.

The ground before Gammon exploded, raining dirt and gravel and a filthy, rag-limp Bess. Julian dropped his fire-thrower, catching her before she could sink into the morass again. The girl's eyes were bright, blue moons, waxed with panic. Just visible under her white-knuckled grip, the book looked all but perfect, its plain, unlovely bindings disturbingly clean.

Jane joined Julian in looking Bess over. The girl shook, lips blue, stammering noises Gammon was certain weren't words in any language.

"Haadi, we have to go. Now," Jane urged.

Gammon held Dor's gaze a moment longer. Just past the lanyani leader's shoulder, she spied a battered Rahielma clamping Nasrahiel's ruined legs around her waist, twisting what remained of them in a rude knot. Then she hauled his body against her back and clutched his arms like a rope in one clawed hand. She wore the wreckage of him like a mantle. Her eyeless face turned, nostrils flaring, fixed on the humans' scent. Without a word, Rahielma sprang into the canopy, climbing, and disappeared, bound for the shattered glass of the ceiling and the starry night beyond.

"We'll see her again soon," Gammon murmured.

Jane scowled. "Too soon. Now come along, before they change their minds."

Gammon shrugged under one of Bess's shoulders. Julian took the other. They carried her from the hothouse of Crystal Hill, walking into the darkened streets under a cindered umbrella of acacia.

Gammon wondered how long it would be before the whitefly eggs Bess left behind hatched, and how soon the larvae would grow wings and feast on the Pit Masters there.

She had only promised not to release the loosestrife, after all.

The hothouse air remained silent once the humans had gone, but its earth sang with battle-cries and lamentations.

Why? Lir moaned through his swollen roots. *Why did you give up our people's birthright? Are you not our prophet?*

Dor stared at herself, examining her hands and arms admiringly. *Oh, indeed. More now than ever before.*

The Pit Master's thousand eyes opened, their buds blinking, then fixed upon her.

Dor's mane of leaves spread down her back, a carpet of glory spilling over her shoulders even as her bark sloughed away like a discarded cape. She ran long, twigging fingers down her arms, peeling them bare. The fresh fibers below wept gently, sap bleeding forth . . . In shapes. Sigils. The markings, familiar as sun and rain, wound up her hand and around its wrist. Down each finger. They marched slowly, creeping like a skin of moss, the sap darkening and hardening in the warm air. Dor tore her bark away, bare and bleeding, laughing with triumph as the words of the book appeared upon her, a suit of armor made of truth.

There was no space left in the book, she explained. *But there is space unending upon me.*

Lir reached for her, willow whips caressing, winding her in an embrace.

Prophet, tell us what happens next.

Dor beamed up at him. Even her eyes filled with the dark ink of glyphs and words, rolling in on waves of syllables unspoken. Lir read the present in them, watched it rise up like crocuses from the snow.

There is so much to tell my people, Dor replied. *Now the story changes forever.*

48.

Madame Kurowa set down the report on the writing desk. The Curator lay on her divan, bundled against a chill the younger woman could not feel. The day had passed very quickly, the sun already ebbing toward the horizon. Exhaustion, perhaps. She was very old for the sort of dramas that day had furnished.

"Is there anything else you wish for me to add, senpai?"

The Curator's white hair was coppered by the setting sun. "No," she murmured. "It is a good report. Very thorough. And now, you must take what His Grace has offered you."

Kurowa's hands stalled in the midst of winding the report to fit in a message cylinder. "It is . . . not a request I am eager to fulfill."

The ancient woman responded with a snort which dissolved at once into wet hacking. "You have been eager to take my place since you were a child, Miyako-chan. Three generations of First Literates before you hung their every breath from that hope. And now you spurn it? Aie, children. You are such fickle creatures."

Kurowa put the message in the vacuum chute installed behind a bronze stamping of a crane and carp. Its cylinder disappeared with a gasp of air, whisked off into the bowels of the building.

"Grandmother, it is true I asked Bishop Meteron to see that I would succeed you in exchange for delivering him the Cormarrans. But I had thought, given a little time—"

"The Bishop and I had an arrangement, my child," the old woman interrupted. She struggled to right herself on the divan, finally managing a propped position. "I honor my agreements. It is the way it must

446

be, when one speaks for the whole of the Library. Here." She patted the cushion with a gnarled hand, nodding toward the floor. "Come."

Kurowa knelt at her grandmother's side.

"Research," the Curator said, stroking a lock of Kurowa's hair, "is a very different matter than collecting or curating. We have held the Amanuenses safe against time and treachery, until the very recent past."

"I know. It gives me shame to broker with the man who stole—"

"Stole?" The Curator's wizened eyes blinked, looking for a moment altogether lost. "Oh, no, my child. Nora Pierce took the book, it is true. But she took it with my blessing, even if the Literates who served me did not know it. She took it in Allister Meteron's name, for a most sacred purpose. It was that *purpose* she stole, not the book."

Kurowa stared. "What do you mean?"

"I am one hundred and eleven years old, Miyako-chan. I have lived long enough to see how much the world can change, and to be frustrated at what little good its changes bring. We have held these books for time uncounted—carved the first of them from the boles of trees that bore words we had never seen before, words that wrote themselves on and on, in defiance of all Reason. We held them knowing they were of great moment, but without understanding their purpose. It was Scholar Cyddra's work that helped me see my own part in this drama. One hundred years, a subject of the experiment, and yet there I was, ignorant and undriven. What good had I done mankind, heedless of my purpose in the Creator's eyes? I knew the Scholar's skills as a translator would only grow. And I knew holding the books here forever would only maintain the status quo. If the Creator has made us to shape the world with His wisdom and insight, should we not have it in our hands?"

The Curator's bloodless lips twisted in something that, on a younger face, would have more plainly been a smile.

"Bishop Meteron was an older man and a wiser one when I asked him about the Grand Experiment again, all those years ago. He had learned something from his youthful arrogance at the Decadal Conference of Aerion. It had bought him notoriety and power, yet still no closer to the truth he sought. I offered him the chance to hold the truth, and its future."

Kurowa sucked in a shocked breath. "You offered to give him the book. So he could begin the library anew."

"In a more public place, yes. We agreed that he should continue the library, and that when it was established, we would . . . test how the Vautnek status transmits. Poor Doctor Pierce. She must not have been told what to expect in that package. Perhaps, she had been forbidden to open it. We had never before made the active text accessible, apart from indulging the Tsunetevas. When she realized what she held, she fled. Perhaps she feared it would be used for ill. Not an unworthy fear. It speaks well of her intentions."

"Why did Meteron let her keep it so long? Surely he could have sent agents after her, taken the book back?"

"Perhaps he could have. But he knew nothing of Scholar Cyddra's translations. In fairness, I did not myself appreciate the connection between their obsession with the lanyani and their facility with the ancient books. I did not offer Bishop Meteron any help making sense of the book. I trusted he would find his own method. Perhaps that brilliant, arrogant son of his could be brought back to the fold, coaxed into working the cipher. Anselm Meteron was always very skilled with patterns. A musician by training, you know." She chuckled at Kurowa's evident distaste. "Not a field much respected in the seminaries, but it was the only course he had the discipline to see through. There is, at least, a lot of mathematics in composition. When His Grace learned Pierce was making progress deciphering the text, he made the only reasonable decision."

Kurowa nodded. "To let her do the work for him. And then the Conference happened."

"Yes." The Curator gazed out the window, sighing. A wind coiled up in the courtyard below, sending cherry blossoms in flurries like snow before they settled between benches and statues, bathed in the fading sun. "Everything spun out of his control. The book, lost. His translator, dead. But part of our agreement can still be kept. The part you must do, to take my place."

"I won't."

"The Curator's successor must be endorsed by at least three members of the Logicians' Council. Meteron is, ostensibly, retired." The Curator smirked. "That seems in vogue in his family, doesn't it? Nominal retirement. But he wields great influence among his peers. He need only ask, and the whole of the Council will place their seals upon your name. But nothing comes from nothing, Miyako-chan. You know this."

Kurowa bowed her head. Why had words abandoned her? How could she have been so sure of her future, so certain she'd held all the trumps, just days before? Hours before, even.

"And Meteron has a means of . . . watching," she murmured. "Despite the loss of the active book?"

"He swore to it in his letter. Allister Meteron is many things, but he would not seek harm without the promise of benefit."

"And you are . . ." Kurowa began.

"I am," her grandmother answered, "one hundred and eleven years old."

With that, the Curator said no more, lowering herself with painful care, lying with hands crossed upon her sunken chest. She closed her eyes. Kurowa watched the sun disappear and the glowplants come to life, their long, ivy trains wound among the bare wooden rafters.

Kurowa stood and took a cushion embroidered in gold and red from beneath the old woman's tiny feet. She lowered them gently, tucking a blanket over them.

The Curator's face settled. Unknotted. She was almost asleep, the weariness of her last, long day rising out of her bones like steam. The First Literate studied her, committing every crease of the old woman to memory, tracing the lines of her face with stinging eyes.

She bent forward as Miyako Kurowa, First Literate of the Grand Library of Nippon, and pressed the cushion to her grandmother's face.

Two minutes later, she straightened and stood framed in the night-darkened window, the Tower of Water rising in the distance: First Curator, the Grand Librarian, the Keeper of Reason, until the Creator claimed her.

⋈

Clara Downshire was not a strong reader, but she knew her maps and had a good memory, though it was always a little jumbled. The Bishop had given her so many things to study, those last two days. So much to remember. Ambrotype pictures from indices of members of the Ecclesiastical Commission. Biographical notes from research extracts. Maps of a little island somewhere off Nippon, so old they were crumbling all around the edges. Her task was, put into words, very simple: to learn so much about the Grand Librarian, the First Curator, that she would see the woman in her mind's eye as she saw everyone else, a swarm of young-old-present selves, faces merging into one another, trying to settle into a moment.

The machine, Clara had been told, was only there to help. It made her feel very funny, and it itched her scalp terribly, though that may well have been from the doctors shaving her hair.

She had wept when they did it. Her husband had always loved her hair, and even Master Meteron buried his face in it, breathing deep as he ran his lips up her throat and his hands down the laces of her bodice. But sacrifices had to be made. Somehow, knowing this ancient woman inside and out would bring her Rowie back. Clara didn't know how, or why, but the Bishop swore on it, and mother always told Clara the bishops and the clergy were people you were meant to believe.

And so, her mind tangled up in grief for Rowena, and the memory of her lost hair, and a warm ache between her legs for a lover she sensed was already gone—already bound for his promised place, where desperate men ate one another and the hateful trees ate the bones left behind—tangled amid all of this, Clara almost missed the moment when a vision of red and gold stitching stuttered before her eyes.

The long-fingered writing machine beside her chair jumped. It drew new lines that rose and fell and peaked on a long, long paper that puddled on the floor.

Rabbit sat up from his flop across her feet, whining, and buried his muzzle between her hands.

All the air in Clara's lungs was gone, as if she'd been punched. She rocked, tried to gasp, but her throat didn't know how to open. Her mouth was full of cotton and her body wailed for air. She dug into Rabbit's fur, clawing his ears. He yowled, but stayed with her, and as suddenly as the fit came, it passed.

Clara sagged, heaving, her eyes streaming.

Someone had come into the room. A jumble of voices bounded off the bare walls. Deliverance Tegura crouched beside the chair, holding Clara's pale hand in her dark one.

Ana Cortes scampered up, pushing a map past Deacon Fredericks, who had appeared at Clara's opposite side, proffering a glass of water.

She took it in both hands and gulped, sloshing down her chin and breasts and dress, still gasping.

"Show us where," Ana Cortes cried, pushing the map forward again. "Where do you see her *now?* Where has she gone?"

Clara stared at the paper. It was the whole world, skimmed off a globe and laid out before her. She heard something—a baby's cry. She looked around, her mother's instinct searching for its source.

"Where?" Cortes shouted.

"Clara, please." Tegura took Clara by the chin and pulled her face round, pointing it toward the map.

The baby's cries were definitely . . . definitely coming from . . .

"Here," Clara said.

She placed a trembling finger on an island east of Leonis, far below the Arabias, far from the aigamuxa that had gutted the mighty continent of its native peoples.

"*Here,*" she repeated.

Tegura stood, nodding toward the window Clara could not see through. It looked like a mirror. But there was someone on the other side, watching. Listening.

"Subject One location, Seychelles, 19th Eightmonth, 277, 1900 hours," she called. "Mark it on the record."

Leopold Fredericks beamed down at Clara, his florid face alight with pleasure. Clara stared at him, uncomprehending. Didn't he know his weak heart would give out before he turned fifty? The poor man. Barely a line on his face, and gone already. The smell of death swelled around him. Clara struggled not to gag.

"You've done it, Mrs. Downshire," Fredericks crowed. "Proven that we can trace the transference of Vautnek status through the exact moment of death coinciding with birth. It's a breakthrough!"

Clara nodded absently. Rabbit had wormed his way past the deacons and seminarians buzzing all around, checking the wires connected just below her scalp, injecting things into the tubes in her arms. She didn't like the tubes, or the one running up her skirt—the unmentionable tube, which emptied her in the most convenient, humiliating way into a jar beside the long-fingered stenography machine.

The dog rested his head in her lap.

A voice—an aged version of the one she had imagined purring in her ear moments before—sounded from a vox box near the mirrored window's frame. Clara choked back a sob.

Rabbit growled.

"Thank you, Mrs. Downshire. You have been most helpful. You must be very tired."

She nodded, though only a little. The bonnet of leads hurt so much. A tear ran down her lip, and Rabbit stood on his hind legs, lapping at her face in sympathy.

"I've asked Miss Cortes to prepare you a place to rest. Your duties can be taken over by our new guest, until you feel properly recovered."

The door to the chamber opened. Two guards wearing the EC's black and gold ushered another man in between them.

The dog barked wildly.

AFTER

Mayeline held the cards in her right hand, though it left her feeling a bit naked, only her wounded off-hand free to draw one of her knives. That off-hand wasn't exactly what it ought to have been, at least not since a certain Amidonian toff had run a knife up it.

She flexed the fingers of her left hand slowly, trying neither to strain her stitches nor let her hand go stiff from lack of use. Three weeks and it still *hurt*. If she hadn't known the blade wasn't poisoned—it had been her own, after all—she might have suspected as much. Then again, the sawbones she'd employed had been more than a little drunk on the whiskey used to purge the wound. Reason only knew what corruption he'd sewn back into it.

"So are you *playing*, or admiring your bloody manicure?"

Mayeline looked up at Muragan through her lashes, knowing that head-tilt looked more ferocious than comely on her furrowed face. The Indine cutpurse flinched.

She smiled. "I'm *thinking*." Her voice was a tumble of gravel, a souvenir of her years inhaling sulfur dioxide at the Cardiff refineries.

Whatever hand Muragan held, he didn't seem in such a rush to play it anymore.

She closed the fingers of her left hand once more, dragging the gesture out until the other players shifted uncomfortably.

One by one, the cards fell.

"Forfeit," called the Chaldean girl. Just a slip of a thing. She'd nearly been cleaned out, anyway.

"Forfeit." The Gaul. The word fell thick from his tongue. Given the number of glasses turned over in front of him, Mayeline couldn't be sure if it was an accent or sobriety he was struggling with.

Muragan growled something in one of the dialects of the Indines and put his cards down.

Kneeler, Scribe, Machinist, and two tengears showed in a fan before him.

"Three men and tens," he announced.

Mayeline opened her right hand and let the cards fall dramatically, one after the next.

"Deacon," she said, and it fell. "Reverend." It fell. "Bishop . . . Scales . . . and the ninegear. Grand Experiment trumps all."

The Gaul and Chaldean whistled softly. Muragan groaned, his hands in his hair.

"I was counting!" he cried. "The ninegear came out already!"

"Five hands ago," slurred the Gaul mournfully. He stacked his chips, though it wasn't much of an exercise, seeing as he had only six left. "Been a shuffle since."

"A shuffle twice," the Chaldean girl agreed. "We mulliganed the fourth hand when we all caught gears and no symbols."

"No, no, I was *counting.* It was two hands back!" Muragan kicked away from the table, not trying to hide his hand reaching for the blade at his belt. "You've got cards up your sleeve, Mayeline."

Mayeline crossed her arms across her bulky chest. "You mean to check 'em, then?"

"I mean to—"

"*Excuse me!*"

The Maiden's Honor was a riot of noise, like always, but they could hear the voice over the din because it came from the bar, and it didn't belong to Keeper.

All the heads at the bar turned toward the girl standing on it, her hands still cupped around her mouth.

The room fell silent.

Mayeline had been spoiling for Muragan to try something. She'd stored up enough pain and bad temper in her left arm, she had to *do something* with it soon and he looked ready to be the thing done. She glared at the bar, and the thought of introducing the little man to her good fist passed completely from her mind.

The hollering girl stood atop the lacquered bar, but even then, one could only spy her from the waist up. Shy of eight stone by more than a little mortar, pale faced, dark-haired, with a scar slicing across one elfin eyebrow. The perfect size for a second story job.

The girl squared her shoulders and scanned the room. "My name's Rowena Downshire. This is Doc Chalmers." She waved a hand toward a man of about Mayeline's age with a soft chin and a treasonous hairline. He looked more like a vermin flushed from its burrow than any Reverend Doctor Mayeline had known.

"Rowena, please," Doc Chalmers said. He tugged her trouser leg. "Cyddra said they won't wait for us more than an hour, and this place—"

"I'll do this with you or without you," Rowena Downshire snapped back. Her rude little face went positively feral. That was when Mayeline remembered her.

She *knew* this girl. Oh yes. *Stupid Douglas.* His arm was still in a sling, but only because he was scaring up the last of the clink he'd need for a clockwork replacement. Busted clean through at the elbow by that old Leonine's cane, the one Keeper called the Alchemist. "A limb destruction," the sawbones had called it. Nasty business.

In a way, Mayeline had got off lucky with that long, slick slice up her arm. Another scar to tell a story about, once she decided how to spin its details. But she'd keep the arm, no question.

This girl and her pet Reverend weren't likely to get off that lucky.

Mayeline rose. That was enough to make the heads staring at the girl turn, if only for a moment.

"Oy, Keeper!" she called.

The old Ibarran looked up from polishing a copper mule. "Yeah?"

"You've got a mess on your bar. En't you gonna see to it?"

He shrugged. The mutton chops flanking his mouth did a little rope-skip. He spat into a jar somewhere down at his feet. Or maybe just on the floor. Nobody ever put their face behind Keeper's bar, let alone their boots on it.

"Paid me fifty sovereigns for three minutes standing," he drawled. "Got two left." He nodded at the girl. "Talk faster."

The Downshire girl pursed her lips, jerked her leg out of her colleague's grasp, and looked around. Her fingers worked into fists, gathering something up from the air. Courage, probably.

"Who here's looking for a job?" she shouted.

A general murmur. A woman at the back barely managed to answer through a rough laugh. "You're not so bad!" she howled. "I'd take you home for free!"

The girl's face burned like a cinder, but she kept going. "I'm on the charter of the Corma Company." She pointed to Mayeline's left. "That's our table, number forty-nine. I need to hire on two campaigners to get my partners back."

The Chaldean at Mayeline's table leaned in, talking to no one in particular. "Can she do that?"

"Takes half or better of a group to agree to add people on their charter," Muragan answered. "If she and that wet handkerchief are the other half, it's legal."

"Where'd these partners go?" another voice called.

The girl turned, trying to find the voice. She settled on speaking to the room at large. "One of them's been taken by the Logicians. To Vladivostoy, where Bishop Meteron does his work."

"If it's a legal arrest—if he's gone beyond what the charter protects—" someone at the bar suggested.

"It's *not legal*," Rowena cried. "They've taken the Alchemist."

A murmur traveled through the room. Nobody needed to ask why the old man had been taken. The Maiden's Honor and half a dozen other campaigner haunts had been percolating stories about the Bear of Amidon for longer than most in the room had been in the business. No one had seen him in a decade, and then he was back, grayed and limping, maybe, but still fierce and strange and as dangerous as his namesake. Someday, someone would find out how he managed to know everything about anything. It seemed that "someone" had turned out to be the fanatics with scalpels and microscopes.

A few folk at the bar looked down at their drinks and muttered vague consolation. But Mayeline hadn't forgotten the plot so quickly.

"And what happened to the other?" she asked, weaving closer to the bar through a maze of chairs and tables. "You said there were two."

"Taken to Fog Island."

The bar boiled up with noise—shouts, laughter, chairs scuttling back.

Keeper tried to haul the girl down, one callused hand wrapped clear around her skinny forearm. She leaned away, was grabbed at by Chalmers, and all they managed was to send her tumbling behind the bar in a crash of bottles and glassware. The two women tearing it up in the fighting pit had lost interest in each other. They clambered up the ladders, bloody and staggered, to see what had drawn away their crowd.

Mayeline reached the bar in time to see Keeper looming over the girl. His voice barely cleared the din, though she was only paces away.

"You get your fool arse off my floor and out of my pub!" he snarled. "Fog Island? *Fog Island?* We don't talk about that place here!"

To his credit, the Reverend Doctor Chalmers had scrambled round to Rowena's side, trying to shelter her with his body. He was talking, though what was said, Mayeline couldn't hear.

Rowena put a hand on the Reverend's chest and shoved him back. She popped up like a jack in the box, seething. "I have *one minute left.*"

Keeper glared at her. The tumult through the Maiden was dying down, all eyes turned toward the girl whose head and shoulders alone peeked up behind the bar's brass rail. The hulking barkeep stared storm-fronts down at her. Mayeline doubted the half a hundred people jostling either to get out of the pub altogether or get closer to its bar could see the flecks of glass prickling Rowena's right arm, or the swell in her lip from the fall. She held her ground, teeth gritted against the pain.

"One minute," the girl repeated.

Keeper subsided.

The girl ignored the Reverend's bleating and swiped a path of crockery aside, clearing her space on the bar. With a nimble vault, she took her pulpit again, almost treading on the fingers of the patrons leaning too close.

"This is the Alchemist and Anselm Meteron I'm talking about," Rowena called. Her arm was bleeding freely now, dripping down her knuckles. "You know them. Some of you have even worked with them. I can get them back, but I need your help."

"Nobody leaves Fog Island!"

Didn't matter who'd shouted that. It was true. No one left the island, even in a body bag.

"They didn't before, maybe," Rowena said. "I mean to change that."

Mayeline's arm throbbed again. Anselm Meteron. She could almost laugh. *Anselm fucking Meteron.*

"What's the take?" Mayeline bellowed. The rest of the Maiden's clientele seemed to have solved their problem with the topic by turning their backs on the girl.

Rowena's head snapped toward Mayeline, like she'd spotted an island after days adrift. She looked around, then crouched down on the bar, eye to eye with Mayeline as she edged forward.

"I remember you," said Rowena, studying Mayeline warily. "How's your friend?"

"Waiting on a new arm."

"Master Meteron's the one who cut you."

"I know."

Mayeline glowered at the girl. If she apologized—if she tried to make nice over it—then fuck her. Mayeline would walk away. She had to see for herself if the girl had sense enough to do more than just play at being tough.

"Good thing it wasn't deeper," Rowena said, smiling crookedly.

Mayeline felt her own grin turn feral. Reverend Chalmers's face blanched at the sight of it. Good. If he was some shit-pantsed tosser, that was no more than she expected. At least there was hope for this girl.

"Good thing," Mayeline agreed. "Meteron's rich, en't he?"

"Richest bastard in Corma. Maybe in all Amidon."

"So what's the take?"

The girl sat back on her heels, wary again. "Are you interested in his money, or getting a chance to cut him back?"

"Both, maybe. But I'd have to help you get him to have a chance of doing for him, wouldn't I?"

"Twenty-five thousand sovereigns."

"From the richest man on a whole continent?"

"Fifty."

"Don't waste my time, pup."

"Seventy-five, or I'm gone," Rowena snapped.

Mayeline raised an eyebrow. "And what makes you think you can just afford to walk away?"

"This en't the only pub on this island. You en't the only campaigner looking for hire."

But the girl's voice, wobbly at the edges, told Mayeline she'd been to those pubs already. Probably that same night. It would explain why word of her coming hadn't run ahead of her yet. There'd been no time. And table forty-nine at the Maiden's Honor might be home to the Corma Company, but they'd been gone long years and drawn blood when they came back. There wasn't a lot of love to be had for them.

This Rowena Downshire was clearly out of options.

"But you'd want to get your Bear first, right?"

Rowena looked down at her boots, then slid off the bar on the patron side, shouldering her way toward the railing of the fighting pits. The women from the last round had slunk off to nurse their bruises with a pint. Two men were climbing down to take their place.

Mayeline followed. The Reverend Doctor scrambled round the bar to stand on Rowena's other side, casting suspicious glances Mayeline's way.

"We would, um," he said, rolling the air with a gesture. His gaze landed in the pit just in time to see a Leonine man drive his fist into his opponent's solar plexus. "We'd like to get him first, if we could," he continued hastily. "But we need Master Meteron."

"He's the brains of the operation," Rowena finished. "We need him to get Bear back, because I don't even really know for sure where he, where they—" She dug her palms into her eyes, like pressing out a headache, and sighed. "We don't know for sure what to do about him."

Mayeline studied the fighters in the pit. Not bad, if a little too ready to stay in the clinch with each other. They wouldn't make much of a show.

"The Old Bear really your da?"

Mayeline couldn't say why, but the answer mattered to her. Not enough to shave even one sovereign off the seventy-five thousand promised, but . . . enough for something.

"Yeah," said the girl, in a voice that didn't wobble. She turned to face Mayeline—pale and dusty and fat-lipped from her fall, blue eyes just a little too bright, a little too close to going wet. "He's my da. He's my whole world."

They stared down into the pit. The Leonine polished off the other man, some washup straight off the anchor yards. The victor stood there, shirtless and panting, collecting himself.

"Seventy-five for the lot," Mayeline mused. "Both jobs, innit?"

Rowena jerked, as if coming loose from a nightmare. Her eyes had filled, but they weren't spilling over. She reached to pass a hand over them, saw the blood on her fingers, and scrubbed her hand down her trousers, instead.

"If you'll take both. Yeah. Seventy-five."

Mayeline considered the Revered Doctor Chalmers. "You can swear to that, EC man?"

He nodded. "On my honor."

"Well, we'll see what that's worth," she muttered. "Fog Island. Meteron must have really stuck his dick in the wrong place."

"Sort of," Rowena answered.

"I, um, don't suppose your experience has taught you anything about the ramifications of using a legal charter to employ oneself in the *illegal* release of a prisoner from Lemarckian authorities?" Chalmers inquired.

Mayeline noticed Rowena rolling her eyes. Clearly she'd been round this bush with the Reverend already.

"Stands to reason there's enough legal and illegal kicking around in that situation that it all gets a bit *gray*." Mayeline chuckled. "Research it, if you want. It's what you're supposed to be good for, yeah?"

Chalmers bristled. "And if we're to give you a fortune on which any reasonable person could comfortably retire, I should ask what *you're* good for."

Mayeline tapped her bandolier of blades. "You're not very good at making deductions, are you?"

The girl threw up her hands, silencing them both. "Stop. *Just stop.* I'll go to stupid bloody Fog Island myself if it means I don't have to listen to you running your mouths at each other."

Chalmers blinked in surprise. Mayeline tilted her head. The girl crossed her arms in a clearly borrowed pose, aping a toughness a little too large for her tiny frame. Mayeline remembered that look when she and Douglas had tried to buy her up, hoping they could fit her down a chimney and into a second story job. The Alchemist had worn that toughness like a tailored glove. All the tears gathered in Rowena's eyes had disappeared, poured back inside her.

He's my da, she'd said. *He's my whole world.*

Mayeline sighed.

"Best get my name on the charter, then. The notary's open all night."

END.

ACKNOWLEDGMENTS

Second books and second children have a lot in common. They are doomed to constant comparison, for one thing, though every comparison proceeds from the faulty premise that they will be—or ought to be—the same. They won't be good at the same things, or have the same sense of style, or the same sort of friends, or even the same circumstances coming into the world.

Seconds come into a world portioned out by the firstborn. There is rarely enough time for them. Everything is loud and busy and distracted. They haven't a lot of options about how to respond to that stress. If they turn difficult, they're the problem child. If they're facile, people wonder if they're simply unimaginative.

Second-borns can't win this race. It's a difficult truth, but it comes with one consolation: seconds never have to run alone.

I have been fortunate beyond words for the support of many people in my private and professional life. I am sure to forget someone, or to fumble what say in thanks. Any omissions or errors are entirely my own.

I'm second-born myself. I can handle that criticism.

In the writing world, I am indebted to the heroics of my agent, Bridget Smith, who dances with editors and authors alike backwards and in heels. I will never know quite how she does it and never thank her enough for it.

My editor, Rene Sears, earns a gold star for talking me out of more than a few creative panic attacks, and surviving those I likely gave her. It's fortunate that emails *don't* always capture tone. If they did, I suspect she would know how to spell the sound of me hyperventilating.

My critique partners, Michelle Barry and Maura Jortner, were often the sole force spurring me through my worst writing days. They accepted sections of this manuscript with the most emotive of online grabbyhands, shrieked with glee, roared with anger, hectored me on my plot inconsistencies, and kept coming back for more. I would still be on page one without them.

Others in the writing world did much to buoy me during a tumultuous debut year, professionals and fans alike: Lynne and Michael Damian Thomas, for the love of tacos and real talk; Curtis C. Chen, for adopting me and accepting my macaroni necklace in return; Sam J. Miller, for treating me like a rock star when no one else had heard of me; Max Gladstone, for enduring my most awkward efforts to be a grown up despite being his biggest fangirl; David T. Palmer, co-founder of our con glomp; Brandon Crilly, fellow Writer-Teacher multi-class and his +2 blazer of Getting Stuff Done; Lawrence M. Schoen, the first pro writer to loudly, repeatedly, and aggressively demand an ARC of the sequel *the actual moment* it was ready; Cat Rambo and Mary Robinette Kowal, for their reading, their honesty, and their love; Angus Watson, for inspiring me to entirely new levels of creative profanity; Laura Merz, my first fan in the wild; Joel Hruska, for finding the Easter Eggs and solving the mysteries of agnomination; Justin Gash, for playing publicist. And there are more—many more than I could possibly name.

I am forever grateful to my fellow faculty at the Illinois Mathematics and Science Academy, especially my peers in the English Department and my forever-supporters in the Information Resource Center (other folks call it "a library," I'm told). My students, current and former, seem to think I've become famous. They're wrong, but I appreciate the vote of confidence, and their seemingly endless patience.

And of course, there is family.

This book would not exist without the special heroics of my mother-in-law, Diane Bronson, who would whisk my children away to loving arms and rampant nonsense while I plunged deep into drafts and edits. Thank you, Mom-O.

Hemingway liked to say that every writer needs a built-in, shock-proof shit detector. I married mine, and have rarely felt luckier for it. I love you, David.

And though this book and they were often mortal enemies in the competition for my time, I thank my children. They were the first truly great things I ever made. How could I want anything less than to do it again?

ABOUT THE AUTHOR

Tracy Townsend holds a master's degree in writing and rhetoric from DePaul University and a bachelor's degree in creative writing from DePauw University, a source of regular consternation when proofreading her credentials. She is a past chair of the English Department at the Illinois Mathematics and Science Academy, an elite public boarding school, where she currently teaches creative writing and science fiction & fantasy literature. She has been a martial arts instructor, a stage combat and accent coach, and a short-order cook for houses full of tired gamers. She lives in Bolingbrook, Illinois, with two bumptious hounds, two remarkable children, and one patient husband.